Praise for *Hannah, Delivered*

"*Hannah, Delivered* delivers the goods. Compelling, controversial, thought provoking, and beautifully written. I could not put it down."

—Patricia Harman, author of *The Midwife of Hope River*, *The Blue Cotton Gown: A Midwife's Memoir*, and *Arms Wide Open: A Midwife's Journey*

"Elizabeth Jarrett Andrew's novel takes the reader deeply into the essence of the midwife's calling--honoring connection, passion, and the profound stories of life and love.   There is no denial of pain and death here, only the woman, family and midwife, together, asking "what is being born?" From my perspective of straddling the two cultures of homebirth midwifery and hospital obstetrics, *Hannah, Delivered* illuminates how even a radical homebirth might be the most life-affirming choice possible.

—Heidi F. Rinehart, MD

"This novel is delicious to read, from start to finish—a wonderful addition to the literature about midwifery and birth."

—Suzanne Arms, author of *Immaculate Deception* and Founder-Director of Birthing The Future ®

Hannah, Delivered documents Hannah's trajectory from midwife wanna-be to solo practitioner with grace, veracity, heart, and passion.

—Peggy Vincent, *Baby Catcher: Chronicles of a Modern Midwife*

Hannah, Delivered
by Elizabeth Jarrett Andrew

ISBN 978-1-940192-18-5

Published by

◤ köehlerbooks™

210 60th Street
Virginia Beach, VA 23451
212-574-7939
www.koehlerbooks.com

Cover design by Linda Koutsky

Hannah, Delivered

Elizabeth Jarrett Andrew

VIRGINIA BEACH
CAPE CHARLES

1.

The Quickening

HAVE YOU EVER noticed that a midwife's quickest route to fame is screwing up?

I'm a lucky exception—my screwiest birth was a success, and that's what rattled the authorities. A soft-faced mother, a glowing father, a filmy newborn flopping into my hands . . . Birth done quietly, naturally, in the bowels of night, can make medical institutions go ballistic and upend our country's laws.

You asked about my night in jail and how I felt the next morning when I found my name headlined on the front page of the Minneapolis *Star Tribune.* If you want to be my apprentice you need to understand that the sensational births are insignificant compared with the thousand ordinary moments that come before, private moments when we choose life over death and allow ourselves to be imperceptibly changed. These are what make a midwife.

So yes, I'll tell you the story.

It begins with a mother, as do all midwives' stories: *my* beautiful mother, her silvery blond hair clipped back, hands clasped, the wedding ring a bit loose on her finger, her cheeks more heavily blushed than she would have liked, her mouth relaxed. Against white satin her practical wool skirt and chunky shoes seemed dowdy. Before the doors opened for the viewing, I hesitated over her, shocked, regretful, trying to trace my origins back into her elegant body. She seemed so self-contained. I wanted desperately to touch her hands, but didn't.

She'd been collating the church newsletter, walking around a Sunday school table piled with multicolored pages with her Elsie Circle friends, stacking one sheet of mundane church happenings beneath the next and smacking them with the stapler, just as she'd done on the fifteenth of every month for as long as I could remember. Those women had worn a path into the Berber carpet over the years. She collapsed—an aneurism. She was sixty-one. After the funeral, her friend Maggie placed one frail hand on my shoulder and handed me a stack of pastel pages. "Her body hit the floor first, dear," she said. "Then these floated down, like angels' wings. You should have them."

I'd taken the unstapled pages and passed them to Leif. Later, when he slid them to me across the kitchen table, we couldn't stop laughing at the absurdity, but in that moment after the service, I was numb, robotic, shaking hands with the parade of Chester Prairie folk in their gravest summer church clothes, nodding at condolences I couldn't comprehend. I kept glancing sideways at Dad, who despite wearing a suit and tie seemed naked without his clergy robes. The narthex closed in on me. I'd known this same stranglehold as a teenager, only now, standing shoulder-to-shoulder with Dad, I felt strangely complicit.

Here I was once again, the pastor's daughter, object of sad, sympathetic smiles. Mom, I kept reminding myself, was *not* down in the kitchen filling warming pans with ham and mashed potatoes. Mom would not dote on Leif over dinner, nor would she fold my hand around a paper bag of soup containers, left-over roasted chicken, and fresh-baked cookies when we headed home. Leif hovered respectfully behind my right shoulder; I was glad for his company. I couldn't wait to relax into his arms, and yet I wanted Mom more.

Mom had adored Leif, and now she wouldn't be at our wedding. Leif's quiet Danish demeanor made up for what I had worried would be three serious counts against him—that he sweated for a living, preferred to go birding on Sunday mornings, and cohabited with me. But Leif grew up two towns west of Chester Prairie. He had straw-blond hair and limbs like a yoga instructor. We'd bonded in community college English class when we discovered we were both recovering Lutherans. Leif had been my passport to freedom. After graduation we rented a studio apartment in St. Paul and consoled one another in the early, overwhelming days of job hunting and city driving. I scored a desk job in a big city hospital, Leif began trimming trees for St. Paul, and we toasted our liberation with cheap champagne.

I loved seeing Leif tethered to high elm limbs, swinging from branch to branch with his chainsaw. When he came home after work, he smelled of gasoline and sap. I picked woodchips from his hair. Sometimes he brought me abandoned bird nests. When we visited the parsonage, Mom poured him black coffee in her best china and inquired about his parents. Dad glowed as though Leif were the son he'd always wanted. With Leif I knew the rare satisfaction of having done something right.

Down in the church basement, I ate pickles for lunch while Mom's friends relayed fond anecdotes ("She was a dear, bringing over hot dishes when Toby was sick") and Dad worked the room with his shoulders strangely hunched. Once the crowd thinned, I couldn't bring myself to return to the parsonage where Dad would stoically wander from room to room, touching Mom's knickknacks as though for the first time. I told them I needed to be alone and drove out to Little Long Lake.

The lake had been my refuge ever since I'd been old enough to walk a mile on my own. In a town where kids avoided me because I was the pastor's daughter, where I monitored my every decision for fear of reflecting poorly on my father, the lake was a wide, expansive breath. It dissolved me. Upheld by glacial melt, anything was possible.

I parked at the public boat launch. Our bags were still in the trunk. I pulled out my suit and changed in the port-a-potty at the edge of the lot.

The south and west ends of Little Long were swampy, bordering the sparse woodlands of a county park. Houses sat to the north and east, their lawns littered with boats, picnic tables, and half-inflated inner tubes. Given the heat the beach was strangely silent, but it was early September, a weekday, and kids were in school. A few maple leaves floated at the lake's edge. Geese had left their slimy mess and webbed prints all over the sand. I strode into the shallows, grateful for the sharp cold.

With a gasp and push I was under, madly paddling and kicking until I could breathe again. Then I stopped, my arms and legs splayed, all of me suspended. Air was a warm bubble in my chest. *Where is Mom now?* Released back into creation, surely, part of the water's chill, the comforting sun, the enormous darkness holding me. I hadn't connected with her dead body but now I imagined a cord spiraling like pondweed from my center downward through tannin-stained sunlight into muck, into her. The cord swayed in the lake's currents. Quiet pressed my eardrums. Here, finally, I knew her. I accepted the silence, the water's embrace, and the sustenance seeping up, up.

* * *

Not two weeks after Mom's memorial service, there was a rush on the maternity ward. Birth always comes this way, coupled in a twisted dance with death. You don't learn that in medical school.

I was a health unit secretary, thirty-two years old, and I had admitted five women that night since my coffee at eight. I kept misplacing things—files, messages, my keys. The phone's perpetual buzz and nurses' requests, usually so stimulating, now grated on my nerves. I couldn't wait to get home to Leif for our Friday night ritual. He would warm Chinese takeout in a two hundred-degree oven. We'd crawl into bed, eat egg rolls, and have sex while ignoring a movie. I trusted Leif not to mention Mom.

You have to understand: Back then I navigated the world in a tiny bubble of competence. Now I see that Leif was a safe bet and what I'd thought was an adventurous job—Spanish and Hmong spoken in the hallways, doctors passing me orders, new babies wailing from the nursery—was dead-end and secretarial. In school I'd earned a business degree and an accounting certificate because, unlike the looser liberal arts subjects, success had measurable outcomes. I could organize a ledger or file drawer; I could manage orders and schedules. As it turns out, being capable gets results but isn't exactly an inspiring life goal.

I'll grant myself one thing, though: I had heeded a barely discernable nudge when I sought out hospital work. I wanted to care for people. I did it the best way I knew how—by pushing paperwork.

That night I was still clumsy with grief. Nearly every room on the ward had a laboring woman, and we were grossly understaffed. Maryann, the midwife on duty, steamed down the hall, muttering darkly and shooting nasty looks into the full rooms. She rested her huge brown elbows on the counter and pointed at the calendar. "Give me that."

I spun my chair and lifted the pharmaceutical wall calendar from its hook.

Maryann was the first nurse midwife to work at St. Luke's Presbyterian. Whenever she leaned her fierce face into mine, I suspected she saw through my city-savvy façade to my small-town self, the kid who put herself through college by ringing up broccoli and baking soda at the Red Owl—or, that night, the girl who just wanted her mama back. There was little Maryann didn't notice.

She removed her reading glasses from her hair, perched them on her nose, and found the date. "Knew it!" she mumbled and harrumphed back to the nurses' station.

A small black circle marked the day. At our last staff meeting,

Maryann had argued for increasing the number of doctors on call during full moons, but two of the younger OBs had made a stink, saying she was superstitious and that was no way to determine a schedule. I was surprised. We'd always made adjustments for the full moon when I worked down in ER. I suspected the docs were wet behind the ears. Maryann had muttered, "Lazy schmucks."

The elevator opened and another patient entered, this time off the street—no insurance, no prenatal care. I took her information and rang for a nurse.

An hour later, as I moved my magnet from the "in" to the "out" box and slipped into my jacket, Maryann and the single doc on call were frantically crisscrossing the hallway. "You!" Maryann shouted, mid-stride. "I need another pair of hands."

I froze. In seven years of hospital work, I'd never set foot in a room with a laboring patient.

"Now!"

I rehung my jacket and locked the cupboard. Raised voices from 146B reached the front desk.

Embarrassing to admit it now, but I'd always blocked out the screams and groans behind the ward's closed doors and imagined instead TV births, the woman laboring on her back, demurely covered with a paper sheet, the husband sweating and holding her hand—maybe not violins in the background but at least a routine of pain and arrival. Instead I saw an older Hmong woman and two teenagers chatting cross-legged on the bed, another woman wringing out a washcloth in the open bathroom, and, on the far side of the bed where there was barely enough floor space, Maryann crouched beside a naked woman. The mother was on hands and knees on the linoleum. Her brows were contorted, her eyes strained, but otherwise she seemed under as much duress as with a bowel movement. Maryann's left hand was spread across the woman's tiny back. Her right hand hovered between the woman's spread legs. Yellow liquid pooled on the floor.

My muscles went slack.

"Get me some chux pads and close that door," Maryann ordered.

The nurses must not have resupplied the room. Adrenaline surged, and my limbs swung into action. From the hall supply closet I pulled a stack of pads and raced back.

"Here," I said, even though Maryann's hands were full with a wet black-haired head. The mother gasped.

"One downside and one up. Gloves!"

Avoiding the sight of the woman's naked body, I found a box of latex gloves and took an inordinate amount of time fumbling them on. The cotton chux pads were lined on one side with blue plastic. I opened two and sidestepped between the bed and birth huddle to get to the puddle of urine.

"You're doing great," Maryann cooed to the mother. "Okay, push now." The sister translated, unnecessarily.

Shaking, I reached around the woman's legs and Maryann's big arms to lay down a pad. I didn't know how to get it under her knees, so I placed it and the second on top of her calves just as she grunted, jerked her body back, and the baby somersaulted out in a burst of blood.

One human being emerged from another! There he was, glistening, brown, a breathing creature cupped in Maryann's palms. He thrashed his arms and, finding no uterine walls to push against, snapped open his eyes. They were black pools rimmed with long, sticky lashes.

He looked at me first.

Maryann ordered me to hand her the bulb syringe, and I groped my way into awareness. The baby began to wail. His grief at the harsh air could have come from me, it felt so close. Finally a nurse arrived, chiding, "Hannah! Why are *you* here?" Maryann snapped, "Doing *your* job," and I was shooed out.

On the winter street, tears freezing on my face, I reached into my jacket pocket for my bus pass and finally noticed the latex gloves on my hands, blood splattered, like an extra layer of skin. I peeled them into a trash can. The baby, that stunningly aware, miniscule body, had erased everything: my mortification at the woman's nakedness, my aversion to blood and urine, the awkwardness of squatting so close. My fear of Maryann. The strangeness of being the only white woman in the room. The unbearable reality of being motherless.

Suddenly, I knew that baby had emerged from the same place my mother had gone. I didn't believe in heaven but how else could I explain that profound sense of continuity? He filled a hollow place in me, forcefully, irrevocably.

Later, Maryann said I had caught the birth bug. Her story's not so different from mine, only she was stuck in a traffic jam outside of Chicago. As she tells it, the combination of a Cubs game and a tractor-trailer accident had the freeway stalled for fifteen miles. The July heat was relentless. Most cars had their air conditioners blasting. Maryann's station wagon was a clunker; her kids hung out the windows panting like dogs. Her husband had turned off the ignition. The next lane over, "within spitting distance," another car with open windows held a couple in obvious distress.

"The lady moaned like a ghoul," Maryann told me, "and her husband kept saying, 'No! Don't!'" When Maryann realized what was happening, she jumped out and offered her help despite having no medical training. Knowing Maryann, I imagine she just took over, setting the woman up in the back of their station wagon and sending her kids running down the line of cars looking for a doctor. "When that sweetpea popped her little head out," Maryann said, "I got high. Been a birth junkie ever since."

Maryann called it an addiction. For me it was more like I'd been living in murky darkness, the basement of my life, and then a match was struck. Birth flared my world with light. My father would probably call the synchronicity God's grace—a death followed by a birth, releasing me from all I'd known. Grace may be the right word, although there's no way I'll concede the grace to God. It was falling in love—irrevocable, fearsome, and blazing.

* * *

In the weeks that followed, my attention on the ward began to shift. I pretended otherwise, but sending orders to the pharmacy had lost its charm. I wanted more than forms, names, and dates. I studied Maryann bustling about the ward in a silk blouse and white nursing sneakers, always purposeful and sharp. After seeing how calmly she'd squatted in urine to catch that baby, I felt awe toward her, even envy. When Maryann was on duty, I hand-delivered forms to the nurses' station so I could peek into rooms. She spent far more time with her patients than the doctors did. She joked with the dads and shared smiles with the moms while pacing the hallways; she almost never wheeled anyone into surgery. For the first time I really looked at the mothers—everyday women, often my age, sometimes teenagers, sometimes older, Hmong, white, Latina, black, brave or fearful, burnished with sweat, riveting participants in this activity I'd never fully considered but for which my body was made. They were captivating. I revered them.

Maryann was too sharp not to notice my awe. She leaned into the reception counter, pushing her nose close to mine. I conspicuously shuffled some paper. "You're spying. Have you got the bug?"

Her full, meticulously made-up face showed no judgment. A patch of flush tingled my hair roots. I shrugged.

"Listen. If you want more, I'll show you more. Just ask." She swung away then added, "On your own time."

A week later, amid my stutterings and profuse disclaimers, which Maryann slashed with her big, jabbing finger, I asked. This, I discovered, was Maryann's gift: She ferreted out cracks in peoples' hard shells, inserted her confidence, and did her best to pry them open. The doctors use Pitocin or prostaglandin gel; Maryann used her wily, fearless heart.

Thus began my year of shadowing, at first once a week during Maryann's night shift, later in my every spare moment despite Leif's protests, using even my two-week vacation to observe Maryann's day-time clinic appointments. Maryann treated me like a puppy, telling me to sit, to hand her the blood pressure cuff, or wait in the hall. Banished, I'd lean against the wall and imagine the prenatal exam, Maryann attending the emergent drama inside the woman's womb, their touch and talk more intimate than anything I'd experienced in my Swedish Lutheran upbringing.

When she'd let me, I bought Maryann cafeteria spaghetti and meatballs. I couldn't articulate the jumbled ache in my chest and instead asked her for technical information. How long was it appropriate for women to labor naturally? How did Maryann know when to tell a mother to push? Why did she remove the baby monitor after the first hour when the doctors never did? Maryann would transfer her glasses to the bridge of her nose, pause, sigh, and answer.

Finally one Tuesday night, I was washing up at the nurse's station when Maryann grasped either side of the doorframe, blocking my exit. I'd just watched my fifteenth birth. The clock read midnight. I had to be back behind the desk by eight. Leif had left a message with the answering service saying we had to talk. I pulled out a paper towel and wiped my hands thoroughly.

"How long are you planning on being a passenger?"

Maryann's questions always felt like accusations.

"Sorry?"

"When are you going to get behind the wheel? Admit it. You want to catch a baby."

"I don't think—"

"Try making a decision using some part of your body other than your brain."

I stuttered something about being thirty-three and not able to afford six more years of school. "Can't I just watch? For fun?"

She crossed her arms. I looked at my feet, cramped in their low-heeled secretarial pumps, and felt my body flush with heat.

"Forget nursing school and go the direct entry route. You can manage it in two years."

I looked up.

"Lay midwifery. Homebirth. The real deal."

"I don't know," I said. My hospital career had unfurled with terrific ease. I'd climbed up to the plush maternity ward in seven years. "I'm not really cut out for it."

"Bullcrap. Change your shape."

That night, unable to sleep, I pictured my cookie-cutter self shaped in the safe mold my parents had helped me perfect. But my mother's death had dented me. That first birth had stretched me, and all my other borders were shifting to compensate. Leif, breathing warmly beside me, wanted marriage and kids and a little bungalow in South Minneapolis. Until now I'd agreed— isn't that what every woman wanted? In the morning he would challenge my new priorities. I didn't know what I'd say.

Change your shape. I lay perfectly still, as though the slightest movement might expose my thoughts. Mom had been the good pastor's wife and I supposedly the good pastor's daughter. While growing up I made decisions as though always peering around her, trying to do what she'd consider proper, a wad of her dress balled in my fist and a tangle of desires in my stomach. I looked to my magnificent father, trying in devious and undetectable ways to catch his attention. But then I stopped. I left. I exploded out of that stifling parsonage into a place of responsibility and independence.

Or had I? What if my impending marriage to Leif was yet another grasp for my parents' affection? What if my every decision, even my fast-paced hospital job, was motivated by insatiable longing? The idea of having a baby seemed perfunctory and safe, but *catching* one—welcoming life, touching skin so new it smelled like the spring thaw! It was the most joyous act I could imagine. I wanted to get on my knees like Maryann, right at the axis of activity. I didn't want to die holding an unstapled newsletter in some back room.

Lay midwifery was an outrageous idea—impractical, not even legal in Minnesota.

I could think of nothing else. A year after my mother collapsed, a month after Maryann's confrontation, I yielded and called the Birth House.

2.

The Birth House

PLEASE DON'T THINK I'm some iconic earth-goddess who single-handedly changed Minnesota's midwifery laws. Others sat on grueling task forces, rallied at the capital, and lobbied legislators while I stumbled backward into my private passion and, unwanted, into the limelight. I'm an accidental poster child. That's my point: Even the most unlikely of us can unleash change on the world.

Who'd have thought I'd wind up in New Mexico? Not Leif, who up until then had treated my interest in midwifery like the blip in good sense that it was. When I asked him to come with me, he gripped my shoulders and said, "New Mexico doesn't have trees, Hannah." I was happy with Leif, happy about who I was with him. But this new fire razed everything in its path. "I have to do this," I told him. "I have to catch babies." I hated myself for leaving him.

Leif's features hardened, although I recognized hurt in his Danish blue eyes. "I've arrived where I want to be, Hannah. I thought you had too. I thought we were going to settle down, not pick up and move."

I cried more then than anytime since my mother died, as though she'd dragged my engagement with her into the grave. Leif was conciliatory. Maybe we needed to go our separate ways now, but that didn't mean the relationship had to end. Frequent phone calls and visits could sustain us. I believed him because I needed to. The day I left, he had to work.

Dad stored my belongings in the parsonage basement and drove me in sad but companionable silence toward the airport. We passed two dozen lakes rimmed with exploded cattails, crossed three rivers, and bisected stubbled October fields until we reached the parade of strip malls outside the metro area. Minneapolis rose and receded. At the airport, Dad stood beside his Lincoln, hands stiff at his sides. "Now, if things don't pan out there . . ."

I felt myself falling away from Dad, away from Leif, away from my birthright of black dirt and glacial lakes cradled by plains; away from home and a job full of promise and the future I'd expected. I clung to the image of Maryann wringing a washcloth, then wiping a laboring woman's brow. It ignited me with desire. What could I do but move forward?

Dad lifted his broad hand to his neck and pulled at the ring of clerical plastic. He'd lost his wife and now was losing me. I wrapped my arms around him.

"It's not forever," I said. "I'll come back." He clutched me. My whole life my father had barely acknowledged me, and now, *now*, he was holding on? "I promise," I said.

* * *

I landed in Albuquerque and climbed into a taxi van with a front bumper twisted upward like a malicious smile. Forty-five minutes past our scheduled departure time the driver leapt into the front seat and drove north at a life-threatening velocity. A plastic Virgin of Guadalupe spun from the rearview mirror. When I went to buckle up, I found myself holding two metal outies and began to panic. What if this was a sign?

Once we left Albuquerque, the landscape revealed itself, parched and plain and rimmed with mountains. My hands began to sweat—this place was so foreign! Maryann had recommended the Birth House because the midwives were exceptional and because homebirth was legal in New Mexico. Medicaid even footed the bill. Now I know it's because the state's so poor, and residents so dispersed, they're desperate for whatever medical services they can get. When I told friends I'd be there two years, their eyes had widened with envy. The sky! The rock formations! The way Minnesotans exalt it, you'd think New Mexico is closer to heaven. I expected an exotic, inspiring landscape, worthy of abandoning my beloved prairie.

Instead it terrified me. After passing Santa Fe the road began a relentless climb until it seemed an ill-advised civil engineering project carved haphazardly out of a cliff. I uselessly gripped my armrest. The gully to my left cut so sharply downward I couldn't see what it held until the road skirted the edge, my stomach lurched, and I glimpsed a slim thread of whitewater. "Is that the Rio Grande?" I asked my seatmate.

"Yep. Someone died right there last week." She pointed to a slope that met the river at right angles. Her fuchsia lipstick outlined a smile. "Happens all the time. A boulder gets loose and flattens a rafter."

I closed my eyes.

At the top of the pass, we made a stomach-lurching switchback and emerged onto the rim of a bowl. Craggy blue peaks circled miles of dusty mesa. I'd never seen anything so vast. Down the center, a jagged gorge ripped the land apart, exposing a glint of brown. The Rio Grande! That trickle had cut through the mesa's dry shell and sliced splendor from aridity. It looked like a wound, only beautiful, the way I imagined the birth passage to be beautiful. My breath quickened.

By the time the taxi van dropped me and my two suitcases one block off Sangre de Cristo's main drag, I was a jangle of elation and nerves. A ragged fence of hand-tied poles hid the private houses, and to my right I could see the edge of town, its low-lying, earthen buildings crouched under mountains bloodied by the sunset. It was six o'clock on a Friday night. The midwives had expected me at four thirty.

I secured my purse strap over my shoulder and hauled my bags through the gate. The Birth House was adobe, rambling, with deep-set windows and a small second story over the southwest corner. The front door was painted purple. A braid of garlic garnished the doorframe on the left and a vibrant strand of chili peppers on the right. I smoothed my wrinkled skirt, ran my fingers through my hair, raised my pale knuckles, and knocked.

No one answered. The evening light shimmered, the air was cooling. During a lull in street traffic, I heard voices inside. Only then did I remember this was a clinic and I should just enter. The door had one of those colonial latches that made a satisfying, wrought-iron click. A cowbell hanging inside rang dully.

I entered a blaze of activity. Two children chased one another around a sagging couch upholstered in rust plaid. A gray-haired woman glanced at me distractedly before turning on her heel. Down the hallway a woman with a thick braid carried an aluminum mixing bowl out of one room into another. I was interrupting a birth.

I set my bags beside the reception desk and pretended to examine the floor-to-ceiling bookcases. My favorites were there: *Spiritual Midwifery, A Midwife's Story, Birth Reborn*— books Maryann had slipped into my hospital mail slot over the previous year. I had paged through them while riding the bus to and from St. Luke's. Their covers opened onto dream worlds where intuition guided women, where they squatted like Neolithic goddesses to birth babies, where midwives coached and coaxed and caught slippery new life in a seamless continuity between the unborn realm and this one.

I pulled a ragged copy of Michel Odent's book from a shelf and flipped through softened pages to a sequence of black and white photographs, facial portraits of a woman in labor. The Frenchwoman's head was thrown back, her neck arched so fiercely that her esophagus bulged. The black gape of her mouth shifted from photo to photo, here turned left, here lifted to heaven. Dark curls cascaded to her shoulders, until in the final pictures they were wet and clung to her skin. Her expressions of pain and ecstasy were indistinguishable. Even the women under Maryann's care had never displayed such rapture. If these books were to be believed, the hospital prevented it. But here a woman might be laboring ecstatically on the other side of the waiting room wall. I imagined holding her hand. She knew something intensely human, an unstoppable power, a glory stretched into her every cell.

I closed the book. Behind me, the children jumped on the sorry couch.

Beside the bookshelves hung a framed bit of needlework that read, "A mother is not a person to lean on but a person who makes leaning unnecessary." I smiled. If Leif had been there we would have laughed at the kitsch. But the thought of Leif was wrenching, and I desperately wanted to lean against my mother. I clung to memories instead—how she gripped my small fist when crossing the street; how she sewed frocks in subdued colors with just enough ribbon to delight me; how she smoothed wrinkles from tablecloths, from my father's robes, from altar linens, her fingers fine and young-seeming, always passing over fabric. I remembered her silken hair. She used to pin it back in a droopy bun that in her last years showed silver amid the fading blond.

Once when I was little, she let me comb it. She sat on the back porch at my grandparents' house, gazing out beyond the barn to the pond rippling with morning sun. I liked how the wind lifted the strands I pulled from the comb and carried them away, to a patch of grass, I imagined, where a sparrow would retrieve them for its nest. For a moment Mom was lost to the land and accepting of my touch. "Blue-eye blue," she said of the summer sky. The immense sadness in her voice became my own. I stroked the comb's teeth lightly against her scalp, as though I could untangle her sorrows. Eventually she said, "You're dawdling," and took the comb.

My interest in midwifery would have disturbed Mom. Conversation that veered into the realm of bodies had made her glance away. Dad, despite his reserve, at least talked about bodies, although mostly in connection to the flesh being redeemed by Christ. But to Mom, human physicality was an affront. When I first got my period at age fourteen, she unfolded the directions from the Kotex box and closed me in the bathroom to read them alone. Any medical gossip I brought home from the hospital she met with thick silence. When I shared news of twins or, once, preemie triplets, Mom winced and changed the subject. Baby names were safer. I loved reporting a gem like Tracy Stacy Casey or Alison Wonderland, because Mom would gasp and together we'd bask in our expert common sense.

I tried to lean on memories, but they offered little support. Standing awkwardly in the Birth House waiting room that first day, as far from my mother's dreams for me as I'd ever ventured, I doubted my lifelong need to lean on her would ever dissipate. If the cross-stitch was right, she'd not done her job. I tucked this secret away.

I glanced at my watch—nearly six thirty. Next on the wall was a bulletin board layered with flyers. "Sufi Dance Night," childbirth class schedules, AA meetings, a baby massage workshop, "Support Group for Abduction Survivors"—whatever that meant—a Domestic Violence Center fundraiser, a woman looking for a boarder—I copied her number—a grief support group, a drumming circle, and a few dozen business cards advertising everything from tarot reading to adobe repair. I'd never seen a bulletin board like it. Excitement shivered through me.

The woman with the braid came into the hall again, this time holding a clipboard. She approached me, her dark eyes sparking.

"You must be Hannah. Welcome." She was a good foot shorter than me, her fingers small inside my pale, farm-stock palm. "Maria Ortiz. The shuttle service made good time. No accidents? No breakdowns?"

The ride had been harrowing. I laughed.

"At least you're alive." Maria tilted her head to look at me. Her hair was parted sharply. She reminded me of a house sparrow, her calm exterior harboring a flitting energy. "Would you like to meet our latest arrival?"

It took me a minute to realize she meant a baby. I was travel-weary. I felt unduly large and blundering and definitely not prepared to leap in. But in community college, I had taken a workshop called "Polish and Protocol"—an acting class where we learned to make eye contact and add deceptive oomph to our handshakes. At first you pretend and eventually your confidence grows to match the behavior. "Absolutely," I said.

I followed Maria down a hallway wallpapered floor to ceiling with photographs of weary, smiling mothers, grinning fathers, wrinkled infants in cotton caps, and the occasional, uncertain sibling. Maria passed me the clipboard. "Wait a sec."

A moment later she pulled me inside. The room was steamy. A damp-haired mother leaned against the headboard trying to position her newborn against her left breast. A man looked on with bleary eyes.

"Has she latched on?" Maria asked.

"I don't think she gets it. It's in her mouth but she doesn't suck."

"That's a start." Maria radiated calm. "This is Hannah, our new apprentice. Josh, Kelly, and baby Agatha."

"Good to meet you," I said, feeling stiff. "Congratulations."

The couple looked stunned, as though they couldn't take in anyone outside of their small triangle.

"Let's see." Maria folded the receiving blanket away from Kelly's breast and with a single finger, lifted the infant's chin a notch. "So sleepy! You worked hard just now."

"Can we weigh her?" the father asked.

Maria lifted the squirming bundle. Agatha's feet were the size of my thumbs, her shock of red hair feathery and wet. When I saw how new she was, my trepidation about appearing capable was trumped by my heart's thumping.

"Will you grab that scale for me, Hannah?"

I pulled an odd contraption from the closet, one side hung with weights and the other dangling a Guatemalan cloth bag. In every birth I'd witnessed at the hospital, a nurse had immediately whisked the baby off to wash it and get the height and weight. Here there was no hurry. I held the balance while Maria tucked Agatha into the sling and adjusted the weights. "Six pounds two ounces. Would you write that down, Hannah? That's great. Eighteen inches. She's going to be tall."

Agatha began to whimper. Maria picked her up and placed her at her mother's breast, nudging the nipple into her mouth. Maria's touch was graceful and motherly. Agatha's eyes popped. She sucked in surprise, and Kelly said, "That's it!" Josh thrust invisible pompoms into the air—"Go, Aggie! Go, Aggie!"—and we all laughed.

"We'll leave you to yourselves," Maria said. "Let me know when you want to call in your mother." Maria clasped my arm and led me from the room. "Let's sit in the office." She passed the photographs as though the miracles they exposed were humdrum.

"Such a tiny baby," I said.

"It's the altitude. We rarely get babies over eight pounds up here." She turned into a back room crammed with desks, bookshelves, and filing cabinets. A window offered a view of a shadowy yard. "Have a seat." Maria rolled out a chair for me and perched, feet dangling, from her own. Our knees almost touched. I sat on my hands.

"How about a quick orientation to get you through the weekend? Stuart's with a woman in early labor, in the other room. Stuart Rizzo. He has dinner for the two of you in the fridge."

Because Maryann had intervened on my behalf, the Birth House midwives had agreed to forgo the customary three-day trial visit and instead interviewed me over the phone. One of the questions they'd asked was whether I'd be comfortable working with a man. Apparently a male apprentice had started training a few months earlier. I had worked in a hospital with many male nurses and on a ward where men oversaw the majority of births, so of course I said yes. But a male midwife? It had seemed odd.

"You're arriving at a busy time. I've told Stuart to come get you when Ava Gomez starts pushing."

My stomach flipped. She wanted me at the birth? The speed at which I was hurtling into what felt like someone else's life was unsettling. I needed time to take in the place, to call Leif, to remember why I'd come.

"I'll show you the crash room in a minute. It's yours until you find an apartment. We're really glad to have you on board. Did I say that yet?"

"No. Thanks." I felt ridiculous sitting on my hands and placed them on the armrests.

"Here's a key. The phone will ring off the hook. Don't feel you need to answer it . . . over the weekend, at least." She picked up a notepad, scanned its contents, then scooted her chair to a bulletin board to point out the phone list and call schedule in case of a walk-in. Stuart would orient me to the building and routine on Monday. We'd start at eight with a staff meeting. I would work the clinic eight to five Monday through Wednesday, with academic intensives Thursday and Friday. Reaching the quota of births in two years could be a challenge; I'd be on call twenty-four-seven to get exposed to as many as possible. She handed me a pager.

"Here's our first text and the National College guidelines." Maria heaved *Heart and Hands* and a mammoth three-ring binder into my lap. I scanned the covers with a dose of apprehension. I hadn't paid much attention in high school biology. "Stuart's studying chapter nine for Thursday. Skim through the first chapters, and we'll go back later." She checked her list. "Would you like to have dinner with my family Sunday night? Nothing formal, just a chance for you to meet Luis and the kids."

"Sure. Thanks."

"What else?" With a little push she spun, scanning the room.

"Is it all right?" I looked at my knees, bulbous under the

wrinkled linen. "I mean, I'm pretty overwhelmed. Can I opt out of the birth tonight?"

Maria raised her thin eyebrows. She was beautiful—no makeup, a natural flush across her small brown face, probing black eyes, and an eager posture. Her energy was pointed and seemingly limitless. I regretted asking. I should have been prepared to launch in.

"Of course," Maria said. "Here, I'll show you the crash room." She stood. "It's Justine's third, so it should go quickly if you change your mind."

3.

Partero

DURING ONE OF our cafeteria lunches, Maryann once said to me, "Girl, never underestimate the mightiness of a willing heart." We'd been discussing mothers in prenatal care and how midwives can prod women imperceptibly toward a warmer, calmer welcome for their newborns. Only today, as I put these stories together for your benefit, do I realize Maryann really meant *me—my* heart, and the mightiness available to any of us if we're open to change.

Over two intense years, that crash room would encompass my blundering transformation. The room was towerlike, protected. Maria had explained that they used it to grab sleep during all-night labors. It doubled as the apprentices' study. Three walls of windows were set into thick adobe, with a full-sized bed taking up most of the floor and two desks along the wall. That first night I stood at the window, collecting myself. Orange houselights pooled in the yard. Scrawny aspens shook dark leaves and, in the distance, the mountains shimmered. An October chill drifted in along with the sounds of traffic and barking dogs.

I kicked off my shoes and launched onto what turned out to be a waterbed. Waves bounced off the wood frame.

The desks abutted a corkboard wall, the right one empty and the left piled with books and papers, above which were pinned artsy black-and-white Southwestern nature photographs, a few poems, and a greeting card that read, "There's no moment like the present." *Ugh.* You can only push yourself so much in a day. I undulated and watched the blue light fade across the baked mud ceiling. I considered calling Leif, but hesitated. How could I share this peculiar place with him? I barely recognized myself here and was afraid of Leif's estrangement.

A brisk knock launched me to my feet and set the bed sloshing. I turned the knob. A lanky, bright-faced boy, outrageously tall, with California blond hair, ponytailed and glowing from the hall light, grinned at me. From each ear dripped a tiny loop of gold. His shirt was white cotton with drawstrings at the neck and cuffs, the kind you'd expect on a lad at the Renaissance Festival, and his road-construction-orange pants ballooned down to gathered elastic at knobby, bare ankles.

"Hi," I managed. Whatever I'd expected of Stuart, it wasn't this.

"Hey, sister!" He wrapped gangly arms around me, undaunted by my stiffness. "My long-awaited fellow apprentice! Welcome to the land of baby-mania." He raised his arms like a ballerina preparing to bow and turned a full circle, embracing the town of Sangre de Cristo. "You, my dear," and here he took my cheeks in his hands—I stepped backward—"are the answer to my prayers." He kissed my forehead.

I backed up another step and hit the bedframe. "It's good to be here," I told his chest.

Stuart glided across the room, flicked on the light, and elegantly levered his rear atop the loose papers on his desk. "Mama Gomez still has a ways to go. We can't go out or anything, so I made us a pasta salad with roasted bell peppers, kalamatas, feta. Are you vegetarian?" I shook my head. "I'll toss in pepperoni. You could catch a baby tonight. How's that for timing?"

I stood uncertainly in the little square of floor. "I think I'll pass."

"You're kidding." Stuart craned his neck, inspecting me. "Why?"

"I'm beat," I said.

"You do look tuckered. Sit." Stuart kicked the chair out from under the second desk, and I took it. "Maria give you the low-down?"

"Briefly. They'll work me into the schedule Monday."

Stuart raised both hands, smacked his knees, and hooted. "Schedule, smedule. Either you're a midwife or you're not. And you and I, sister, are midwife, laundry-boy, full-time student, and pot-and-bottle washer. I don't blame you. Catch up on sleep while you can." Stuart's face was tan except for a rim of burn along his hairline and some skin flaking at the tip of his nose. I guessed he was mid-thirties. "Say, I read your file. Turns out we're both hospital refugees."

Mentally I reviewed my application to find out what Stuart knew. The biographical essay had been grueling. Maryann's response to my writer's block? "You're enough to drive an old woman to drink. Just tell the truth." I finally landed on an acceptable version: my story from behind the reception desk, observing the nervous couples, the bustling nurses, the commandeering obstetricians, and Maryann with her generous hands. How my decision to pursue midwifery was no decision at all but a pull, a silent undertow that I'd only recently recognized. The application portrayed me as a go-getter looking for a career change, dedicated to the well-being of mothers and infants. Stuart assumed I was that woman. I straightened my back.

"What did you do?" I asked.

"Nursing, in hospice care. Down in Albuquerque."

I tried to imagine Stuart's boyish enthusiasm beside a lung cancer patient, wheezing his last breath.

"Did you burn out?"

"No, no, I loved it. It'd just been fifteen years"—I

recalculated; with nursing school he was likely ten years older than me—"and insurance kept cutting back what we could do. Totally suffocating. Besides, hospice and midwifery are sister professions. You usher them in the door"—he swept his long arms from his left to right—"you usher them out. I want to be on the receiving end for a change. Say, will you be okay working with me, Hannah? Does it bother you that I'm a guy?"

I hedged. A single wrinkle sliced his forehead, transfiguring the boy into troubled man. "All the OBs on the ward where I worked were men," I said.

"Well"—Stuart tilted his head against the bulletin board—"that's a relief."

The windows were now dark, blotting out the town and tightening the room around us.

Stuart slipped his hands, palm to palm, between his knees. "Guess I'm controversial. I didn't know it before I got here, but it was a tough decision for Maria and Sunny to take me on. My references impressed them, though, and then my dazzling personality won them over. A client last week said it's impossible—there's no such thing as a male midwife. It got Maria and Sunny going. Stuff came out of the woodwork."

"Like what?"

"Like that Sunny had advocated for me. She's on some bandwagon about inclusifying midwifery. Maria had to be persuaded. She's concerned my presence will intimidate women. What she actually said was, 'Men put out different vibes that can interrupt the labor process.' And something about preserving wisdom that's traditionally women's." Stuart took a breath. "What if she's right?"

Yes, these were the reasons a male midwife seemed strange. "Then most maternity wards are in trouble," I said.

"Which they are." He paused. "I don't want to defile something sacred."

Stuart's worry seemed overly dramatic. "I don't know," I said. "It's just birth." But this was precisely my fear as well: that by entering that hallowed moment, I'd defile it, with clumsiness, with insufficient reverence, or because I somehow wasn't worthy. I scratched a nonexistent itch on my ankle.

"True, true," Stuart said. He plucked a Kleenex from a box, wiped his brow, and stuffed the tissue up his sleeve. He was so different from Leif, from my father, from most men I knew. "Let's eat."

In the little kitchenette next to the crash room, Stuart doctored up the salad and tossed it into two cereal bowls, mine with pepperoni slices. The noodles twisted through an oil dressing. He tore two hunks off a loaf of French bread and swiped butter across the end of each.

"Take. Eat," he said, handing me the bread.

"Watch it," I teased. "My dad's a pastor."

"Scary."

"Not half as scary as having the pastor's wife for a mom."

I had told myself and Leif that I'd put my Christian baggage behind me when we moved down to St. Paul. Why, then, turning back toward the crash room, did a knot rise to my throat at Stuart's blithe joke? He plopped onto the bed. I turned on a floor lamp, the second circle of light making the room feel less intimate. Even though I lowered myself carefully, the waves made Stuart into a bobbing Buddha. For a few minutes we ate in silence.

When I was nine I had begged my father for communion the way other girls pleaded for ponies, with equivalent results. My desire was stoked not by envy of other kids parading down the aisle but by my father, standing with his back to the congregation, the chalice raised over his head in a gesture so contrary to the withdrawn man I knew at home that I was certain the Eucharist itself had transformed him. I wanted that magic. I wanted to burst out of my mousy-girl self into someone solid and fearless.

Dad considered the Eucharist a privilege, granted at confirmation.

Eventually my ardor wore him down. I followed my mother up the communion line one Sunday, my stomach churning with nerves. When we neared the dais, I heard Dad's low voice, "Body of Christ, broken for you," holy words he'd willingly spoken into every other ear but mine. I watched the adults and other kids and my mother accept the wafer and miniature glass then turn to the chancel rail to kneel. That's what I would do. I saw the hem of Dad's white robe covering his feet. I cupped my hands. "Hannah," Dad pronounced softly, and my head snapped up. He hadn't said other people's names. He paused, making the line wait. My chest thumped. My mother glanced over her shoulder. Dad held my eyes in his. "The body of Christ, given for you. The cup, spilled for you." Neither of us looked away. His fingers pressed my palm.

I turned, stepped forward, knelt. My knees trembled against the cushion. The wafer tasted like snow. The splash of wine made my eyes tear. The congregation and church and all that I knew, even my body, even my awareness, slipped away. I was nothing. I was God's throbbing heartbeat.

My mother's fingers grabbed my skinny arm and shook. "Stop that."

I'd been sobbing. She yanked me up the side aisle and into our pew. "Don't ever make a scene like that again," she whispered.

And I didn't, because communion became as mechanical as the rest of church. Eventually I considered Mom cruel, too willing to damage my heart for the sake of external appearances. All through my teens I hated her and berated myself for it. As a young adult I wondered what pressed her to edit my life so fiercely. Certainly the intensity of that first communion had frightened us both.

"Don't worry." I tried to dismiss my seriousness. "I'm not a churchgoer anymore."

"What happened?"

"Confirmation." I bided my time from age fourteen, when I'd made my first conscious decision about church, until graduation, when I could act on it without incurring my father's wrath.

"That'll do it."

"How about you?" I asked.

"I worship at the altar of hard knocks." He hooted. "Seriously,

I miss it. The robes, the incense, the bowing. I was Catholic until sixth grade, when my folks stopped going. At heart I'm a ritualistic kind of guy. But the church wouldn't want me, and I've got better things to do with my time. Walk the walk. The talk's not worth much."

The baguette was excellent, the butter salty.

"What happened with that patient?" I asked. "The one who had an issue?"

"We call them clients. She's refusing to work with me. It's only fair. If she wants a woman, she should work with a woman. Trouble is, she's on the board of directors."

"Yikes." This wasn't a big city hospital. "Why don't you become a nurse midwife? It wouldn't be much more training for you."

Stuart's expression soured. "I want out of the hospital. Jeez, I've seen enough unnecessary interventions on the dying end. Insurance companies were getting to me. Twelve minutes per visit? It's bullshit. Those folks are *dying*." With his fingertips he rubbed circles into his brow.

"Did you run into trouble being a guy there? There aren't tons of male nurses."

"Foot rubs, that's my secret. Even super-duper macho guys forget their hang-ups after a foot rub. I have prodigious hands." He spread his fingers wide. They were slender and smooth, with a thick silver band on his left ring finger. "Speaking of which, I should check on the mama-to-be." His empty bowl clattered when he put it on the floor. I still had half of my dinner left—it was a tad too garlicky. In a seamless motion, Stuart rose, strode across the turbulent bed, and stepped off. "You can change your mind if you want. The papa's not interested in catching, and they're not picky about who's there."

I shook my head, longing and weariness too snarled to sort out. Stuart cascaded down the stairs.

I picked up his dish, tidied the kitchen, and shut the crash room door, glad for solitude. I changed into my nightgown. As soon as my head hit the pillow, labor screams rose through the floor, amplified by the water. I was still hungry. The waterbed made me nauseous. Tossing, trying to accustom myself to the waves, I thought about confirmation. Dad had assigned us to write credo statements to read to the congregation. Mom had disapproved of what I'd written. We'd spent a teary hour at the kitchen table reworking my beliefs with a red pen until they were presentable. I was fourteen, old enough to spit and flail. But I hadn't.

Why? The bed sloshed. I missed Mom; I wished she were alive so I could ask her why she'd been so harsh. With each of Mrs. Gomez's groans, remorse shot through me. I had accepted my parents' bending of my will, colluded with them even, for fear of losing their love. And Leif, dear Leif—that he couldn't embrace my passion for birth now seemed like an extension of my parents' limitations, as though I'd left one beautiful cage for another.

No more. I was in New Mexico to pursue a glimmer of desire entirely my own. At this thought I sat up, untangled myself, staggered off the bed and back into my sour-smelling clothes. My body was heavy, but I descended the stairs anyhow, Hannah the Apprentice, determined to push against what I had presumed was my fate. I knocked on the birth room door. Stuart opened it and smiled like sunshine.

"In the nick of time," he said.

4.

Fear of Falling

STUART ONCE TOLD me a story about circus families. Shortly after a baby is born, the whole community gathers— acrobats, clowns, tight-rope walkers, and lion-tamers, stripped of their makeup, wearing jeans and T-shirts, and milling around the mother's bed. They crack jokes and slap the father's back. He hands out cigars. Then he reaches for the newborn. The mother, pleased, removes it from her breast. In a chorus of "hip-hip-hooray!" the father raises the naked baby for everyone to see; "hip-hip-hooray!" and it's thrust skyward a second time. On the third jubilant hooray, he releases the infant into a dramatic air-borne spin, heels over head, tiny body flipping upward toward the ceiling then descending in a slow, final turn to sink into the adept hands of its father. So the newborn's first experience of the wider world is flight. Its second is the safety of the catch.

That, my friend, is a beginning free of fear.

Mine was the opposite, and I've paid a lifetime of consequences. I was born on January 7, 1962, in a cement-block hospital in Chester Prairie, Minnesota, population seventeen thousand three hundred and forty. Outside, the cold was severe.

Inside, a young country doctor attended my even younger mother. Surely she pinched her lips through the labor pains. Surely my father called upon the Lord. I arrived, Hannah Abigail Larson, first and only product of the constrained conjugal affections of a Lutheran pastor and his new wife, at the ungodly hour of three twenty-eight in the morning.

As early as I can remember, I was curious about my birth, perhaps more so than other children because of my mother's reactions. She would be stirring a drop of red food coloring into a bowl of butter frosting or ironing linen napkins or tucking me into bed, her body warm and steady yet somehow distant. Even when she was near I longed for her. "What was it like when I was born?" I'd ask and she'd bristle, then place her hand on my shoulder.

"You were a miracle baby," she'd say.

"Tell me," I'd plea.

"Thank heavens for Dr. Jorgenson." She'd kiss the top of my head and turn away.

Bill Jorgenson was our family doctor and a fishing buddy of Dad's, despite his ardent atheism. When he was invited for Sunday dinner, Mom would make pot roast, set out the wedding china, and light new tapers. I had to wear my Sunday dress and shoes all afternoon. Dad would bounce impatiently on the balls of his feet from the appointed time until the tardy bachelor-doctor arrived. When Dr. Jorgenson finally filled the doorway with his protruding belly and coarse laughter, my parents showered him with gratitude. He'd ruffle my hair and bellow, "How's the babe I brought into the world?" Of course I wasn't a baby then, and though I felt like saying so, biting my tongue was how I helped my father spread Christian kindness.

Once I even asked Dr. Jorgenson. I was eight. His eyebrows leapt like jumpy caterpillars. He glanced at my parents. "Ho, ho," he said. "That day was a record breaker. Forty-something below. The kind of day your spit freezes on its way to the sidewalk. Kind of day your eyelashes glue shut with frost." He pinched his fat fingers and thumbs together in front of his brows. I waited, looking up the hump of his checked flannel stomach. His Santa-eyes saw my thirst. "You were in a hurry to come out, missy. Must have been excited. We said, 'Whoa, Nelly!' " He pulled back on invisible reins.

I wanted more, a detail, a handhold on this beginning that felt more like an absence, but Dr. Jorgenson chuckled and Dad gave him a hearty whack. "Here's your hero, Hannah," Dad said. He was wearing black pastor clothes with the strangling collar. "God works in wondrous ways."

Gradually I began to understand my mother's fancy meals and my father's chummy punches: Fearsome and blessed, the fat doctor had saved me.

* * *

That first Monday morning in New Mexico, a door slammed and I floundered out of the waterbed, snatching the plastic travel clock from the sill—it was only six thirty. The staff meeting wasn't until eight, and yet someone was downstairs already, bumping around. I paused, trembling. The room was icy.

After a shower and a yogurt cup, I sat at my desk to review the National College guidelines. In two years, if I passed the NARM and New Mexico state exams, I'd get a national certification and license I could frame for my office wall. That Minnesota wouldn't honor either was a distant and inconceivable problem. The Minnesota Board of Medical Practice was in the process of evaluating the exam; surely by 1998 they'd approve it. Midwives' status was changing. The governor of Florida had just declared a week in October "Florida Licensed Midwives Week."

The Gomez baby had arrived just before midnight on Friday, and while I didn't catch him, I'd wrapped him in warming blankets and pulled the knitted cap over his perfect ears. After that I slept soundly. Saturday I scoured the town and by late afternoon signed a lease on a furnished room beginning the next week. Sunday I couldn't find an open store that sold twin sheets. Dinner at Maria's had been a generous chaos of homemade enchiladas shoveled from three pans onto eight plates laid out carelessly by Maria's eldest around a picnic table. As far as I could figure, four of the kids were Maria's and the fifth was her husband's nephew. I never got their names straight for all the wiggling and switching places. Adult conversation had been limited. Maria seemed like the ideal mother—calm, certain, and clear in her affection.

The cowbell clanged against the front door. For the umpteenth time I glanced at my watch, double-checked my hair in the bathroom mirror (helplessly limp in the dry, high desert), tightened the sheets across the bed, and followed the scent of coffee downstairs.

Two women bent over the front desk. The older one leaned on her elbows, her graying blond hair tied in uneven ponytails. She wore loose culottes and a slack-sleeved cotton shirt with elaborate floral embroidery draping the neck. A younger Latina woman was seated, her hair teased upward and outward, electric with hairspray.

In modest heels and gold jewelry, I looked like I'd been beamed in from some corporate planet. "Good morning," I managed.

"Jesus, Mary, and Joseph!" The Latina woman touched manicured fingers to her throat.

The blond turned. "Hannah!" She strode toward me, leather flip-flops snapping at her heels, and wrapped me in wiry arms. "Good to meet you. I'm Sunny. This is Anita, our receptionist."

Anita stood. "Where the hell did you come from?"

"We're lending Hannah the crash room," Sunny said. She placed her hand on my shoulder. Her movements were willowy and swift, the heavy jewelry around her wrists studded with turquoise, and her eyes bleached. "Give me a minute here, Hannah. Can you bring out a few chairs?"

From the back office I maneuvered a squeaky-wheeled swivel chair into the hall. According to Maryann, Sunny had been instrumental in rejuvenating lay midwifery in the Southwest. She had created the Birth House twenty years before and brought Maria on shortly afterward. My breath quickened with the prospect of learning from her.

As I reached the waiting room, Stuart burst through the front door and pronounced, "Good morning, good morning!" to no one in particular. Anita waved without looking up. Sunny scolded, "Too much cheerfulness." I just gaped. Stuart was wearing a sarong tied around his rectangular waist, fringes dangling at his ankles, and a white T-shirt. "Cheer is the order of the day," Stuart retorted.

Before I could place the chair properly, he plopped down and began spinning. "The sun is out, Hannah has arrived to be my partner in crime, and there are five babies due this week. What's not to be cheerful about?"

Sunny and Anita ignored him. I waited for him to take his skirt off, to show us the shorts underneath so the joke would be over, but he just leapt up, grabbed my elbow, and ushered me back down the hall.

"Don't worry. The initiation rites aren't too painful. Lots of bad coffee and an hour on our butts. We always start the week reviewing charts. They'll probably subject you to a mild inquisition."

"About what?" I let him corral the second chair.

"Skills, interest. They'll want to know what you do well so they can plug you in. Do you have grant writing experience? Like to cook? Can you rub your tummy and pat your head at the same time? We'll also go over the calendar since it's going to be one doozy of a week."

Walking behind Stuart, I got a good view of his scrawny ankles and the strange, straight way the batik sarong hugged his hipless middle. There were no shorts. When he turned his head, I lowered my eyes. "Maybe you and I can squeeze in some study time together," he said.

"Can we play it by ear? I still need to settle in."

"No problemo. Say . . ." He stopped just shy of the waiting room. "I was sorry to hear about your mom's death. In your application, I mean. What a blow."

His sympathy, coming from nowhere, ripped me apart. I stumbled into Mom's absence again and again, my sorrow always fresh and quickly extinguished. "Thanks," I said.

Maria arrived bearing a steaming loaf of banana bread between oven-mitted hands. Anita swept the scuffed coffee table clear of magazines and toys and dumped down a colorful pile of file folders. When Stuart flopped onto the sofa, I chose an office chair. Sunny made rounds with the coffeepot and a fistful of mismatched mugs. "Don't say I didn't warn you about the coffee," Stuart said.

I took a sip. It was coffee from a can, church coffee, the kind my people drink unadulterated like a satisfying penance. Wonderful.

"¿Listos?" Maria asked, sitting beside Stuart. Side by side they were comical, Stuart lanky and sprawled, Maria dark and tidy. She propped herself forward with an overstuffed pillow. "What's with the skirt?"

"I got it in the Punjab. Told the guy it was for my wife."

I felt vindicated by Maria's slight frown.

"Bueno," Maria started. "First of all, a warm welcome to Hannah." Stuart ululated. "We're really glad you're here. We've never had a student from Minnesota."

"Maryann Parker says hello," I said. Maryann had interned at the Birth House in 1985.

"How is she?" Sunny asked.

"Thriving. The maternity ward will never be the same." I was acutely aware that Maria and Sunny had spoken with Maryann recently in reference to me. I clenched the hot mug between my palms.

"That's our girl," Sunny said. "Social revolution, one baby at a time."

"We've all read your application, Hannah, so I'm afraid we know more about you than vice versa. That won't last long." Maria's hair was pulled back in a bun this morning, into which she'd stabbed a yellow pencil. The eraser bobbed. "Is there anything else you'd like to share?"

I shrank minutely. "Just that I'm happy to be here." *More*, said my polish and protocol coach. *And sit up!* "I haven't always wanted to be a midwife. I mean, it's come as a surprise. Last year I got pretty obsessed, though. I hope I can make more of a difference actually participating in people's health care rather than pushing papers around." I winced, thinking too late of Anita. "Thanks for taking me on."

"Tell us about your last job." Sunny leaned forward. "Can you do Medicaid claims?"

I endured a barrage of questions about tasks I could perform blindfolded and skills I thought I'd left behind until Sunny determined that billing would be an excellent use of my know-how and Anita and I had set up a time to review Birth House procedures.

The week's schedule was mind-boggling. With the exception of lunch hours, we would see clients back to back from nine to five, Monday through Wednesday, with a handful sprinkled in at the end of the week, when Stuart and I were exempted from clinic. That much seemed reasonable, but then Sunny reviewed the five women with impending due dates. I didn't understand how we'd do clinic *and* attend the births. Sunny blitzed through the charts, highlighting a woman's blood pressure here and a potential abusive relationship there.

"What do you do in a situation like that?" I asked.

Sunny smiled encouragingly. "Depends. Some moms you can ask outright. Some are ashamed or want to keep it secret, so you can always express concern for the baby—'Do you feel that your baby's safe?' It's good to get the guy involved too, if possible. Let him know he's responsible for the baby's well-being."

"The hotline number's posted in the bathroom," Maria added. "The moms test their own urine, so the bathroom's the best place for resources like that."

"You can practically get your whole midwifery education while taking a dump," Stuart said. They all laughed.

Ten charts later, the pregnant women had dissolved into an abstract statistical mess and my head was pounding. The first clients would walk through the door in fifteen minutes. Maria extracted the pencil from her hair and tapped her clipboard. "Before we finish up," she announced, "I want to review the Simic case."

Sunny looked up. Stuart crossed his arms and sank deeper into the sofa. Carol Simic, the woman who would teach me about fear. Her name charged the room with tension.

"I got a phone call from Carol over the weekend. She was grateful for our willingness to exempt Stuart from her appointments, but then she remembered our policy about students at births and wanted to be sure he wouldn't be there either. We need to discuss that. Now that Hannah's here, we have more options."

The boyish brightness vanished from Stuart's face. "If she doesn't want me at her birth, that's her choice."

"What's there to discuss?" Sunny asked. "Our policy is all students at all births. If we make an exception this time, it'll be a slippery slope. You two need to reach your quota." Sunny adjusted her bra strap. "There's no good reason for him not to be there. This is a chance to do some educating. If women hold exclusive rights to birth, it's like a secret club. Isn't that shooting ourselves in the foot? We're for accessibility when it comes to clients but not for practitioners?"

Anita looked at her watch. "I'll get ready."

Maria tapped her pencil through the pause. "That's fine in principle, Sunny. But can we really risk clients like that? Carol's a bad place to start an uprising."

"Board members shouldn't get special privileges. If Carol doesn't want apprentices at her birth, she shouldn't come to a learning institution."

"It's more than that. We're about mother-centered birth, right? If a woman wants only women at the birth, that should be her right."

"I don't want to be a teaching tool." Stuart pouted.

Sunny ignored him and crossed her arms. "In that case, we need to reexamine our policies."

"With all their infertility struggles, Carol and Benito don't need more *problemas*." Maria leaned forward to gather the spent napkins and leftover banana bread. "Besides, Hannah's here. She can be the extra hand."

I glanced apologetically at Stuart, who didn't notice.

Sunny rose, brushing her gray-streaked ponytails over her shoulders. "We need to bring this to the board, Maria. We committed to giving Stuart an education, and I want to fulfill that obligation. Hannah—" I straightened. "Now that you're part of the team, you have a voice in this matter. We'll want to hear your opinions too. We run things by consensus. Give it some thought."

I assented blankly. When Maria stood, I did too and remembered the chairs. I started to wheel mine back.

"Stuart," Maria said, patting his knee, "take the morning to give Hannah a thorough tour. You can pick up clinic this afternoon." Her voice was calm and authoritative. She took the file Anita had left on the coffee table and went back to a birth room.

Stuart remained slouched in the sofa, his knobby knees showing through his skirt. I didn't know what to say. Then he sprang into action. "Another day, another learning experience," he proclaimed, grabbing the second chair and trailing me down the hall. "Could be worse, you know. That's what working with dying people teaches you."

"Still," I said, "it's a hard place to be."

"Eh!" He brushed the whole conversation away. "I appreciate Sunny fighting for me. I doubt I'd be here if it weren't for her. This is what midwifery looks like, I guess. Better face it now than be sheltered until graduation and then get slaughtered. Maybe if I'd approached her differently . . ."

We arrived at the back office and sat. Stuart threw his exceptionally long feet up on the desk.

"Carol?" I asked.

"Carol Simic, board member and local bank dominatrix. A woman you don't want to cross, as I found out too late." Stuart gave himself an internal kick—I recognized the wince. "Not that I really crossed her. Maybe I just came on too strong."

I could believe that. "It doesn't sound like it was your fault."

He considered this seriously. "You're right. It wasn't." He picked at the sarong's red fringe. "I should tell you the details since you're supposed to have an opinion and since Carol's your client now."

I hadn't arrived at that conclusion.

"So I was working with Maria maybe three weeks ago, and partway through the afternoon she took a phone call from her mother-in-law about one of the kids. I got Carol, took her weight and blood pressure. I'm being Mr. Friendly, you know, chatting about the drought and who'll sell frito pies at the Chili Festival, while she's getting quieter like this thunderhead's moving in. When I sit her down and ask how the pregnancy's going, she says, 'Where's Maria?' even though I'd already told her. It was her second or third prenatal, so I figure she's attached to Maria.

"Then she says, 'I'd rather wait.' I took it in stride. So we sit there in silence for an eternity, because I couldn't ask her anything clinical and it'd be strange to say, 'How about them Cowboys?' Finally Maria comes in. 'I want to talk to you in private,' Carol tells her, and I hightail it out of there. That's when Carol throws a hissy fit you could hear all the way down the hall, laying into Maria about the Birth House being a women's refuge and my presence a huge violation." He drummed on his thighs.

"It sounds like it's because you're a guy. You can't help that." At the hospital, I'd never thought twice about men doing births. With Stuart, though, I wasn't sure. Was it because he was a man, or because he was a man in a skirt?

"Truer words were never spoken." Stuart raked his fingers through his hair, his face suddenly troubled. "I didn't realize they'd struggled with infertility until this morning. Maybe that's part of it. Anyhow," he looked at the wall clock, "we've got a ton of material to cover."

With that, Stuart launched into a tour of the office, the shelves of three-inch binders, the aging copy machine, the reference books, the computer and its various antiquated databases, and minutiae I was determined to master in a month, as Stuart had. I jotted notes frantically.

In a pause between appointments we entered a birth room. The floor was earthen ceramic. White batiste curtains drifted in front of open windows. The jumble of birth art crowding the rest of the Birth House was absent here, and instead, a single, abstract spiral of energy, beginning with a red splash and spinning the color spectrum outward into a field of heaven-blue, graced the wall directly across from the bed. I breathed in as though I could inhale the room's possibilities.

Out in the reception area, Stuart talked me through the color-coded scheduling book and file drawers behind the desk. Anita chatted leisurely on the phone. By the end of the morning, I'd stopped jumping every time his fingers touched my forearm or when he'd burst out in generous, cascading laughter. He leaned close to explain the nuances of charting, and I began, tentatively, to trust his dedication to *our mamas*. When I stopped my gaze from descending to his waist and when I wasn't sidetracked by the dramatic sweep of his arms or his witty wisecracks, Stuart seemed competent and, potentially, even a friend.

5.

Primip

"DO YOU WANT to feel this?" Stuart palpated the firm balloon of a teenager's belly. Janice was sixteen. Her pink T-shirt was hoisted just below her diminutive breasts, and she'd rigged a button extension to her designer jeans. Sunny sat beside her, holding her hand. "Hannah?" Stuart twisted to find me. My back was pressed against the cool adobe wall. I'd been trying to imagine my way into a pregnant teenager's life—unsuccessfully.

"Do you mind?" I asked Janice.

Her head flopped sideways on the pillow. "Whatever." Janice had full, pouty lips, bleached blond hair pulled back with a terrycloth band, and dramatic sea-green eyes. She was probably missing algebra class. When I placed my hands on her smooth abdomen, she steadied her gaze on Stuart.

Stuart guided my hand until I felt the curved knuckle of a skull tucked in her pelvis: a child, electric and stunning, within a child. So wondrous, I pulled away.

"Feels like the little one's getting into place," I said. In my notebook, I listed the topics Stuart had addressed in this thirtieth week appointment and recorded how, in the future,

I might distinguish a baby's head from its butt. After a dozen appointments, I had accumulated a mess of random and increasingly overwhelming information.

Stuart finished measuring Janice and offered her his hand. "You're doing swell," he said.

She sat up, beaming a pretty smile.

"Let's talk about plans," Sunny said. She sat beside Janice on the bed while Stuart rolled a stool close. "You're into your third trimester now. It's time to think seriously about the birth." Sunny pulled out a photocopied handout entitled *What To Bring to Your Birth House Birth* and talked through each item—loose clothing, light snacks, onesies, diapers—while Janice bobbed her head impatiently and focused puppy-dog eyes on Stuart. She began to annoy me. By the time Sunny asked, "Will you have any family with you?" Janice had forgotten to feign attention.

"Who will be at your birth, sweetie?" Stuart asked.

"Oh. Maybe my sister. I don't know."

"Who do you want there?" Sunny tried. "Who would be supportive?"

"I don't care. Will you?" she asked Stuart.

"Definitely. Hannah and I will both be there. We're serious students, and you're going to be our teacher."

"Hardly." Janice giggled and rolled her eyes. Her insouciance grated on me. She'd gotten herself into trouble. She should take this seriously.

"If you'd like your sister here, invite her in for an appointment," Sunny said. "What about your boyfriend?"

"No friggin' way. I don't want him to see me shitting myself."

"Your mom?"

Janice turned away sharply. "She works."

"She could come over a lunch break. Whoever you want, it'd be good for us to meet them."

Janice exhaled impatience.

"All right. That's enough for today." Sunny helped Janice off the bed before she could reach for Stuart. "We'd love to have you at birth class Wednesday night. We're showing a few videos, so you could get a sense of what to expect. Wednesday night. Seven o'clock. Birth class." Sunny handed Janice the list she'd left on the bed. "Make an appointment with Anita on your way out, for next week."

When the door closed, Sunny whispered, "That kid—and I mean *kid*—is expecting a Cabbage Patch doll to pop out." According to New Mexico law, girls could make prenatal and custodial decisions at age sixteen, much to Sunny's dismay. I doubted I could ever be a midwife to someone like Janice without shaking her silly. The realization distressed me. "And you"— Sunny swung accusingly toward Stuart—"I don't know whether you're a hindrance or our only hope to get her attention. Don't encourage her by calling her 'sweetie.' That's all she needs."

Stuart's jaw dropped. "I could be her father!"

Sunny swatted him with Janice's file. "Wish you were. She wouldn't be in this predicament."

"Shouldn't she put the baby up for adoption?" I asked.

"She claims her mom's against it, although God knows what the woman's thinking, leaving her daughter alone with this." Sunny tucked the file under her arm. "Kids have babies here. That's the norm. Five minutes, *amigos.*"

In the hiatus before the next client, I sought refuge in the bathroom. The walls and ceiling were plastered posters and bumper stickers advertising abuse hotlines, drug hotlines, what to do if your child's choking, and ten activities to save the planet. With the onslaught of medical information and appointments and glimpses into strangers' lives, my stomach felt soft, as though I were still careening down the mountain pass in the taxi van. How would I ever measure up to Sunny, with her fierce ideals? Or to Maria, who seemed infinitely capable? I wished my mother were alive so I could draw on her steadiness. I wished I had my father's bolstering faith.

Compared with Janice, sixteen and pregnant, I was taking risks that were trifling. Even so, my breathing was shallow and quick. I hung my head between my knees, soaking up the cool comfort of porcelain and tile. Our moments of greatest courage are hidden and humble. Most of mine took place in that absurd bathroom where I retreated again and again, and then, with fresh determination, flushed away my reticence.

6.

Grand River

LEST YOU THINK these stories are the indulgence of a rambling middle-aged midwife, I'm making a point here: To recognize what's being born, you first have to know what doesn't exist. You think it's simple—no baby, then *voila*! A pink and wrinkled human the size of a hoagie. But that newborn is only the outward and visible sign of an inward and invisible reality, which was my father's definition of sacrament. You're a midwife to the insides too.

Of course I didn't learn that lesson with any alacrity. Carol Simic and Janice, the uppity teenager, were my teachers. Maria and Sunny facilitated, probably sharing a smirk when I wasn't looking.

By Thursday of that first week, I'd moved into my rented room and was enjoying the mile between it and the Birth House. The blue of the New Mexican sky, I'd discovered, was deceptive; in the morning I needed a coat that noontime made unnecessary. Past the boxy chain grocery and some fast food franchises, downtown Sangre de Cristo was a nonsensical collection of laundromats, thrift stores, pricey art galleries, and T-shirt shops. Large kettles on the sidewalks belched green, roasty smoke. Magpies teased from scraggly branches, and traffic stalled in the narrow streets. Behind low buildings and across the distance, mountains sliced the horizon. The town was exotic and hopping.

Up in the crash room that morning, I found Stuart wearing an orange tank top and denim overalls rolled above his pointy ankles. He sat downing coffee, shoulders hunched, nose close to the desk. "*Hola, hermana. ¿Cómo estás?*" He barely looked up.

"Bushed."

We crammed for an hour. The textbooks, unlike any I'd studied previously, read like good murder mysteries. How would I recognize a normal pregnancy when this woman wasn't gaining weight and that one had terrible leg cramps and the next hadn't slept for two months? Each small-print fact could be applied to real human beings who would walk through the door at any minute. I had never been so motivated.

At nine sharp, Sunny entered and dropped a thick binder onto the crash room bed. The sheets rippled. "Okay, kids. Today's lesson is on uterine inertia and sphincters. I've given it the title, *Sphincters Aren't Egyptian*." Stuart and I looked up from our respective desks. "That's a joke. I guess you need the lesson first."

We joined Sunny on the bed in a disciple-esque flotilla. Sunny leaned against the wall, skirt hoisted above her knees, her unshaven legs splayed. Her agility, her floppy ponytails, and especially her clothes belied her age, which I guessed to be mid-sixties. A bit older than Mom. Sunny was utterly different. I hardly knew how to relate to her.

"Okay. If you ask most women what scares them about birth," Sunny began, "they'll say pain or finding out there's something wrong with the child. If you ask me what keeps women from natural childbirth, I'd say fear of pain, fear of things going wrong, especially for the fetus. So we need to be smart about what fear does to women physiologically, because no matter how educated or emotionally prepared a mom is, at one point or another during the birthing process, she'll be afraid. Almost all first-time moms think they're dying during labor. Do we abuse that or work with it?"

I sat with my pen poised above my notebook, considering whether my mother thought she was dying at my birth. Very possibly. She'd called me a "miracle baby." Not for the first time, I'd wondered what exactly had happened to make me a miracle and Dr. Jorgenson my hero.

"There's economic value in women feeling afraid," Sunny continued, "at least to the medical and pharmaceutical industries, so fear doesn't get addressed much." As it turned out, this was one of Sunny's favorite diatribes—thus my clear memory.

She delineated for us the swift progression of chemical shifts that happen during labor. When a mother becomes afraid, adrenaline surges, heart and respiratory rates increase, and blood gets shunted away from internal organs to the large muscle groups. "Adrenaline's the body's natural emergency brake," she said. "How often have you heard of a woman progressing fine, checking into a hospital, and *wham*—her labor stops. Adrenaline neutralizes oxytocin, the hormone that stimulates uterine contractions.

"But oxytocin also instigates the mother's affection for the infant. So, fear," Sunny said, punctuating the progression with her turquoise-studded fingers, "then adrenaline, then no contractions, no motivation to bond. Are you tracking?"

Stuart and I nodded as if we understood, but it would take me years to grasp the implications.

"Another casualty of adrenaline is the endorphins. Which . . ." Sunny left a test blank.

"Help the baby swim," Stuart said. Sunny *tsked.*

"Block the pain," I said. "Like in a runner's high."

"Good. We release endorphins when we're under major physical strain, especially if we're also feeling safe, warm, and loved. They're ten times more potent than morphine. When you see laboring women in ecstasy, it's the endorphins." I pictured the French woman in Michel Odent's book—her open-mouthed smile that was also a shout, the sheen of her skin, pleasure and pain locked in a love embrace. "Unfortunately that's rare, because adrenaline always neutralizes the effect of the endorphins. And the brain doesn't get an endorphin high if it's on pain meds."

Most women didn't know this secret about their bodies. The thought made me tremble.

"Ergo, if a whole society's convinced birth is scary, it really is. Questions?"

"I thought the pain was because Eve goofed," Stuart quipped.

I shifted, trying to put distance between us.

Sunny pushed her forefinger into Stuart's arm. "Injury pain is constant, while birth pain has a rhythm, in and out, in and out." Sunny punched the air with her fist. "Then it ends. The question you should be asking"—I reflexively reproached myself—"is what we can do about fear. Which brings us to sphincters. They're the circular muscles that form the vaginal opening. Where else do we find them?"

Stuart deferred to me. "The rectum?" I ventured. Despite my excitement at Sunny's lecture, or maybe because of it, a headache was slowly working its way across my temples.

Sunny nodded. "And the bladder. You learned about controlling your sphincters during potty training—we hope. Think of what it sometimes takes to poop. Privacy. Safety. Familiarity with the people around you and the surroundings. The same conditions open the cervix. I always get constipated camping because of the daggone stinky latrines. You definitely can't *order* a sphincter to open. Adrenaline shuts 'em down." Sunny crossed her arms. "We know how sphincters work, but only instinctively. It's that animal-self we need to bring forward for birth to do its thing."

I had assumed we were supposed to help *make* a birth happen, that midwives were different from doctors only in that they had friendlier, gentler methods. But nobody, not even the mother, could force a sphincter open.

"Then it's not about getting the baby out," I blurted. Amusement flicked across Sunny's face. "I mean, mostly what the midwife is doing is psychological. Helping the mom relax."

Stuart elbowed me. "Right on, sister."

Sunny shifted, and we rode the waves. She described Odent's research, which showed how environment is the one controllable factor that influences birth results. "I'd say the literal environment isn't nearly as important as the psychic environment, which the midwife brings with her into the room."

Sunny missed Stuart's grimace. I rubbed my forehead while Sunny plowed forward, describing the link between a woman's emotional state and her birthing experience, the importance of the relationship between midwife and client, and how trust affects hormonal responses.

Periodically she'd make grand pronouncements like "Accepting natural childbirth is fundamental to a culture's ability to love women. If we loved women, we'd trust our bodies," and I scribbled them down, hoping time would help me comprehend. Amid a tumble of oxytocin and prostaglandins, I released myself into the headache, which now throbbed and blotted out the room. I tried to catch a thought swirling hazily at the edges—something about a midwife needing to be passive, not active. Sunny turned to Stuart. "I've missed your charming wit this last bit."

Stuart leaned against the wall and shut his eyes. "It does beg the question whether a man's presence in the room is detrimental."

Sunny placed her binder on the floor and flexed her ankles. Her toenails were painted scarlet. Her face grew still. "That's an important question."

Stuart ran his narrow fingers through his hair, loosening his ponytail.

"Your wondering shows sensitivity, Stuart. I value that in a midwife."

"Carol Simic's not some bizarre anomaly. There will be moms who won't have me. Hell, I sympathize. My sphincters wouldn't cooperate if some hunk were hovering over my bathroom stall."

Hunk—I felt suddenly hot despite the breeze creeping through the windows. Stuart was gay. Of course! Was I that clueless? I wanted to leave the room. I couldn't handle the overload of information. Sweat trickled between my breasts. I monitored the static between Stuart, hair mussed and eyes anxious, and Sunny, whose arms were crossed.

"Okay, you're right. There will always be women who refuse to work with you. That's life. We all deal with it one way or another, with personality differences—"

"Or prejudice."

"Sure. My point is we have to find within ourselves hospitality toward birth. Women respond to that. Just think of all the well-loved male obstetricians. If you're squarely in that welcoming place, others' rejection isn't about you. That's your challenge, Stuart." Stuart's lips were thin. "After you interviewed, I said to Maria, 'That kid has one of the widest hearts I've ever seen.' Have I told you that? I want that heart available to women. You just have a few extra hurdles."

"That's me." Stuart spread his arms and hung his head. "Atoning for the sins of men."

"Don't get a complex." Sunny glanced at the wall clock. "For me it comes down to this: Is midwifery a secret society for women? That doesn't serve women's best interests." Sunny stood, creating an unsteady sea. "I need to be downstairs for a phone conference. The pizza comes at noon."

She left.

Stuart turned to me, arms crossed. "You'd think women'd feel safe around a fairy gayer than springtime."

What could I say?

"You're blushing!" Stuart laughed then sobered. "You didn't know?" His cool fingers wrapped around my knuckles. I shook my head. I should have known; there'd been gay orderlies and nurses at St. Luke's.

"Oof," Stuart said. "Lesson learned: Never assume the obvious. Cal runs a photography gallery down in Albuquerque; we rendezvous in Santa Fe when I'm free. Together three years, Cocker Spaniel, condo in the university district, a shared obsession with Victorian romance novels. All that's missing is the two and a half kids, which isn't an option, much to my remorse. My first partner died of AIDS, thus the hospice career. What else? Sunny and Maria know. The clients don't, but I'm not into deception." He released my hand and dug his fingers into his hair, pulling his eyebrows up and releasing them. "I'll answer whatever questions you've got. No holds barred." Beneath the words his tone was pleading.

"I'm sorry," I said, meeting his eyes. We had a half-hour until lunch. "I've got a splitting headache. I'll be back. I need a quick walk." I struggled off the bed.

"Sure," Stuart said uncertainly.

* * *

Outside the October sun was searing. Heat from the concrete rose through the flimsy soles of my sandals. Downtown bustled with locals grabbing lunch and tourists (after a week, I could distinguish them) blocking the sidewalk as they window-shopped. I turned down a residential side street lined with latilla fences. It meandered uphill, the houses thinning until I arrived at empty, brown pastureland with a few mangy horses grazing on God knows what. I scuffed my toes in street sand— no sidewalks here—and felt a sudden sadness about this place with its barren yards and unleashed, ceaselessly barking mutts, its acres of clay-colored homes, and the way strangers with dark faces turned to stare at my white-blond, too-thin hair. The mountains were glorious, but where were the lakes? To assuage the sickening swirl in my stomach, I needed to dive into water, to pull through that initial shiver into the familiar oblivion that makes everything bearable. The Rio Grande, I suspected, would not do. I licked dust from my lips. Clumps of sagebrush spotted the sand. For all its ski resorts and happy-go-lucky chili peppers, Northern New Mexico was a desert.

You didn't know?

I missed sane, straightforward Leif, who called sex "making love" and never asked probing questions. I had finally called and we'd talked for two hours straight. He offered to visit at Christmas. Striding down the street I longed for egg rolls in bed with Leif's quiet body next to mine. I wanted marriage and kids. I did not want Stuart and cocky pregnant teenagers and sphincters that refused to open.

Gravel cut the thin soles of my sandals. Above, the sky was blue-eye blue. On Sunday afternoons during my childhood, we'd sometimes drive out to my grandparents' farm near Bemidji, passing over country roads that offered nothing but sky, planted horizon, and a continuous ditch of butterfly weed, wild asparagus, sow thistle, and black-eyed Susans. Wind roared through the car like the Holy Ghost. In my parents' silence, I sensed the effort of Sunday's services, the weighty demands on my father, my mother's grave social obligations, and my own effort to make myself invisible so as not to reflect badly on either of them, all gathered up and released. Looking out the passenger window, my mother would say, to no one in particular, "Heaven on a hillside, and my heart's happy."

I wanted to feel my mother in me, the part of her I cherished, soaking Minnesota from the moist black soil, up. I wanted to be a midwife too, but the deeper in I got, the more I suspected I was betraying Mom.

Back in town, pickups with cracked windshields were parked carelessly along the curb and clean rental cars trolled the streets. I pushed through the Birth House gate, strode up to the dangling braids of chilies and garlic, and opened the door.

Sunny handed me a pizza box. "Margrita's in labor. Let's go."

And so I slipped into the grand river which is birth, speeding across town to a small canyon nuzzled up against state forest land and a ramshackle house full of kids and the sounds of labor. I readied warming blankets in the kitchen oven and charted with an unsteady hand into the night. Margrita lay sideways on a four-poster bed, legs bent and feet thrusting against Sunny. "That's it," Sunny crooned. "You're doing great. Push through the pain. Your baby's on the other side of that pain." Pain was a threshold to cross over and back and over again until, with

Margrita's gasp, a baby girl arrived—a stunned creature Stuart cupped in his lithe fingers. Sunny gave her a once-over, passed her to Margrita, and motioned to me. I fitted the cotton cap on her head and tucked her in blankets. Stuart and I burned our exhilaration afterward by scrubbing the bedroom floor on hands and knees, pouring peroxide onto bloodstained sheets, loading them in the washer, and charting the night's events with unnecessary fervor, our mutual glee temporarily distracting me from any boulders teetering overhead.

7.

OPENING

"HAVE I BEEN drinking coffee?" Sunny asked the ceiling. She lay spread-eagled on the Birth House waiting room rug, her ponytails skewed and mussed, her eyes sunken with exhaustion. It was five a.m. Saturday morning, a week later, and the last of three families had just walked out the door.

"No," Stuart said. "I poured you adrenaline, straight up. Hope you won't need your sphincters."

I shut my eyes and let my body sag in the too-soft sofa. In the past seven days I'd spent a total of thirteen hours in my tiny rented room. I was "beyond-beyond," as my mother would say, too weary to move and too wired to sleep.

"*Por el amor de Dios*, why do they always come at once?" Maria said from the easy chair.

At the beginning of my second week, Sunny had handed me a blood pressure cuff and said, "Give it a whirl." The midwives expected us to be the clients' primary human contact as we were training, which meant careful and casual banter with them during lag times; showing new clients how to test their urine for protein, a signal of preeclampsia; discussing the birth class schedule with them; holding hands or cooling brows during contractions, and other tasks that accumulated until the stakes seemed high. I was in constant terror of tripping up. I didn't want to defile something sacred. And I didn't want to be rejected by a client, like Stuart.

He charmed most everyone else. The young mothers teased him about his appearance, batted back his witticisms, and begged him for back rubs during labor. Since he'd said I could ask him anything, during a coffee break I had blurted, "Why the skirt?" Stuart angled his chair against the wall. "I don't play gender games. People think you have to look a certain way to be a man. I'm a man; I like skirts. I want people to see me, not a confirmation of their stereotypes." He shrugged, as though it were no big deal. During lessons and appointments, he deferred to me because I was the newbie. He was a man, he was gay, he wore a skirt, and yet I couldn't help feeling he was better suited to midwifery than me. I could barely palpate an abdomen without worrying I'd burst the mother's spleen.

Anita saved me. One afternoon she persuaded the midwives to let me skip clinic. She showed me the stack of rejected Medicaid forms, which caused her to grip her puffed bangs and pull them heavenward. I'd never done billing, and yet each time I asked a question or made an observation, Anita proclaimed, "*¡Gracias a Dios!*" Once, she put her hands on my shoulders and kissed both my cheeks just as Sunny passed. "Did we bring you a present?" Sunny asked.

Anita cast Sunny a dark eye. "It wears thin, working with you creative types. Hannah here actually believes in accuracy."

Anita was systematic, dogged, and swamped. She squeezed an old typing table between the bookshelves and filing cabinets so we could both work up front. With my help on billing, she hoped the Birth House might break even. The cramped corner behind her desk became my haven of competency.

And then the backlog of births that had been delayed my first week hit us like an autumn storm, beginning Thursday evening with one woman grunting in childbirth on each side of the Birth

House hallway. A third began her pre-labor in the crash room. At one o'clock Saturday morning, Maria ordered me to put on gloves and join her on the floor. The mom was squatting beside the bed, her elbows propped on the edge. She squeezed her husband's hand as she blew through the contractions.

"*Ya viene. Aquí está la cabesita. Estás haciendo muy bien,*" Maria told her, and showed me the bulging perineum, the waves of the baby's advance and retreat.

"Put gentle pressure against the head—there," she guided my wrist toward the wet crown—I had no choice—"and support the perineum with your left hand."

The mother let out a victorious "Aiii!" and there was the baby, creamy with vernix, open-eyed, breathing. In my palms. Just like that, I'd caught my first baby. She glistened under the floor lamp; she smelled clean, like earthworms in the spring.

Maria helped the mother into bed while I followed closely with the baby, white loops of umbilical cord trailing between us. "*Chulita,*" the mom said when I placed her child against her bare breast. "*Angelita.*" Maria handed me a towel, and together the mother and I dried the baby and bundled that fragrant and glistening skin. Afterward, in the hall, Stuart gave me a high-five and I squealed.

"I'm famished," Sunny said from the floor. "How about breakfast out?"

"Felipe's," Maria said. "Bacon and eggs."

My head sizzled, my mouth was sour. At the mention of food, my body mustered an extravagant hunger and my spirits plummeted. Could I survive another hour without sleep?

We piled into Sunny's truck, four of us squashed in the front without seatbelts. I braced myself against the door. Sunny accelerated to hit the pothole at the bottom of the driveway. She and Maria raised their hands and shouted, "Yee-haw!" When Sunny braked to turn onto the empty main street, we slid forward.

"What's with the cowboy routine?" Stuart asked.

"Cheap thrills, Stu."

We drove the five blocks to Felipe's, not one of us apologetic for not walking. Downtown was so quiet, at the red light Sunny said, "Screw it," and plowed through. She made a lazy U-turn up over the curb, setting off another artillery of laughter, and pulled the brake in front of the restaurant. As we tumbled out our separate doors, Stuart whispered in my ear, "Punch drunk."

"Breakfast's on the Birth House." Maria led us in, her black braid swaying across her back.

Felipe's was a quirky combo of fifties diner and Southwestern burrito stand, the booths and chrome-top tables empty so early in the morning. A waitress greeted us. Her black minidress was tied tight around her thick waist and a ruffled white apron hugged her breasts. "¡Parteras! Sit." She handed Maria a stack of cushioned menus. "Coffee's coming."

I scooted down the cracked seat. Stuart followed, throwing his arms wide across the booth. I longed to lay my cheek against the menu's cool plastic surface. I could barely make out *huevos rancheros* and remain upright.

"So here's what we never told you two about becoming apprentices." Sunny tucked her Guatemalan bag under the table. "You have to pass the Postnatal Agility Test." Maria snorted. "Can you hang a spoon on your nose after not sleeping for forty-eight hours? Don't laugh," she scolded Maria.

Stuart dug into the swaddled silverware. He breathed into the bowl of his teaspoon and balanced it on the boyish upslope of his nose. The handle dangled in front of his Adam's apple.

Sunny followed, licking her clean spoon for traction then conversing with Stuart between precariously hung stainless. Maria *tsked* and left for the restroom. When the waitress dropped off a carafe, she clucked something in Spanish. I pressed a hot mug to my face, thinking of the nine hours of hard labor I'd just watched. Sunny had reached up to her elbow inside the mother to shift the baby's position from posterior to anterior. The moment should have been tense but wasn't. Sunny had radiated calm; the baby cooperated. Was that really what I'd seen? I wished my misfiring synapses would clear.

"Hannah, don't let these *idiotas* get to you," Maria declared, sitting back down.

The waitress returned with her faded pad and a ballpoint pen. "*¡Ay, caramba!*" she said. The suspended silverware clattered to the table. I rested my head against the window while she took our orders.

In the pause that followed, Stuart said, "I totally freaked when you changed that baby's position." He demonstrated, as though we wanted to picture the poor woman's invaded uterus over breakfast. "Made me wonder what was the scariest birth you've seen."

Sunny sat across from me, her feet squarely on the floor. Maria, dark and delicate-boned, perched on the bench with an occasional bounce. They both cocked their heads.

"Well, there's medical-scary and then there's scary-scary," Sunny said. "The time I was most scared shitless was three months after we opened the Birth House."

"*¡Ay, Dios!*" Maria declared, forehead sinking to her hands.

Sunny glanced around the empty restaurant and lowered her voice. "So it was a weekday night, and I'd stayed late to do some paperwork. About eleven, I hear someone open the front door. This was back when we were still using my kids' twin beds in the birth rooms, remember that?" She looked to Maria. "So I go down the hallway saying, 'Hello?' and find this couple I'd never laid eyes on before. He's this hulk of a guy. I mean enormous pecs, broad shoulders, the kind of guy who makes women think twice about walking alone at night. He could beat you to a pulp without working up a sweat. He's supporting this waif who's totally in labor. She's pushing right there in the front doorway. I swear, the baby's about to pop out any minute, and I've never seen either of them in prenatal. 'Are you the midwife?' he asks. I say 'yeah,' and he reaches around to his back pocket— he's holding the girl with one arm—and pulls out a gun."

"What?" Stuart's mug hit the table. I perked up. Maria must have heard this story hundreds of times, and she still looked interested.

"Yep. He pointed it at me and said, 'Buffy's having a baby—"

"Buffy?" Stuart repeated.

" 'Buffy's having a baby, and I want you to do your thing. Lamaze or whatever it is.' So I'm thinking, holy shit, this guy wants me to do *Lamaze* with this woman—she was *maybe* twenty— after Maria and I had just worked out the legal requirements for our practice, none of which this couple met, and he's holding a gun. We got her onto the bed screaming and pushing, and I barely had time to put on gloves before the baby crowned. The whole time he stood two paces behind me pointing that damn thing at my back. Thank the universe everything went fine. I don't know what he might have done if I'd had to resuscitate."

"That's crazy," I said. The waitress set down platters of soupy eggs, bacon, and toast glistening with butter. I almost swooned.

"And guess what they named the baby. Mom was Buffy, dad was Brute or something like that—"

"Tyrone," Maria corrected.

"Tyrone, and they named the baby Charity. I signed the birth certificate. I can prove it."

"Why would someone hold up a birth center? For its services, I mean," I said.

"Pretty ingenious," Sunny answered. "If they'd said, 'We can't afford to pay you'—heck, even if they could've afforded it, I would have sent them to the hospital. My guess is they were in trouble with the law and didn't have a penny between them." Sunny took a generous bite of waffle. "How's that for a primo midwife's tale?"

Maria thrust a fork at her business partner. "You always play that story like it's the only trump card in the pack."

My eggs were greasy and undercooked and tasted divine.

"I'm hooked," Stuart said. "Bring 'em on."

"*Bueno.*" Maria bounced on the booth cushion. "There was the time this woman showed up at the Birth House *de mirada furiosa*, her eyes wild, crazy hair, her mouth hanging open. She stood in front of Anita's desk grunting, and when Anita got up to show her the door, she noticed this bulge in the woman's crotch.

We laid her right down in the entryway, and I had to cut her pants to deliver the baby. But that doesn't count—" she cut off Sunny's protest with the flash of her knife, "*porque* it's really Anita's story."

I put down my toast. "She was giving birth in her *pants*?"

Sunny and Maria nodded.

The hot eggs slathered with salsa, the side of steaming black beans and the coffee were entering my bloodstream, shooting my brain with disproportionate bursts of energy. My whole body heated up. The unexpected was normal here. The midwives had shed their professional demeanor and were treating us like friends. I could no longer calculate the hours I'd been awake, and now women showed up with babies half-born in their pants. I'd lost my balance and was afraid they might notice. "So the moral is be prepared for anything," I said.

"*Exactamente.*" Now Maria jabbed her fork at me. "Which brings me to my story. One thing you'll learn about living *aquí* is that there's a lot of people off the grid, out on the mesa or tucked in the mountains, a few old-timer Latinos and Native Americans, but mostly gringo hippies evading taxes and saving the world. Which means that sometimes we're doing homebirths in dug-out houses with no running water. You'll get to see that. So this couple comes in for prenatal care. Stargazer and Honeysuckle."

"No!" Stuart protested.

Sunny jumped in. "You have to picture this: Stargazer is maybe six-four, skinny as a rail, wearing a white monk's robe or something and this huge, dangling pentacle pendant around his neck, and Honeysuckle is this petite thing, probably some East Coast banker's daughter, in tie-dye and a gold band around her head."

"*¡Es la verdad!*" Maria said. "They lived in Las Alturas squatting on national forest land. Somehow they'd gotten a railroad car dumped there which they were using for their house, and Stargazer told me they'd buried their VW bus in the ground to use as a septic tank. It's hard for me to imagine them that enterprising. Anyhow, at their first prenatal they were cautious, wanting to know if I'd go out there, if I'd be comfortable without running water and electricity, would it be okay if Stargazer played drums during the birth, if I was open to herbal remedies for problems during pregnancy—all normal stuff. They kept looking at each other, like they were testing me. Finally I asked if they had any concerns. Stargazer gives me this intense stare, comes over, puts his hands on my temples"— Maria leaned across our breakfasts to grip my forehead—"and says in this woo-woo voice, 'The baby in Honeysuckle's womb isn't mine. It was conceived during a consensual abduction, and we have the honor of welcoming this new commingling of the species onto the planet. Will you, Maria, take responsibility for midwifing this precious union?'"

With the explosion of my laugh, the eggs in my mouth sprayed across the table, narrowly missing Maria. Horrified, I reached over my plate to hide the splattering of yellow and knocked my water glass over, sending icy water into Sunny's lap. I took a humiliated moment to realize Sunny's howls were hysterics and that the only thing funnier than Maria's alien baby was me. I caught their laughter, squeezing out tears which Stuart was swift to point out through his own sleep-deprived hilarity, and the four of us rocked the booth. Between bouts, Maria told us how Stargazer drummed himself into a hypnotic state at the birth and totally ignored Honeysuckle, who made little "oo-oo-oo" noises with each contraction, and how both of them were shocked and a little disappointed when Maria declared the baby entirely normal.

I reveled in our joint lack of manners, in the absurdity of my being there, in Sunny's complaints that she was going to pee in her pants and Maria's refusal to let her out of the booth, and in the waitress's reluctance to refill our coffeepot as though she were a bartender at closing time. Having relinquished my good image, I laughed as I'd never laughed before, uproariously, helplessly. When Maria finally rose to pay the bill and Sunny dashed to the ladies' room, Stuart put his arm over my shoulder and said, "Life's grand." He gave me a squeeze, and I accepted it.

Out on the street, I insisted on walking the four blocks to my room. Maria stood on tiptoe to give me a hug and then there were hugs all around, quick and friendly, the four of us a team. I walked away as Sunny flapped her skirt, drying the wet spot. I couldn't stop thinking about Honeysuckle and her baby, conceived by aliens. Maria had treated them with respect. I admired that. I wanted to be that generous. The New Mexican winter sun warmed my hair, and I felt a burst of gratitude for being seven thousand feet nearer its glory.

8.

Blood Pressure

THREE BIRTHS A week wasn't uncommon during my apprenticeship, some in quirky adobe homes, some in shacks out on the mesa, most at the Birth House, always consecutive or overlapping so that our bodies muddled elation with exhaustion. Sleep became a drug. Years later, Stuart told me that the constant rush of births reminded him of marathon sex. Ha! It reminded me of the ecstasy of my first communion, a fuzzy tingling in my temples and a maniac heart. In blood and sweat and the pungent scent of amniotic fluid resided eternity. Every few days I inhabited a limitless space of origins and ends.

Clinic jerked me back. Clients had leg cramps or no insurance or concerns that their previous C-section would prevent them from having a vaginal birth. Inexplicably, they looked to me for answers. My throat dried, my hands thickened. I fumbled the tape measure from pubic bone to fundus across bellies so taut the skin rippled with marks. Maria handed me a checklist; I did intake interviews. Women's faces softened as they related their medical histories. They asked *me* questions. They smiled warmly at *me*. Appalled, I deferred to Maria or Sunny, and the women's affection shifted away.

During my third week, Carol Simic appeared on the schedule—Stuart's 'nemesis.' "Don't take her personally," he advised. "Kindness is tough when you've got a spike up your ass." He was sitting on the desk in the back office, feet on the chair, knees knocked.

"My, we're bitter." I lifted her chart from the filing cabinet. I wasn't going to let Stuart's issues spill into my work.

Stuart waved dismissively. "Water under the bridge. You two will probably hit it off."

Out in the waiting room, a man and woman leaned into one another on the couch. Uncertain, I glanced at Anita, who nodded. "Carol?" I walked around. "I'm Hannah Larson, the new apprentice." They struggled up. On heels, Carol was almost my height. Her cream business suit looked more like Wall Street than the wily backwaters of New Mexico. Her haircut, strawberry-blond waves, was expensive. Her fingers tightened around mine.

"My husband, Benito."

"Nice to meet you."

Benito removed his cowboy hat. He was stocky and short, with glistening brown skin. He smiled broadly.

"Why don't you take care of your urine test and weight," I told Carol on our way down the hall. "We'll be in the red room."

"Benito! ¿Cómo estás?" Maria grasped Benito's shoulders. They exchanged cheek kisses and happy, cascading Spanish. Benito's bass voice dominated the room. I made myself inconspicuous, laying the chart open on the desk and moving chairs to accommodate everyone. "You've met Hannah," Maria switched to English when she saw me fidgeting. "Benito is Luis's second cousin. Do you know Jimenez Lumber, out at the north end of town?"

I didn't.

"My empire," Benito said.

"Hannah's come all the way from Minnesota."

Benito shuddered. "Aren't there glaciers up there?"

"Sure," I said lightly. "And herds of moose. And ice-fishing huts, where people spend the winter." His eyes widened.

A sharp, expensive scent entered with Carol. "Everything was negative," she reported. "I'm at one thirty-six."

"That's great," I said, then regretted spending my enthusiasm so liberally.

Carol sat on the bed and crossed her ankles. She caught us up on the past month—she'd survived a rough first trimester and could now enjoy her morning orange juice. Sleep was wretched. Did Maria have any suggestions? Carol was decked out in gold jewelry; her hands covered a nylon-tan knee. As yet she wasn't showing, although her cheeks had probably puffed with the hormonal shift. She was older than most of the Birth House clients—thirty-nine, her chart said. At our Monday staff meeting, Maria had relayed the history of their late marriage, two-year struggle with infertility, and the final, happy victory of conception.

Beside Carol on the bed, Benito dangled his hat between his legs. His upper arms bulged against the limitations of his shirtsleeves.

"Let's check your blood pressure." At Maria's cue, I stood with the cuff and stethoscope, their rubber tubing bouncing every which way. Carol peered down her left arm. I rested my knee on the bed. Velcro gripped her upper arm; I pumped, trying to distinguish Carol's internal thumping from my own, and followed the needle's swing. "One thirty-five over ninety," I said. "A little high."

Following protocol, Maria double-checked my work. "Wasn't that true last time?"

I read the chart. "It's getting better."

Benito cleared his throat. "I got us enrolled in a yoga class that starts next week."

"*Bueno.*" Maria smiled. "What about diet? Are you cutting down on empty calories?"

The couple looked penitent. "No more doughnuts," Benito said.

"Reduce your stress at work. Use the baby as an excuse. Go for a walk. Meditate. I don't care, just interrupt those long stretches."

"You know that's hard."

Maria raised her eyebrows.

"A friend taught me some breathing exercises," Carol conceded. "I'll give them a go."

"Lunch!" Benito shouted. "I'll treat you a couple times a week."

We took Carol's measurements, felt for the baby and listened for heart tones. Each time I touched her, Carol flinched. Maria must have noticed because she stepped back, put her hands on her hips, and said, "Carol, I want to make sure we're on the same page about apprentices. We've discussed it as a staff and decided to make an exception to the policy—with Stuart, I mean. Given the circumstances. So we'll assign Hannah to your birth. How is that for you?"

I slunk back to my stool. Carol tucked in her blouse then fluffed it uniformly.

"It's not just him. I want to surround myself with people who *get it*. Real midwives. Or women who've given birth. Have you?" Shame flooded me reflexively, and I shook my head. "See?" Her voice was ragged. "It's my rite of passage. Isn't that what the birth movement's about? Empowering us to make our own decisions? At least that's what I've been volunteering for all this time."

Maria's pager, clipped outside her jumper pocket, vibrated loudly. She switched it off without looking. "Of course. But when you chose to work with us, Carol, you agreed to participate in a learning institution. Training new midwives is part of our mission. You can always go someplace else."

"You know I adore you." Carol flicked her head, cascading curls.

Benito rose just as the minute hand hit the hour. "Give Hannah a chance, *dulcita*. Maybe you'd choose to have her there anyhow."

I pretended not to notice Carol's frown.

"Is it about feeling safe?" Maria asked tenderly.

The room quieted. When I looked up, Carol's eyes were shiny. She touched them with the tip of her ring finger, careful to avoid the mascara. Benito pulled a folded red bandanna from his rear pocket and pressed it into Carol's hand.

"Maybe that's it," Carol said. "It creeps up on me sometimes. Jesus, I'm a wreck. I didn't mean to explode, Maria. It's the damn hormones." She stood. "I'm giving you and Sunny trouble."

"Not at all."

The handkerchief was wadded in her fingers. "Two weeks?" she asked, referring to her next appointment.

"Four."

Benito gave Maria another peck and shook my hand violently. After they left, Maria checked her pager. "Flora Whitewater. I bet she's in labor. Hannah, I've got to take this call. Keep in mind that Carol and Benito have been through a lot. Carol's testy. Don't take it personally." She squeezed my elbow and left.

Stuart's exact words. Still, I wanted to throw myself on the bed and fold up into nothing. The door was open so I retreated to the corner instead, inhaling the residue of Carol's perfume and testing myself against her fear. Perhaps motherhood was the password into this profession, and not training; perhaps I didn't belong here any more than Stuart did. A moment from my childhood swelled inside me: Mom carrying a hot dish to a neighbor's, me trailing behind. Before pushing the doorbell, Mom had crouched down to my seven-year-old height.

"Now, Hannah, I know you love babies. But this one is brand new. Don't ask to hold her. It's not polite." Then Mom went right for the squirmy bundle, which the neighbor handed over gladly. I peered at the newborn, feeling strangely dirty.

In the empty birth room, I realized that fate had not relegated me to the outskirts of others' lives, as I'd always assumed, but Mom's inexplicable dictums. Enough. To hell with her nay-saying and anyone else's. My passion for prenatal care would exceed that of any experienced mother. Carol would beg to have me at her birth.

I slammed the desk drawer. If I picked up a sandwich on my way home, I could get in five hours of studying before bed.

9.

Flesh Boundaries

FRIDAY MORNING, SUNNY stood in the crash room doorway, hands on hips. "Stuart, would you give Hannah a blood-draw lesson?"

Maria had assured me I could proceed through the apprenticeship requirements at my own pace. She may not have minded my taking my sweet time, but I suspected I was trying Sunny's patience.

Stuart hooked my elbow. "Let's play vampire."

"Poor you," I said.

I liked Maria better. Her precise instructions, her no-nonsense attitude toward our education, and the firm, motherly way she cared for clients suited me. Sunny's imposing stature and unpredictable, hippie ideals made me self-conscious. Despite my suspicion that a dark underbelly of judgment lurked beneath Sunny's passion, I wanted to climb a ladder of skill and daring and arrive in her ranks.

Stuart grabbed a kit from storage, and we took seats at a desk in one of the clinic rooms. I'd observed dozens of blood draws: the stretchy band, the gentle slap of two fingers, the cold alcohol swipe and then the stab, the catch, the crimson collection. Sunny was right: I could do this. Stuart scrunched the sleeve of his white T-shirt up over his pointy shoulder blade. He looked like a macho-wannabe. I snapped on latex gloves.

He extended his arm. "It's like your first driving lesson. I'm your empty parking lot."

I cinched the elastic band around his shockingly slender upper arm. "I failed my test the first time," I told him. "Hit the curb parallel parking. Like that's a skill you need in Chester Prairie."

"Tighter," he said. "You'll probably fail this one too."

"Thanks."

"Tighter."

I didn't want to dig the band into tender skin. Stuart's Ichabod arm was even paler on the underside. I held his wrist and tapped the inner elbow. A vein popped up blue and thick. I washed it with the alcohol swab, inhaling the sharp hospital fume.

"Carol Simic wants only mothers at her birth," I said, readying the equipment. "People who 'get it,' whatever that means. Giving birth would be the ultimate midwifery training, don't you think?" I footed the trash can pedal and prepped the needle.

"If that's the case, I'm a goner," Stu said. "You want kids?"

"Maybe. How about you?"

"Sure, but it's not an option. Be firm with the needle."

I gripped it like a thick mechanical pencil.

"Now hold it firmly." Stuart's sudden gravity reminded me of my father shouting, "Easy on the brakes!" After one spin around the church parking lot, he'd signed me up for driver's ed.

"Ready?" I asked. I sucked in air.

"Are *you* ready?"

I tossed the packaging onto the desk and gently sank the needle down. Nothing happened.

"You've got to break the skin, Hannah. Ouch."

"Sorry." I pushed another degree. Suddenly there was blood

everywhere, streaming down his arm, splashing to the floor, smeared across my glove and up my bare arm, an untamed gush of red everywhere except in the vial.

"Hard!" Stuart shouted. "Get the bevel into the vein. Cripes."

I cocked the vial against his elbow pit and thrust the needle into the vein. The tube filled darkly. I loosened the tourniquet, detached the tube, and slid the needle from his skin. Too late, I fumbled for gauze.

Stuart blew out air and raised his arm. I raced to the bathroom for wet paper towels. "God. I'm so sorry." I mopped the floor frantically. From my hands and knees, I noticed a splattering on his pant leg and was too humiliated to mention it. "Are you okay?"

"I'm fine." Stuart blew a long, narrow breath.

I wiped the table, handed him some damp towels, and went back to wash my trembling hands. I ran cold water and scrubbed and soaped, trying to wash away my blunder. Head throbbing, I finally dried my hands and reentered the birth room.

"I'm really sorry."

"Cut it out, Hannah." With his hand raised, Stuart looked like the teacher's pet. "It happens a lot the first time. It's hard, that's all. Here, wipe me off, will you?" Still holding the gauze tight, he lowered his messy arm.

I washed his scrawny wrist, his white palm. Between Stuart's easy physicality and the way Maria or Sunny leaned against me as they demonstrated how to measure a cervix, I'd experienced more nonsexual skin contact in the past month than since I was . . . five? When had my mother withdrawn her body from me? And now to become a midwife I had to push even further, across that social boundary meant to protect us from one another into the fleshy substance of another person, where I inflicted pain. I wiped a soggy paper towel over the muscles and bones of Stuart's lower arm and tossed it into the biohazard bin. I taped down the gauze. I didn't want to hurt people. I didn't want to violate anybody.

Stuart heaved a breath. "Okay, here's what I have to say.

You've got to be more assertive. None of this lollygagging. It's possible to jab the hell out of someone, but you've got a long ways to go before that will happen. You need guts. *Be a man*, as my father would say."

I imagined the sensitive, bruising arms of a pregnant woman. Drawing blood was only the beginning; I'd yet to do a pelvic exam or (I didn't want to think of it) rupture a water sac. If midwives believed so much in the body's inherent wisdom, why did we perform these invasive procedures? I wanted to provide a safe container for birth, not pierce women's skin with sharp metal instruments.

"Buck up." Stuart stood, smacking me on the back. "I'll tell you what. Just to prove my confidence in you, I'll offer you my left arm to mutilate on Monday. Not today. My blood cells need regeneration. But it's all yours next week."

I gathered my books and walked home for lunch. Tourist traffic was at a standstill down the main drag. I adored the hunkered adobe buildings with their spiral-carved posts silvering in the sun, desert molded perfectly into town and sculpted against sky, but I passed through as though displaced, neither tourist nor native, wanting to belong yet knowing I belonged elsewhere. Then my mind skittered with schemes to avoid Stuart and drawing more blood, and I saw only my own dusty shoes.

10.

Round Ligaments

I DON'T MUCH like remembering myself then, living out a belated adolescence, blundering through my apprenticeship with an unattractive mix of ego and insecurity. Please don't think that by sharing these memories I'm implying you're similar. We each have our own demons. What I want to understand about my New Mexico years, what I want you to know, is how change happens. This, above all, is a midwife's wisdom. We each must give birth to ourselves before we can assist others.

No wonder Janice, dubbed by Stuart "my little girlfriend," got under my skin. She was brazen, mouthy, rebellious as teenagers need to be but my parents had somehow disallowed. That she appeared at the Birth House early in my tenure now seems a splendid happenstance. That Stuart invited me to help with her care was, I'm sure, deliberate.

After avoiding Stuart and his blood for three and a half days, I joined him and Sunny in the birth room on a clinic afternoon. Stuart had an orange silk scarf tied around his neck that bobbed each time he swallowed. Janice's chart rested on Sunny's lap.

"She's in her thirty-second week. Healthwise she's great.

My main concern is she's uninterested. Never did show up for childbirth class. She says her mom's not letting her put the baby up for adoption, but then the mom hasn't shown up at any appointments either. I've left half a dozen messages. Who is going to care for the baby?"

"So the challenge is convincing Janice to take responsibility," Stuart said.

"Not necessarily. We've got to ask, 'What's she ready for? What's the next step?' It'd be great if she paid some attention to her body."

The cowbell struck the front door, and Anita offered a warm hello. We heard the bathroom door click shut—Janice knew the routine.

Sunny leaned in. "Let's try a new tack. Stuart, since she won't look at anyone else anyhow, I'm putting the reigns in your hands. Hannah, stop being a wallflower and at least stand next to Stuart. She might listen to you; you're closer in age. I'll play bad cop since I probably remind her of her mother."

Water flushed through the plumbing in the walls, and Janice strutted in wearing a T-shirt with torn sleeves and *Bad Girl* flashing in sequins across her perky breasts. Her jeans had been rigged into low riders, showing a good three inches of budding abdomen. She twisted her torso and bounced onto the bed.

"How's the cheerleader?" Stuart dragged a chair close and straddled it backward. Sunny retreated to the desk. I perched awkwardly on the corner of the bed, willing my eyes not to drift toward the bouncing orange knot at Stuart's Adam's apple, grateful for Leif's good taste.

"Pissed about missing practice." She exaggerated her lower lip. "What's with the fashion statement?" She raised slender fingers to her neck. "Got a hickey?"

The knot jerked downward. "Are you still rehearsing? Doing games?"

"Just watching. It's too hard. I'll be able to jump after the baby's born, right?"

"Not for a month or two." Stuart looked to Sunny for

confirmation.

"No jumping for six weeks," she said.

"Man, this baby cramps my style. I have to piss constantly. Today I got all geezerish just going up to science. It's like, pitiful. Only three flights and . . ." She gave an unconvincing performance of a dying asthmatic.

I said primly, willing Sunny to notice, "Your body's got fifty percent more blood in it, to support the baby. It's hard work to get oxygen pumped into all that blood."

"Whatever." Janice flashed Stuart a coy smile.

"Janice," Sunny said, "the baby's going to cramp your style a whole lot more once it's born. It'll need care—feeding, changing, lots of attention. Tell us about your plans."

"I'm *not* going to that program for loser teenage moms, if that's what you mean."

"No," Stuart interjected. "We're wondering what's next and how we can support you. A baby's not just a health class project. Did you have to carry around a sack of flour for a week?"

"We used eggs. Mine got smashed by third hour. I dropped a book on it in my locker."

I winced. Janice giggled.

"And the plan is—"

"Mom. This is her fault anyway, with her freaking Catholic guilt trip."

"She said she'd take care of the baby?" Stuart pushed. Janice shrugged.

I had the disturbing impulse to shake her until her teeth rattled.

"You're getting close to your due date," Sunny said. "If your mother's going to be at the birth and care for the baby, I'd like to meet her. I've left messages, but she doesn't return my calls. How can I get in touch with her?"

"Do you think that scarf makes you look sexy?" Janice touched Stuart's neck. "Because it doesn't."

"Janice!" Stuart cautioned, pulling back. "Answer Sunny's question."

"Beats me. She's home sleeping all day. She works a late shift at Tres Cervezas. I guess you could catch her there."

"If that's the case, what about the baby?" Sunny said.

Panic flitted briefly across Janice's eyes. "That's her problem."

"No, Janice. This child is your responsibility. You're the mother."

"Can we get on with this?" She hurled herself back on the bed and hoisted her shirt.

Stuart and I looked to Sunny, who tightened her lips and gave an exasperated nod. I measured the perfect mound of Janice's belly (thirty centimeters) and palpated for the position—I could do that much—while Janice babbled about the baby's hiccups waking her at night. When Stuart double-checked the position, she squirmed, suddenly ticklish. He found the heart tones immediately, the whoosh-whoosh of fetal life filling the room.

"Nice and healthy," Stuart said.

He helped her up and took her blood pressure. Janice cocked her head while Stuart pumped.

"I think it's sweet that you're a midwife. I like gentle guys. You can get really sick of the machismo stuff."

"Ninety-six over sixty-four," Stuart said. I recorded for him. Stuart did his darnedest to delineate what to expect—that first pregnancies often go past their due date, that contractions can be erratic, to call when they're regular, four-to-five minutes apart and lasting at least a minute. Janice twirled a strand from her ponytail between two fingers and stuck it in her mouth. Stuart's voice trailed off. He turned to Sunny for help.

"Have you put together a birth bag yet?" she asked. "From the list I gave you?"

"I forgot."

In a swift and decisive movement, Stuart tossed the blood pressure cuff onto the bed and gripped Janice's shoulders. "I'll make you a deal," he said in her face. "You bring your birth bag next week, and I'll run down the street during your appointment and buy you a tall mocha. Decaf. With whipped cream. You're having a baby, woman. It's time to get ready.'"

Janice beamed, pushing his chest away with her index finger. "You called me woman! Okay. Bribery works." She smiled devilishly. "That's how I got into this mess in the first place." She reached out as though she needed Stuart's hand to rise.

"Meaning?"

"Tickets to see Alice in Chains in 'Querque. It was a damn good concert."

My stomach lurched. Stuart and Sunny were speechless.

Janice stood but then doubled over, clutching the bulge of her abdomen. "Oh!" she said, sounding pained.

Sunny leapt to massage Janice's hunched back. Stuart dropped to his knees. "What's up, *chica*? What happened?" he asked. I sat stupidly on the bed.

"Fuck, that hurt." Hesitantly, she righted herself and turned to Sunny. "I'm not going into labor, am I?"

"Was it a cramp?" Sunny asked. Janice pressed her hands to her groin in assent. "You probably pulled your round ligament. They can be sensitive. It's what attaches your uterus to your pelvis. You're not going into labor, not yet." Sunny had become a paragon of patience.

Janice's voice trembled. "I'm going to flip out."

"Yep," Sunny said. "You might flip out. You also could be really strong and just push that baby out. There's three things to learn about labor. It's work. It hurts a lot. And you can do it. Think you can remember that?"

Janice scrunched her brow. Then, with a flick of her ponytail, she batted away the previous minutes and peered down her nose at Stuart, still on his knees. "I prefer caffeinated, you know. I went cold turkey for the baby. I'm not drinking either, in case you were wondering." She pranced to the door. "'Til next time, *amigos*."

Her tennis shoes squeaked down the hall, and we listened to her brief exchange with Anita over the schedule book. Sunny closed the door.

"Unbefuckinglievable," Stuart said.

"I'm curious about where her mom stands," Sunny said. "Legally, Janice can make these decisions, but if her mom is really taking the baby, we should know. Especially if she'll be at the birth. Stuart, you did a good job. Tread lightly on the bribery thing. We don't want her conning you into muddy boundaries. Also," Sunny said, scratching her wrist, "you weren't inappropriate, but I'm going to suggest no touch here. She's too much of a firecracker. If it's not work related, I don't want casual physical contact."

The orange knot jumped. "Ever?"

"Just in Janice's case. She's too young. We should be careful. Okay. See you both shortly." Sunny turned and left.

Stuart looked at his hands.

"Are dying people any easier?" I asked.

He reached to the ceiling, cracking his back. "Nope. Some people fight death their whole lives. This isn't any different." He rolled his shoulders vigorously. "The amazing thing is she could have this baby without ever acknowledging it exists. Hannah, this is exactly why I need to be a midwife." He grabbed my hand pleadingly, as though I could make it happen. "I get death. I totally get how we can live through it, and it's beautiful."

"What does that have to do with Janice?"

He released me. "She's not a kid anymore. The kid part of her is dying, whether she wants it to or not, and the woman's being born. At least that's how I see it."

I squinted at him, puzzling over how this stork of a man could understand a pregnant teen's inner life. In these rare cracks in his façade, Stuart's eyes looked pained and old. It frightened me a little, the unspoken weight of his experience.

"Shall we call it a day?" he asked, and when I nodded, he gave me a high-five, job well done, *hasta mañana*. I trailed him down the hall, wondering what part of me was dying and whether Stuart noticed.

11.

Needled

A HALF-MOON LIT my rented room. Spiders skittered across the adobe walls. Night after night, my adrenaline-rattled mind evaded sleep; I kicked my way free of knotted bedsheets, retrieved milk from the mini-refrigerator and a lone box of cereal from the shelf. I ate at a card table by the window, flannel nightgown tenting my bare feet. Camino Central, the spine of Sangre de Cristo, was empty. Small shuffling sounds rose from the brush. The air was luminous, electric. Sometimes a high-pitched *yip-yip-yip* traveled from the mesa, an eerie wail rising and fading. The corn flakes were always soggy, the spoonfuls of whole milk an unsuccessful sedative.

Crossing Stuart's thin threshold of skin had made me an insomniac. At midnight I jabbed a navel orange with a stolen syringe, the pitiful fruit softening with repeated tries. My aversion to drawing blood ballooned into a full-fledged phobia. I envisioned the quivering needle's entrance into an expectant mother's vein, the prick painful and troubling, the act a precursor to other horrors like pelvic exams or uterine invasions to turn a baby or help remove the placenta. Others weren't crippled with panic. Why was I? Fear was my curse. The more I hunted for its origin, trying to rip it out from the roots, the stronger it grew. When Stuart cornered me for a second try, saying he was dedicating his body to medical science post mortem but he might as well get a head start, it took me six stabs and one dry heave into the sink before I caught his vein. He treated me to *chimichangas* anyhow.

I missed so many times, I came to expect it.

Not nearly enough days passed before Sunny leaned her hip into the crash room's doorframe and declared, "I've got a spare minute. Let's see you do your thing." I was sweating before I shut the textbook. Downstairs, Sunny set the crook of her arm across the desk. I examined her pale flesh, a bit loosened from the bones and smeared with freckles: no evidence whatsoever of blood vessels. I wanted to make up some excuse: I wasn't ready, the sight of blood made me break out in hives. Instead, I cruelly bit my lip.

Sunny had me mark with a ballpoint pen where I was going in then watched my needle jiggle across the spot and miss. She emitted an inadvertent grunt and made me try again and again. The dot of ink vanished into a spreading bruise. Finally the bevel caught the vein. I cleaned up my mess.

"Tell me what happened," she said.

Tears welled. Sunny watched without sympathy or distress.

"I don't know," I sniffed. "I don't want to hurt you, and then I do. I'm so scared, I screw up."

"No. Tell me what went wrong. Why didn't you hit a vein the first three times?"

I swiped my face with my sleeve. "I was shaking too hard. I couldn't direct the needle properly."

"True. But I also have recessed veins. They're not obvious. Even lab professionals miss them. When the vein didn't appear after using the tourniquet, you might have asked me to pump my fist a bit, get more blood down. You find this in older women and people who are overweight. Ask where techs have succeeded in the past. Now let's try again."

Sunny rolled her stool around to my right and matter-of-factly extended her unmaimed arm. Her lack of judgment was unsettling. I poked her again, hands calmer but no more successful, the welts swelling while inside I reeled with shame and this new possibility that I should keep trying regardless.

In the end, Sunny declared I was getting the hang of it.

"Really?"

"Sure. Half of it's the skill, the other half is your presence. You're getting the skills. At some point, though, you've got to be less nervous than your patient. Drawing blood isn't just routine, Hannah. It's part of your relationship with the client. If you're upset, you're not taking care of her, you're needing care yourself, which puts the mom in an unfair position. Don't let your own hang-ups get in the way of good care." Sunny studied me with her arms crossed. I felt wrung out. "And that means dealing with feelings, not just stuffing them. I'd like to see you leading clinic next week."

I nodded because Sunny would have been annoyed otherwise.

As an antidote to Sunny's fast-paced expectations, I directed my thoughts to small handholds of competence. I was thorough in my studies. Anita and I were bringing order to the mess of Medicaid billing. Leif and I had found a new normal—in my rare spare moments, I'd phone him, we'd share tidbits from our day and then together hash out the Associated Press crossword puzzle. I could tell Leif all the bizarre things about New Mexico—the low-rider cars that cruised through town with their undercarriages lit bright blue, the mystical hum that supposedly emerged from the mountains, the enclave of vegetarian hippies living off the grid who fed their unruly packs of dogs raw chicken, the alien babies—and our mounting laughter always set me on my feet again. Talking with Leif gave me a dose of good common sense.

Gradually the half-formed idea niggling in the back of my brain since Sunny's sphincter lesson emerged as a working theory: If the mother was the active agent in childbirth, the midwife's work resided at the margins. The Birth House was set up on the premise that the mothers themselves, or at least their bodies, were the authorities on childbirth—not us, not the hospital. The midwives simply created an environment, a safe container, within which the families gave birth.

Drawing blood, I reasoned while stabbing another sorry orange at midnight, was part of providing the safe container. Testing for blood type, rubella immunity, Hepatitis B, syphilis, and the blood count was critical. Like asking tough questions, drawing blood was not a violation but rather a hard necessity that guaranteed the container's boundaries would hold. With midnight milk souring on my tongue, I determined that I would create the environment, step away, and let the clients do the work. Perhaps the midwives had chosen me for this very reason—because, unlike Stuart, I knew how to take a backseat.

12.

Backseat Driver

SUNNY STOMPED AROUND the couch, shaking her fist at invisible insurance salesmen. "Eighteen-fricking-thousand a year! They rob us blind then ditch us."

Maria pressed her hand to her brow. Her black hair was knotted tightly. The waiting room reeked of sweat, and it was only eight o'clock, Monday morning. Anita had opened the weekend mail to find bad news: The last insurance company in the U.S. to provide malpractice coverage to midwives had changed its policy. Roberta Devers-Scott, a midwife in Syracuse, New York, had been arrested after two undercover agents from New York's Office of Professional Discipline had posed as clients. Roberta was charged with practicing medicine without a license, and in response insurance companies were running scared.

"At least we're not alone," Maria said. "Everyone's in the same boat. But *en realidad* that doesn't help."

Sunny was furious. "Two decades! Two decades of payments with zero claims. And now this!"

Some people say that any sense of security is a false sense of security. When it comes to the insurance industry, I agree.

Midwives and our clients must make our own insurance from of a web of trust and effort. There are no financial shortcuts.

But at the Birth House the bulk of our clients were covered by Medicaid, which endorsed homebirth in New Mexico so long as the midwives had malpractice insurance. Sunny and Maria were dedicated to serving Northern New Mexico's poor. Without Medicaid payments, they were sunk. They had until June—seven months—to find coverage.

"I'll call first thing," Anita said. "Maybe they'll make an exception."

"Bastards!" Sunny punched the air with a one-two, her culottes flapping. "Watch. They'll double the premium."

From our slump in the sofa, Stuart and I followed the midwives with the wide-eyed dread of children whose parents have gone bankrupt. In my mind's eye, I saw the Rio Grande, its whitewater rushing rafters down the pass. Two or three casualties each year was an acceptable death rate, a risk the culture was willing to take, like automobile accidents or smoking-induced cancer but, ironically, unlike natural birth. And I thought of a story I'd heard about a laboring woman who drove herself to the hospital through a raging ice storm because, in her own words, "Giving birth at home is dangerous." The disconnect between real and perceived danger baffled me.

Maria's pencil tapped rapidly on her clipboard.

The phone rang and Anita jumped.

"We should call a board meeting," Sunny said. "Maybe contact the governor."

Anita waved the phone at Maria. "Your daughter." Maria frowned and rose from her chair.

"The governor?" Stuart asked.

"We've got sway. No one else does maternity care up here. Even the docs can't afford the malpractice insurance. The state takes *some* responsibility for making sure its residents get health care. It's a long shot." Sunny quit her frantic pacing and checked her watch. "Shit." We looked at the untouched stack of files on the coffee table. "Quick, who's coming?"

From her desk, Anita opened the schedule book and announced, "Sanchez, White, Simic, Dominguez, Frontinak, Valasquez, Tutorson." I sucked in air at Carol's name. Stuart fanned through the multicolored files, plucking out the morning lineup. "Here you go, sweetie." He handed me a blue folder. "She's all yours."

Behind us Maria slammed down the phone. "*Ya me voy. I've got to go.* Luis cut his hand in the shop and needs a ride to the hospital. Sorry, guys, it'll be all morning. You can cancel my appointments."

Sunny told Maria we'd be okay, to take her time, and Stuart offered to babysit. The kids were with their grandparents, Maria said, and "Don't forget the lab order's due today."

"I say we go ahead." Sunny bustled the furniture back into place. "Hopefully we'll get a no-show." Anita emitted a grunt of disgust. I opened Carol's file. Sure enough, she was in her twenty-eighth week, time to test for hematocrit, hemoglobin, platelets. I put my head in my hands. In the whirlwind of Birth House business, Maria and I had never talked through Carol's last appointment.

Stuart rubbed smooth circles between my shoulder blades, rocking me back and forth on the couch. "Don't worry," he said. "You're a charmer." The gesture was so kind, so unexpected, that for a moment I believed I could bear anything with a touch like this.

"Each of you take a room, except I want Hannah drawing blood for Carol and Tita. Stuart, would you supervise?"

"Not with Carol Simic, I won't." Stuart stood. "That's a majorly bad idea."

Sunny slammed her palm flat against the desk. "Damn it all, we can't function like this."

"Shoo," Anita said.

The wrought-iron latch clinked up, and the front door swung inward. We stared into the hot crack of daylight. A baby stroller wheeled in, followed by a young Mexican mom whose cheeks blushed with pregnancy. The baby interrupted a monologue with a coquettish grin. She was so beautiful, I laughed.

"Morning, Sonia," Sunny said. "Morning, sweet pea." The girl grabbed Sunny's finger. "We're just finishing a staff meeting. Why don't you do your own weight and urine test? We'll be with you in a minute."

I grabbed an office chair and wheeled it down the hall behind Sunny and Stuart.

"I'll talk to Carol," Sunny continued loud enough for me to hear. "She shouldn't have a problem if you're just in the room."

"She shouldn't, but she will," Stuart said.

"If you're going to give me a hard time, Stu, we can just cancel Maria's share."

"That's your call. Don't make me responsible."

One of the wheels stuck, momentarily screeching against the tile. I kicked it.

"I'm asking you to be professional, Stuart."

He tossed his hands above his head. "Fine. But I want pre-absolution for any damage."

Sunny gave him a locker-room punch. "That's a good one." She turned into the office.

Stuart stopped me, whispering, "Is this crazy? Shouldn't we have canceled?"

I shrugged. "I'd appreciate your being there."

His shoulders sank. "For you, Hannah. Although I might be more of a detriment."

Stuart and I handled the basics while Sunny passed between rooms, too busy, after all, for the supervisory work of letting me lead with clients. Two chaotic hours later I ushered Carol, who was finally showing in a maternity business suit, into the red room. Carol measured four centimeters bigger than a month prior. She answered my questions with snipped noes and yeses, offering nothing in the way of idle chat. When her blood pressure read on the high end, she got impatient with Sunny's suggestions, the same ones she'd already heard from Maria. Sunny asked, "Anything else?" Carol, close-lipped, shook her highlighted curls. "Did Maria explain about the blood test?"

"Yes. I'd like to have it." Carol wrung her hands in the curved juncture of her lap.

"Okay. Since Hannah's still learning, I've asked Stuart to supervise your draw. He's got a nursing degree and is fully qualified. I know you requested that he not be your caregiver, but we're shorthanded this morning because of Luis's accident. If it makes you uncomfortable, you can come back later."

Carol gave it serious consideration. "Go ahead."

"Good."

Here was Carol in a pricey maternity outfit she must have special ordered, most likely having postponed some teleconference at the bank for this appointment, rising from the bed to sit on the stool, slipping a pearl button from its hole and folding up her sleeve, extending her narrow forearm. Here was her china-doll skin, and me cinching it with the tourniquet, unwrapping the needle, footing the trash can, swabbing her skin, preparing to insert metal into flesh. Stuart lurked beyond my right shoulder, sending silent telegrams of encouragement, his hands behind his back. Carol turned away, biting her pretty lip. I willed the trembling from my fingers and plunged. The draw was quick, tight. When I withdrew the needle from under the gauze, a bead of blood escaped. I nabbed it and guided her arm above her head.

"There we go," I said cheerily. Behind me, Stuart emitted a long exhale. "We'll have the results tomorrow morning. We can go over them at your next appointment. If anything's wrong we'll call right away, but I don't expect it."

Here, I thought proudly, was the container. I was holding space for Carol's birth.

"That wasn't so bad," Carol said.

"Is blood scary for you?" I tried.

She lowered her arm for me to tape down the gauze wad. "No. Working with amateurs is."

I cut the tape without touching her.

"We've got to learn somehow," Stuart said.

Carol checked her arm for blood and buttoned her cuff.

"We'd never do anything that put you at risk," I offered, trying to patch up the cracks in Carol's confidence. I imagined my words reaching out like motherly arms, embracing Carol and her unborn child and her mistrust that I suspected was really fear squeezed sideways. By modeling faith in the natural process, I was finally wearing the midwife's mantle. I would touch others. I would be with them during their most vulnerable and human moments. I remembered the question Maria had asked that had made Carol cry—*Is it about feeling safe?* "I promise you'll have a safe birth here." I said it boldly, glad for the conviction in my voice.

"Hannah!" Stuart's voice was harsh. "You can't—"

I spun around. Consternated wrinkles fanned from the corners of Stuart's eyes. He actually looked his age.

"I *will* have a safe birth here," Carol faced Stuart, "and I don't appreciate your saying otherwise." She swung her gold-chain purse strap over her shoulder. "I've got a meeting. Thank you, Hannah." She left.

For a moment I hovered on the fulcrum between surging pride and sinking shame. "What?" I demanded of Stuart. "What was that about?"

"I can't believe you said that!" Stuart ran his fingers through his hair. "You can't go promising anyone a safe birth. It creates false expectations." The disbelief written across his forehead made me want to duck.

"That's not what I meant."

"What *did* you mean? Because that's sure what it sounded like. And even if you meant something else, that's not what Carol heard. Cripes, Hannah."

Stuart had his hands on his hips like Sunny, and suddenly I hated him. "I don't have to justify it to you." I busied myself cleaning up. He had no right to question me in front of a client. I let the metal lid of the trash can clang shut.

Stuart stood stock-still.

I flipped the cotton sheet off the bed, tossed it in the laundry basket, and grabbed a clean one from the drawer. With a wrist flick inherited from my mother, I let it billow over the bed. Stuart instinctively reached for the sheet's hem and tucked it in. "Think, Hannah. It's a setup for disaster. You promise her a safe birth, which no one can guarantee, and then what happens when she hemorrhages or has a stillbirth? She'll blame *you*."

"I don't want to talk about it."

"You can't make things dandy just by saying so."

Did he think I was an imbecile? Sunny leaned into the room, a stack of charts tucked under her arm, coffee cup in hand. Stuart and I stood straight. "Anita got an earful from Carol on her way out. What happened?"

Stuart pursed his lips.

"It went fine," I said.

"So?"

"Stuart thinks I shouldn't have said something."

"Write a verbatim. Stuart, I need you across the hall."

Up in the crash room, I ripped a page from my notebook and recreated the scene—the smell of rubbing alcohol, the terse exchange about blood and professionalism, my attempted reassurances. A breeze passed through the open windows, along with the sounds of traffic wending down dusty, narrow streets.

On paper my words looked cheap, a veneer of platitudes. As far as I could figure, my mistake was a matter of semantics. I didn't mean to promise anything so much as convey my conviction that all would go well. What could be wrong with that? The midwives radiated this faith, as did the Birth House. Why then the horror in Stuart's voice? I saw again the surprised splay of wrinkles beside his eyes, how he caught the bedsheet as though he couldn't help but help me. Perhaps I was such a rotten midwife I couldn't even recognize my mistakes.

No—Carol had appreciated what I'd said. Stuart was meddling.

I leaned over the window ledge, soaking in cool sunlight. Every minute I spent upstairs meant more work for Sunny. In my mosquito-ridden home state, screens protected every window and door. The screenless, flung-wide windows of New

Mexico made me feel overexposed and subject to vertigo. The sky, predictably, radiated blue. White mountains jagging against such clarity were too bright. Going downstairs, I slid my right palm along the earthen wall for balance.

* * *

Two days later, Sunny and I carried our lunches out to the picnic table to discuss my verbatim. I had managed to keep the fallout from Carol's blood draw below Maria's radar; Luis's injury had put him out of commission, so Maria was working half-days and was otherwise preoccupied with insurance troubles. Sunny, to my dismay, had not forgotten. I'd brought egg salad; Sunny microwaved fish sticks on a cardboard tray. With the exception of a bed of dry, bushy weeds against the house, the yard was sand and tall fences and a swing rigged from a neighboring cottonwood tree. The picnic table was weathered silver. Sun flared overhead, barely warm enough.

"Are you sure you don't want one?" Sunny dipped a breaded chunk into mayonnaise. I shook my head. "Then let's hear it."

Forty-eight hours had tarnished my confident assurances to Carol. Stuart was right: I should have kept my mouth shut.

When I looked up from reading the verbatim, Sunny was massaging her forehead. "Okay," she said. "How do you understand what happened?"

"I wanted Carol to feel less afraid."

"Why?"

"Because fear makes birth painful."

Sunny crossed her broad, freckled arms. "No. Why did *you* want that? What would *you* gain if she were less afraid?"

"I wanted her to trust me." I looked down at my salad.

"Hannah, you'd just done a stellar job drawing her blood. You've given her no reason not to trust you. I'll admit, Carol's testy. Even so, it's your job to take care of *her* needs, not yours."

My scalp burned. "I was trying."

"Assurances build false confidence. We want the real thing."

I wished someone would explain the difference.

"It's a Band-Aid, Hannah. The wound needs air. Why's she so afraid? What's the origin of her testiness?"

I mumbled that I didn't know.

"Well, ask. You're the one who needs to be less afraid, Hannah. Applying Band-Aids is easy. It's poking people with needles that's hard. You've shown you can do that, so let's see it with words too." She looked from her clean tray to my untouched salad. "Why don't you journal about it for the rest of lunch? Let me know if you want to talk more."

Sunny left. I sealed the Tupperware lid over my lunch and held my thick head in my hands.

* * *

Stuart and I sidestepped one another until study day, Thursday morning, when I claimed the crash room waterbed and arranged my books around me in an undulating barricade. Stuart arrived carrying two fragrant mugs of coffee.

"It's fresh," he offered.

"Thanks," I said. I was too embarrassed by my screwup to meet his eyes.

Stuart sat at his desk. Within minutes, he'd tilted his chair and hiked his feet up, textbook in his lap. I tried to read but found myself instead puzzling through Sunny's advice. I did not want to poke Carol Simic with words. I couldn't see how doing so would help create a safe container for her birth. Invasive questions punctured the easy dynamics between people; they put me on edge. Stuart turned a page, and I snapped back to my reading. I couldn't afford to get behind.

Two hours of silence later, Sunny shouted for us and we stampeded down the stairwell. She was halfway out the back door. "Clarissa Alvarez. I've got the kit. Grab the oxygen. Get a move on. This could be precipitous."

Stuart gave me a puppy-dog, surely-you'll-forgive-me look and jingled his keys.

"Let me get my lunch," I said.

Out on the street, we climbed into Stuart's rusty Civic, slammed the doors, and skidded off. Stuart eyed my paper sack. "Any chance you'd share?"

I pulled out the waxed-paper-wrapped sandwich. "It's PB and J."

He grimaced and extended his hand.

Clarissa was a grade school teacher who lived forty minutes out of town on the mesa in a house she and her husband had built. As the crow flies it wasn't far, but the roads had bumper-sized potholes and had to be taken at five miles an hour. Stuart's car ran too low to the ground. Every few minutes we felt the crunch of rock. The dust wake from Sunny's truck was miles ahead.

"I knew when I bought this tin can I wasn't taking the terrain into account."

"Why did you, then?"

"Because it makes me look hot." Stuart flexed his arm out the open window. Grit billowed in from the road, which was why my window was shut. The peanut butter felt heavy in my mouth. Loops of plastic Mardi Gras beads thrashed from the rearview mirror.

"Hannah, I know you don't want to talk about what happened Monday, but we're going to a birth. We need to get Carol Simic out of our system."

I put an uneaten crust back in my lap. "Leave the correcting to Sunny, okay? It's not your business."

Stuart pursed his lips. He swerved to avoid an errant boulder. "We've got to work as a team. I don't want us giving anyone happy illusions. What you say reflects on me, and vice versa."

I grabbed the sandwich before it bounced off my lap and wrapped it up, ignoring Stuart's hungry glance. "Then I'll keep my mouth shut."

"Come on, Hannah."

I looked through the film of dust on the window. Outside, the mesa stretched bleakly in every direction. Sagebrush and the brown chamisa that everyone assured me would bloom a beautiful yellow in the fall dotted the dry earth. The sun was sheer and cruel. We passed one barebones pickup, the driver offering a single-finger wave. Our car lurched.

"I can't believe they don't grade this road," I said. "What kind of town lets people live like this?"

After a pause, Stuart said, "I hope we don't have to transport."

I grunted; that would be bad. This was Clarissa's fourth child. She had pushed out the last two in under an hour, and there was no reason to expect otherwise today.

The car shuddered and the tires spat gravel. I thought of Mom, how much I needed to push her away but never did, how much I longed to bury myself in her arms. I turned from Stuart to hide my welling tears. I couldn't stand having anyone manage me as Mom had. I couldn't bear not being held. I wanted to be solid, both resistant and receptive.

"You don't trust me." There. The words were out of my mouth. They sounded like a grade-school whine, but at least I'd named what was bothering me. I had no experience arguing. My parents agreed about everything. Even through my departure, Leif and I had been amicable.

Stuart took one hand off the steering wheel, wiped it on his pants, and replaced it. "I trust you. I trust you as a friend and colleague, but . . . I mean, *and*, you're still learning. We're both learning. So that means we make mistakes."

We reached Clarissa's drive. Her house was a two-story clapboard with dormers on the second floor and a green roof— so Midwest-ordinary it put me at ease. Stuart parked behind Sunny's truck and yanked the emergency brake.

I released my seatbelt. "Except it's not up to you to call me on my mistakes. Especially not in front of clients." I slammed my door against the humility of it. When I saw worry edging Stuart's eyes, I wanted to cry.

Inside, the kitchen thumped with salsa music. Two women who introduced themselves as Clarissa's neighbors were helping the older children spoon cookie dough onto sheets. The youngest sat on the floor furiously banging a pot with a wooden spoon. Despite the open doors and windows, the hot oven made the kitchen a sauna. A box of Materna-tea sat open on the counter beside a pitcher. "Take this up, will you?" The neighbor waved her oven-mitted hand toward the stairs.

We heard a low moan. When I reached the landing, Stuart grabbed my elbow. "Hannah," he whispered, "I want you to know I value your friendship."

I couldn't look at him. "Me too," I said stupidly.

Clarissa let loose a full-blown wail. Stuart and I exchanged a guilty glance and took the remaining stairs three at a time.

13.

What Midwifery Needs

SOMEHOW ANITA CONVINCED Lloyd's of London to sell the Birth House malpractice insurance for an annual forty grand—an insurmountable sum that the midwives nonetheless tackled by brainstorming in a hot tub. Sunny's house was a rambling straw-bale structure nestled against state forest land, seemingly humble with its clutter of Navajo rugs, hand-hewn sofas and miscellaneous saddle gear hanging from the walls, yet sprawling, with a view of the mesa through floor-to-ceiling windows. On the south side was a solarium with tiled floors, monster geraniums, and a generous Jacuzzi. Frida Shoemaker, the board president, had called the meeting. Carol Simic came too—she was the treasurer.

I thanked my stars for mixed company. Had Stuart not been there the meeting would have been held nude, and the idea of orchestrating a major fund drive while soaking bare-skinned beside my mentors and Carol Simic gave me the willies. Instead I wore my navy one-piece. Carol perched on the tub's edge in a perfect-fitting maternity swimsuit; she carried the growing sphere of her center beautifully. Sunny soaked in bikini bottoms, whose elastic had given out, and a mismatched top. Maria lit a dozen candle stubs along a shelf, set a notepad and pen on the tub's tiled ledge, and eased herself down. I slid in next to Stuart, whose plaid trunks floated up from his knees, reminding me of my father. The water burned. I sank to my chin.

"Does take the edge off," Stuart said.

"Mmm," I replied, knowing he meant Carol's presence. I averted my eyes from his scrawny chest.

"Just what we need," Sunny said, adjusting her straps.

The women chatted a bit about whether or not the legislature could pressure Medicaid to pay midwives regardless of insurance coverage and whether a consumer advocacy group might hold some sway down in Santa Fe. Finally, Maria reached for the notebook, having had the foresight to keep her hands out of the water. "Ideas?"

We listened to the tub motor whir. The glass room reflected the candlelight. Then Sunny began—"Art auction"—and the women brainstormed everything from appeals on the local radio to selling bumper stickers: *Midwives help people out*; *Peace on earth begins with birth*; *Push ahead with midwives*; *Say no to drugs—beginning with birth*. I couldn't wait to laugh about them with Leif. Stuart suggested a display at the local library showing birth photos next to photos of the kids now—to raise awareness of how many children we deliver—and offered Cal's photography services. That sparked Maria to imagine a "family reunion." Carol doubted we'd make much money off former clients since most of them were on welfare, but she guessed the sentiment would appeal to local business owners and some Albuquerque benefactors. Conversation spun toward a huge outdoor party, starting with kids' games and ending with a high-price banquet donated by a local "chichi" restaurant.

"We could call it The Big Birth Bash," Stuart suggested.

"That sounds like it's from *Sesame Street*," Sunny said.

Carol shifted. "I'd go with something more . . . respectable. And inclusive. We want investors there, not just mothers."

I felt a poke in my ribs. The hot tub gurgled. "How about

Family Fest?" I offered.

"Another country heard from," Stuart said.

Carol frowned. "That's good. With some tagline like, 'Celebrating birth and growth in Sangre de Cristo.' "

I jabbed Stuart back, perhaps a bit too hard.

"Growth being the size of our wallets," Sunny said. "Everyone agreed? Okay, we've got it. I don't think we should eliminate these other options," she said, gesturing toward the notebook, "but for now let's move forward with the Family Fest. We need a task force, maybe one of us, two board members, one alum and someone from the community." Everyone nodded. "You're gregarious," Sunny said, turning to Stuart. "Want to represent the midwives?"

Stuart straightened. "Sure."

Carol's body grew still. Maria asked, "Carol?"

"Is that wise? I mean, this festival will be the public face of the Birth House."

"What about me do you find so objectionable?" Stuart whipped his hands out of the water, sending spray in Carol's direction. I pulled away. "You've been on my case since we first met. Jesus, you've never given me a chance."

"It has nothing to do with you," Carol snapped. "It's a matter of principle. Do we want a man representing us when our work is about empowering women?"

"It's just a committee to plan a party," Sunny said.

"If we're going around soliciting donations, we need someone with a professional demeanor." Carol crossed her arms. I looked around the candle-lit tub, at Sunny's sagging bikini top and Frida's dripping curls. "Why not Hannah?"

"Me?"

"Hannah," Maria said, "we'd like you to be a full member of the team."

"So I'm not professional enough," Stuart continued. "I didn't realize a cosmopolitan demeanor was a requirement for this job."

"It's not." Sunny pulled herself out of the tub and perched on the tile rim. Water spilled over the ledge. We all looked up. Sunny was the founder, the Birth House's creative genius. "Stuart, you're an exceptional person, and you'll make an exceptional midwife." She turned to Carol. "You need to know I'm behind him. If the board wants more say over who we take as apprentices and how we treat them, we need to make a policy about it. But in the past that's always been the midwives' prerogative."

Maria followed Sunny, stepping outside the tub and groping for her towel. "A lot's at stake now, Sunny. Let's put it on the agenda for our next meeting. But I also need to say how important it is that we maintain a respectful working environment. We have mothers to serve."

I wasn't sure to whom that comment was directed but felt chastised nonetheless. Perhaps we all did, because a tense silence followed. My reluctance to participate was habitual, a relic of the person I no longer was. Or, rather, the person I no longer wanted to be. I might not be good at soliciting contributions, but I certainly could organize and track a budget. I climbed out and, shuddering in the chilly desert air, wrapped myself in a towel. "I'd be happy to do it," I said. "I don't want to go door to door, but I can handle the money."

Sunny slung her arm around me in a gratifying sideways hug. We both watched Stuart stand, trunks clinging to his scrawny thighs, his shoulders slumped. "Buck up, champ," she said, releasing me and handing Stuart his faded Mickey Mouse towel.

The others left the solarium discussing who else might fill out the committee. Once they were out of earshot, Stuart gestured at Carol's roost, now abandoned. "You want my take on this?" he asked. "People feel threatened when they meet someone who doesn't play by the rules. It's like I undermine every restriction Carol's ever placed on herself, and she blames me for those constraints. There's always a Carol in my life."

Sunny gave him her sideways squeeze. "Don't let her get under your skin, Stu. You're just what we need. Just what midwifery needs. I'm going to put the kettle on. Want tea?"

We both nodded, although really I wanted coffee.

After she left, Stuart said, "That's well and good, but why do I feel like some queer pawn? Pushed into the center and sacrificed. I don't know, Hannah. Sometimes I get worn down."

Sadness pressed his eyes, a fine blond and white stubbled his jaw. I resented how naturally midwifery came to Stuart and how Sunny favored him, and at the same time I wanted to champion him—he should be the midwife, not me. "Don't give up. We need you."

"That's exactly it, Hannah. Midwifery may need me, but do I need this?" He pointed his chin toward the tub. "I'm not so sure. I won't squeeze myself into someone else's image just to keep them happy."

Or to be normal, I thought. I pulled the towel tighter across my shoulders. "Some compromises aren't the end of the world."

He eyed me sideways. "You *would* say that." When I turned to leave, he caught me. "You're still mad. Hannah, any time you want to talk, I'm game."

"I'm not mad," I said, and left him in the glass room of reflected candlelight.

14.

That Bolt of Fabric

A FEW WEEKS later, I was charting in the crash room when Janice's high-pitched voice pierced the walls. Curiosity got the better of me. She was two weeks from her due date and as recalcitrant as ever, although she had managed to bring a garbage bag of birth supplies to her last appointment. I thought I was drawn to Janice because she was headstrong in a way I should have been as a teen. Now I suspect only a life as troublesome as Janice's could have jerked me into becoming the midwife I am today.

So I went down to join Stuart. In the hallway, Sunny spoke sternly with a top-heavy woman who looked too young to be Janice's mother. I slid past them into the birth room. Stuart mouthed, "Warning, warning" just as Janice stormed in, ponytail thrashing. "Mom's a prude," she announced, and told Stuart her weight and urine test results.

Janice was flouncy and unstoppable. Sunny had said teen pregnancies were the easiest. "An unfortunate biological fact. Women are meant to give birth young. That's when our bodies are most limber, our pelvic muscles elastic." Nine months pregnant, Janice could have aced cheerleading tryouts.

Stuart patted the bed and Janice bounced down, arms crossed between her growing breasts and the taut bubble of her belly. "Why are you always here?" she said to me. "I feel like a zoo animal."

"Me?" When Stuart didn't come to my rescue, I added, "Stuart and I help out with all the births."

"She's underage!" Mrs. Holback's voice rose in the hall. "She doesn't get to do whatever she wants."

From Sunny's responding murmur I caught the words *commitment* and *mutual decision-making*. Janice scrutinized Stuart. Today he was in a purple top and baggy gypsy pants, a scarf with a hundred tiny bells dangling from the hems tied around his waist. I may have snickered inside, but I never shared such details with Leif.

"What kind of freak are you, anyway?" Janice asked him.

"One with exceptionally good taste." Stuart rocked his hips to make the bells jingle, his ear cocked toward the hallway.

"I'm just looking out for my grandson. I don't like the idea of—"

"It's not a boy!" Janice screamed. "I hate it when you say that."

The hall quieted and the women entered, Sunny controlled and alert, Mrs. Holback with her neck extended, back rounded, gripping the straps of a patent leather purse. She was solid, her dark curls hair-sprayed in place and her lips painted a thick magenta. When she saw Stuart's outfit, she scowled.

Sunny swept between Janice and her mother. "Why don't we sit down and talk this through, from the beginning. Margaret?" Stuart pulled the rocker forward for Mrs. Holback and took the stool. Sunny and I joined Janice on the bed. "Up until last week I was under the impression that you supported a Birth House birth. Neither you or Janice gave us reason to suspect otherwise. What happened?"

"She flipped out," Janice said.

"I'm looking after my child's best interests. I want her to see a doctor."

"I wish you'd told us sooner. It's best to have everyone on the same page, especially if you're going to be at the birth. What do you think, Janice?"

"I'm having it here. Jeez, that's what I said from the beginning. Juana had her baby here and said it was cool."

"This isn't about being cool, Janice Rose. You're way past that."

"It's unfortunate how this has transpired," Sunny said. "Margaret, you've missed a lot of the work we do by not coming to appointments. Why don't we address your concerns."

"I'm concerned that Janice is being disobedient. It's high time she learn what's good for her."

I agreed and yet felt strangely protective of Janice, who stared her mother down with well-matched ferocity.

"Margaret, many women choose to have their babies with us. Perhaps you can share your concern about Janice's choice."

"She's being an asshole," Janice said. She pushed off from the bed and stood inches from her mother's knees, thrusting her belly in her mom's face. "You don't give a shit. You're up in Vegas for weeks and then swoop down on me like you can control my every move? Fuck that."

"Watch your mouth. Who do you think's going to take care of the baby, huh? Let me ask you that."

Sunny rose to intervene, but Janice stomped, "I will!" and marched around the bed and back. "I will, I will, I will. Dammit. It's my baby. I get to choose where to have it."

Mrs. Holback stood, swinging her purse in a tight arc. "You do that, and you're not welcome back home, Janice Rose."

Janice scoffed. Blood thumped in my head. I wanted to shield Janice from her mother's rejection.

"Whoa." Sunny stepped forward. "Let's all take a deep breath." Sunny demonstrated with a full-chested heave. "According to New Mexican law, a mom over age sixteen has legal custody of her baby. Officially this is up to Janice."

"See?" Janice fired.

"But the best scenario," Sunny continued, "is one where we're working together. What can we do to make you feel comfortable with a Birth House birth, Margaret?"

"Lay off. Let me parent my own child."

"Some parent," Janice spat.

"Mrs. Holback," Stuart said, "this is a big transition for Janice. She could use your support."

"I don't have to put up with this." Mrs. Holback turned and strode out of the room. Sunny's jaw dropped; she ran out after her.

"Asshole!" Janice screamed, flinging herself next to me on the bed.

"Hey, kiddo," Stuart said, sitting beside Janice, "don't you worry. We won't abandon you. We'll work something out."

Janice fumed. I watched her furious breathing with new admiration. Her consistency with clinic visits was remarkable, independent, courageous. That Janice had managed to get prenatal care humbled me. I didn't trust myself to say something helpful, so I reached over and took her hand. She pretended not to notice.

Sunny returned looking ragged.

"I don't want to be pregnant," Janice announced. Her hand was clammy and limp.

Sunny sank onto the stool. "Oh, honey, you *are* pregnant. We've got to make it the most wonderful experience we can. Now, your mother prefers a hospital birth. You can still choose that. We would be with you in the hospital too, only a doctor would deliver your baby."

Janice pushed my hand away. "Fuck that."

"Give it some thought. Do you have a place to stay?"

"My sister's. I'm there most of the time anyhow."

"Can she be with you at the birth? Or a friend?"

Janice shrugged.

"Do you have transportation once labor starts?"

"Mhm. Francesca's got a car."

"I'll try talking with your mom again. I'd rather she were on board."

"Whatever."

Stuart looked grave. "We've discussed this, but it's worth bringing up again—what about making an adoption plan? Your mother doesn't want you to. How about you?"

Janice's face contorted; she bit her lip.

"Adoption's nothing to be ashamed of, honey," Sunny said. "You could finish school, figure out what you want to do with your life. We have connections with good agencies and could help you set something up. I'd be happy to get you more information. You're a good mom whether or not you keep the baby."

"I don't know." Janice's voice was small. Compassion for her, affection even, filled my eyes with tears.

"How about you come back later this week?" Sunny patted Janice's knee then pulled her upright into a maternal hug. Janice's arms were flaccid, her face pressed into the blue batik of Sunny's dress. "Whatever you decide, it's a fine choice. There's no right or wrong." Sunny stroked Janice's hair. "You're a trooper, you know. I'm convinced you'll come out the other end of this stronger. You already are. You know that?"

The ponytail bobbed.

Sunny released her. Janice mumbled something to her feet and placed her palms on her distended abdomen. Janice was a *mother*, I realized, loving and caring for her child as best as she could. The intricate weave of genes and temperament and story that bound Mrs. Holback to Janice had already begun tying Janice to her child. I too shared my every fiber with my mother, and held within me this fearsome capacity to unroll that bolt of fabric another yard. I shunned its power.

No wonder Janice was combative and recalcitrant. She left without looking back.

15.

Mothering Instincts

THE BIRTH HOUSE forced me to learn the only way we learn anything—through application, until I was stretched far enough that my reticence fell away. Four months into my apprenticeship, that moment arrived with a woman named Jennifer, pregnant for the third time. She was on her back, a cotton sheet draping her naked body for a routine thirty-seventh week checkup. Sunny asked, "Do you mind if Hannah does the pelvic exam?" Jennifer turned to me with pity in her eyes and said, "Go for it."

I didn't have a chance to protest. After it was over, what amazed me most was not her privacy spread open before me or the firm elastic rim of the cervix under my fingers' pressure, or even the crazy fact of having my hand deep in a woman's body, but Jennifer's lingering and relaxed smile, as though her insides were no more secret or mysterious than the curve of an ear. "When I was a grad student, I freelanced as a pelvic model at the med school," Jennifer said. "I was strapped for cash."

A finger's width was apparently a good enough measure for a centimeter, and Jennifer was dilated two. With my hand exploring Jennifer's hospitable body, I thought of all the miserable gynecology appointments I'd endured and wondered what role adrenaline played in my suffering. I thought of Leif, who, like my father, would likely wince at this dimension of my work. To this day I'm grateful to Jennifer, whose open comfort taught me we can only ever be as easy with others as we are with ourselves. She helped me across a formidable boundary.

* * *

Black sleep, heavier than gravity—I was lost to the world, sunken as the dead, when ringing jarred me. Body pounding, I thought *Janice*, and sure enough, Sunny was on the line saying Janice was in early labor; her sister would drop her off at the Birth House on her way to work a graveyard shift. "She'd be alone otherwise," Sunny said. "Will you and Stuart walk her and call me when she's close?"

I threw on jeans and a sweater and tossed a few English muffins, packets of soup mix, and some Family Fest task force paperwork into my bag. Once outside, I shivered; the temperature plummeted at night. The streets were empty, luminous with moonlight. Whitewashed mountains rimmed a sky pitched with stars. Somewhere a pack of coyotes yipped, and the town's dogs piped up, wailing into the great bowl of desert. The adobe buildings slipped back into history, and I was walking across the mesa toward a woman in labor just as women have done since the beginning of time. Once the barking dwindled, the only sound was my tennis shoes grinding grit into pavement. Even at the center of town the air was pungent with sagebrush. The hinges of the Birth House gate rasped. Yellow porch light washed the yard. I opened the door.

Stuart and Janice paced the waiting room arm in arm. "*Hola, amiga,*" Stuart waved. "Join the party."

I stashed my bag under Anita's desk. "How's it going?"

Janice was pale, her hair disheveled. An oversized torn sweatshirt hung down to her thighs. She looked like a kid in her father's clothes. I had never wondered about her father before.

"Okay. Guess I'm missing school tomorrow."

"I'd bet money on it. Where are we?"

"Every ten minutes or so," Stuart said. "The contractions are pretty light."

"My friend Juana's birth was painless. She didn't feel a thing. And it was natural."

I frowned. "That's unusual."

"And when Juana was born, her mom was asleep. She just woke up and there was a baby halfway out, lying in the bed. They have painless births in their family."

"Are you sure she wasn't drugged?"

"Just asleep." Janice tossed her hair proudly. Limp strands strayed from her ponytail. "It could happen for me."

"Don't get your hopes up, kiddo." Stuart released her arm and looked at her head-on. "Childbirth's intense. Your job is to ease into every moment, whatever it brings."

Janice bent over, gripping the back of the sofa, distracted by internal movement. She left us, as laboring women do, to search some distant cellar at the foundation of the world. Then she righted herself, declaring the contraction "weird." "It's like tossing your cookies without feeling sick."

"Maybe you should try to sleep now," I suggested. "Save up your energy."

"You can if you want. I'm wired. Can I have a smoke?"

Stuart sank into the armchair with his arms crossed. "What do you think?"

The next hours we spent pacing, listening to Janice gripe about there being no TV at the Birth House, discussing the supposedly dire prospects of the Sangre de Cristo football team, and heading out to circle the block a few times. We could see the Milky Way stippled across the night. The stars were sharper here than at home, less blurred by humidity. Under the streetlamps, Janice's cheekbones glistened.

Back indoors, I asked if anyone wanted a cup of tea. Janice stripped down to her T-shirt and sweatpants, saying she was too hot. Stuart accepted. Halfway up the stairs, I heard the cowbell clank against the front door. I paused with my palm against the wall; we weren't expecting anyone. Janice snapped, "Get out! I don't want you," and for a moment I wondered if it was the baby's father or some boyfriend gone bad. Then I heard Mrs. Holback's chesty reply, and a chill ascended my neck. I continued upstairs and called Sunny.

"Already?" Sunny never sounded sleepy, no matter when you called.

"Margaret Holback just walked in."

"Shit." Muffled movements. "I'm on my way."

Since Janice's last appointment, Sunny had left four messages for Margaret and finally stopped by Tres Cervezas. Margaret had been fired. Sunny found her at home, weepy, 'Woe is me, how can things go so wrong'—a puddle. They'd made an appointment to talk. Margaret never showed.

Back downstairs, I hesitated just outside the waiting room. Mrs. Holback's broad back was tensed, her fuchsia polyester blouse tight, her head and torso thrust toward her daughter. Her lipstick was fresh and a bit skewed. Janice clenched her fists at her sides; she showed no signs of labor. They were shouting epithets: Janice a scathing commentary on her mother's lack of parenting skills and Mrs. Holback a graphic account of her daughter's sexual promiscuity.

Stuart saw me, held an imaginary phone to his ear, and raised his eyebrows. I nodded. From their argument I deduced that Mrs. Holback had had an intuition—at least she claimed Janice's sister hadn't ratted—and when she saw light in the Birth House windows, she knew Janice was in labor. Between flourishes of Janice's cussing, Mrs. Holback managed to call her daughter a whore, an ungrateful bitch, and "no blood of mine." I looked on in horror.

From the sidelines, Stuart tried, "Now let's . . ." and "How about we . . .," but Janice just stepped within inches of her mother's nose, butting her with her distended belly and screaming, "Get the hell out of my life!" Mrs. Holback lunged, grabbed Janice by the forearm, and yanked her toward the door. Janice's neck jolted like a rag doll's. Stuart sprang between them, guarding Janice and trying to get Mrs. Holback to let go.

I ran in and pulled ineffectually at Mrs. Holback's arm, remembering to feel scared only when her muscles tightened, jerking Janice forward a second time. Stuart stumbled. Mrs. Holback's hot whiskey breath enveloped us. Stuart leaned back and I worried Janice's arm would tear. "She's in labor! Stop it!" I flailed, suddenly protective and infuriated, slapping Mrs. Holback's chunky arm, digging my fingernails into her skin. In a sudden movement she released Janice, who stumbled backward with Stuart, and swung her fist into my jaw.

Stuart yelled, "No!"

First there was the smack, bone hitting bone, and then I reeled, ear throbbing, hand to cheek, onto my knees. Stuart backed Janice into the bookshelves, ignoring her pounding fists and one neck-snapping wrench on his ponytail. Her screams were shrill. "Get out of my life, you bitch! It's my baby! Mine!"

Mrs. Holback turned her red countenance toward me, eyes narrowing. "You damn hippies have no right. Just you wait." She spat a glob that smeared across the tiles. And she was out the door. The cowbell clunked on solid wood.

We listened to our frantic bodies. A car started up and peeled away.

I probed my cheekbone. The skin was throbbing but no bones were broken. I opened and closed my jaw. In the corner, Janice gasped for air and shuddered through the exhales. She bent over her tremendous middle. Stuart leaned against the wall and whispered, "Holy crapola." Janice began to weep the comfortless weeping of a child. She dropped to her knees and curled into a protective crouch.

"Oh, sweetie." Stuart knelt down. "I'm so sorry. I'm so very, very sorry." He rubbed small circles into her hunched back. Her choking sobs filled the room.

I got up and steadied myself against the chair. My heart knocked madly. When the spinning stopped, I squatted beside

Stuart. Janice was knotted up. I rubbed her pointy shoulders. "Hey," I said gently. "Hey." Tingling life returned to my palm. Janice's keening faded with exhaustion. She wept into her knees.

The back door slammed. Sunny rushed up the hall. "Jesus Christ. Is she hurt?"

"Just scared. Hannah's the one who got hit."

I turned my head for Sunny to see. She brushed my hair aside and cupped my chin like a mother. Her fingers were feathery and cool.

"I'm fine," I said.

"You're swelling. Let's get an ice pack on it." Sunny dashed upstairs.

Janice's sobs slid from private grief into pain—her contractions were returning. She released a full-throated groan. "Make it stop! Make it go away!"

Stuart and I rubbed her back until the contraction passed. "Janice, can you roll over so I can listen for the heartbeat?" Janice fell to her side. Stuart pressed his ear to her belly. "Good," he said.

"I don't want a baby!" Janice convulsed. "I don't want to be a mother."

I held Janice's shoulder with one hand and accepted Sunny's ice pack with the other.

"Look at that bruise." Sunny stroked Janice's right arm where fingerprints were purpling. She helped Janice sit and took her face in her hands. "You are beautiful and strong and loved," she said into Janice's glazed eyes. "You're going to have a baby, and we'll be here to help you and protect you. Do you understand?"

Janice gave the barest assent before her body seized again.

"Remember? It's work, it hurts a lot, and you can do it."

"Here," Stuart said. "Let's try walking again." He waited out her contraction and pulled her upright, offering his waist for support. They hobbled down the hall.

"Drunk?" Sunny asked me.

I gave her the details. "She also threatened us."

"Let's call the police. Did Stu tell you I finally talked with her? I should have done that months ago. Janice covered up her home life like a pro. I mean, maybe the situation hasn't been this bad all along. Margaret only lost her job recently, but I suspect food's been scarce. I alerted Social Services last week."

I pressed my fingers to my temples. My theory that midwives should create a safe container for birthing women took on new dimension. Danger could come from anywhere.

"I had no clue she'd get violent," Sunny said apologetically.

"Who would?" I said. "It's not exactly maternal."

Sunny snorted. "Whoever perpetuates the myth that mothering's an instinct doesn't know jack shit."

From the hall, we heard Janice gasp between contractions then release an ardent wail. Sunny and I rose at the distinct, unbidden quality in her cry.

"They're coming pretty quick," we heard Stuart say. "Let's get you into the bedroom."

"Teenagers." Sunny shook her head. At the threshold of the birth room, Sunny and I stepped over a puddle that exuded a familiar, faintly bleachy odor—her water had broken. The room was dim, lit only by the hall light. Janice thrashed across the bed with soggy underwear and sweatpants pulled down to her knees and the baby obviously crowning. Stuart tried to nab her feet to untie the high-tops. She whipped her limbs about, unabashed, her freedom from constraint or protocol glorious. And sure enough, despite Janice's howls that she wanted to die, that she couldn't stand it any longer, that she hated our guts and hoped we went to hell, the baby was descending at a stunning pace.

I slid a chux pad under Janice's hips just in time to catch a spot of blood. Janice, straining forward to witness the action, saw red on white and commenced screaming. "I'm dying! Fuck, fuck, fuck. I don't want to die." She arched her back as though jumping from a cheerleading pyramid, and I watched, amazed, as the perineum thinned, disappeared, and a mound of wet black hair crested. Acrid moisture filled the room.

"Hey, hey!" Stuart said, having stripped off her pants and

abandoned her socks to hold her hand. "You're fabulous, Janice. You're doing just great."

At my back a tall form blocked the doorway and our light. "Out!" Sunny commanded. She shut the door before I could see who had arrived, and turned on a table lamp. "Pay attention, Hannah!" Sunny barked and with one more push, the head popped out and mine were the nearest gloved hands. I cupped a face and then a slippery boy body emerged with a gush of blood and Janice's dwindling howl. I held him, pink-skinned and baffled. Everything happened so quickly. Janice—even distracted, rebellious Janice—could bring life into the world. When I looked up, Sunny was watching me with an equal portion of delight. His skin tone was perfect, his breathing steady, his eyes open and trusting.

"It's a boy," I told Janice, placing him on her chest. The thick cord of translucent skin dangled between his legs and across her now flaccid abdomen. "You delivered a healthy baby boy."

He wriggled against the damp cotton of her T-shirt. "Holy shit," she said.

Stuart helped Janice wipe him down with a warming blanket and slip a tiny cap over his head. He propped Janice up with pillows while I replaced the soiled pads. Sunny checked her fundus.

"Hey, peanut." Stuart tickled a wee chin.

Janice's mussed, wet hair clung to the pillow; her features were flushed and shining. She cuddled the infant like a teddy bear, rocking and whispering bits of affection.

"Hey, dude," she said. "Where did you come from? Look, he wants to nurse. He's not going to pee on me, is he?"

I took her pulse and blood pressure, then helped her maneuver her shirt off so she could position herself to breastfeed. The little guy rooted hungrily around her chest. I showed Janice how to nudge her bloated nipple into his mouth.

"What's his name?" I asked.

"Jordan. He's going to grow up to be a big famous basketball player. Right, pumpkin?"

"We're going to cut the cord, Janice," Sunny said. "You'll have a few more contractions with the afterbirth, but they won't be nearly so bad."

Janice beamed adoration at Sunny. "That's okay. It was a blast! I could do it all over again."

The three of us snorted, and then when Janice asked, "What's so funny?" we laughed outright. My skin thrilled with life, and with love.

"You did a super job." Stuart took the clamp. "I'll take over," he said, directing Sunny and me to the door with his chin. "Your body's so strong and capable."

"I know!" Janice said brightly.

* * *

Sunny took my arm and marched me to the waiting room. A police officer stood propping the front door open with a booted foot, his neck stuck into the dark. Chilly air streamed in.

"Just who the hell do you think you are?" Sunny's voice was exasperated. "I can't believe you barged in on a private birth."

The man turned, shutting out the first wisps of morning. He was wiry, with a ruffled mustache and dark circles under his eyes. He tucked his blue shirt more tightly under his belt, looking like he'd prefer the crossfire of a drug bust or a bout of drunken fisticuffs over two angry midwives.

"I'm sorry, ma'am. It was a mistake. When I heard the screaming, I just rushed in."

"Are you thick in the head? This is a birth center. Women scream."

He held up his palms. "I was responding to a call, ma'am. Lady said something about coercion. Must admit, it wasn't really clear." He was awfully pale. He started to unbutton his collar then changed his mind. He extended his hand. "Officer Billy Martinez."

"Sunny Sampaio. And my apprentice, Hannah." His handshake was decisive. "Have a seat. Who was the caller?"

Officer Martinez chose the straight-backed chair. His head thudded against the wall. "No I.D. Said she feared repercussions."

"Margaret Holback," I said, touching my cheek.

Sunny collapsed into the couch. "Your anonymous caller attacked my apprentice and tried to kidnap my client in the middle of labor. We were going to report *her* to *you*."

"Ma'am?"

"Is it possible to put a restraining order on a sixteen-year-old's mother?"

He smoothed wrinkles from his pants. "Call Child Protection. We refer out matters like that."

"Figures." Sunny bent her neck wearily and massaged the taut muscles. "I did, four days ago. Tonight was retribution."

"Sixteen?" he said.

"Take it up with the state if you have an issue with it, Billy."

"Yes, ma'am."

"Damned bureaucracy. We're supposed to help this kid, not make matters worse."

Perched on the sofa arm, I identified the dread that had lurked around the edges of the past hour.

"She threatened us," I said. "I mean, calling you was one form of revenge."

"Pretty tame. I can mention it in my report." He stood up to examine my profile, making me blush. He smelled like toothpaste. "Do you want to file assault charges? That looks nasty."

I shrunk. "It's okay." The lump on my jaw throbbed. "Unless it'd help Janice."

"Documented violence? Sure would." He extracted a pad from his back pocket and thumbed a ballpoint pen. Once again I related what happened. This time I felt strangely exhilarated—I had entered the fray. My instinct had been to help! The events struck me as bizarre, humorous even, and I realized I had acquired my first genuine midwife's story.

The next day when I tried to relate it to Leif, the long-distance wire sapped the story's power. Leif didn't laugh. He missed my point entirely. "What are you getting yourself into?" he asked. But in that moment, with Officer Martinez growing animated, his questions probing for more drama than I could provide, I knew what had happened was significant.

Martinez had seemed satisfied. "Two witnesses," he declared. "If you corroborate, you've got a case. Can I talk with this Stuart guy?"

"I'll send him out." Sunny rose. "I also want you to see the bruise on Janice's arm. It's ugly."

Down the hall the baby started to wail and Stuart called out, "I could use a hand in here."

"The afterbirth," Sunny explained to Officer Martinez.

He blanched. "Aiii. I'll wait outside."

16.

False Labor

AFTER A MORNING stuffing envelopes addressed to the entire population of Cerco County plus a few choice Santa Fe and Albuquerque health care and government officials, I came away from the task force meeting with two paper cuts and an increasing suspicion that Carol Simic liked the idea of me better than the reality. At one point she'd turned to Frida and said, "Hannah's got experience with medical billing. Anita says she's streamlining our books," and yet when I suggested that we create a separate line item for recording donation income from the fundraiser, Carol unequivocally shot it down—she wanted to track the event's income and expenses together. I clammed up. The mess of nonprofit bookkeeping would yield its own consequences. A good working relationship with Carol was more important.

Not four hours later, Anita handed me the phone. Carol's voice was tight—she was having contractions every five minutes. "For how long?" I asked.

"A half-hour. I thought they would stop, or that they were Braxton Hicks."

At thirty-two weeks, this was not a good sign. "Is the baby moving?"

"Somersaults."

"Any leaking of fluid?"

"No."

I told her to drink lots of water and come in right away then alerted Maria, who said, "We should check to see if her cervix is opening. Are you up to it?"

I leaned against the wall of family snapshots. Between mopping up after Janice's birth and my morning meeting, I'd gotten two hours of sleep. I nodded.

"Sunny said you did great with Jennifer. With Carol, be gentle and slow. Explain every step and ask permission. Got it? If it's really labor, we'll have to transport."

Maria's instructions for Carol were always specific, detailed, and insufficient. She offered nothing about Carol's testiness, and I didn't ask. "Is it possible her high blood pressure is bringing this on?"

"Unlikely."

Carol arrived a half-hour later, and Anita delayed a well-woman checkup to squeeze her into the schedule. When I met her in the waiting room, Carol asked, "What's this about an abduction call? Benito saw the police report."

"We had a vengeful client," I said. "I mean, the mother of a client. It was a false alarm."

"Even so," Carol said, "it's not good publicity."

I led her to the birth room, where Maria was studying her chart, and closed the door.

"Let's start with what you noticed, so Maria can hear too," I said.

"Well, they've stopped now." Carol smoothed her black linen skirt. "It's possible I was imagining it."

"Doubtful," I said.

"You'd prepared me for the Braxton Hicks contractions, so at first that's what I thought they were. But they were coming steady, every five minutes or so." Carol looked at her gold-encircled wrist. "For about forty-five minutes. Hard enough I left a meeting."

"And the baby's still moving?"

"Yes."

"That's a good sign. And it's good the contractions have stopped. It's hard to know yet what's going on. The first thing I'll do is check your vitals."

Once again her blood pressure was high. Maria interrupted my gentle and unoriginal suggestions to give a lecture: If Carol couldn't get it under one forty over ninety, she was in danger of preeclampsia or placental abruption. "Step down from the Family Fest task force. It's too much."

"Benito and I just started yoga . . ."

Maria raised her eyebrows.

"Fine. I'll take some vacation. Half-days this week and next."

"Better think about sick leave."

Carol agreed. Maria deferred to me.

"It's not uncommon to have bouts of contractions," I explained. "It just becomes a concern when it's early labor. So we need to take a peek at your cervix to see if it's opening. That will tell us if we should take precautions. I know pelvic exams aren't much fun." I grimaced in sympathy. "Are you up to it?"

Carol lifted her hands a centimeter from her thighs. She suddenly seemed small. "Sure," she said.

From the dresser I pulled a daisy-patterned bedsheet. "I'll need you to undress from the waist down. You can throw this over yourself."

Carol got off the bed and turned her back toward me. "I'm so damn big I can't reach the zipper. I'll need help with the nylons too."

Officially we were supposed to leave the room while the woman undressed. Maria signaled her permission.

I unhooked and unzipped Carol's skirt. The inside was lined with slippery silk, so finely made I wished we provided hangers instead of an empty stool. Carol pushed her stockings as far as her knees; I rolled them the rest of the way and waited as she lifted each foot. Her toenails were painted gold. Goosebumps dimpled her legs and, for that matter, my arms. Carol dropped her panties to the floor. I picked them up and tentatively set them on the stool.

Carol lay down, arranging the sheet over her lower body. "Can you nudge your heels up to your butt? Then butterfly your knees open. There you go." Maria sat on the desk to watch me. I snapped on latex gloves and placed a hand lightly on Carol's knee. She twitched.

"Can you scootch forward just a bit?" I said. Carol's head was flat against the bed, twisted far to her right so she could see what I was doing. I should have offered her a pillow but now my hands were sterile. "That's it. I'm going to insert my index and middle fingers and touch your cervix. It won't feel nearly as bad as a pap smear. And it won't affect the baby at all."

"You're sure?" Carol's voice was weak. Maria got off the desk to hold her hand.

"I'm sure. Take a deep breath."

Carol did her best, and I breathed with her, hoping to steady my hands. *The mother is the active agent*, I reminded myself. *I create the safe environment.* I wanted to promise Carol that everything would be okay, especially since my assurances had helped her relax after the blood draw, but Stuart's know-it-all reaction and Sunny's caution—did I want this for my own sake or for Carol's?—left me tongue-tied. Instead, I mimicked the midwives. "Good. You're doing fine." With my elbow, I slid the sheet up to her knees. The air between her legs was warm. As quickly as I could, I parted her folds and slid my latexed fingers in.

Carol sucked air through her teeth.

"There's the cervix. Nice and firm." Carol's pelvic bones were small. I scrunched my hand as tightly as I could and touched the encircling rim of muscle. "It's closed." As quickly as I could, I retreated. "There. You're not in early labor. That's great."

Only then did I look over the tent of Carol's legs to see her face, wet with tears, her right cheek twisted into the sheets, her body quaking. She closed her legs into a fetal curl. Maria held her hand and smoothed back her hair. I stood dumbly, gloved hands dangling at my sides. What had happened? I'd watched dozens of pelvic exams, none any different from this one. And my words of assurance were parroted from my mentors—how could they be wrong? Carol tightened her body into a quivering knot. "*Chiquita mía*," Maria crooned. "*Pobrecita*. It's okay. You're okay." Shame crept its red fingers up my neck. I turned to the desk.

This was what I'd feared from the start—that extending myself into others' lives would cause harm; that despite my best intentions, I'd defile the sanctity of birth. I might scratch and claw at Mrs. Holback, but the consequences of a midwife's smallest actions were too heavy for me to bear. I stripped the latex from my hands, the translucent fingers turning themselves inside out, and dropped them silently into the wastebasket. Meanwhile, Maria murmured in Spanish. She knew exactly what others needed. I pretended to be busy with the chart.

Carol blew her nose. Maria said, "There you go."

"What if I can't do it?" Carol whispered, as though she didn't want me to hear. "I want this baby so bad, I don't think I can stand it. The memories crash in, only they're just the feelings of memories. I can't tell what's now and what's then." She sniffed, and I heard the shush of Kleenex pulled from a box. "Shouldn't this be a joyful time? Instead I'm living that crap all over."

I felt ridiculous looking at the wall. I sat down and studied the floor instead.

"Oh, don't I know it." Maria's voice was soothing. "It's the darnedest thing. We have to tunnel through hurt to get to the other side."

I glanced up. Maria was stroking Carol's hair. The fist of Carol's body had relaxed its grip. Tucked under the daisy-strewn sheet, she looked ready to fall asleep.

"Can you imagine the baby blessing you on its way out? Maybe it graces every inch. Maybe it transforms a place of violation into a place of birth."

I finally saw what should have been obvious, what Maria had hinted at but couldn't name because Carol had likely asked her not to: Carol had been violated. I felt a loosening in my chest then a wrenching sadness.

"Maybe," Carol said.

The cord holding me responsible for griefs I couldn't control was cut, and now I saw Carol as she was, untangled from me. I was absolved, and in that new space I saw what Maria was suggesting: that having this baby could heal Carol just as tunneling through the humiliations of my apprenticeship was healing me. Birth can balm the harshest hurts and move us from fear to courage. I wanted to correct my error in this encounter, that I'd retreated instead of reaching out, so I joined Maria alongside the bed. Carol looked scared of me. I wanted to say, *Maria's right; there's a way through*, but I wasn't sure what that meant and instead said, "I'm sorry that was hard."

Carol's head moved in what might have been a nod. She raised herself on an elbow and turned back to Maria. "Please," she said in a low voice, "will you do my care from now on?" Her face was streaked. Her request came from an old wound.

"Of course." Maria touched her cheek then offered her hand. "Hannah." My exit cue. I left without guilt or shame but terribly, terribly sad.

17.

Aftermath

SUNNY, STUART, AND I descended on Janice's sister's house two days after the birth for a postnatal visit. Janice was camped on the living room sofa, one shoulder bare of her sleeveless T and Jordan flailing in her lap wearing a dirty onesie that asked, *Got Milk?* We clustered around, exclaiming at his perfect toes and the tuft of fine black hair on his crown. He flashed us adorable, gas-induced smiles. Janice beamed, soaking in the attention, bouncing, talking nonstop about Jordy's poop coming out yellow and how much he liked hip-hop, but he started screaming when they tuned in to the classical station and she couldn't wait to take him to the teen parenting class at school "because he's so much cooler than those other grubs." Her hair hadn't been combed; two wet splotches stained her shirt.

Stuart gave Janice a high-five, yelping, "You did it!" Janice squealed.

I moved the pile of dirty laundry and Pampers bags from the couch and found a few folding chairs in the kitchen for us to sit on. Stuart brought out the sling scale and slipped Jordan into its fabric hammock. "He's weighing nicely. Good work with the breastfeeding."

"I feel like a cow," Janice pouted.

"Jordan's job is to eat and grow," Stuart said, lifting Jordan free. He frog kicked in the air. "Your job is to make sure that happens. What are your plans for feeding once you go back to school?"

Janice hugged her chest. "I want to breastfeed. Bottles aren't as good, right?"

Stuart sat beside Janice and took out a stethoscope. "Formula's not as nutritious as breast milk. Stay open, though. Nursing can be a challenge, especially in public. Especially in high school. What's most important is that he gets what he needs and it's manageable for you. If that means using a bottle at school, fine. You can always pump."

Stuart warmed the metal disk between his hands and we waited, quiet, while he listened to Jordan's heart. By now I'd seen Stuart hold dozens of babies, and yet something about the easy way he sat beside Janice, the natural cradle of his long arm and how his whole being encompassed Jordan, lifted the remains of my bitterness. Stuart was radiant, an oddball Madonna. I'd been envious. Stuart so cavalierly defied social norms and yet entered others' lives with flawless grace. Now, I realized, I could too. I had, when I left Leif and St. Paul behind, when I stepped forward to protect Janice from her mother. I'd acted out of instinct, and care, and curiosity. I'd helped a new mother emerge.

"One forty-four," Stuart said, and I remembered the chart in my lap. "Hey, little guy, you've got a good, strong heart."

Jordan yawned.

The social worker knocked at the door—Sunny had arranged for her to meet us there to, as she put it, "open communication lines." A Pueblo woman whose smile folded into her cheeks, she took copious notes and nervously fingered the keys to her Toyota Previa minivan whenever she spoke. Motherhood must have calmed or distracted Janice; the worst thing she did was look the woman up and down and say, "*You're* supposed to protect me from that bitch?"

Janice reported accurately on her mother's behavior and offered details about home life—Margaret's drinking, hitting, boyfriends—that made even Sunny *tsk*. I held Jordan while the social worker helped Janice fill out Medicaid paperwork and sign up for a home-visiting program for at-risk moms. His tiny body relaxed in my arms. He watched me with black, absorbing eyes.

Sunny walked the social worker to the car. Janice said, "My mom's going to beat that softie to a pulp."

I reached for a bag of donated nursing bras I'd brought from the supply room and asked Janice if she wanted to try on a few.

Her face lit up. She poked Stuart in the chest. "*You* can't come." He tussled her hair like an uncle and took the baby.

In the bathroom, I ignored the toilet bowl's orange film and the wet Kleenex on the floor, instead giving my attention to Janice, who playfully wriggled her "gazongas" into the cups, wailed about "old lady hooks," and got me giggling by lowering a flap like a mouth—*"¡Hola, bambino!"* I showed her how to insert the extra pads should the leaking get bad. "Cool," Janice said. And with that resounding endorsement, a warmth began in my chest and seeped out to my hands—a capable, emergent agency. Janice had made me a midwife. There was no turning back.

18.

Good Enough

THE FAMILY FEST task force occupied the Birth House the following Thursday, hauling artwork and other donations for the silent auction into the waiting room and tying up the phone lines. Carol Simic had taken Maria's advice and stepped down. After an initial reshuffling, we'd managed just fine without her. The large challenge grant she'd procured had piqued the public's interest, and checks were arriving in the mail—ten or twenty dollar donations from former clients, a few hundred here and there from local businesses, and four-digit doozies from the rich and famous who vacationed in sprawling outposts in the New Mexican mountains. I was confident we'd bring in enough to pay the insurance bill, at least this year. Even so, this was a stopgap. The Birth House's long-term future was uncertain.

I had Officer Martinez on the phone arranging for the police to block off the street Saturday morning. The front door was propped open so Frida, the board president, could direct her teenage kids to stack the paintings under the window, the electronics by the bookshelves, the fabric items on the sofa. Carol walked in. We locked eyes. Her palm was pressed to her chest. She was wearing a crisp white blouse and maternity jeans. The sight of an elastic waistband on Carol was alarming.

Over the phone line, Officer Martinez assured me that a lackey would drop off the barriers Friday afternoon. "I'll come Saturday. After what I saw, sure, I'll give you ladies a donation."

Carol approached me hesitantly as I set down the phone. "Hannah, something's not right. Any chance Maria's available?" Her voice was tight.

"She's out running errands. What's up?"

"I'm having heart palpitations. What if the baby's not okay?" Carol's voice shook. "It doesn't have to be Maria."

"Have you felt any movement?"

"Yes, this morning. I think."

I glanced up at a teenager with an upside-down rocker on his head. "Would you like me to page Sunny?"

"No, no. I'm probably being irrational. Would you check?"

"Of course."

Down the hall, I flicked on the birth room light and followed Carol in. She sat on the edge of the bed, her hand to her face. I pulled a stool close. Whatever momentary satisfaction I felt that Carol had agreed to work with me dissolved in the face of her distress.

"My heart keeps fluttering. What if the high blood pressure's giving me a heart attack or hurting the baby?"

"It's good you came in. Even if it's nothing, it's better to check." I grabbed the cuff and stethoscope from the desk. Her skin was clammy. "I don't know if it's any comfort, but lots of women have panic attacks mid-pregnancy. It's completely normal. I guess we're always anticipating the best on the surface and the worst underneath." Her blood pulsed through my head; I counted. "One twenty-eight over seventy-eight. Isn't that what it was last time? I didn't grab your chart."

"It's the same."

Sitting so close, I could see sweat glistening through her foundation makeup. I willed myself to be calm, to retrieve that source of confidence Janice had brought out of me. "It's also common to get heart palpitations during pregnancy." I pressed the stethoscope's disk below her collarbone. She sucked in air and waited. "Breathe normally. There you go." The thump was regular and strong, if a bit fast. "Again." Steady, confident, forceful. I listened, searching for any sound out of rhythm.

"I'm fine, aren't I?" The vibrations of her voice came through the earpiece.

"You know, we're not heart specialists. If you're worried about a heart attack, you should go into your doctor and have an EKG." I folded the stethoscope in my lap.

"No. It's stress. I know it."

I looked at her clenched jaw and new, protective hunch. At her final Family Fest meeting, Carol had reported soliciting significant contributions from three major banks, matching donations from a chain of baby supply stores, and landing in-kind donations for the auction from local businesses. Single-handedly she'd raised half the money we needed. Without her connections, I doubted our motley committee members could have pulled off such a feat.

"I'm trying too hard to be good enough," she said. "For the baby."

I swallowed and pressed my weight into the stool. Her pumping blood still echoed inside me. "Oh, Carol. You *are* good enough. As is, without having to do anything." I spoke with conviction. It was true.

Panic flared in her eyes. "I forgot to tell anyone about Rio Hardware."

I touched her hand. "They called. You can let it go. Your job is to take care of yourself and the baby. Drink lots of water. Rest. Eat lots of protein. Nothing else is as important."

"That's right," she said, surprised. "That's the priority."

I taught her to monitor the fetal kick counts. I had her lie down so I could test her ankles for pitting edema, a sign of preeclampsia, and check the baby, whose heartbeat was stable. I passed the fetoscope to Carol so she could hear. "Oh," she exclaimed, and shut her eyes. I waited. With the fetoscope pressed below her left rib, Carol attended the quickening inside her. Her back relaxed, and her face went slack. I closed my eyes too, grateful for this still moment, aware that Carol was allowing me to care for her. Down the hall the kids burst into overwrought laughter. After a while, I realized Carol was watching me.

"A small miracle, hmm?" I said.

"Huge." She sat up and pulled down her shirt. "You're right about priorities, Hannah. Thanks. I get caught up, you know, in proving . . . my worth." Her laugh was short and pained. "You get it, don't you? Earn your way into heaven and all."

I wound the fetoscope's rubber tubing around the metal staff. "Sure," I said. Then I floundered, unable to find an appropriate way to end the appointment.

Carol arranged her blouse to hide her waistband. "Anyhow," she said. "I hope the Family Fest is a roaring success."

"Me too," I said. "Say, come back Monday so we can take your blood pressure again, okay?"

Carol nodded and shut the door behind her.

I stalled, yanking the bedspread flat and putting equipment away. I knew exactly what Carol meant. If only I could be good enough . . . then what?

Then Mom would forgive me.

I sat down. Forgive me for what? So much of my energy had been drained by insatiable longing, to be seen by my parents, to be accepted, to receive something more . . . Forgiveness? Below my every action and reaction was a dark, defining smudge. I wanted it lifted, or loved. Mom was gone and still the longing governed me, a lifelong habit and perhaps older than that, perhaps inherited from Mom, whose every criticism was a punishment and whose every kindness, I now saw, an act of atonement. The altar cloths, the hot dishes delivered to shut-ins, her service as a pastor's wife, her perfunctory mothering, all sprang from generosity, yes, but also from a pervasive need for forgiveness. Why? Mom was incapable of any crime big enough to warrant two generations of ache. What a waste.

Carol was good enough. I was too. The appointment had gone well. Perhaps we could both relinquish our inheritance.

19.

The Family Fest

THE MORNING OF the Family Fest was, predictably, New Mexican brilliant. I missed the wait-five-minutes-and-it'll-change weather of Minnesota, especially its spring swings from eighty degrees to snow flurries, and scoffed at Sunny's fretting about the March wind. Stuart loaned me his car; I drove onto the mesa and into the foothills to retrieve clients and their kids who otherwise wouldn't be able to make it. Our hope was to fill the street with alums so potential donors would see the breadth of our service, and, as Maria put it, to guarantee a good time.

Out on the expansive basin and up in the steep piñon-spotted mountains, I found my spirit lifting, reaching, opening. When I'd first arrived, the mesa had seemed exotic from afar and barren up close, dust and sagebrush and tumbleweed parching my throat. I'd been accustomed to nearsighted beauty: a shock of orange butterfly weed in a ditch, a flash of bluebirds, the enduring black wealth of soil. But now the yucca had sprouted white bloom stalks and odd pink tufts of hair sprung up on otherwise bare bushes. My thirst for lakes was unsatiated and yet the broad bowl of the mesa embraced me within its sculpted rim as though *I* was the water it held, *I* the contents.

Back in town, orange barriers blocked either end of our street. I parked on the commercial road and let out my last passengers. Maria's husband directed a crew to unload folding chairs and construct picnic tables out of sawhorses and plywood. Felipe's Diner had hauled in a kettle grill and a pig was rotating above red coals; smoke barreled eastward. Directly across the street from the Birth House, Benito's lumber guys had erected a small stage and Benito stood, legs spread, cowboy boots planted, hands on his hips, before the microphone, repeating, "*Uno, dos, tres.*" The speaker system crackled. I waved; he lifted his broad-brimmed hat.

"How's Carol?" I called out.

"She'll be by later," Benito said into the mike, his voice booming through the speakers. "We thought it'd be better . . ." He swept his arm across all the activity, and I held up my hands to show I got it. "Party on!" he said. A cheer went up from the scattered volunteers.

I found Stuart in the front yard with a full-sized helium canister and a flock of Maria's kids, their number somehow doubled, jumping for balloons. When he saw me, he put his mouth to the valve and sucked in a long hiss.

"Hello, folks!" He sounded like a castrated Donald Duck. The kids squealed. "Let's give a big hand to Hannah, who helped coordinate this show." The group turned their brown, elated faces to me. I'd bought a playful red sundress with white polka dots that made me self-conscious in a celebratory way. I curtsied.

The waiting room sofa, coffee table, and chairs were hospitably arranged in the dirt yard—another bit of Southwestern overconfidence in the weather. Inside, the Birth House had been transformed into an art gallery/appliance store. White bidding sheets taped to each item flapped as the wind blew through. Anita's desk held baskets of soaps and cheeses and a collection of gift certificates from local psychics, massage therapists, and fruit tree sprayers. If this stuff sold, we'd ride pretty.

I found Sunny in the back office studying a clipboard and wearing a scoop neck goddess dress that turned her eyes a piercing, otherworldly blue. Heavy turquoise-studded jewelry wrapped her neck and arms. Her silvery blond hair was twisted and pinned back. "Oh, good," she said, looking up. She was flushed with excitement. "Did the Hernandezes make it?"

"Mm-hmm." I sat on the desk. Sylvia Hernandez would tell the crowd the story of her hair-raising homebirth. A forest fire had ripped through the mountains and lapped at the chamisa in their front yard while she pushed out her second child. Sunny checked her off. We reviewed the lineup, which included Jill Whitehart performing an original birth ballet, Sunny's unassuming husband doing stand-up comedy about being married to a midwife, the local Community Ed belly dancing group leading the crowd in developing their abdominal muscles, occasional pleas for money, and Sunny as emcee, interspersing her own harrowing tales. Anita had asked a dozen clients for their permission. My job was to arrange the performers at the stage's steps, in order of appearance.

Sunny rubbed her temples. "I sure hope Nadine doesn't go into labor. You and Maria will have to run out. Are you wearing your pager?"

I patted my hip.

"Reliable Hannah." Sunny put her hand on my knee and pushed herself up, already moving toward the next task. Was that all she was going to say? I wished she would give me her approval as freely as she gave it to Stuart. I wished she would acknowledge my part in making this event happen or affirm that I was becoming a fine midwife. And then I let the wish go.

By two, the street was crowded with kids, their cheeks painted with crusty white baby-toting storks, and adults biting into barbecue pork burritos or dancing to the marimba band up on stage. The task force had strung wires at eye-level up and down the sidewalk and invited people to clothespin their birth photos in long rows. Snapshots flipped and spun in the wind. A few houses up, I saw Janice hanging a Polaroid. Her face had the shocked, beat-up look of all new moms, and her maternity bra straps were showing under her halter top. Jordan was zonked in an umbrella stroller. I went to greet them.

"Let's see," I held the photo against the wind.

"My sister took it."

A bit off-center, with an unfocused fast-food counter in the background, Janice pressed cheeks with tiny Jordan, whose mouth and eyes were perfectly round. "That's a keeper," I said.

A gaggle of children trailed Stuart down the street, trying to snatch balloons out of his hand. I watched him do a handstand, balloons bobbing between his legs. A man nudged my elbow and said, "Too bad he's not a papa, huh?" I'd seen Stuart's wallet photo, and even so, Cal's blue button-down shirt, khaki slacks, and stocky build surprised me. Cal was head-turningly handsome, with a natural smile and keen eyes.

Stuart landed and dashed over to give his lover a kiss that made me blush. "Hannah, Cal, Cal, Hannah." He lifted the balloons out of the reach of leaping hands. "Fellow pragmatists, introverts, and conservatives, you should have a lot not to talk about."

Cal shook my hand. "Don't listen to him."

Cal's and Stuart's ease wrenched my heart; Leif and I would never love that way. With relief and a flood of sorrow, I admitted to myself that Leif would never satisfy me. I would leave him. The calm with which I accepted this told me I'd known it for a while.

The band announced their final set. I found Sunny, gave her the five-minute warning, and darted through the crowd to corral performers at the south side of the stage—not an easy task, since half of them were changing diapers inside the Birth House or still squeezing into costumes. After some handwringing on my part, Sunny ditched our plan and just introduced whoever was ready at the stage steps. The belly dancers came out in gold-stitched bikini tops that accentuated their nipples and jangly, fringed skirts over which their tummies rolled. When I recognized Anita jiggling in their ranks, she raked her fingers seductively across my cheek and laughed. I was happy enough to watch them clang their finger cymbals and rotate around the stage, but when they asked everyone to stand and draw hip-circles, arms undulating, I opted to tally imaginary figures on the clipboard.

Mark, Sunny's husband, listed in reverse order his ten most embarrassing moments as a midwife's husband. First was an evening out drinking with the guys when he accidentally used the expression, "The meconium hit the fan." His climax was the story of a neighbor arriving at their house in labor while Sunny was out. The woman lodged herself in the doorframe and refused to budge, dismissing Mark's protests that just because he was married to a midwife didn't mean he knew squat about delivering babies. He knew enough to catch the infant when it fell out, though. A high school kid in the crowd shouted, "That was me!" and we applauded.

Sunny swatted Mark's butt away from the microphone. "What he's not telling you," she confided, "is about the birth of our second son." Mark, back on the pavement, groaned and ducked his head. "So we're living on the mesa in a dugout back then. This was in the early sixties, back when the idea of being a midwife hadn't crossed my mind. Mark and I thought it would be groovy to give birth at home—how hard could it be, right? I'd already given birth once in a hospital. Mark had read everything he needed to know from *A Barefoot Doctor's Manual*, you know, the one Chairman Mao loved." The crowd snickered. "So I'm in labor, contractions coming bam-bam-bam, and—"

Someone touched my elbow—Carol, eight months pregnant. I almost didn't recognize her. Her face was drawn and blotchy, her hair uncombed, her head turning frantically to scan the crowd. Her breath came in jagged gasps. She must have run the few blocks from her car.

"God, Carol."

". . . Mark comes in carrying a chicken from the backyard coop. So I say . . ."

Carol grasped my arm with both hands. "Oh, Hannah. I'm so scared. I may just be panicking again, but I haven't felt the

baby move since . . . It's probably another false alarm. I thought
about calling, but I knew . . ." She pressed the corner of her eye
as though to stop tears.

I found a board member nearby, gave her the clipboard with
brusque instructions, and led Carol around the periphery of the
crowd. "Let's get Maria."

"No. Don't interrupt her." Carol smeared her palm across
her brow.

I scanned the crowd, but Maria was short and dark-haired
and hidden. Carol pulled me.

We passed the barbecue and bake sale table. The front gate
was tied open. Stuart and Cal lounged on the sofa, feet on the
coffee table. Stuart raised his eyebrows; I ignored him. In the
waiting room we elbowed past shoppers, Carol acknowledging
the occasional greeting but then tucking her chin, allowing me
to pull her forward. Sunny's voice over the speakers dimmed
when I shut the birth room door. I left the lights off.

I retrieved the fetoscope from the desk drawer, our silence
magnifying the sound of wood scraping on wood, and pressed
the cold metal disk between my palms. Carol lay along the edge
of the bed with her head sunk into a pillow, her hands hiding
her face. In the afternoon half-light I pulled over a stool and
scrunched up her shirt.

Her glistening skin, her pale stretch marks ascending, her
exuberant, popped navel, all were stunning the way a loaf of
bread steaming from the oven is stunning. I found the curled
baby-form head down and passed the fetoscope across the thick
organ of Carol's skin. I revered her and her unborn child, and I
adored this work, so much bigger than myself and yet, finally,
within reach. I steadied my left hand against the bed. And
then I listened: the great, steady rush of arterial blood; Carol's
tight, controlled breathing; my own heartbeat, surprisingly
exaggerated.

I drew the scope along the lower left quadrant. Where was the
baby? I cast the fetoscope on the bed and took out the Doppler.
The windy static of a long-distance telephone call filled the

room. I dragged the instrument along her abdomen, I traced the rounded meridians. I couldn't locate that steady helicopter beat. I began again at the base and heard nothing but the increased thumping of my own chest. "Breathe, Carol." I lightly touched her cheek. "I'll be right back. I'm going to get Maria."

I carefully pulled the door shut then rushed to the bustling front room. My skin had lost heat; I was shaking, adrenaline clanging in my head. "Frida, where's Maria?"

Frida turned from her conversation with some art buyer. "She just came in for the prize bag. They're starting the children's games."

"Get her for me. Carol's . . ." I gestured wildly toward the room.

Frida held her palms up to the art buyer and headed toward the door. I turned back to the darkened room where Carol lay eerily still, pulled a stool over and took her hand. It was dry, limp, and small. Her head was twisted to face the wall. We sat in silence until Maria opened and closed the door.

She paused, reading the panic on my face, Carol's hand in mine, the equipment cast on the bed. "*Dios,* " she whispered. I moved out of the way. Carol turned, her face pale and eyes rimmed with red, allowing Maria to rest a hand on her exposed belly. "*Caro*, let's see what we can find." Maria maneuvered the Doppler across Carol's skin. I clamped my lips between my teeth.

The awful, adult pulsing of Carol's womb once again filled the room.

Maria had Carol shift positions; she nudged and listened. The air grew heavier. Then Maria set the Doppler on the bed to take Carol's hand in both her own. "I'm so sorry, Carol. We're not hearing a heartbeat. *Lo siento mucho.*"

"No." Gurgling disbelief, and then a rising, insistent "No!"

"Let's get you down to Española," Maria said. "Maybe we missed something."

I sat on the stool. I knew there was no mistake, nothing we could do to bring back that hummingbird heartbeat. My throat cracked, and my knees felt untrustworthy. Maria held Carol and rocked on the bed, back and forth, while I sucked in ragged gasps of air. Then I thought of Benito and broke out of the room, out of the house and into the festivities, which now seemed to lack substance, like heat waves distorting the air. Benito's cowboy hat bobbed above the grill. I squeezed through the meal line and told him I needed him inside.

"Now?" he asked, and I must have looked scared because he handed off the carving knife. "*Madre de Dios. Mí nene, mí nene.*" The massive bulk of Benito's fear propelled him forward.

I followed, gasping now, but stopped short of the doorway. Suddenly Stuart was at my side. He corralled me in one arm and led me around back to the dirt yard where I could sob freely. We sat on the picnic bench. The high fence cloistered us from the activity on the street. The sky was perfectly blue. A magpie landed on a tall post and nagged, fanning its tail feathers. I leaned into Stuart. My grief was ragged and snotty, racking, pure. Stuart held me, his arm heavy across my shoulders. Weariness steeped my bone marrow, my head, my skin. Finally, I fell quiet.

On the other side of the house, a horn blared and car doors slammed. Maria would speed down the mountain pass, managing the curves expertly, her voice an accompanying stream of compassion.

"It's not fair," I sniffed. I wiped my nose on my hand. "I thought birth was going to help her heal. She's a rape survivor."

"Jeez." Stuart put his face in his hands.

"They wanted that baby so badly."

The magpie's ruckus attracted the attention of the dog next door, who leapt at the fence, barking. The bird hopped from post to post. Out in the street, the band whooped and the crowd continued its humming conversation.

Stuart shook his head. "That's awful." The deaths of Stuart's former partner, his parents, and hundreds of hospice patients were carved into his brow. Now death trumped his resentment toward Carol.

I rested my head on his shoulder. "Babies shouldn't die."

"They shouldn't but they do." Stuart's voice vibrated through my body. "Know what I think? Death's a vital organ. You can't extract it without everything going haywire. Better to admit it's right here." He clutched his ribcage. "Better to live with it."

Stuart inhaled deeply and I imitated him, expanding my lungs to try and still my trembling. Perhaps grief was elemental. Grief—for Carol, for my mother, for my marriage that wouldn't happen, for Janice and a messed up world—wasn't worth fighting. Loss was part and parcel of everything. Next door the dog barked sharply, its toenails clawing the wood slats of the fence. With a scornful flap, the magpie rose, flaunting its black and white against the sky.

20.

At Home

BY THE END of my second year down in Sangre de Cristo, I'd caught eighty-three babies, lost a fiancée, made the best friend I'll ever have, and mustered gumption enough to go into business for myself. But mostly I grieved my mother. After Carol Simic's baby died, I was paralyzed by sorrow, followed by a pointlessness that drained even blue New Mexico of its color. Like so many people, I had conflated creation with life and destruction with death. I thought life should be triumphant. That was Dad's version of the resurrection, and Mom's, as I came to find out. But reality isn't like that. Creation and destruction are dance partners; what comes of their separation is death of the spirit and what comes of their tight intertwining is life. Midwives serve life, which means opening our arms painfully wide. Thank goodness for Stuart, who knew this and could nurse me back to wellbeing.

Much as I came to adore New Mexico, I needed to return to central Minnesota's lakes and pines, its land swells and agricultural ditches, and the humus scent of soil in the spring. I might not have remembered my birth, but the land reliably linked me to my origins. So a month before graduation, when New Mexico's aspens shivered yellow against a blue sky and before I'd aced the North American Registry of Midwives exam, I flew back home to explore the possibility of setting up my own practice.

You probably think me noble and brave. Really I was naïve. I figured my biggest hurdles would be finding office space and a backup doctor. Sure, I'd heard Maryann describe the "push-me, pull-me status" of Minnesota lay midwives. The law said we could deliver with a license, but the Board of Medical Practice, stacked with physicians, refused to issue licenses due to "the lack of an exam." They could have required training; they could have developed an exam. Without any enforcement arm, the Board referred complaints to the Attorney General's office, which made midwives' transgressions into finable offenses. So the laws contradicted enforcement. That's why Maryann wound up working in a hospital under physician scrutiny with oodles of malpractice insurance—she had kids and a mortgage.

"Want to know why state policy favors the docs?" Maryann liked to ask. "Midwives don't play golf." Even today, if you drive the highway north from St. Paul to Chester Prairie, you'll pass one billboard after the next advertising, "We Deliver; You Recover," or, my favorite, "Where do babies come from? Midwestern Regional Hospital." There's money to be made in babies.

After two years in New Mexico, homebirth seemed so natural, so normal. Surely the Minnesota Medical Board would come around.

What worried me more was money. The apprenticeship had drained the little I'd saved, and I knew income would be scarce while I got my business off the ground. Dad had been dropping hints for months—"I'm considering closing off the third floor of the parsonage, unless someone needs it, that is," and in the expectant, long-distance pause that followed, during which I was supposed to respond, "Gee, Dad, why don't I come live with you?," screams of protest bounded in my skull. Dad may have wanted me home, but he didn't want my profession. He skirted the topic as though I was entering the sex industry. And when I pictured Dad in his study communing with God and parishioners slamming car doors in the parking lot outside while in an upstairs room a pregnant woman trusted me to measure her cervix, I gagged.

"Don't you dare!" Stuart said when I asked his opinion.

I determined to scrimp in other ways.

So when Dad mentioned that Esther Lundgren's children were renting out her tidy brick house and offered his help with the security deposit, I boarded a plane. The house was perfect. It had a single attic bedroom and a downstairs parlor I could use as an office. The parsonage was five blocks away, and Little Long Lake a mile west. Leif would have loved the large silver maple out front. Even a year after our break-up, the thought of him filled me with a potent mixture of relief and regret.

My dream was to serve the families of Chester Prairie, much like my father. I wanted to return to the community that had formed me, that my mother had loved. Perhaps I needed the completion that comes of settling your adult self on the site of an unsettled childhood. Perhaps I needed to test my newfound strength against the forceful backwaters of my hometown. Dad was aging. If I were ever to grow close to him, now was the time.

Chester Prairie also has the magnetism of small towns—I wasn't the only one it pulled back into its clutches. A high school friend returned to teach math and still sits in the faculty lounge with our old nemeses, calling them by their first names. My friend Cathie took over her father's floral business. My classmate Zarida left long enough to don nursing sneakers; she now defends the supremacy of the hospital's maternal care. Fifty-plus years later, Dad continued to mount the pulpit every Sunday. And Bill Jorgenson, white-haired, nearsighted, and careless about tucking in his shirt, was still Chester Prairie's primary obstetrician. I found it uncanny to have as a potential colleague the very man who rescued me from the womb.

I planned to screen my clients carefully, turning down high-risk cases and accepting only healthy women with standard pregnancies. Sunny and Maria taught me that, with screening, the vast majority of homebirths are safe, yet there's always the possibility of a rare, surprise moment when things can go amiss. That two percent chance of complication rests heavily against the uneventful ninety-eight. I had to find backup—a way through the hospital doors. I knew that much. Which is why I asked Bill Jorgenson to the parsonage for Sunday dinner that week home, much to Dad's delight.

The meal stretched my culinary skills: a steaming roast, mashed potatoes, boiled carrots, even Mom's French-cut green bean hot dish. The recipe cards, propped on the windowsill, were browned with age, the blue ballpoint ink seeping beyond the bounds of her handwriting. I hoped my attempts to replicate Mom's cooking were passable. Especially the apple pie, with its jagged patchwork crust and ridiculously lumpy filling.

Bill showed up at the kitchen door dressed in weekend jeans, red suspenders, and flannel. "Smells tasty," he said through the screen.

I put down a potholder to let him in. "Dr. Jorgenson."

His eyebrows rose. "My, my." He gripped my fingers in a meaty palm. "Welcome home. You haven't changed a lick." He fumbled me sideways into an embrace.

In the nine years since I'd left Chester Prairie, seven in St. Paul and two in New Mexico, I'd seen Bill only peripherally, on visits, as a hand wave and a honk from his rusting truck when he picked up Dad for a day on the lake. Occasionally I had called on a day he was visiting, and Mom's voice would be hushed with reverence. I'd seen him last three years ago at Mom's funeral. Bill had donned a suit and bowed his head at the service despite his aversion to "that religious claptrap." Whatever the friendship between Bill and Dad was founded upon, that gesture sealed it. Ever since, the two men huddled at the Hitching Post every Wednesday at six a.m., downing coffee, bacon, and wet eggs. I was glad mine wasn't the only shoulder Dad leaned on.

The likelihood that Bill would back me was slim. Any doctor

in Minnesota caught supporting a homebirth could lose hospital privileges or his license. Most would scorn my apprenticeship as inadequate training, despite the fact that I'd assisted more births than most doctors entering family practice. With some searching I might have found a hip doc down in the Cities willing to take a political stand. But Chester Prairie tethered me. I held out hope that Bill's friendship with Dad and our shared history might prove persuasive.

My father's measured steps descended the stairs. "Jorgenson," he bellowed. He had changed into his Sunday casuals. "Cindy Lundeen saw you out on the lake this morning. Fishing on the Sabbath's a sin, you know." The men shook hands.

"I taste heaven on earth every day while you rack up points for a later date. How's it going, Loren?"

"Not bad, not bad." Even in khakis and a navy cardigan, Dad's presence was charismatic. His sweep of graying hair, his gold-rimmed reading glasses, and long features brought authority and substance into the room. Without him our lives— the entire community's life—would lack direction.

The men took seats at the table, Dad regal at the head, Bill at his right, rumpling the tablecloth with his elbow. I had polished two years of tarnish off the silver and ironed the linen napkins. For a centerpiece I'd considered buying a potted mum but figured it was an expense the men wouldn't notice and arranged some reddened maple leaves under the candlesticks instead. The dishes steamed pleasantly. Dad stretched out his long legs. The men joked with each other, intoxicated, I supposed, by the heady scent of a home-cooked meal after months of bachelor diets, and by the privilege of being served. Precisely what I'd planned, but it irked me nonetheless. The last thing I wanted was Dad's expectation that I fill Mom's empty apron.

Wine, I remembered, and descended to the cellar for a bottle of red. I wiped off the dust, found a corkscrew in the kitchen drawer, and caught myself about to turn both over to Dad. Mom had never opened wine. Unlike me, Mom had excelled in her role as straightener of my father's crooked collar and orchestrator of unnoticed niceties. She would have bought a potted mum. I jammed the bottle between my knees. The pop of pressure and velvet, fermented scent gave me a tiny vindictive thrill.

"Wine?" I asked.

"You bet," Bill said.

"What's this?" Dad sat up.

"I thought we'd celebrate my homecoming." Bruised red splashed up the crystal. I sat and raised my glass. "To Chester Prairie. Let's hope I can stay."

"To Chester Prairie." We grazed glasses and sipped.

By the time I'd set down my wine, Dad's head was bowed. Bill and I exchanged a contrite glance during the awkward and lengthy pause. Finally Dad cleared his throat.

Other than the roast being dry, the meal was a success. Dad's eyes welled up when I lifted the lid of the green-bean hot dish sprinkled with curls of store-bought fried onions, a titch burnt on top. For the duration of the first serving, I allowed them to bypass conversation about my past years in New Mexico and current plans. I had told Dad, but, like most things he disapproved of, he kept silent about how much he'd heard or whether he'd divulged anything to his friend. So instead we discussed Bill's catch that morning—two small-mouthed bass he would pan-fry for tomorrow's breakfast—and Dad complained at length about the new intern the seminary had sent. Apparently this Chuck fellow had persuaded members of the youth group to shave their heads in solidarity with a high-schooler going through chemotherapy.

"Don't get me wrong," Dad said, leaning back in the armchair. "I appreciate the display of compassion. Only now I've got a hoard of grumbling parents and a bald guy with a nose ring serving communion next to me. There're better ways of being compassionate, surely."

When the conversation swung around to me, the men gnawed on the subject of Esther Lundgren's sloping front porch and monstrous gravity-gas furnace.

"It's going to conk out one of these days," Dad cautioned.

"Don't count on those Lundgrens for beans," Bill said. "You'll be calling your own plumbers."

I basked in their paternal doting until Bill asked, "Now what happened to that dashing young man I met at your mother's funeral? The Danish fellow?"

I'd called off the relationship more than a year ago but still felt embarrassed.

Dad glanced my way. "Not in the picture anymore," he said, and I was grateful. At the time Dad had taken the news evenly, as though I was simply canceling the appointment I'd made with him to officiate the wedding. His feelings were unfathomable.

Finally, in the lull before the serving dishes went around again, Dad emitted a throaty sigh, Bill eyed the potatoes, and I said, "You've been practicing obstetrics in town for how long now, Bill?"

"Finished practicing ages ago." He winked and succumbed to the potatoes. "Since the mid-fifties. Just before you were born. Damn, that makes me old."

"Set the retirement date?" Dad asked, and I endured a digression on tax shelters and health benefits and the scarcity of new OBs due to the burdens of malpractice insurance.

"Sounds like you're still in demand, though," I reentered.

Bill waved his fork. "No shortage of pregnancies in these parts. Too many loose teenagers, too many Catholics. The clinic's looking to hire another OB part-time but can't afford it. I'm run ragged. Jeff Skogel pinch hits for me so I get a couple of days off each week, but he's got a commute. Lives out past Princeton. Got to admit, I'm getting tired."

"I don't know if Dad told you. I'm just finishing up a midwifery apprenticeship and hoping to set up a practice." Dad's jaw clenched. Both men's foreheads wrinkled. "I might be able to relieve you of some work. I don't want to be any competition, just take the pressure off and do some natural birth educating."

Dad raised his hand midair, as though bringing worship to a close. "Hannah, I don't think it's appropriate—"

"What are you saying?" Bill interrupted. He rested his fat chin in his fist.

I took a deliberate sip of wine. "I'm wondering if you'd back me up. I need to be able to transfer my mothers in an emergency."

Bill opened his mouth.

"Wait," I said. "I have ethics. You know that. You know my family. I'll use Guild standards—no preemies, no twins, no malpresentations, no high blood pressure cases, no diabetics, nothing high risk. I've had excellent training, seen about a hundred and twenty births, caught eighty-three. I'm no novice. I'm licensed in New Mexico. If Minnesota had licensure, I'd get it. I'd never put a laboring mother in danger." I pressed my fingers into the whorls of the armrests and thought of Maryann's expression, *white-knuckle labor.* "I won't practice if I have to abandon my clients at the ER entrance. I want to provide continuity. I just need a way in."

Bill rocked in his seat for a moment then patted my father's arm. "Stalwart, Loren, that's what your daughter is. And well-intended. But homebirths aren't safe. No birth is. Hell, *you* of all people should know that." This last he fired at me through a pointed finger. "What happens when you get a shoulder dystocia or they start hemorrhaging?" His jowl quivered. He stabbed the potatoes with his fork.

"The women I bring into the hospital will have chosen to be at home until then. Their choice, not mine." My plan suddenly seemed hopeless, but I was in too deep to stop. "Here's what I need: You accept their choice and help them through emergencies, turning a blind eye toward me."

"Hannah Abigail!" Dad slammed his palms into the table; I flinched. "Bill has done enough for this family. I won't have you—"

"Now, Loren. This is between your daughter and me."

Dad glared at him.

Bill continued. "A buddy down on the Medical Board says the legislature is pressing to get the midwifery problem resolved. No more legal wishy-washiness. This stuff's a hot potato, Hannah. If the insurance company ever found out, I'd be up a creek. No." His face, his nose especially, had turned crimson. "The only thing you midwives bring is liability."

Blood throbbed in my fingertips. I feared that blotches were inching up my chest and neck. Without backup, I'd have to look elsewhere for work, perhaps down in the Cities but more likely in Oregon or Washington State or back in New Mexico. I moved cold green beans around my plate and tried to disregard the crease in Dad's brow. People give birth at home no matter what the law declares, no matter what the health insurance companies require; they give birth at home out of personal conviction, for religious reasons, due to poverty, always on the fringes. If Bill truly cared about the welfare of Hiawatha County moms, my threat to proceed regardless might prove persuasive.

And I knew that much about Bill: He cared. Over the years he'd delivered half the town, been a guest speaker in our high school health classes (where he'd advocated abstinence until marriage with sweeping, moralistic pronouncements), spear-headed the hospital's remodeling of the maternity ward, and run twice, unsuccessfully, for mayor. He was rooted in the community and unquestionably dedicated. Mom had thought the world of him. Even after twenty-some years, she had called him "Dr. Jorgenson" over rhubarb crisp at her own table.

"What about the population of moms who already give birth at home? Wouldn't some care be better than nothing?"

Bill winced. "Damn hippies and Jesus freaks." Dad's chin jerked up and Bill amended, "Pardon the language. There's always a few wackos that wind up in the ER at the eleventh hour with baby feet dangling between their legs saying it was God's will." Bill leaned over his plate. "So you're going to work with *those* people? They need all the help they can get. I had one couple once, show up in the emergency room after zero prenatal care and thirty-four frickin' hours of labor. The nurse comes and gets me, we're going to induce, and when we walk in we catch the guy in bed with her, sucking her nipples."

"I don't need this." Dad stood, the chair teetering behind him, and began clearing the dishes.

"It stimulates labor," I said.

"Oh, come on," Bill said. "Have some decency. There're loony people out there."

"With no one to respectfully deliver their babies."

Dad stacked the china precariously, with the silverware between, and disappeared into the kitchen. I realized I'd never before seen him perform a domestic chore. Two years had changed us both. I listened to him put coffee on the stove and pressed my hands into the chair's arms.

"You won't make a living that way," Bill said.

"Cathie Johnston's asked me to do her books." Cathie had made a mess of the Bountiful Bouquet's financials and was too ashamed to ask her dad for help. Keeping her books could provide my bread and butter.

"You," Bill pointed his thumb at me, "are not like your mother. Rest her soul." Folds deepened in his chin; he looked around the dining room as though Mom might be listening. "No multiples, no malpresentations? What are you going to do for hemorrhaging?"

Once hemorrhaging starts, there's no time to transfer to the hospital. I planned to buy my Pitocin from the New Mexico Birth House where Sunny and Maria could acquire and ship it legally. Bill, I knew, would disapprove. It's one thing for a midwife to help women with labor and another entirely for her to use medications over which doctors want sole dominion. Even though I only ever use Pitocin for hemorrhaging, the drug is tricky because hospitals use it to induce labor. How do you prove emergency use of a drug that can also be seen as a medical intervention? "There are methods," I said.

"What? Moss? Cobwebs? Witch hazel?"

"Bill," I tried, "consider this: The state of Denmark, which we know you love"—he slapped his heart in knee-jerk patriotism—"has one of the lowest infant and maternal mortality rates in the world. Why? Because their births happen at home with easy access to the hospital. That should make you proud. There are fewer complications if women give birth in a familiar place. I see it all the time."

"Denmark doesn't have crack babies screwing up their stats." Bill plucked a carrot from the serving dish and leaned back to chew.

"My point is, women's hormones work better in a relaxed atmosphere. And women need to move around. They need a good birth coach. You know what a difference doulas make." Bill scoffed. "Besides, I'm licensed. I could practice in a dozen states. I'm just asking for your cooperation so I can practice safely here. I want to give back to my community."

Bill swallowed. I held his gaze.

"Coffee?" Dad filled our teacups with double-strength Folgers. His stocky fingers looked strange curled around the black handle.

"Dad, will you cut the pie?"

He nodded and left.

Bill and I took long, quiet sips. Finally, in a voice so low it took me an instant to register his meaning, Bill said, "I was born at home."

"You were?" I met his blue eyes. My esteem for Bill went up a notch.

"On the farm. Everyone was then. Well, not everyone, but certainly us country kids. Nearest hospital was St. Paul. Doctors made house calls." He leaned on his elbows. "I remember the black bag. It's one of my earliest memories. Mama and the doc consulting across the kitchen table and me rifling through his medical bag for the shiny tools. How old fashioned is that?"

He laughed sadly. "We've advanced since then, Hannah. I mean, medicine has. We know more about sterilization and pain control and how to start and stop labor. And technology makes everything safer—ultrasound, and the fetal heart monitor's a great gadget. But you're right. There'll always be people who don't want that stuff, who like it the old way. If you want to help them out, who am I to stop you?" He rubbed his eyes and when he looked up, I saw the doctor who had birthed two generations of Chester Prairie's children. He had identified innumerable miscarriages, caught stillborns, grasped at any solution that might prevent loss, and now he was tired. He wanted to sit in his metal dingy in a shady nook of Little Long Lake and not catch a blasted fish all week.

I leaned forward, puzzled. "You'll back me up?"

He harrumphed. "Nothing in writing. If I see you in ER, you're a doula. Don't go handing me any records."

"I appreciate it, but what—"

His eyes on the kitchen, Bill cut me off with a sharp shake of his head. "For your mother's sake." His voice was a harsh whisper. "She was . . . kind."

Dad came in bearing huge, collapsed slices of apple pie.

"I don't understand," I said.

"Enough." He turned toward Dad. "You can rest easy, Loren. I'll keep your daughter out of trouble."

Dad scowled and sat down. Bill's dismissal irked me, but the culture of my parents' household prevailed. The men took bites of pie, their dessert forks clinking on china.

"Did you hear Jesse Ventura joined the governor's race?" Dad said. "Politics. It's a three-ring circus."

The small burst of elation I felt at my victory—*I could try out this crazy dream!*—was tainted by misgiving. Why would Bill agree against his better judgment? Weariness seeped through my veins with the wine. I picked up my fork. The pie looked like a failure but tasted perfect.

21.

God's Heartbeat

I SET OUT to hide my birth kit early on a December morning, a month after moving back, two years before the beginning of the new millennium. Chester Prairie was hushed. Streetlamps lit our first dusting of snow, which squeaked underfoot. From Esther Lundgren's bungalow I walked westward into puffs of my own breath. The bulky kit bumped against my ribs; I shifted the oxygen tank, swaddled in towels and a duffle bag, from arm to arm. Lights blazed from kitchen windows along the street, and in a few driveways exhaust billowed from the tailpipes of empty, warming cars. Five blocks later, my shoulder sore, I passed the parsonage. Dad, I knew, would be praying in the back study. The church staff wouldn't arrive for work until nine.

Chester Prairie First Lutheran stood apart from the neighborhood, its white spire hoisted over the treetops. The front steps were broad, concrete, and exposed. I glanced up the street. Two kids in letter jackets trudged toward the high school. A car rounded the corner, cold engine squealing as it gained speed.

I heaved my bags up the steps and yanked at the oversized

door. Dad insisted the church remain unlocked, a tradition few congregations kept anymore. The poor trustees had a rough time of it as the candlesticks kept disappearing. They grumbled that it was only a matter of time before bored hoodlums entered one night with cans of spray paint. Dad countered that a church should be a refuge always, not just on Sunday mornings. Up until then I'd considered his policy quaint. *Church* and *refuge* were opposites, as far as I was concerned.

Pulling the door closed required my full weight. The slam reverberated. I held my breath.

The narthex was dark. I passed through the entrance into the sanctuary, where silence floated with the dust motes. I hadn't been inside since Mom's memorial service three years before. The white walls still harbored my numb disbelief and the final, anguished alleluias of "For All the Saints." I hurried down the aisle as though to escape my former self. Crimson carpeting muffled my steps. The armrests of the pews had darkened with hand grease, and the cushions were a tad more threadbare than I remembered. Except for a new advent banner made of paste and purple felt, everything was the same: simple, pointed windows staining the morning's first light gold and scarlet, the angled ceiling, the tired hymnals. Mom's hand-stitched paraments still draped the lectern and pulpit. Each detail was familiar, dear, and stifling. At the dais, I placed my palm on the decorative knob of the chancel rail, where I'd dangled and swung as a child. It was the size of a newborn's head.

The steps up the dais were lined with kneeling cushions and a railing wide enough to lean on in prayer. I paused. Here's where I'd taken my first communion, where wine and bread had dissolved me. I tried to remember the sensation of being nothing, of being God's heartbeat. What had happened? I'd tasted sweet unity, then whiplash as my mother shook me. I was nine. Almost three decades later, the sensations still resided in the sanctuary—glorious, bewildered, shameful. It was impossible to squeeze the miracle out from the inky childhood dread of having done wrong.

The altar, an enclosed semicircle of polished oak, was tucked into an alcove; red velvet curtains hung between the half-moon wall and the table. Only a pastor's kid, bored brainless, would discover the hollow hiding place inside. As an adult I could easily reach over the altar top, draw back the heavy drapery, and peer beneath. Paint chips and chunks of plaster littered the floor. The space was smaller than I remembered, yet plenty big enough to stash the kit, oxygen tank, and records. Of course Dad, the janitors, and the trustees knew the altar was hollow, but they were unlikely to look inside. With sheepish excitement, I levered the bags over—evidence that could incriminate me for breaking a nonexistent law.

I'd have to be diligent about retrieving the kit in time to avoid Sunday services and choir practice, and I needed an excuse to frequent the church at odd hours. The hiding place wasn't ideal.

A thunk echoed from the narthex. Heart racing, I arranged the curtain and scurried up the aisle. Dad, I knew, would come in the side door through the office, so it had to be someone from town. My watch read seven twenty-five. So early! At the back of the church a young man stepped into the sanctuary.

"Hello?" he said. The rich vowel of his surprise expanded and faded. He wore a black leather jacket, a silver ring glinted in his nostril, and bright red ears stood out from under a black knit cap.

"Morning," I said cheerily.

His bare brow furrowed. "What are you doing here?"

"Praying," I said as though offended. "I'm done." I pushed past but then hesitated—what was *he* doing here? Pierced twenty-somethings weren't common in my father's church. His eyes were hazel and teary, probably from the cold. When I realized I was staring, I looked at the bicycle helmet under his arm.

"Praying," he repeated skeptically. He had seen me messing with the curtain, I was sure of it.

"Yes." I crossed my arms.

He grinned. "Well, it's nice to know someone else in this

town appreciates silence. Usually I have this place to myself. I don't mind company if you want to stay."

I decided an early-rising winter biker probably wasn't a threat. "Thanks, but no. It's all yours." I brushed past.

"Have a blessed day then," he called after me.

The pastor-speak stopped me—this man was Dad's intern. What if he ratted on me? The gold candlesticks were in place, and the communion plates. He wouldn't know about the hollow space. I waved casually and put my shoulder to the door, my body pulsing with adrenaline. Outside, the cold was bracing. I stood on the top step overlooking Elm Street and the first blocks of downtown, trying to recognize myself. New Mexico had stoked my inner fire until I'd become this *rebel*, this *apostate*. Then it occurred to me: All I needed to secure my hiding place was an erratic prayer practice. I was the pastor's daughter; everyone expected it of me anyhow. After years of Dad using guilt to try to leverage me through the church doors, what finally worked was my own deceit. I descended to the street, the alarming pleasure of my secret thumping in my chest.

22.

Insurance Policy

THAT FEBRUARY A Minneapolis midwife got busted. Maryann called with the news. "Undercover agents, a forced entry. Held her thirteen-year-old daughter at gunpoint, ransacked her office, took her computer, everything. She's out on bail now, but holy Jesus."

It was a blow. Until then, plenty of Minnesotan midwives practiced under the law's radar. The consequence was a steep fine, something I figured I could handle. But arrest? This was a new development.

"Look out for yourself, honey," Maryann said.

So I refined my cover. Should the police ask, I did prenatal education and massage. Over the winter I converted the front parlor into a small office with a desk, overstuffed armchair, basket of toys from the parsonage basement, and a massage table. Floral curtains and the east-facing window made the room cheery and expectant.

By early April, I'd already done three births and had one looming. I drove down to St. Paul to have cafeteria coffee with Maryann. We sat at our favorite table. Dirty snow melted on the other side of the plate-glass windows; pedestrians sidestepped the puddles.

"Give me the lowdown," Maryann said.

Two Christian fundamentalists, neighbors and both in their last trimester, showed up in January. Until they heard about me—from a high school buddy, the small town grapevine working in my favor—they had planned to be each other's midwife. "You won't believe it," I told her. "They gave birth three days apart. When one went into labor, the other started baking a chocolate layer cake and served it up once the baby was born. Warm."

"Speedy. Did you shine?"

"I guess."

"Go on."

My third didn't really count. A guy I'd grown up with at church had taken his wife as far as the car when she started pushing. He was a dairy farmer, unafraid to catch the baby. They went back to bed rather than trekking the twenty miles to the hospital and called me.

My current clients included two mothers without health insurance; I was the cheap alternative. One was a sweet Mexican student at the technical college who I guessed was here illegally, and Katrina, the other, had called me in December not an hour after I'd posted my birth class flyer in a women's bathroom stall at the community college. She and her husband were in Chester Prairie on a professor exchange, Bernard teaching German and Katrina working on a doctoral thesis. Something about orangutans. "She gave me an earful about American prenatal care," I told Maryann.

"Uh-huh." Maryann's enormous gold hoop earrings swung back and forth.

"She's due in a few weeks."

Maryann continued nodding. "Folks always fall through the cracks," she said. "But you're catching them."

Yes. This was my work.

By early April I had slipped into the sanctuary to retrieve my kit three times, all unhindered. A fourth time I just sat, deepening my meditative ruse. The sanctuary breathed around me. My mother was present in the altar cloths and the space's crippling expectations. She was also absolutely, irrevocably absent. I couldn't leave fast enough.

* * *

Then one morning the plastic thermometer outside Esther Lundgren's kitchen window read sixty-two; the bare willows sweeping the Rum River west of town were yellowing with life, and lilac hedges all over the neighborhood were thick with buds. I took down storm windows and hooked up screens—premature, I knew; we could still get a hard freeze, but I wanted to catch the first whiffs of fragrance as soon as they drifted off the bush. The shining office, my business, my return to Chester Prairie all seemed expectant, the way things do at the close of a long Minnesota winter.

After cleaning the parlor, I checked the street for my client. Melinda Hollinger had gotten my number through church. Her husband, Mike, was a parishioner, one of the ushers, although goodness knows who he'd spoken to. Melinda kept a produce stand at the end of their drive ten miles west of town. I'd never stopped. Rumor was her prices were high—she farmed without pesticides and the neighbors grumbled about her weeds. Melinda hadn't discovered she was pregnant until her second trimester, the result of an irregular cycle and the failure of birth control. When she called, she'd seemed oddly ambivalent. To my suggested time she replied, "I guess that will work."

Two backlit forms approached the house, one adult, rail-straight, the other a toddler with his arm stretched upward, stumbling, eyes on his mother. The third being, I knew, was hidden, heart thumping, bones solidifying, intrinsically and unknowingly itself. I love that presence in a pregnant mother, how it's at once dear and forceful, already asserting itself into relationships, cravings, personal finances and, who knows, world politics, before even sucking its first breath. I love how pregnant women have secret power tucked away. From behind the screen, I sensed Melinda's child-to-be and warmed with anticipation.

I pushed the door open. "Hello."

Melinda pressed her callused hand in mine; with mute judgment, she surveyed my five-feet ten-inches of Swedish farm stock, denim jumper and flat sandals. Her look made me feel like a first-year apprentice again, desperate to please. Disconcerted, I knelt to greet the boy, who was maybe two and a half. "Hello, there."

"Kevin, are you going to say hi to Hannah?" Kevin rubbed his cheek against his mother's thigh.

Women usually sequester a part of themselves during pregnancy, dividing their attention between the outer world and the dark churning interior. But not Melinda. In her twenty-second week, belly just beginning to push against a navy stretch-top, she perched on the edge of my overstuffed armchair with such perfect posture that the chair, which I'd dragged in from Goodwill and which other women sank into gratefully, seemed a bad idea. She held her jaw at a tough angle. Her bare arms were thick with muscles. Her stare was critical and uncompromising.

The frizz of Melinda's curls, barely tamed by a stubby braid, caught the sunlight from the window behind her. At her feet Kevin rustled through the basket of Lincoln Logs, toddler-sized Legos, fabric dolls, and a rusted Slinky left over from my childhood.

"How are you feeling?" I began.

"Fine. Everything's fine."

I groped unsuccessfully through memories of our phone conversation for a more engaging start. "You weren't looking to have another child?"

"No." Melinda broke her stare, glanced at Kevin's towhead, and corrected herself. "Well, yes. Mike and I both want more children. We're on a farm. Mike comes from a big family. I love kids, and we want siblings for him." Kevin found the one matchbox car in the basket and raced it along the paths in the

braided rug, brrrming throatily. "But after his birth I swore I'd
never do it again."

"What happened?"

Melinda's green eyes stripped me of my midwife trappings—
the jumper, the pencil, the manila folder. "I said from the start
I wanted a natural birth. Dr. Jorgenson knew it. Mike knew it. I
told the nurses I didn't want an epidural and not to ask. Hell, I'm
an organic farmer. I didn't want to load up my baby with drugs
before he was born."

Under her gaze, blinking seemed a weakness.

"My water broke at home. They'd said to come in then, but
I didn't want to, I wanted to labor more first. Mike had a fit. I
warded him off for a while, maybe six hours, but then he called,
and, no surprise, they tell him to get my butt in there. They didn't
want more than twelve hours of active labor to pass. That scared
me, so I agreed." She glanced at her lap. "Wouldn't you know,
my labor stalls. We're barely in the door, and they're hooking me
up to the baby monitor. I'm friggin' stuck."

"The stranded beetle position."

"Ha." Melinda's brow softened. "Exactly. Hell, even bats
have sense enough to give birth upright. What's with the twelve-
hour thing?"

I was surprised; most hospitals allow twenty-four. "They're
worried about infection. There's a greater risk once the sac isn't
protecting the fetus. The trouble is, longer labors don't introduce
bacteria. Foreign objects do."

"Like drilling wires into my baby's head?"

I nodded.

"They let me labor a little more, but by that point I was
so exhausted that when they checked and I was only three
centimeters, the fight in me drained out. I'd asked Mike to be
strong when I lost it and instead he's freaking out, saying things
like 'No one should have to go through pain this bad' and 'It's just
an epidural.' As soon as that needle sunk in my spine, this cold
crept over me and it wasn't my birth anymore. My body went
on autopilot. Jorgenson ended up using a vacuum extractor. I

didn't have a birth, I had a medical procedure." She yanked her chin up a notch, pinning me with her eyes. "Reminded me of having an abortion."

I hesitated. "When?"

"College. I swore I'd never dismiss my intuition again, and then . . ." She glanced at Kevin, then down. Her arms, freckled and pink, were folded between her breasts and belly. Kevin thrust an odd clump of red and green Legos into her lap. "Look what you made!" Melinda said, her voice harsh and unchanged. "Can you make me a truck now? A dumpster truck?"

"Dumpster twuck." Kevin's face brightened. He turned back to the pile of plastic pieces.

"So when he's born, they whisk him away without telling me why. As far as I know, he's missing a lung or something. My tongue's thick, and there's part of me that didn't care. That was the drugs. When they faded, I was furious." She still was; her anger sprung from her like her untamed curls. "I could hear him screaming in the next room. He needed me, I needed him, and there was no"—she mouthed the word "fucking"—"reason for Jorgenson to be in the way." She smoothed Kevin's hair as he played. "I've done my research now. When Mike said there was a rumor going around that you did homebirths, I wanted to check you out."

"You want a homebirth?"

"No question."

"How does Mike feel about it?" When she'd set up the appointment, I'd invited them both.

"Mike. He thinks a midwife is better than nothing." Her fingers drummed on the arm of the chair. "Besides, it's my body."

She wielded the feminist maxim like a weapon. Melinda reminded me of Sunny, who not only caught her second and third babies but cut an episiotomy on herself during labor just to see if it was true that the body produces its own anesthesia. It does. Mid-contraction, at the height of pushing and pain, Sunny bent over with surgical scissors and snipped. When I heard that, I thought, *Holy crap*. Melinda's fierce self-reliance troubled me, perhaps because I couldn't imagine it for myself or perhaps because I had an inkling I'd suffer its consequences. I shifted in my seat.

I steered our conversation toward the safer terrain of Melinda's medical history, the ambiguity of her due date (she and Mike speculated that conception had been mid-November, which meant roughly mid-August), and nutrition. Her health and diet were ten times better than mine—all those greens right out of the garden. I gave her my handouts and talked her through the scope of my practice: low-risk pregnancies only, no malpresentations, no multiples, births in the thirty-seven to forty-two week window.

"You're aware homebirth isn't entirely legal here?" I asked.

"Minnesota's screwy."

"It means I'm putting myself out on a limb." I'd determined the best way to protect myself from the law was flat-out honesty. "That's why I need to be strict about my protocol. I'm using the Minnesota Midwifery Guild's guidelines because they're similar to New Mexico's, and that's what I trained under. They're important; they help me maintain a high standard of care. It means we need to collaborate, in every way. I'd like both you and Mike to read this informed consent carefully, ask me any questions, and sign it. Next appointment, we'll find a time when you both can be here to discuss if this is a good fit."

I'd worked hard on the release. Maryann, Sunny, Maria, and a Minneapolis lawyer had all reviewed it. Firm boundaries that excluded the risky cases gave me freedom within the cases I took. If the state and the Medical Board were unwilling to define safe, normal birth, I would do it myself.

Melinda set the papers on the armrest. I hesitated. "You should also know that Bill Jorgenson is my backup doc. I wish I could offer you an alternative, but he's the only OB in town. If there's any complications at the birth, he'd be the one you'd see."

Melinda's face hardened. "Then there won't be complications."

We listened to the plastic clack of Legos. I noticed my fingers clenching the pencil and loosened them.

"I'm not interested in homebirth at all costs," I said. "There are times when the hospital's essential. Even if you're right and all goes well, we need a contingency plan."

Melinda took Kevin's latest red and blue amalgam in both hands. "What a great truck! Are these the wheels?" She swung her gaze back at me, jade with amber darts. "Tell me what a birth with you would look like."

So I described how I encourage movement, eating and drinking, how I listen to the baby's heartbeat with a fetoscope or Doppler, don't limit who can be in the room, ask for family involvement in decision-making, support labor in whatever position is working best, use intervention only when necessary, and facilitate bonding and breast feeding immediately after birth—the spiel.

"If you feel at ease," I told her, "you're statistically more likely to have a safe birth. My job is to help make that possible." When I mentioned the home visits, once prenatal and twice post, Melinda leaned in.

"I knew this could happen," she whispered. "I was sure there were other ways."

This is the moment I savor in initial appointments, when the woman arrives at a clearing and realizes that the path she's been walking is only one of many. The possibility of homebirth awakens our dormant instincts—birth can be as ordinary as an April morning. A woman's capacity for motherhood resides in her every cell. We can surrender to the body's wisdom.

Melinda's eyes sparked. I knew then we'd work together.

We did an exam and said our goodbyes. I scratched down some notes, including the fact that Bill Jorgenson induced after only twelve hours of labor; bit by bit I had to figure out how he worked. Then I asked my new-client test question: *If something went wrong and the state got involved, would this woman stand by me?* Mutual trust was my only insurance policy.

Melinda was adamant. She would fight for homebirth with or in spite of me. I filed the chart in my metal cabinet, locked the drawer, and hid the key.

23.

This Is My Body

YES, THEY HANDCUFFED me. No, I wasn't surprised. By the time of my celebrated dead-of-night delivery, I had realized the stakes. What stuns me now, a dozen years later as I reflect on my work with Melinda, is the timing. A ragtag group of women with babies strapped to their chests had spent months waving homemade signs in a rotunda empty of legislators. Powerhouse midwives worked the committees behind the scenes. One senator, miracle of miracles, had given birth at home. An unpredictable, anti-party-line, pro-wrestling governor was about to be elected. In the midst of all this, news of my arrest sparked the press's interest, and they swung their cameras from woman to baby to woman. For a brief and beautiful moment, birth at home seemed reasonable, and the legislators legalized it. Attention turned the trick.

So you never know. Every birth matters, and some—who can tell which?—matter a lot. Maryann had tried to hammer this lesson into my head when I first began trailing her, long before I claimed my desire to catch babies. "I'm going to tell you something I don't often share," she had said conspiratorially over a cafeteria lunch. Conversation around us was muted. Forks clinked on china. I stopped eating, my heart fluttering.

Maryann paused, holding my eyes in hers. "I remember being born."

"That's impossible," I blurted, and instantly regretted it.

Maryann's eyelids narrowed. She crossed her substantial arms and leaned into the tabletop, sloshing my coffee. The silk paisleys of her blouse scrunched at the armpits and her St. Luke's Presbyterian I.D., strung on a gold chain, disappeared from view.

"It's written in the body, honey. Whether you remember or not, how you're born always matters. Comes through the pores and gets into the bloodstream. Then you have to live with it."

I watched her silently file me with the vast population of naysayers whose skepticism was the bane of her existence. She rolled her eyes toward the ceiling and added, "Or live in denial." I ducked my head and mopped up the coffee with dispenser napkins.

"That's why we birth them gently, Hannah. Because it matters." She tore open a second sugar packet and dumped it into her milky coffee. "I can still feel the tight passage sometimes, and the slap of light at the end." She dropped her spoon and splayed her hand across the table, palm up. "It's written down, Hannah. Right here."

I had wanted to believe Maryann, but my own birth was so inscrutable, it had seemed absurd that for someone else it might be otherwise.

* * *

A week had passed since that initial appointment with Melinda. I let the back screen door slam behind me—such a confident, homey sound—and reached for the ringing phone.

"Morning," I said.

My kitchen was cool and dim.

"It's one in the afternoon."

At the sound of Dad's voice, affection exploded in me like caffeine. "Really?" I glanced at the stove clock. "I was just at the most amazing birth, Dad. Katrina Schultz had a baby boy. He floated out. She only pushed for an hour. Gerard caught the baby and cut the cord like a pro. It was perfect."

"Did you get any sleep?"

"No. The call came around ten last night."

"Don't know how you do it." Dad's deep-grained tenor was a touchstone. In the four months I'd been in town, we'd gotten into the habit of sharing a spontaneous dinner or two each week. I hoped he had an invitation brewing.

"I wish I could have filmed her. She was awesome." I stopped myself from blathering about how the Schultzes and I had walked circles around the house at four a.m. while robins woke up the neighborhood. The air had turned steely then radiant. Gerard had massaged Katrina's shoulders as she hunched on the living room floor. He'd quoted German poetry in a dramatic sing-song that sent us into hysterics. During hard labor, Katrina swore she'd never again make inferences about human experience based on the behavioral patterns of orangutans. Then she pushed out a seven-and-a-half pound baby boy. I could still smell Katrina's sweat. The spilled weight in my palms, the shimmer of translucent skin, the sweet, sleepy threesome I tucked into bed that morning—*this* was living! *This* was the work I was meant to do, perhaps from the beginning. I could barely believe my good fortune.

"You say the father delivered the baby?" Dad asked.

"Gerard wanted to touch him first. He was great, not at all nervous." Once Gerard handed the baby to Katrina, he'd given me half a dozen bear hugs. "Catching's pretty straightforward. The only risk is that newborns are slippery. A towel helps."

"Well. That's something."

I heard a wisp of regret in Dad's voice and pictured him angled against the stove in the parsonage kitchen.

"I guess you couldn't even watch when I was born."

"No."

Dad would have been relegated to the waiting room, informed only about what the nurses and Bill deemed appropriate. He probably accepted his second-class status without question. When Sunny birthed her first child, her husband had bought a pair of handcuffs and locked their wrists together before they entered the hospital.

"That's changed. Although hospitals still won't let the father catch."

The gravid scent of black, tilled earth entered my open window. If Dad felt sad about missing that momentous occasion, he wasn't going to admit it. In the pause that followed, we orbited the gravitational weight of my birth. Dad didn't speak, but I heard the words just the same: *Thank heavens for Bill Jorgenson.* Bill's rescue simultaneously gave me life and negated it. A familiar ache filled my chest, and I realized for the first time that it was grief. Suddenly self-protective, I changed the subject.

"What've you been up to?"

"Not much. Meetings. Confirmation's wrapping up. That Chuck fellow"—he cleared his throat—"wants to try some new-fangled way of taking the Eucharist."

"What?" The mention of my father's intern set my blood racing. Had he looked behind the altar?

Dad's mouth worked faintly. "Supposedly communion's not communal enough. He wants families to take the elements together at various stations up front."

I suppressed my smile in case Dad might hear it across the phone. I found it entertaining that the pierced seminarian gave my father liturgical pause.

"That doesn't sound so bad," I said.

He harrumphed. "It's the principle. Tradition serves people. It's how they relate to God. We shouldn't mess with it."

Years ago, the Worship and Music Committee had lobbied Dad to use home-baked bread for communion. You'd have thought the admonition to use wafers was one of Luther's Ninety-Five Theses.

"So what are you going to do?"

"Let him try." He sounded bruised. "His contextual ed rep will be there. I think they get extra credit for innovation. Then I'll field complaints all week."

"Really?"

"What Chuck's up to might work in Minneapolis, but not here."

Lack of sleep must have made me reckless. "It might be comforting to share communion with loved ones. Less lonely."

"The Eucharist," Dad pronounced, "is between yourself and God."

Anger rose to my throat like bile. The Eucharist, I wanted to retort, is man-made, flawed, and too detached from reality to carry any meaning. Or if there was something to it (the fragile flutter of memory), humans had mangled and manipulated that holiness until it'd become downright destructive.

I'd always acquiesced to Dad in such discussions. He had theological authority, and what did I know? But New Mexico had changed me. Dad needed to see that.

"I met a woman in Sangre de Cristo who told me she always thought communion was barbaric. You know, the Christianity-as-ritualized-cannibalism argument." My voice was pitched too high. "Until she began having kids and 'This is my blood, shed for you' suddenly made sense. Turns things upside down, doesn't it?" Her comment had dogged me during births, where blood was a precursor to babies and mothers offered themselves not as a sacrifice but as full-bodied gifts. *That* I could believe in.

Dad was silent. Dread moved across my heart and clamped down.

"Dad?" I asked meekly.

Over the telephone line, a distant lawn mower revved up, most likely from the cemetery.

"Well then," Dad said. "You get some rest."

The click of the receiver, sharp and punitive, switched me from *on* to *off,* from elated midwife to heartless, exhausted daughter. I had no idea what I was talking about, why Christ supposedly died for our sins or what it might mean to love a baby enough to give your life for it. I opened the refrigerator door and stared at a quart of milk, bag of bagels, three McIntosh apples, and my plastic army of condiments. Tonight both Dad and I would eat alone.

24.

Gifts

HALF OF WHAT you need to learn to be a midwife is external stuff, pretty straightforward—textbook knowledge and bedside manners and how to interpret vital signs. The other half is subterranean. You learn by plummeting through your personal history to the molten core. No one goes there willingly. I certainly didn't. Sure, I can coach you to draw blood or measure a cervix, but how can I convince you to dig under your easy actions and reactions down to the fiery furnace of your heart? This story is my best attempt.

* * *

Not long after I moved to Chester Prairie, the postman delivered a box labeled *Juan's Pizza and Burrito* and plastered with Mexican stamps. I sat on the hall stairs to open it. Inside, atop a mat of shredded newspaper, lay a black and white card of Frida Kahlo with her hair in a power braid and those undaunted eyebrows. Stuart had written, *Chica! You go, girl. Here's something so your mamas will know they're coming to a happy place. Don't do anything I wouldn't. Ha-ha.*

I lifted the newspaper to find one of those wrought-iron suns you see in Mexican import stores all over the southwest—an exuberant smile, curvy rays spiraling in every direction with tin bells dangling in the open spaces. With it came the memory of dusty chili peppers and terra cotta lawn ornaments, the heavy wool of Mexican blankets, and the expansive joy of the New Mexican sky. As much as I didn't belong there, New Mexico had wrought a change in me I was still trying to unpack, and I'll forever think of it fondly as a result. I opened my front door and took down the "Home Sweet Home" plaque I'd borrowed from Mom's old stash. The jingly, radiant face felt like Stuart's, grinning at Chester Prairie with determined optimism— something I needed on those long days of not enough work.

A second housewarming gift arrived in mid-April, this time with a knock at the front door. The window framed Maggie Hendricks's pink face and white curls. Maggie was my favorite of Mom's quilter friends, a cheerful bundle of a woman who sewed her own housedresses and spent Election Day chauffeuring nursing home residents to the polls. When I opened the door, she grinned mischievously and handed me a basket of fabric.

"Welcome home, dear. A few months late. Not as many nimble fingers as there used to be."

"Goodness." I lifted out a quilt, full-sized, hand-stitched, with hundreds of faded floral gingham squares, lemon and gold and spring green. The quilt, heavy between my spread hands, must have taken the women forever to make. "It's gorgeous, Mrs. Hendricks."

She scrunched her round cheeks. "In memory of your mother, dear."

"She would have loved it," I said. "Thank you. Won't you come in?"

"No, no. I'm heading to the pee-wee game. My grandson's playing." Maggie bobbed her head. "Your father tells me you're a midwife now. We had a brouhaha at Circle last week over it, and I figured you could settle things. I said it's this newfangled trend to have midwives in the hospital. Trudy insisted I was wrong, that you're going into people's homes." Maggie had more laugh lines than my mother; she was more direct in her curiosity and freer with her touch, and yet I found myself flustered and wanting her approval as though Mom had commissioned her friends to continue where she'd left off.

"Yes, that's right. I'm doing homebirths."

"Oh, how quaint!" Her hands flitted like birds. "Who would've thought? And you can make a living doing this?"

"Well, I'm also teaching childbirth classes. And keeping books for Cathie Johnston."

Maggie's fingers on my arm were lighter than tissue. "Your mother would be proud. She always wanted to be a nurse, and now look at you."

A nurse? I searched Maggie's warm eyes for any sign she was joking. My mother, who couldn't speak to me about getting my period? Who took me aside when a boy first asked me out and said, "You will have . . . special feelings. Don't let them override your principles." Her words had made me hot with humiliation. I hugged the quilt to my chest. True, Mom had been attentive during my illnesses, concocting honey-lemon brews for sore throats and singing hymns to sooth my feverish sleeplessness.

"When?" I asked Maggie. "When did she want to be a nurse?"

"Oh, before you were born. She'd just registered for classes when they conceived. Right after your dad's appointment." Maggie frowned, and fiddled with the clasp of her purse.

"I never knew that."

"Ancient history." She glanced up. "You can pick up where she left off."

While the idea of Mom as a nurse seemed bizarre, the way the information sank heavily in my stomach told me it was true.

Maggie leaned forward to brush my cheek with her lips. "Glad to have you back, dear."

Later, I opened the quilt onto my bed. The one-inch squares formed a yellow diamond in the center and radiated outward in deepening green. The border and back were done in a classic

1950s floral, although the material seemed stiffer and less
worn than the rest. This was exactly how I'd always been loved,
so wrapped in intricate and practical care that my need for
something more was surely greed.

My mother had set aside a dream to raise me. Somehow I
felt responsible. I remade the bed, folding up the old chenille to
return to Dad. Mom would have considered the gray attic walls
too dark, the windows too bare. The room was unworthy of the
quilt. Amazing how a gift so resplendent could pull my spirits
down.

25.

Midwife to the Father

MELINDA HOLLINGER RETURNED after a week, dragging her husband Mike along with little Kevin. Mike was on lunch break from clerking down at the county seat. He stood through the appointment as though the overstuffed chair might muss his suit. The materials I'd sent home with Melinda he held rolled in his fist, ready to swat something. I looked up from my desk chair and asked if he had questions. He smoothed the paper against his thigh. Notes were scrawled in blue ink along the margins. Outside the window a cardinal called *birdy birdy birdy*.

"It says here you don't recommend ultrasounds because we don't know the full effects on the fetus." He pointed to underlined text. "Now, aren't they routine? Wouldn't we know by now if they caused some damage?"

Melinda, sitting on the massage table, kicked her legs impatiently. I was careful not to meet her eyes. I needed to be Mike's midwife too.

I explained that, while there have been studies disproving any immediate harm, no tests have been designed to measure long-term neurological or emotional ramifications. "That said, there are lots of circumstances where I'd recommend one. If we suspect twins, for instance, or if there's any concern about Melinda or the baby, then the benefits outweigh the unknowns."

A frown distorted Mike's otherwise handsome features. Melinda's crossed arms rested on her belly, within which the little one was curled, flexing fingers, floating, growing at a phenomenal rate.

When I outlined the scope of my practice, including the restrictions, Mike said, "Oh. That's reasonable." He reread the details of the informed consent. "Honestly, Ms. Larson, this isn't my first choice. It's just, until you came along the only person I could think of who might help us was the vet." He said this with dark brows furrowed.

"I'm having a baby," Kevin declared from behind his pile of toys. "It's in Mommy's tummy."

I smiled. "And you'll be a big brother. I think you'll make a fine brother."

Kevin nodded gravely.

I reiterated that Bill Jorgenson was my backup. "Really?" Mike said. He finally sank into the chair beside his son. "Why didn't you tell me *that*, Mel?"

"What about just using the ER?" she asked me.

"You can do that," I said levelly. "I couldn't join you. And you might end up with Dr. Jorgenson anyhow. It's a small hospital." I explained the disclosure of medical information clause of the release in case we needed to transport, and how sharing information meant better continuity of care. Transporting directly into Bill's hands would be best for everyone.

Melinda lingered over the form. I admired the blond wisps springing from her braid. Sparrows bickered in the lilacs on the north side of the house. The buds had split, and their dizzying scent entered the room. The ballpoint hit the clipboard with a thwack. "Of course I'm responsible for my own health," Melinda said. "Why do I need to sign this to state the obvious?"

"For heaven's sake," Mike said.

"Fine, fine."

Melinda's handwriting was illegible. At the door, Mike shook my hand, saying, "You're a gift, Ms. Larson." I sensed him heaving the burden of this pregnancy off his shoulders onto mine. After they left, Melinda's careless squiggle made me decide, just in case, to stash a photocopy behind the altar.

26.

Ministry

THAT NEXT SUNDAY morning, low clouds plodded in from the west, blotting the May sky and promising much-needed rain. I bought tuna, noodles, mushroom soup, and the makings for a green salad and let myself into the parsonage. Dad was still at church.

I usually avoided sharing Sunday dinner. In those hours after church I felt Mom's absence too acutely, and I dreaded Dad's expectation that I carry on her traditions—linens, candles, all that food. But he and I had spent the weekend repainting my attic bedroom to accommodate the Elsie Circle's quilt, prepping and priming the grim, gray walls, the physical work and old-timey radio neutralizing any theological tension between us. Plain white had done the trick, brightening the eaves and setting the patchwork fabric aglow. While the paint dried, we hauled a dresser and rocker over from the parsonage—simple, worn-out furniture left over from Grandpa and Nona's farmhouse. "Looks good," Dad had decreed.

In thanks, I broke my Sunday dinner moratorium. I set the kitchen table with everyday dishes, put the hot dish in the oven, and had half an hour before Dad finished church to plunder my mother's drawers for some green-checked curtains that had hung in the attic years back. They would tie my new bedroom together nicely.

Upstairs, the door to Mom's sewing room was shut, possibly to save on heat through the winter, although I doubt Dad had entered since Mom died. Inside, everything was just as she'd kept it, chair pushed squarely under the sewing table, felt turtle pin cushion bristling atop the machine, the rag rug worn but perfectly centered, a wall of closed-mouthed dressers. In the corner was a squat four-legged stool she'd had me stand on to hem my dresses. Mom seemed eerily present.

I opened the window. Outside, the low front bruised the sky and turned the canopy of new leaves chartreuse. I switched on the overhead light. Mom had floor lamps on either side of the sewing table; I remembered this room bright, with my mother's foot pressed firmly to the floor and the machine's high-stress whine. Now the stillness felt uncanny.

The three dressers had fifteen drawers between them, not counting the smaller ones where she kept spools of thread, spare zippers, and earring boxes of snaps, hooks, and eyes. I started at the top and worked my way down, left to right, sliding drawers open, fingering swaths of aging material, and occasionally recognizing a scrap from a sundress or a bolt from a Sunday school bulletin board. All this material, ironed and stacked, sorted by fiber and pinned to the past, helped me remember Mom as the seamstress behind the scenes, her sewing machine puncturing millions of minuscule holes where she concealed her love. I wished I could feel fondness for the fabric rather than a tangle of resentment and longing. I was sitting on the floor, in my lap the blue satin remnants from a Mary costume I'd worn in fourth grade, when Dad entered.

I held up the slippery fabric. "Recognize this?"

He shook his head, pulled out Mom's chair and sat. His eyes were tired.

"It's from my Mary robe. Remember when we did the live nativity?"

"Oh, yes. The lutefisk." Dad's long face brightened.

The women's social had made a famous mistake that night, cooking dinner during the service, the scent of hot lye permeating the sanctuary. I'd concentrated so hard on not dropping the Baby Jesus that I hadn't noticed everyone's distracted looks. The story had circulated long enough that I know the adults hadn't paid attention to the drape of my gown or how I'd held the newest church member, a six-week-old girl with a scarce breath of blond hair, at a loving, gentle angle. Mom saw, though. While we lined up on the basement steps for dinner, she placed her warm hand on my head and infused me with happiness.

Dad surveyed the sewing room as though for the first time. When Dad had needed his trouser cuffs hemmed, Mom carried the stool down to his office. We hadn't touched Mom's things after she died. Her clothes probably still filled a closet in their bedroom. "I suppose I should go through all this," he said without conviction. "Your mother saved everything."

"And used it. It's not like stuff went to waste."

"No, that's the truth."

Dad wore black pants and a clerical shirt with the plastic collar unbuttoned and dangling. He set his elbows on his knees, a posture that made me hopeful and eager. *Maybe we can talk.* He knew how. His parishioners lauded him for raising essential questions and for offering the balm that soothed, beside hospital beds and in premarital counseling and through every variety of hurt. But his warm proficiency as a pastor had never translated into fatherhood. I wanted to share with him my fears about self-employment and the precarious state of midwifery. I wanted him to know how much I loved my pregnant mothers. I wanted to ask if he missed Mom constantly, like I did, and why she'd given up her dream of nursing. "Do you think the Quilters could use this stuff?" I asked.

"That's exactly what she would want."

I folded the slick fabric and replaced it. Rain began to blow through the screen, so I shut the window. The room grew cozy, the air tender.

"Mom would love to see another Mary wearing that blue,"

I said.

Dad dangled his hands between his legs. His fingers had swollen with age, locking his wedding band forever below the knuckle. They were long farmer's fingers that had brought a burgeoning pride to his parents for harvesting a congregation of souls. I wasn't one of them. Or I had been as a child, fawned upon by grandparents and elderly church ladies, but then my faith snapped and I no longer had it in me to be the pastor's kid, the child graced by a God who looked an awful lot like my father. Dad still treated my churchlessness as temporary—someday I'd come to my senses. He was simple that way. Once I overheard him and Bill in heated conversation; Bill insisted that he could never believe in a transcendent deity and Dad countered that of course Bill believed, he just worshipped God in the splash of walleye and the healing capacity of the human body. "You're not hearing me, Loren," Bill had warned. I respected Bill's ability to distinguish Dad's poor listening skills from some ultimate truth.

Two drawers later, I found the checked gingham curtains, a bit yellowed at the edges but, I was glad to see, hemmed, with fabric loops for the rod. "Here they are." I shook one out.

Dad looked up. "What's that from?"

"The attic. Mom had these up before she bought the blinds."

Dad grunted and undid one button at his neck. "Tell me again what you're up to, Hannah. I want to understand. People are asking, and I don't know what to say."

"What do you mean?"

"Your work."

I leaned back against the dresser to receive Dad's admission— he hadn't listened. "I've set up a homebirth practice. I'm teaching childbirth classes through Community Ed and doing prenatal care and attending births. And balancing Cathie Johnston's books for some steady income. What don't you understand?"

"Why not the hospital?"

I vacillated between hurt—Dad had dismissed the last two-plus years of my life—and hope. Perhaps he'd listen now.

"That's not what I want to do. Nurse midwifery takes

different training. I just want to do the average birth, at home."

Dad studied his polished shoes. I leaned toward him.

"They're different approaches, Dad. As soon as you walk through the hospital doors, birth becomes a medical condition, because of the drugs and technology and the doctors' training. Sometimes that's really important, like in an emergency. But when the mom and baby are healthy, it can become a problem."

"Seems to work fine for most people."

"Seems to, yes. But it doesn't really."

I careened forward with a tirade about how hard it is to prove that hospitals spoil normal deliveries, how even Russia and the Czech Republic do a better job preventing infant and maternal mortality than we do and how no one tallies the hidden costs to a mom's or baby's well-being, from the drugs, from the surgeries . . . bluster that evaded Dad's real question—*how can I relate to you?*—and avoided telling him how scared I was that my fledgling practice would fail or, worse, land me in trouble.

Dad bent forward, listening, trying to understand—just what I'd always wanted. But now I was angry. "The mom's blood pressure goes up, she's more likely to tear, she picks up infections. Did you know more people die of hospital-acquired infections than of car accidents and homicides combined? The hospital's not a safe place for healthy women to give birth. Naturally. How God made them," I added for persuasion's sake.

"I don't know, Hannah. Doctors do things with good reason."

"Doctors have one kind of knowledge, Dad. Midwives have another." I mustered my courage and said, "It's not like Bill Jorgenson has magic powers."

Dad sat straight. "You owe your life to that man. From what I can tell, he's doing you a big favor. What's come over you?" He crossed his arms, almost hugging himself.

Blood surged to my head. "Why haven't you paid attention?"

Dad jerked his chair back.

"I'm providing good maternal care, Dad. Bill's a good man, a good doctor, but some of his policies . . . He still routinely cuts episiotomies."

"I don't know what that means."

"An incision in the perineum. They used to think it created a bigger opening and prevented tearing. Turns out it just makes the mother miserable."

"I'm sure he has reasons."

"Not at the rate he does it. OBs sometimes create problems that they profit from fixing." I wiped sweat from my eyes and parroted Stuart's conspiracy theory to pack a punch, not because I believed Bill was greedy. "The only reason anyone would cut episiotomies these days is convenience. Or habit."

He stood, punctuating the conversation. "I don't recognize you, Hannah Abigail."

"Dad," I pleaded. "I thought you wanted to understand."

He extracted the plastic strip from his shirt collar. It hung between his fingers like a slivered moon.

"Listen." I clamored to my feet—I had to try while I had the chance. "I've never loved anything like this before. Surely you get that. It's like I've found my ministry." Only arguing with my father would steer me to such language. I was surprised to find I meant it.

The rain fell steadily against the window, steel gray dimming the daylight and leaving us high and lonely in the old house. Dad ran fingers through his graying hair. He looked frail, thin, and shaken, like in the months after Mom died. Only this time I was responsible.

"I just wish—" His voice cracked. "I wish you wouldn't be so—"

The stove timer began to buzz downstairs. Neither of us moved. After a minute it lost steam, as we both knew it would, and became a low, electrical moan. I caught a whiff of browned breadcrumbs. "I made tuna pea wiggle," I said.

"Ha." Dad glanced at the hall. His eyes were bloodshot. If I hadn't known better, I'd have thought he'd been crying.

I tucked the checked cloth under my arm. "Come on," I said by way of apology. I had returned to Chester Prairie to be near my father, not to push him away. We could hash out our misunderstandings another time. "Let's eat."

27.

Prayer Ruse

WEDNESDAY NIGHT WAS my birth class: nine women and most of their husbands on folding chairs in the library basement. I stretched the plastic demo pelvis to show how loosely joined our bones are, how capable of spreading, and watched the pregnant women gain respect for their bodies' sturdy construction. In such moments I was pierced by conviction so pure that my fears about Minnesota birth politics fell away.

Before I arrived back in Hiawatha County, prenatal education had been limited to the hospital's occasional day-long Saturday workshop. My blurb in the school district's Community Ed program's catalogue for an ongoing group found an enthusiastic audience. The administration asked me to add a second class. I agreed, despite the pitifully low pay.

By May we'd gotten through the basic anatomy and chemistry of labor, practiced our Kegels to prevent incontinence and squats to strengthen endurance, and discussed natural options for pain management—the easy stuff. Sunny's voice nagged in my head: "Boring! Birth's about creating. These are *families* in the making, for cripe's sake."

Sunny always taught the academics of birth classes in combination with some outlandish art project like plaster casts of pregnant bellies painted in tempera. Maria would sling her guitar strap over her shoulder and teach everyone "*De Colores*"; she claimed singing from the diaphragm worked better than silly breathing exercises. Both believed the essence of childbirth preparation to be self-discovery. Birth plans, Maria said, invariably get tossed out the window once labor begins. Better to develop confidence and competence and flexibility.

This was especially true for my moms, most of whom would give birth in the complex, technological universe of the hospital where women easily lose faith in their own ability to deliver. I'd begun to understand Community Ed students— single women who punch the service station register overnight, Mexican couples who work long hours processing poultry at the Shoenfield plant, a few farmers' wives weary of isolation, and middle class men and women whose schedules or philosophies don't align with the hospital's offerings. Most needed the basics. Those with health insurance were shuffled through prenatal care in seven-minute appointments, and those without insurance lacked fundamental information about the significance of good nutrition or the advisability of sexual intercourse during pregnancy or the fetus's stages of development. Their ignorance gave me confidence, and their hunger for companionship made me suspect my most important work was bringing them together. In class the previous week, one woman derailed my lesson by asking the group about their secret worries. The circle leaned in, grew animated. They shared visions of deformed babies, cracked pelvises, unbearable pain, humiliating screams.

It was time to expand my teaching methods.

I decided to assign self-portraits—*Draw a picture of yourself giving birth*. The point wasn't to make art but rather to expose the women's hidden expectations, which we could then discuss. Were they realistic? A mom's expectations will determine her satisfaction with the birth experience. For background music, I would play a tape of drumming that imitated the fetal heartbeat which Stuart had dubbed for me. I didn't have a portable cassette player, so I called Dad. He told me to swing by the church on my way into town.

I got to Dad's office around six—early enough to miss the Wednesday night choir and Bible study crowd. His door was open. Floor-to-ceiling shelves of Biblical reference books lined the walls. To one side was a loveseat, where parishioners sat for pastoral counseling, and a coffee table with a chunky, unlit candle on it. I walked in without knocking. Dad leaned across his desk, face-to-face with the shaven-headed intern. A black T-shirt stretched across Chuck's strong back emblazoned with a Che Guevara-style portrait of Jesus and the words, "My man!" He had a tiny, blue-green cross tattooed at the base of his neck.

"I don't know, sir," I overheard Chuck say. "My Christology's pretty low right now."

"The state of your Christology," Dad said, looking up, "is irrelevant. Hannah!"

I balked. "I'm interrupting." I backed out. "I'm sorry."

They both rose. Dad was a pillar of silver and black, his authority augmented by the spotless, broad oak surface before him. Chuck turned, brightened in recognition, and closed the space between us with his hand extended. "So *you're* Hannah. The skulking, early-morning contemplative."

I flushed. Chuck's handshake was solid and lingering.

"What?" Dad asked. "You two have met?"

"Briefly," I said.

Chuck added his left palm to the handshake—an enthusiastic, pastoral gesture—while I silently pleaded for his discretion. "We bumped elbows in the sanctuary one morning." He winked at me. "You must be an early riser. Haven't seen you since."

"I keep strange hours."

Chuck released me. "The buzz around town is you do radical births."

"They're hardly radical."

"Okay, traditional. Still, setting out on your own, beginning a business. Friends of mine who've done it say it takes guts."

Chuck's jeans were torn at the knee, and he was wearing red high-tops. The copper color of his mustache and hint of a beard were incongruent with his shiny, pale skull. His eyes were hazel and confident.

"Dad told me about the youth group supporting the boy with cancer."

"They're a great bunch." His gaze meandered toward Dad, who stood with his hands behind his back, his pressed clerical shirt still crisp, looking strong and handsome and stern. "I'm hoping to take them on a mission trip to Mexico in August."

"Mexico! Where?"

"I haven't decided yet. Somewhere along the border."

"I've got a friend in Allende, not far from El Paso. I could hook you up." Stuart and Cal had moved to Mexico after graduation.

"That's great." Chuck bounced on his heels then stopped. "If it happens."

Dad's mighty brow furrowed. His blanket disapproval made me angry. "I wish I could've done a mission trip as a kid," I said. "Exposure to poverty would've done me good."

"Exactly. It's to educate the kids."

Except for Chuck's defiant nose ring, tattoo, and clothes, he was much like every other overly enthusiastic seminarian who had passed through Dad's office. What he'd likely seen in the sanctuary made me pay closer attention than I might have otherwise. "I'll send Stuart's number through Dad," I said.

"There's the stereo." Dad pointed at the floor. "We won't need it until Sunday."

I grabbed the boom box by the handle.

"Say"—Chuck reached his hand between us again—"maybe we can pray together sometime."

Heat prickled my neck. Behind Chuck, Dad paused in his descent to the chair, his mouth open. I almost said yes just to spite him.

"Thanks," I said. "I prefer solitude."

Dad landed, palms flat on the blotter. "Hannah," he declared. I was dismissed.

With an hour yet before class, I walked through the halls into the sanctuary to reinforce my prayer ruse. Organ music, something relentless and Bachlike, sketched its architecture in the air. The pews were vacant. I took a seat in the back row and closed my eyes. The interlocking melodies lent structure to my fear, my rebelliousness, my regret. Anger wasn't loving or Christian. Anger was not allowed in my parents' house, and yet now it surged inexplicably, toward my father, toward my mother, toward God when I forgot I didn't believe in Him. My anger was out of proportion to my parents' small injustices. Why was my blood pounding?

The organist interrupted himself to rehash a few measures. A door opened into the chancel, and the choir director entered. Abruptly the music halted, residual vibrations lasting a half-second longer, and the two musicians' voices took its place. I ran my fingers along the pew cushion's velvet. Hot gold light crept up the far wall. My breathing slowed. The tension in my back softened. Sitting in the sanctuary was nice, even with the men talking up front. Perhaps meditation was not a ruse after all.

28.

The Mischief Maker

THERE'S A CRAGGY, isolated spot on the coast of the Black Sea where hot springs bubble up, warming the salty water to body temperature. Russian midwives take off their clothes; they enter as naked as the pregnant women and their husbands. Waves pulse against contracting uterine muscles, easing the pain. Women have given birth there for millennia, squatting in a clear pool, the midwives accepting newborns into the element they've always known. Underwater, the little ones open their eyes. The womb becomes this great undulating sea, alight with sun. Only after the midwife lifts the infant from the water does it suck its first breath.

But get this: After the midwife has cut the cord, checked the vitals and delivered the placenta, and after the parents have recovered, they release the newborn back into the water. It thrusts its arms and thrashes its legs. More fish than human, it propels itself from the mother across a span of sun-streaked sea into the father's waiting hands. The newborn knows water, and the parents trust that knowledge enough to let the child go.

You want to be a midwife. You want authority and grace, to

be stripped down to the skin and to kneel in the waves. What I want to teach you is that first you must push off like the baby—vulnerable, capable, your essential self. When you're in your element, you'll know how to swim.

* * *

"I don't much see the need for checkups if everything's fine," Melinda said. She'd arrived for her thirty-week appointment in faded overalls with dirt under her fingernails. Kevin was at a play date. "I know what pregnancy looks like."

"Uh-huh," I replied. Melinda lay on the massage table, her body taut, muscular, and dark with sun. Only her abdomen seemed defenseless. Pale and exposed, it had doubled in size since I first saw her. Her breasts had swollen. I took my time winding up the measuring tape. "Even so, it's good to have someone looking out for you."

The lilacs had burst and faded, exuding a brown, overripe perfume strong enough to make a pregnant woman nauseous. A few tardy sparrows mated in the bushes. It was too warm to close out the fresh air. I sank my fingers into Melinda's skin.

"Okay, kiddo, where are you?" I asked. Just below her left rib I located a lump I assumed was the baby's butt. I inched my fingers downward, tracing the tiny spine pressed against the uterine wall. Across the street the school bell rang, followed by a pause and a burst of children's voices. Down at Melinda's pubic bone I felt a sharp, unmoving edge. "Hmm," I said, keeping my face impassive. Back at the top, I probed through skin, fat, and uterine muscle, and wobbled what was surely the head. "Oh," I said, drawing my fingers back down to the base of the spine to triple-check, and then again. Holding the baby's form within my palms, I felt a sudden chill.

Melinda lifted herself to her elbows. "Look at this," I said, nudging the knot inside her uterus back and forth. "This feels like a head. The little mischief-maker might be breech. I'd like to do a vaginal exam."

"Breech?!" She sat up effortlessly and tugged down her shirt. "Legs first?"

"Rump."

"That's not necessarily a problem, is it?"

"No. A lot can happen in two months. Usually babies flip on their own. I'm not worried. Let's listen for the heartbeat, shall we?"

Melinda eased herself down. I plugged my ears with the fetoscope. It *was* early, and yet the ramifications of a breech stampeded through me in a blind, heedless panic. At what point would I turn her over to Jorgenson? I placed the fetoscope beside her bellybutton and soft ticking filled my head.

"There. Do you want to listen?"

She shook her head. "I'm not telling Mike."

I pulled out my desk chair and sat. "About the position? Why not?"

"He'll freak. He's already convinced I'm suicidal because I want to birth at home." She swung her legs around and sat up.

"Melinda, the baby's still active. It's apt to move quite a bit yet. There's no reason to keep secrets."

I followed her gaze to the white, speckled ceiling.

"Mike's scared," I said. "And the hospital makes birth seem orderly and manageable."

"He's ignorant, and untrusting. That's what gets me. Even if he *is* just scared, he could still believe in me. Besides, it's not just him, it's my whole family." She corrected her posture. "Reminds me of weddings and how people say just elope."

I reached behind me to rub a sore spot on my back. "You don't need to tell Mike right away. But if the baby hasn't turned when we get nearer your due date, thirty-six weeks, we'll have to address it. With Mike, and with Bill Jorgenson."

"Jorgenson?!"

"I don't do breeches, Melinda. I said that upfront. But you've got two months. Babies flip. Let's see what happens. In the meantime, you should do the tilt exercise." I demonstrated how she could sit on a pile of cushions ten inches high and lean backward, jamming the baby's head into her diaphragm. "Not a comfortable place. Twelve minutes, three times a day. On an empty stomach, okay? Kevin will think it's a trip."

The vaginal exam confirmed my suspicion and, despite my confident pronouncements, worry settled between us like the summer humidity. Melinda was brusque, hastily making her next appointment and letting the screen door slam. I retreated to the kitchen's aluminum-edged counters and the stylized tulips, crimson and burnt orange with dusty-green leaves, I'd stenciled along the ceiling. My coffee was cold but effective. I practiced breathing.

Of the three breeches I'd seen during my apprenticeship, two had ended in C-sections. All were clients of a doctor-friend of Sunny's who practiced in Española. He gave her the heads-up when he got unusual cases so she could truck us down the mountain pass to observe. Even though New Mexico considered malpresentations high risk and outside the domain of midwives, babies always had the potential to surprise, and Sunny was determined that we be prepared. "Personally, I'd do them if it weren't for the law," Sunny confided. "And twins." But then Sunny had cut her own episiotomy.

Stuart and I had memorized the standard turning techniques. We studied how to prevent the additional complication of face-up rotation, how to sweep the arms down, perform the Mauriceau-Smellie-Veit maneuver, and reinforce the myriad factors that make for a smooth breech delivery, especially insisting the mother remain horizontal without pushing until dilation. My head knew. My hands were clueless.

I berated myself for signing on with Bill without learning more about his practice. Did he perform external versions, a slow, skillful method of nudging the baby into a new position through the mother's skin? I doubted it. Did he ever deliver breeches vaginally? He'd been around long enough to see feet come out first, or tiny rears. If I could trust Bill to respect Melinda's desires, I could hand her over to his care with a modicum of dignity. Had our arrangement been above board, I might have interviewed Bill first, watched him work, and made an educated decision. Instead he had leaned across an empty dinner plate and huskily whispered he would back me up— because of my mother's kindness. Now I was in the position of needing information I couldn't request without raising alarm.

In the meantime, I had to do some research. I grabbed my grocery pad and made a list. The New Mexican midwives always sent clients to the local acupuncturist who had a seventy percent success rate turning breeches. Believe it or not, burning herb cigars near a women's pinky toes is a fairly reliable means for moving babies. I could probably find someone in the Cities. And external version was an option, especially since Melinda was a second-time mom. I just needed a doc or midwife who knew how.

Then I jotted an embarrassing list of solutions that give midwives a bad reputation—hypnosis, having the father whisper encouragement to the mother's vagina, having the mother imagine a helium balloon attached to the baby's foot for an hour each day or shine a flashlight into her crotch to encourage the baby to turn toward the light. I had no idea how Melinda would react to such suggestions or even if I could offer them with a straight face. Still, you never know what might work. One of Sunny's clients did handstands twice a day. Another had her husband play bongo drums while she was in the bath, and both succeeded in turning. Stuart used to say anything under the flim-flam sun is possible.

I put down the pencil. Flipping the baby was one thing; dealing with Melinda was another.

Melinda got under my skin. She threw her shoulders back and tucked her chin as though everyone else was beneath her. Yes, that was the rub. We were both enterprising, independent women operating at the margins. Folks around town called her fanatic, a hippie. I was sure they were saying the same about me. Couldn't we muster up some camaraderie? Instead she pushed me away, defiant in her idyllic life. Instinctively, I pushed back.

Yield, I told myself. The one great lesson of my training, which I am still and forever learning, is that a midwife's best asset is the capacity to let go. To serve Melinda well, the stubborn part of me had to yield. How, I wondered, did those Russian mothers release their infants into the ocean? I wanted to be like them—abundantly generous and able to trust the body's wisdom.

29.

Red Owl at Night

MY STUDENTS' VOICES were buoyant despite the deadening acoustics of the Chester Prairie library basement. Class had ended a good forty minutes earlier. The banter that started during our maternity yoga stretches had segued into bittersweet remembrances of their parents' child-rearing and what each couple hoped to replicate or avoid. I pushed aside my lesson plans and admired their radiance.

Finally I called out, "Ladies! I need to get groceries," and slung a backpack over my shoulder. They laughed and hauled their bellies around, picking up notes and purses. I locked the door behind them.

Outside, the June evening shimmered, pewter light from the west reflecting in the windows of houses and parked cars, the intersections empty, the sidewalks padded with new-green maple wings. Nighthawks called "eew, eew" over the rooftops, a sound that might have been eerie had I not fallen asleep to it as a child. The streetlamps buzzed on. A lone robin's song swung up and down the street.

At the Red Owl, fluorescent light spilled across the nearly

empty lot. Plate glass blazed like a movie screen playing *Two Lonely Cashiers.* I remembered working closing hour, how the store felt like a bright, self-contained universe, both safe and utterly suffocating. I'd lasted there four years, funding my way through college. When I told Dad midwifery was my ministry, it wasn't just rhetoric. In comparison with that aimless, half-hearted time and my seven years behind reception desks when I was content to be good at something, anything, midwifery was *vocation,* a siren song luring me from smallness and complacency into a bigger self. That Dad had known such clarity his entire life awed me. And mom? Motherhood, committee work, sewing—she employed herself with perfunctory choicelessness. If she'd wanted to become a nurse, why hadn't she? Mothers didn't often go back to school in her generation, but it wasn't unheard of. I wasn't entirely to blame.

I pushed through the door ten minutes before closing. Peppy easy-listening music piped through the intercom, interrupted by smooth, radio-announcer specials for ketchup and Windex. In Produce, the asparagus caught my eye, and I was debating the extravagance when I heard my name. I turned. Behind a grocery cart crammed with bulk toilet paper and bottled water stood Zarida Severson. I'd seen Zarida last at high school graduation. She'd painted a *Y* on her mortarboard, so when her row of popular kids lined up together and tipped their heads, they spelled, "Bye-bye, losers!" She used to smoke cigarettes behind the gym. In fifth grade, we'd played clarinets side by side in the school band. In eleventh-grade chemistry we were lab partners. Once, our test tube had boiled dry and shattered; our stifled hilarity had been our friendliest moment.

"Hey, Zarida."

"I heard you were back in town." Zarida leaned forward for a mock embrace. "You're looking great. Not a day older than eighteen."

"Oh, come on." She was wearing institution-green scrubs and white shoes with silent rubber soles. Her cheeks were vaguely hollowed. She looked middle-aged. I put my empty basket on the linoleum.

"Fun to see you. Dad mentioned you're at the hospital. Emergency?"

"I float. ER, intensive care, post-op."

"For how long?"

"Since I got my degree. Six years. And you're a midwife." She emphasized "mid," as though I hadn't finished wifing yet. I searched unsuccessfully for a hint of cigarette huskiness in her voice. "Risky work, isn't it?"

"I weed out the dangerous cases. You see the worst of it." Her right hand gripping the shopping cart flashed long, manicured fingernails. Someday I might depend on those hands. "How do you like intensive care?"

"You wouldn't expect it of me, nobody does, but it's great. Not just because I feel like I'm on 'ER' either. Adrenaline kicks in and suddenly I'm there, helping people. I amaze myself constantly, you know? Unlike playing that damned clarinet." We both laughed. "You get it."

"Sure. The baby's crowning and the mother's pushing and Super-Hannah bursts onto the scene."

"Exactly! You wouldn't catch me doing what you're doing, though. I mean, the things I've seen . . ." Her words sounded practiced.

I shrugged. "It takes all types."

"Maybe. If I ever get pregnant, bring on the epidural. There's no way I'd go through that torture."

Neil Diamond was cut off mid-guitar bridge. In the sudden quiet before the cashier's closing announcement, we both looked toward the drop-ceiling. "There're other forms of pain relief," I said. "You see some births?"

"I do post-op, so just the Cesareans and preemies and anything else unusual. The stuff *you* don't want to see."

"Say," I winced at my feigned casualness, "just out of curiosity, what do you guys do with breeches? Ever deliver them vaginally?"

Zarida's eyes widened. "Vaginal breech? You've got to be

kidding. Listen, Hannah." She looked at the pink plastic watch on her wrist. "They're shutting the store down, and I've got a long list yet. Great seeing you and all." She reached behind me for a head of iceberg.

"Sure." I decided I couldn't afford asparagus, chose carrots instead, and strode to the dairy case. Over the PA a teenage voice said, "Attention, Red Owl shoppers!" When I caught myself heading directly to check out, I turned around and went back for some soup. Their shift wasn't up for another half-hour.

* * *

Zarida took less than fourteen hours to do her damage. I was scrubbing the hall toilet in preparation for a new client, a friend of Katrina Schultz in the Scandinavian language department— my growing specialty had become ex-pat community college professors—when someone knocked. I answered the front door with a wet rubber-gloved hand.

Bill Jorgenson occupied the stoop, his dress pants and blue short-sleeve shirt wrinkled, comb marks still wet in his hair.

"You got a minute?"

"Bill." I propped the screen open with my foot while blood rushed to my head. "What can I do for you?"

He rocked from foot to foot, the porch boards creaking under his weight. His eyes darted to the foundation plantings.

"Now, don't take this the wrong way. You know I think highly of you. And of course it's not my place to meddle. But in light of our agreement, I've got to look out for everyone's interest— yours, mine, the patients'. Doctorly duty. I don't put much stock in rumors. Still, there's usually some grain of truth."

The eight-inch step allowed me to look down at Bill with confidence I didn't possess. I put my gloved hand on my hip.

"The long and short of it is, Zarida said you grilled her on breeches. Made us both wonder what you're working with."

The little shit! "I'm sorry, Bill. How *do* you deal with breeches? I need to know." I gave myself an internal kick for not asking Bill directly.

"Section 'em." Bill angled himself against the railing. His fingers disappeared under his armpits. "Now don't take that as callous, Hannah. It's a controlled surgery with predictable outcomes."

He was damn right the outcomes were predictable—three times more likely to kill the mom. This was the man my parents revered? I tempered myself and asked, "Have you ever delivered a breech vaginally?"

His eyes darted to mine as though the question was threatening. Then he harrumphed. "A footer once, early on. The woman walked in off the streets fully dilated and pushing before we could even do an ultrasound. Kid slipped out like riding down a water slide. Downright freaky, if you ask me. And the exception. Malpresentations are unpredictable and dangerous. Which is why you shouldn't do them at home. That wasn't our agreement."

I leaned through the doorway. "I'm a person of my word, Bill. I don't practice willy-nilly. I've set professional guidelines, and you know what they are: normal, healthy delivery."

"Normal is a retrospective diagnosis."

"I have a mandate to safeguard my clients too, you know."

Bill's nose was very red.

"Vaginal breeches aren't unheard of," I told him. I didn't want to sound accusatory. "Presbyterian does them occasionally." Maryann had done one that I knew of, and it was precipitous.

"Good for them," he grunted. "Listen. I don't want to see you in hot water, that's all. Or me."

"I appreciate the consideration." I wished his nose didn't look so alarming. "Really. And everything you're doing for me."

"Consider it a gift." His contracted eyebrows, white and in need of trimming, did not strike me as generous. Together we stared at his beater pickup. Rust was creeping up the cab door. Bill was not in medicine for the money.

"We'll figure this out, Bill—how to work together. We're just getting to know each other."

"Right."

He thrust out his hand, and I shook it.

After he left, I raged around the kitchen, slamming the damn kitchen cupboard that refused to latch and cursing Zarida's loose, lipsticked mouth. Medical slut! With two months to go before Melinda's due date and the good chance her baby would turn, I had no reason to feel like a backstreet abortionist caught with a coathanger. I despised the smiling surface of Chester Prairie, its clean white face and smug presumption of normality. In a fit of small-town claustrophobia, I dialed Maryann and arranged another lunch date. My world was bigger than *this*.

30.

Sunday Sermon

THE ORGAN BLASTED the first hymn; the congregation mouthed the words. I accepted a bulletin from the usher, slipped into a back-row pew, and fingered the hymnal like a pro. Robust chords rumbled through the floorboards and up through my feet. An organ makes a building and its occupants into a single, vibrating instrument. I closed my eyes so that bigger sound might fill me, erase me, make me more blast and whistle than flesh.

A momentary lapse. By the hymn's end I was fighting the hypocrisy of Christian worship and berating myself for getting suckered into coming. I'd shown up because, of all things, Dad had asked.

From shortly after high school graduation when I'd first experienced the bliss of a Sunday morning sleep-in until I escaped to New Mexico, Dad had met my firm refusal to attend church with relentless nagging, Dad-style: "See you Sunday morning," or "The Johnsons are getting lax about attendance. You never know what rushes in to fill a void like that." Since my return to Chester Prairie, he'd let me sip Sunday coffee and read the paper guilt-free for enough months that I had dropped my guard. So when I stopped by his office to bring him some clip-art of Madonna and Child from a birth newsletter, he'd asked the unthinkable: "I was wondering if you'd come to church on Sunday. I'd like you to be there." I was so surprised, I said yes.

Dad had two services, at nine and eleven. The nine o'clock he used as a venue for the "contemporary hoo-ha" of his intern. Apparently Chuck played guitar and one of the teenagers pounded bongos. I chose the eleven o'clock. Church without organ music isn't worth squat.

The morning's liturgist was a tremulous middle-aged soprano. The congregation's response, which I didn't join, sounded bored. Was Dad's direct request a new tactic? It went against his nature. He'd asked my attendance as a favor to *him* rather than to correct some defect in *me*. The liturgist stepped down and we sat.

During the interminable pastoral prayer, I smirked at the thought of my birth tools hidden up front. By that point I'd attended eight births, and even the one precipitous labor had given me enough lead time to retrieve my kit. Late evenings, I'd found, the sanctuary was reliably empty. I'd grown to appreciate my pretense of prayer, the dim light, and the still, expansive space sounding in my ears. I released my responsibilities, my spinning worries, and straining dreams into . . . what? Emptiness. I hoped that was enough.

Dad's black robe was corded at the waist; the red stole Mom had embroidered with gold crosses flapped as he strode across the dais. His left hand grasped the pulpit railing, his right, a soft-covered Bible with gilt edges. Mounting the steps, he stooped forward like an old man. *He's changed,* I realized. He would turn seventy in the fall, well past retirement age, and he was beginning to judge his next step before taking it. Yet when he turned, he was again imposing. His cheeks were severe. His hair was entirely gray, standing on end a bit from pulling on his robe. Mom would have smoothed that. He groped below the pulpit for reading glasses and latched them behind his ears. The congregation settled.

Over time I'd learned his formula. He would read the lesson then retell it in his own language while adding tidbits of historical context. I guess it was too much to expect people to absorb the scripture on one hearing. Then he would elaborate on the text's overarching theme, and finally present a single, climactic morsel for the congregants to chew. Presumably one nugget of wisdom at a time was all we could stomach.

Sometimes I wondered if the congregation didn't want more substance after thirty-eight years. But they adored Dad. They requested his presence in their hospital rooms; they wanted his broad hands to invoke the Trinity upon the consternated foreheads of their infants; they wept on hearing his oft-repeated blessings over loved ones' coffins. With Mom gone, the women pampered him and the men shook his hand more vigorously, yet they never invited him to a hunting opener or to watch a Twins game. They revered him too much. I suspect they needed to elevate him to keep holiness at a safe distance. Or they considered their ordinary lives base and unworthy. That's why I appreciated Bill. Outside of their backslapping friendship, Dad inhabited a sphere of grace upheld by Mom, his congregation, and (I couldn't quite shake my childhood conviction) by God Himself.

"Our scripture reading this morning is taken from the first chapter of Exodus, verses one through twenty-two, during Israel's bondage in Egypt." Dad's voice was amplified and came at me from a speaker in the rear corner, with the same broad tenor I'd recognized as a toddler on my mother's lap—resounding, full-throated, grave. The passage began with a monotonous list of Abraham's sons, which Dad intoned as though each name actually meant something.

The odd thing about Biblical stories is that I heard so many so often in my childhood, at church, at Sunday school, over dinner, and while being reprimanded, that, given the slightest instigation, they spring forward in live-action dramas in my mind's eye. And so, while the mahogany timbre of Dad's voice reconstructed the story, I saw the pompous Egyptian king observe his Israelite slaves as they began to outnumber his own people; I saw him turn cruel, forcing the slaves to haul brick and till the fields; I felt his mounting fury at their resilience. Hardship wasn't enough for the captives. The pharaoh dictated genocide.

"Then the king of Egypt said to the Hebrew midwives," Dad read, and I sat up, chest thumping, " 'When you serve as midwife to the Hebrew women, and see them upon the birthstool, if it is a son, you shall kill him; but if it is a daughter, she shall live.' But the midwives feared God, and did not do as the king of Egypt commanded them, but let the male children live. So the king of Egypt called the midwives, and said to them, 'Why have you done this, and let the male children live?' The midwives said to Pharaoh, 'Because the Hebrew women are not like the Egyptian women; for they are vigorous and are delivered before the midwife comes to them.'

"So God dealt well with the midwives; and the people multiplied and grew very strong. And because the midwives feared God, he gave them families."

Dad's voice hung in the sanctuary. I held my breath and surreptitiously scanned the neighboring pews. Was it as obvious to everyone else that he was using the pulpit to speak with his daughter? Surely this lesson wasn't in the lectionary. Even if it was, Dad preferred to preach from the Gospel texts. I slid down an inch.

Dad removed his glasses, collapsed them, and placed them on some unseen shelf. A woman sneezed. The congregation shifted. Dad placed his hands deliberately on either end of the pulpit's sloped surface and looked down at his flock.

"You know what's coming next—baby Moses in a basket among the bulrushes, traveling downriver into the hands of Pharaoh's daughter. Thus begins the Israelites' epic journey from bondage into freedom. That's the more familiar passage. Today we start back a step."

When Dad preached, he ignored his prolific notes and gazed

directly into people's eyes. He deliberated upon every word. Pharaoh wanted the Hebrew midwives to support Egyptian national interests. God, on the other hand, wanted them to protect the captive Israelites. The midwives became "instruments of life." Moses's birth depended on them, as did the Israelites' liberation. Dad's voice was so certain, his pace so unhurried, I felt drugged into agreeing. The midwives were God's servants.

But no: Hadn't the midwives acted out of their own feisty volition? Who *wouldn't* avoid murdering newborns, despite a ruler's edict? As far as I could tell, the only communication between the midwives and God was after the fact, when He rewarded them with children. Most likely the midwives rebelled without any sense of God whatsoever. Dad read the Bible with twenty-twenty vision, hindsight giving the evil people horns and the good people a terrific knack for hearing God's will. He didn't account for how much guts it took to break the law.

Dad paused long enough to replace his glasses—the signal he would soon end.

"Brothers and sisters, God is faithful. God abides with us in our anguish, in our labor, in our birthing and dying. God is ceaseless in seeking our hearts, in His offer of grace. The midwives of today's story serve to remind us how God works through people—God even supports subverting the establishment—for the sake of offering us life. This is the same life he gives us continually with his Son, Jesus Christ. So be it. Amen."

The congregation exhaled and adjusted their hips. A young couple at my right gave me sidelong looks. I was glad I'd sat far enough back that most people didn't know I was there. Dad announced the morning offering; the organist began a toccata and a chorus of check-tearing rose from the pews. Quarters were passed to children, dropped on the floor, retrieved. I sat with Dad's final words, oddly relieved, my breathing less obstructed. His expression, "subverting the establishment," floored me, as though to get his mind around my work, he had to resort to the language of the sixties. Dad *was* the establishment. If I took his analogy far enough, I too was an "instrument of God," a midwife working to preserve the life of her people. The message was overblown but generous. Dad had finally listened. My bitter outbursts must have driven him to seek guidance in the scriptures. Lucky for me the midwives of the Bible fared better than the homosexuals.

My father's peculiar form of love sank to my stomach, indigestible.

The usher handed me a brass plate piled with checks. I reflexively passed it along, then regretted not throwing in a few bucks. We stood for the Doxology and sat for the postlude, during which Dad and Chuck (minus the nose ring) trailed two white-draped acolytes down the aisle within three hands' breadths of my seat. Chuck flashed me a knowing smile. Dad ignored me. The tail of his stole flicked gold and crimson. On my way out of the sanctuary, I shook his hand like every other parishioner.

"Dad."

"Hannah." He dipped his silvery head, looking past me to the next person in line.

* * *

Maggie snared me before I could get out the double doors. She'd gotten a perm since I saw her last, and gray, unsprung curls made her soft face look unnaturally chipper.

"So you've come to hear your father preach about midwives, hmm?" She hugged a white macraméd purse to her belly.

"I didn't put him up to it, you know." I smiled weakly. "How are you, Mrs. Hendricks?"

"Missing your mother." Maggie's gray eyes met mine, and we shared a companionable sadness. "There's six Quilters left. Can you imagine? And I'm the only driver. Last time we went out for coffee, I had to make two trips."

The narthex was muggy; the crowd jostled Maggie and me a foot closer. People I didn't know stared at me and nodded hello. Apparently the mystique of being a pastor's kid hadn't worn off with adulthood, especially when the pastor lacked subtlety.

"I redecorated my bedroom to match the quilt, you know." Every evening when I folded the quilt down to the foot of the bed, I felt humbled by the Quilters' kindness.

Maggie beamed. She patted my forearm. "You're doing so well. Your mother would be pleased."

I flushed with affection and began to protest—I wasn't at all sure what Mom would think. Chuck appeared at Maggie's elbow, his clerical garb hanging open to reveal black jeans and a black T-shirt. "Glad I caught you, Mrs. Hendricks. Are you going to Lutheran Homes today?" Chuck slung his arm around Maggie's small shoulders and squeezed.

"After a bite to eat, dear."

"You can take the altar flowers. Hi, Hannah." He rubbed the tattoo at the base of his neck. "Your dad digressed from the lectionary today. You must be a powerful influence."

"Hannah's delivering babies, just like the Hebrew midwives," Maggie said. "Isn't that something!"

I tried to look politely exasperated.

"Is it true what you're doing isn't legal?" Chuck asked.

"A-legal. It's complicated. The statute and enforcement don't match up."

"That must put you in a bind."

I smiled as though I didn't hear the subtext.

"Well, then. You're courageous."

I examined Chuck, his attentive eyes, his ascetic scalp now bristling with bronze. He was genuine. "I don't feel courageous. Just beleaguered."

"You and midwives throughout history, apparently. You help women, you get into trouble."

The tension in my shoulders slackened a notch.

"Say," Chuck said, "thanks for connecting me with Stuart. It looks like we'll be going to Allende."

"Really?"

Chuck touched my arm. "Want to come?"

However much I'd have liked to see Stuart, there was no way I could leave my practice with babies due.

"I can't. I've got clients—"

"Excuse me. Hannah?" Mike Hollinger shouldered into our threesome, his gray suit jacket slung over his arm and ironed white shirt, sharp against a red usher's tie. My heart sank. I hadn't seen Mike since Melinda's second appointment a month and a half ago.

"Mike, dear!" Maggie enthused. "How's Melinda coming along?"

Mike strangled his bulletin. "Getting huge, still gardening. I tell her she's racing her watermelons to see who'll be biggest. Hannah, may I speak to you?"

"Of course." I glanced at Chuck. "Thanks for the invite, though."

Chuck raised a parting hand.

I followed Mike out the doors into the simmering morning. He stepped into the church's shadow. I leaned against the cool brick. "How are you doing?"

Mike's black shoes were freshly polished. Moisture beaded along his neck. "I can't pretend things are easy. I mean, it's a piece of cake compared with her emotional swings the first time round. But this homebirth stuff's got me rattled. I thought breeches weren't in your purview, Hannah."

So he knew. "They're not."

"Shit," he said, and then remembered my father. "Excuse my language. So you're trying to get her to the hospital too?"

"She won't have a choice if the baby doesn't turn."

Mike placed his crumpled bulletin and pressed jacket onto the low wall and sat, careful not to scrape his pants on the concrete. His hair was trim, his face round and sweet. I saw now that he was younger than Melinda, perhaps by five years. Dad told me he came from a farming family, dairy, out near Princeton. At one point Dad had referred to Mike as "an upstanding citizen of this community," and that old longing I'd felt for Leif tugged at me—I wanted to escape into the familiar safety of such a man's arms. "I've married one hell of a stubborn woman," he said.

I smiled sympathetically.

"What are you going to do?" he asked.

"About the baby? Wait it out. See if it turns." I waved at a family I knew as they exited the church. "I'm researching some options, docs in the Cities who turn babies and might deliver breeches vaginally. Nothing's certain until the baby engages. In the pelvis, I mean."

"When's that?"

"It's different for everyone—two or three weeks before the due date. Usually a woman's second baby doesn't engage until labor."

"You should be firm, Hannah. If she knows you're not an option, she might give in."

"I have been. It's the arrangement I made with Bill. I don't do malpresentations."

Mike swiped his brow with the back of his hand. "She respects you, you know. That counts for something." He eased himself off the wall.

"Next time I see Melinda, I'll give her some phone numbers." I leaned into Mike's shoulder and confided, "Some couples swear the little one turns to hear the papa better. You could always try whispering sweet nothings you know where."

Mike grinned sheepishly. "At this point I'll try anything. Thanks, Hannah." He slung his jacket over his shoulder and reentered the narthex.

From the edge of the cemetery, a high, sweet frog song ascended to a fevered chirp. The sun had reached its apex and was starting to burn my scalp. I took advantage of the lull in the crowd and descended to the street. I couldn't get home fast enough.

31.

Over the Wires

YOU ASKED ABOUT my notorious delivery, but perhaps you're really searching for your own place in this populous and daunting world. What makes a midwife's work significant?

Not a policeman's beefy fingers encircling your forearm; not a night spent in jail, awake, or even attention in the papers. No. Birth is what matters. Our hands touch mothers, their babies and their families, and with each choice we make together, a culture of fear or welcome blooms around us. We're birthing a world. I want you to know this without having the misfortune of everyone else knowing it too.

* * *

I spent Wednesday morning in the kitchen bent over The Sweetest Blossom ledger, taking refuge in columns, totals, the precise buttons of my calculator, and my efforts to help a friend. Cathie's books were a disaster. After reconstructing her financial records, I suspected she owed thousands in back taxes. The first thunderheads of the season rode west winds across the plains and darkened the kitchen. At noon, the skies cracked. I closed the windows and turned on the overhead light. For lunch I ate tuna from a can and drank a tall glass of orange juice with yogurt whisked in. Eventually I pushed the ledger aside and watched the ash tree twist in the front yard. Rain seared air and earth, streaming in the gutters and seeping through the loamy soil. Gusts of wind streaked the rain sideways, battering the glass. A low rumble crossed the flatlands.

The isolated yellow light of the kitchen, the thrashing, dark world outside, and the flooded streets of Chester Prairie deepened my melancholy. Having had a few days to digest Dad's sermon, I began to wonder if his endorsement, generous as it was, arose from fatalism. Had he resigned himself to being the father of a midwife because, for good or ill, this was the path the Lord had placed before him? The thought saddened me; it meant he'd been compelled to speak by theological imperative rather than affection. To Dad, God's will was revealed in the unfolding of events. This had been true for Mom too, although in my case she'd felt free to censor their unfolding. Most likely she understood her pregnancy to be God steering her away from a nursing career. I'd almost followed her example, presuming my skills and success in hospital administration revealed my calling. The thought caught my breath.

I struggled to hold on to the expansive life I'd found in New Mexico. However much Chester Prairie was home, however much I was thriving, building birth classes and a client base and, in fits and starts, my relationship with my father, still, I knew a bigger world, or perhaps my heart itself was bigger. I didn't want to lose what I'd become. I couldn't wait until my lunch date with Maryann the next day, so I rose, grabbed my address book from the window ledge, and dialed the string of digits that linked my phone line to a funky cinder block hut on the outskirts of Allende.

Four rings, and a sleepy voice answered, *"Hola, este Stuart aquí."*

"Stuart, it's Hannah. Did I wake you?"

"Hannah!" He shouted into the background, "Cal, it's Hannah!" and then, "I've missed you, *chica*. Where've you been?"

I untangled the phone cord and sat. "Getting my practice off the ground."

"Jeez, it's good to hear from you." Stuart's enthusiasm carried with it sweltering heat, a shameless passion for birth, and a friendship in which it was fine to be asked, "How are the techno-medical dictators treating you?" and to respond by describing Bill Jorgenson's stretched suspenders, double chin, and perplexing motives.

Stuart told me about working in the slums, offering midwifery services in exchange for a new pair of flip-flops or freshly butchered chickens, which, vegetarian that he was, he gave away. His clients called him *Partero Rizzo* and he explained the joke—the Spanish word for midwife is never masculine. Cal supported them both by exporting his photography, although they lived like ascetics eating beans and rice out of cracked bowls.

"You have no idea what I'd give for a fine Bordeaux," Stuart exclaimed. I rose and added it to my grocery list, then remembered the post office wouldn't ship liquor. "But it's worth it. Most of these mothers would be giving birth alone, with no prenatal care. Some don't have running water. And they've broken away from their village roots, so they've lost their own birth traditions. Totally different scene from the U.S. of A. The biggest problem I deal with is malnutrition."

"God," I said. "Constricted pelvises?"

"Some. Lots of anemia and spina bifida. If I get to them early enough, I can hook them up with some meals-on-wheels missionaries in town. The ones I suggested to your friend."

"Dad's intern."

"Uh-huh."

"Any authorities breathing down your neck?"

"The opposite. The doc at the hospital's a fag. He's got Cal's photos all over his apartment and wants us to join him and his partner down in Cancún for a week this winter. Not my scene. We might go just for cultural edification."

"You lucked out. How much are you working?"

"You won't believe this, Hannah. I'm doing one or two births a week. You caught me catching up on my Z's. Want a job?"

"Ha," I said. Sunny had recommended that we practice in a developing country for a spell, both for the quantity and breadth of experience. Where no other medical options exist, midwives handle twins, preemies, everything. I'd been eager to return home, at a price: Honing my skills would take generations at the rate I was delivering babies. The realization hit me hard. "Well, maybe," I said. "Have you done any breeches?"

"Two. Woo-wee. One my first week here. This kid comes running to my door screaming, '*¡Doctor de bebé! ¡Vente!*' I'm clueless how he knew me. So I grab his miniscule hand, and we're racing down these dirt roads between shacks, all of which looked the same to me, corrugated tin roofs and makeshift walls, and I'm thinking, how am I going to find my way back? The grandmother was there to deliver the baby but instead of a head there were toes. I was like, 'Oh shit!' But what could I do at that point?" I could feel Stuart glowing.

"She was maybe six centimeters, so I'm shouting, '*¡No empuje!*' and I check the heart tones, which were just fine, thank the goddess. I got her to hold off for another hour by coaching her to breathe whenever she had the urge to push, until she was complete. And then, *whoosh*."

I wrestled with awe and envy.

"The other one I had some warning on. Scared the bejeebers out of me. I watched the Gaskin video until I was delivering in my sleep. Turned out slick. Why do you ask?"

I wrapped the phone cord around my wrist and up the length of my arm. Rain beat through the screen and ran in warped sheets down the kitchen window. "I've got a frank breech at thirty-two weeks. If she doesn't flip, I'll have to turn the mama over to the OB." I felt humiliated saying it, as though the baby's position were somehow my fault. "The mom's not happy."

"Not in your protocol, huh?"

"Stuart, *midwifery's* outside protocol here. I check someone's blood pressure, and I could get arrested for practicing medicine without a license."

"So brave," Stuart said apologetically. "Don't listen to me, hon. My judgment sucks when it comes to obeying dumb rules." If ever Stuart spoke a truth about himself, this was it. Lawless Mexico had been a good choice. "I'm sure you're right to go to the OB."

Stuart advocating moderation? He was placating me.

"Don't fret it," he said. "Most babies turn. It's way early."

"It is, isn't it? I don't know why it's getting to me. Do you have any tricks up your sleeve?"

"The only thing new is the rebozo method. You get a long bolt of coarse material, nothing slippery, have the mom lay down face up. Then you grab the fabric like you're the stork and she's the baby, and rock her side to side. Get a rhythm going to lull the twerp and then give it a series of little jerks. Doesn't necessarily correct a breech, but it sure dislodges the fetus."

"I don't know," I said. "I'd have to see it."

"It takes strength. I'll show you sometime."

"I wish you could visit."

Outside, the air darkened another degree and the rain turned downright mean. "Really? You're serious, Hannah?"

"Really. Both of you. You can have my bed, and I'll sleep on the couch."

"Isn't the world's largest ball of twine in Minnesota? That's on my list of things to see before I die."

"I think it's rotting. It stinks."

Lightning bleached the sky; a crack rent the afternoon and the phone sizzled.

"*¡Chinga!* What was that?"

"Maybe I should hang up. We're having a doozy of a storm."

"Don't get electrocuted, babe. Hey, if it comes to it, just deliver the breech. You'll do fine."

His confidence was just what I'd wanted, yet it left me

tongue-tied.

"It's awesome that you called, Hannah. *Amiga del corazón*."

"I love you, Stuart."

"Love you too, sweetie."

I set the phone in its cradle just as the bulb overhead popped and the whir of the refrigerator cut short. Deliver Melinda's breech baby? Stuart was crazy. No, Stuart was Stuart, ever capable, perpetually residing across the border in some country much freer than my own. My practice was bounded by my competence and by the guidance of other midwives. The whole point of hospital birth and OBs and advanced technology was to take care of difficulties like malpresentations. I sat in the odd afternoon, semidarkness closing around me. Damp entered my pores, and, covered by the rumble of thunder, I wept, sweetly, buoyantly, because I was and wasn't alone.

32.

Brink of Extinction

THE NEXT DAY I escaped to the Cities, my mood rising the more freeway I put between myself and Chester Prairie. Two hours over sunbaked pavement and I was in St. Paul, the glistening capitol dome on one hill and the copper-topped cathedral on another like great breasts, erect against the June blue. How many times had I made this drive and not noticed? Cars cooled in the hospital ramp. Sidewalks teemed with business-suited men, teenagers in packs outside coffee shops, a homeless woman carrying a bent umbrella against the sun . . . I needed this bustle and space.

"About time, woman." Maryann's loud pronouncement and chesty hug made the hospital cafeteria diners turn their heads. Her embrace squeezed moisture from my eyes. I hadn't seen Maryann since December.

"I've missed you," I said. It was true, despite how small she made me feel.

"Imagine that." Maryann handed me a tray. "Tough love works."

I followed her silk leopard-print back through the line,

picking out plastic-wrapped sandwiches, juice bottles, and chips. At the cash register, Maryann grabbed two oversized chocolate cookies and paid for us both despite my feeble protests. We took a table with a plate-glass view of Sixth and Exchange.

"Give me the update." We'd talked on the phone, but Maryann detested machines and luxuriated in human company. She ignored her food, folded her arms, and leaned into the table. Noontime sun heated the glass. I was warmed by summer and Maryann's open face. With my old mentor listening, the crazy enterprise I'd begun in Chester Prairie no longer seemed like a blip in common sense; it was the logical next step, a choice continuous with my childhood curiosity, my budding passion, and the hard work of apprenticeship. My life held a larger pattern I could only sometimes see.

Maryann hummed pleasurably at the strides I'd made in my practice, declaring, "Amen, sister," at the story of Katrina's birth and "Hallelujah, Lord" at my birth class successes. I flushed with satisfaction.

"How about that," Maryann declared when I finished. I saw something register in her brain. Her mouth flickered, resisting a grin, and she looked down to unwrap her sandwich.

"What?" I demanded.

"Eat your lunch."

This was what I always dreaded: that she'd exercise her sly midwifery self on me. I sipped my coffee. "How are things upstairs?"

"The usual chaos. They've added another four CNMs since you left. We're giving the docs a run for their money. Turns out midwives bring the hospital a good reputation."

"No surprise." Nurse midwives were making strides in hospitals all over the country.

"Is to the docs. We just got a fresh batch from some highfalutin East Coast teaching hospital, and they're up in arms. Don't like the Hmong families spilling into the hallway and say we take too long. Same old same old. They'll get used to it. So, tell me why you're here."

"To visit you."

"Out with it, white girl. What do you need from me?"

I gripped the plastic seat and nudged back an inch. "I hate it when you do that. Can't we just be friends?"

"Sure." Maryann waved a potato chip at me. "The day you call just to catch up because you love my dynamic company. Now out with it."

I looked at the triangle of white bread, flaccid lettuce, and uninteresting ham. "I could be in a bind. I don't know yet—it's too early. I'm signed on with a mom whose baby's breech."

"And the dilemma?"

"I won't deliver a breech at home, so when do I turn her over, and how?" I delineated—to Maryann and to myself—the obvious, beginning with my insufficient experience and ending with my commitment to Bill. "Plus she despises my backup doc. He's already nervous, breathing down my neck, and the town's scandalized that this witch is delivering babies in bedrooms. I'd be afraid of getting run out of town if it weren't for my dad. He more or less endorsed my work from the pulpit. It was huge, Maryann. He's never paid any attention to me before."

"Now, what does your dad have to do with the breech?"

I prodded my sandwich. "Nothing."

"Good," Maryann said. "Your job is to provide the best care possible to your moms. What your father thinks, or the doc or the town, has nothing to do with it."

"That's not true." The sunshine was too strong on my neck. "What they think matters a lot. You wouldn't know; you're working in a hospital with oodles of malpractice insurance. I'm not just practicing midwifery, Maryann. I have to justify it; I have to educate everyone about it. Seriously. My backup doc still cuts episiotomies." Maryann grimaced. "He induces after twelve hours. That's the climate I'm working in. I *have* to care what people think. I have a serious public relations problem to deal with before I can do anything."

Maryann swung her head, leveling me with her intense eyes. "Amazing. The genie's out of the bottle."

"What's that supposed to mean?"

"You're a spitfire, Hannah. An honest-to-God rebel." She yanked my hand across the table and shook it. "I knew you had it in you."

I retrieved my hand. "I don't know, Maryann. I only—"

"What you're doing takes guts. Listen to me." She thumbed her breastbone. "I know about guts. So you're plunked down in the middle of an uptight state that says, 'Midwifery Is Bad.'" She flashed her palms, illuminating an imaginary billboard. "It's not unlike yours truly strutting her stuff down the lily-white streets of St. Paul. I can't just be me. I've got to justify myself as a black woman who belongs here. Mind you, I say that *only* because I don't think you've got a choice. You find out who you are and step it out, you can't help but rip the social fabric."

I shook my head.

"Listen. Truth is explosive. If you start being real, everything you thought was just going about your business is enormous. Powerful, threatening. I get it, honey." She patted my bare arm.

I pressed fingers to my forehead.

"So," Maryann started in again, "you've drawn an arbitrary line: no breeches."

"It's not arbitrary! I don't know squat about delivering breeches. Even if I did and everything went fine, I'd be out a backup doctor. I'd wind up behind another reception desk for the rest of my life. Or in the slammer. *That's* not serving my mothers."

"Ha! You could write a letter from the Hiawatha County Jail. 'One has a moral responsibility to disobey unjust laws.'"

Maryann was relentless. "That's not me," I said, although later I was forced to reconsider it.

"Exactly what you said about birthing babies."

I *had* said midwifery was beyond my scope then discovered my latent longing. I wondered at what point I could live happily within my personality's boundaries.

I lit into lunch. The Swiss cheese was bland, the crust stale. I might be willing to duck unobtrusively under the law's wire for a practice I believed in, but blatant defiance of my own good sense, of common sense, for a cause as ambiguous as a home-delivered breech?

Maryann pushed the napkin dispenser aside and leaned across the table. "Did I ever tell you about how I was born?"

I recognized her maneuver; if the mother's not progressing, change her position. I crossed my arms. "You remember coming out."

"I do. But this story I learned from my mama, and from my Aunt Mimi, who did laundry for the hospital. So it's South Carolina, 1952. That's the segregated South, mind you, meaning the maternity ward's upstairs near the OR with individual rooms and great staff-patient ratios, and the colored ward's five floors down—one big underground cavern with dozens of laboring women, not enough beds, and a spattering of nurses. Probably the newbies. The white ladies were all narcotized—Demerol, morphine—because, you know, they're delicate flowers, they faint a lot, and they need to be saved from the terrors of childbirth. Sometimes they were so out of it the nurses used four-point psychiatric restraints to prevent them from falling out of bed. They either slept through contractions or got combative and bit the nurses. Mimi says they lost one or two babes for every twenty-five. In the end, docs used the husband stitch to sew women up good and tight, so the menfolk could enjoy themselves.

"Supposedly the coloreds were more primitive and animal-like and didn't need all that fuss. Mama didn't have a bed and just paced the ward with seven other women. They leaned against each other during contractions. Can't you see it? Holding hands, squatting back to back. When Mama was ready to deliver, the nurse comes over and says, "Let's get you upstairs to Delivery." Mama sure as hell didn't want to leave her pregnant friends and have some white masked doctor deliver her, so in the elevator going up she gives a mighty push. And there I was"—Maryann grinned proudly—"screaming bloody murder, unlike those drugged blue babies upstairs. Sometimes privilege isn't all it's made out to be."

My horror at Maryann's story was subsumed by the suspicion that I was being chastised. "Why are you telling me this?"

"Think about it, Hannah. There's a wealth of untapped knowledge down in the basement. You can access it. You stay down there with the women who are awake, or you can say, 'Sorry. My hands are tied.'" She held her hands up in dainty, pitiful surrender.

A flush rose up my neck. I hadn't driven two hours in ruthless heat to be bullied into a dangerous delivery and given a guilt trip about race.

"I've a notion," she said. "Come along." She slid the Saran-wrapped cookies into her purse, rose, and lifted me by the arm. "I want to show you something."

Once again I was trailing Maryann down a hallway, chafing under her preposterous expectations. We walked at her Chicago clip up a sloped corridor that linked the hospital to the clinic, although from inside it seemed like a contiguous blank-walled maze. Framed blotches of pastel watercolors signaled we'd arrived. Here were the exam rooms where, two and a half years ago, I'd watched Maryann interview clients and where my old insecurities still resided. *Who was I, to think I could do this?* We turned into the back office. Maryann's cubical had a window, I suppose due to seniority. She'd draped the gray-speckled plastic of the dividers with bolts of velvet, royal blue and green, and her desk was cluttered with family snapshots.

"Sit." She pointed her chin at the metal radiator box beside the window. I pulled myself up and watched her lift a bristling keychain from her purse. She fingered the keys, plucking out a small aluminum one and fitting it into the lock of her desk's file drawer, which rolled out, empty except for a long black scrapbook. "Here's my misdemeanor." She set the album on the desk, where we could both read it. "We're not supposed to keep patient information. Screw that." The cover was blank. When she opened it, I knew exactly what Maryann had done—created a portfolio. The broad archival pages were black, inscribed with white ink in Maryann's old-fashioned script. Orderly columns were interspersed with photographs and greeting cards I assumed to be thank you notes tucked into black photo corners. Each entry was dated in the left column. Maryann ran her polished red nail down the margin, searching for a date.

"Wow," I said. "How many have you done?"

Maryann's hand flattened against the desk. "I count on New Year's Eve, so I don't have this year's numbers. Last year my grand total was six hundred and thirty-four." I whistled appreciatively. "We do a higher volume than you'll ever get, which means I hardly know them. I've got to write them down or I forget. Each baby's a blessing, you know. Even the ones who don't make it. I can't let quantity numb out my appreciation." She turned another page and tapped a date with her nail.

"Here we go—Trisha. I'd seen her off and on for prenatal care—nothing unusual except she was a bit overweight, which made her hard to palpate. Someone else had done her final visit, Sianna McCollough, and then Trisha shows up on the ward one night in advanced labor. We do an ultrasound, and the baby's breech. I'm spitting nails. I call up Sianna and chew her out. Poor Sianna swears up and down she'd presented fine just days ago, that the baby must have flipped. So I give her the benefit of the doubt. We prep Trisha for surgery because that was the policy—still is, although they cut us more slack these days. Just before the doc cuts her open, he does one final check and lo and behold, the baby's fine, presenting headfirst, just knocking at the door to get out.

"Doc turns to me like I'm some imbecile. I'm thinking, did I read her wrong? So they attach a fetal monitor, get these fabulous heart tones, and decide to go for a vaginal delivery. Next thing you know, the baby's crowning, only instead of a head it comes out buttfirst, with the flipping fetal monitor stuck up its ass. The readings must have been haywire. The baby lands in my hands, no problem, with the doctor looking on in shock— he's never seen such a thing. As far as I can figure, the baby was doing somersaults in labor. Unbelievable." Maryann tapped the scrapbook entry. "Brendon Lee. That's what they named the baby. I'll bet he's a gymnast now."

"That's crazy." Babies in labor usually lodge themselves into the birth canal, too far along to move. But Sunny used to say when it comes to birth, anything goes. Just when you think you've seen it all, along comes an alien baby.

"You know the most amazing part of the story? A couple years later, we're kibitzing in the lounge and I say, 'Remember that breech baby that kept turning?' The attendant nurse and the doc both denied that it happened. They laughed at me and said it was impossible. Made me doubt myself all over again until I came back and read these notes. The truth itself isn't slippery, but our memory of it is." Maryann shut and smoothed the cover. Then she said, as much to herself as me, "Sometimes I think half our job as midwives is to remember the truth."

I stretched my legs flat on the radiator and gazed at the sidewalk. Summer grilled the city. Wet blotches stained pedestrians' armpits, and passing cars were sealed tight. I loved Maryann for remembering her babies despite the rules, for delivering the bottom-down baby under the doctor's nose, for preserving the story, for telling it to me. I thought again of her tender palm reaching across the cafeteria tabletop, exposing its lifelines, and her reprimand, "How you're born always matters." Only now I realized it matters not just for the baby. It matters for posterity, for the sake of birth itself.

"So here's one truth I believe in, Hannah. Vaginal breeches can be safe. The hospitals and insurance companies will regulate them up the wazoo, and that means over time we'll lose the skills to deliver them naturally. That knowledge is endangered, almost extinct."

Maryann strained the springs in her chair-back. Her leopard-print blouse pulled tight around her breasts, and she drummed her fingers on the arms of the chair.

I exhaled. "I don't know, Maryann. I'm all for preserving natural birth for the sake of the human race. But Melinda . . . Is it worth risking my practice for a cause hardly anyone cares about?"

Maryann's face soured.

"*I* care," I said. "*You* care. But what if the rest of the world would prefer a mechanical birth? What if we're fighting to preserve something no one really wants?"

"Your mother wants it."

It took me a moment to realize she meant Melinda and not my mother, who from her grave in the Chester Prairie First Lutheran Cemetery or during her sixty-one years had never given two thoughts, as far as I knew, to the preservation of natural birthing techniques. Still, my momentary confusion opened the possibility—no, the likelihood—that the crisis of my birth had pained my mother, even if her staunch praise for Jorgenson suggested otherwise.

Maryann picked up a fat ballpoint emblazoned with a pharmaceutical logo and copied down a name and number from a phone list posted on the wall. "Here." She handed it to me. "Bessie's down in Florida. She's one of the granny midwives, learned her trade from her grandmother who was a slave. I met her at a MANA Conference a few years ago. She won the Sage Femme Award. She's done thousands of births. I'm not exaggerating. She could tell you about vaginal breeches."

I bristled. "I can't just call her out of the blue."

"Why not?"

A complicated tangle of reverence for this midwife's experience and weird self-consciousness about race constricted my throat. "I'm not going to deliver Melinda."

"You should know how, regardless."

Of course she was right. "Why can't you teach me?"

Maryann huffed. "I've only done a handful, the ones that come out too fast for the doctor to get there. Look, Hannah, you're a big midwife now. You've seen the Ina May Gaskin video?" I nodded. "That's about as good a lesson as you'll get. And talk to Bessie."

I dismounted the radiator. "I'm supposed to learn breech delivery over the phone?"

"No. You're supposed to become a better midwife."

I spread my arms for the obligatory hug—I'd had about all of Maryann I could take. She pursed her lips and stood. Her body was munificent. I held her tight. "You're not much help, you know," I told her. "You always complicate things."

"Good. Here," she said, extracting a mammoth cookie from her purse. Later, on the drive north, while butter and chocolate softened in my mouth, I missed my mother, suddenly, bitterly. Tears blurred my vision, and I had to pull over. Mom was gone. I would never know how she felt about giving up her nursing dream or about the emergency of my birth. She had abandoned me to a world where black women were neglected, white women overmedicated, and birth itself was broken. I didn't know the right thing to do. I was on my own, my mother's only daughter, traffic rushing past and rocking the car in its wake.

33.

Sage Femme

"YOU'RE THE TOWN midwife?"

I leaned into the kitchen counter. "I guess." With my name and phone number posted in prudently selected bathrooms across Hiawatha County, answering the phone was an adventure. I only wished it rang more often.

"Any chance you could help me and my partner inseminate?"

The couple landed on my stoop the next morning, Lori wearing a man's cotton work shirt, her voice husky with cigarettes and a serious set to her jaw, Soo Young hip in narrow-banded sunglasses and a miniskirt. Their being lesbians didn't throw me so much as that they were *here*, in run-of-the-mill Chester Prairie, in my house. Lori explained they were renting an apartment over the Hitching Post while she finished her cabinetry certificate at the technical college. Soo Young did copy editing for an advertising agency in Michigan via the Internet and was desperate for kids.

"We want tons," she said, a mischievous smile spreading across her face. I eyed the faux leather hugging her nonexistent hips.

"I grew up around here," Lori said. "I know better than to try the local docs. We planned to do the insemination ourselves and trek down to the Cities for the birth, but then Soo Young saw your flyer. We figured, hey, it's worth a shot."

The two educated me about the sperm bank they'd chosen and their need to optimize their chances of getting pregnant since money was tight. We discussed vaginal versus cervical versus tubal implantation. I taught them how to chart Soo Young's cycle more accurately and suggested herbal teas and vitamins to increase her fertility. We agreed to try an intrauterine insemination two weeks later at their apartment.

In the meantime, they'd peruse the sperm donor catalogue. "They're all med students," Soo Young whined. "I want an upstanding pipefitter or landscape artist."

How could I have spent a quarter of a century in this town and never have met a lesbian, never conversed with the Mexicans working at the Shoenfield plant, never encountered anyone, really, who didn't drink church coffee or know to turn a check upside down in the offering plate? The phone number of a slave's granddaughter was pinned to my kitchen bulletin board. My best friend was a fairy delivering babies in Mexico. My father's intern had a nose ring, tattoo, and believed in some punk-rock version of Christianity I couldn't fathom. Perhaps Maryann was right, and my whole life I'd been living up on the white ward in a haze of painkillers, assuming the restraints were for my own good. I'd had no idea how compelling the basement ward could be.

With Lori and Soo Young's visit as inspiration, I unpinned Maryann's note and dialed the Florida phone number. Six rings. An elderly voice drawled, "Morning."

"Hi. I'm looking for Bessie Jones."

"May I ask who's calling?"

"My name's Hannah Larson. Maryann Brownson gave me this number. I'm a midwife, and I was hoping—"

"Just a minute." I heard her shout, "Ma! Ma, wake up. It's a member of your fan club."

I heard a loud clatter as the receiver fell to the floor, followed by muffled grunts. I was sure the call was futile and rude. But I'd been second-guessing myself since my trip to St. Paul; I had ordered the Gaskin video, which made breech birth look as easy as turning a doorknob, and reread the relevant textbook chapters with their itemized, can-do instructions. When I'd written my protocol, I copied most of it from Maria and Sunny. The Minnesota Midwives Guild guidelines were similar, so it wasn't like I was out in left field. Except we were *all* out in left field, we lay midwives delivering less than one percent of the U.S. population; we'd made our own set of rules and were playing our own little ballgames. Maryann's suggestion, that we could mess with these rules as well, was crazy-making.

"Hello?" Bessie's voice was a cracked whisper.

"Sorry to disturb you, ma'am." I explained who I was and my connection to Maryann in such a hurry I doubt Bessie understood a word. "It's just that I've got a breech baby coming, and I guess you're one of the few experts on vaginal deliveries."

"You got yourself a footer? That it?"

"Actually, it's frank."

"I done me nineteen hundred and seven births, you know. Only lost one mama, bless her soul. Five stillbirths and one death to complications is my track record. That with folks going hungry. You know I'm ninety-two years old?"

"That's remarkable," I said.

"Started in 1938. I delivered half this here township."

"I hear you got the MANA award for it. Congratulations."

"Them ladies, woo-wee! I tell you, us midwives can party."

I leaned into the kitchen doorway, wrapping a finger in phone cord coils. "I was wondering, I mean, do you have any special techniques for turning babies? I know it's hard long distance and all—"

"Turn a breech? Why would you want to do that?"

I rested my forehead on the doorframe.

"A backward baby's a sign of specialness. Coming into the world on his own terms. You don't mess with a spirit like that, no ma'am."

"So you deliver breeches."

"Wait 'til the mama's open, grease her up, and get on your knees. The good Lord listens when we're near the earth. Besides, the catching's easier."

I waited while Bessie coughed. "And you've never had a problem?"

"Problem? Honey, each birth's how it is. We gotta take what comes our way, and all of us got hardship."

"But what if you could have done something differently? What if you could have saved that one mother?"

"As I see it, the good Lord giveth and the good Lord taketh away."

Bile rose to my mouth. This was my father's line. God willed Dad to serve the Chester Prairie congregation and Jorgenson to rescue me from the womb and the Hebrew midwives to spare rather than murder the newborn boys. I didn't buy any of it. To have a mother or baby die and just shrug, saying the Lord gives, the Lord takes away—it was unconscionable.

"You'll do just dandy with your breech," she said. "Now, what was your name?"

"Hannah. Hannah Larson."

"Oh, yes. I remember you from Pittsburgh. Woo-wee, that was some party. You're sweet to call me."

"I . . . Thanks for talking with me, Mrs. Jones."

"Bless you, child."

That was it. Sure, Bessie was remarkable, but why had Maryann insisted I call? I went out to the front steps for air. The lawn needed mowing. I wanted to trim the lilacs before next year's buds set—the landlords certainly wouldn't. I bent over to yank errant clover from between the spirea bushes. A crow heckled me from the boulevard.

The stats, I realized. Maryann wanted me to hear Bessie's stats. If they were accurate, her results were better than those of the Birth House, better than Denmark's, better even than Michel Odent's hospital, and, given her community's poverty, hers was perhaps the most successful birth practice on record. Bessie had been far from negligent. In light of such good outcomes, I couldn't dismiss her attitude toward breeches as superstitious or her faith as misguided. The turbulent humility Maryann induced in me returned to my stomach. I tossed the weeds and went inside to watch the breech video yet again. At the very least, I had to pay attention.

34.

Nudge

HERE IS THE secret to being a good midwife: In every woman are two compelling and contradictory forces. The first says a mighty NO to birth. Out of safety or familiarity or pride, this force yanks women away from the wellspring of their power. The second shouts YES. It is the creative impulse, the source of our resilience and spark. It desires more than anything to be born.

In childbirth these forces play tug of war with a woman. Your job is to direct her YES inward, downward, until it's concentrated on labor. Only when a woman surrenders to her own life-giving power does a baby emerge. But remember, something else emerges as well: a new woman howling with all of human suffering lodged in her groin, aware now that life begins regardless.

Serve her.

* * *

"I might ask Mike not to be there."

We weren't even seated. Melinda tossed her purse on the massage table and pulled out the toy basket for Kevin. "Of course I really want him to catch the baby and cut the cord. I just can't stand his naysaying." She squared herself on the edge of the overstuffed chair and crossed her arms. "I need to do this, give birth like a normal woman. I won't be robbed of it a second time."

I pulled my chair close and waited while Kevin tugged at her shorts, whining. She asked him cheerlessly to make her a rocket ship.

"We'll do our best." I meant Mike, Melinda, and myself, but it came out sounding haughty. "It's just that birth is unpredictable. You and I can't control it any more than the doctors can."

"Unpredictable I can handle, Hannah. It's abnormal I'm fighting here. Mike keeps saying, 'Someone in your condition,' as though I'm prone to heart failure. I'm pregnant, for Christ's sake. The baby happens to be breech. Breech is a normal variation. How many zillions of women throughout history have been in my shoes and come out fine?"

I smoothed wrinkles from my skirt, weighing a small portion of mortal danger against heaps of normality.

"I'm sick of him harping. Especially about unnecessary suffering, as though I'm torturing *him*. There's worse things than pain. I thought when we found you he'd stop, that we'd settled on homebirth. With the baby breech, he's relentless. And it's not just him—it's my whole family. They're not listening to the facts—they're not listening to *me*." She pressed her hands into the cushion and locked her elbows.

"Melinda." I steadied my voice. "We need to consider *why* the baby's breech. Sometimes the position signals another issue. The cord might be short, for example. And it's easy for breech babies to get stuck. They start descending before you're fully dilated, get their head caught with the cord wedged in, and you've got minutes, that's all, before brain damage starts. We have to take this very seriously."

Kevin turned to his mother, wide-eyed. Melinda ignored him,

lowering her voice. "I'm fully aware of that, Hannah Larson."

Heat flashed in my face.

"I'm sorry," I said. "Let's not get ahead of ourselves. We've got six weeks until you're due. Time for the baby to turn, time to educate Mike about homebirths. Think about it. For as long as women have been birthing babies, men have been scared shitless." Her posture softened minutely. "I'll give him some reading material. Meanwhile, let's you and I focus on flipping that rascal." I gave her the number for an acupuncturist in the Cities, which she received gladly, and for a doctor who did external versions, at which she frowned. My mind spun through the rolodex of bizarre turning techniques. "You could try swimming. Your abdominal muscles relax, and some people say deep water immersion increases your amniotic fluid. More room for the baby to turn."

"I can do that."

"It might not hurt to ease up on the work. This is just a hunch, but the baby might dislodge if you relax."

"Work is my refuge. Besides, most mothers in the world don't stop working to have a baby."

"Most mothers don't have breech babies."

Melinda's body drew back like a bow.

"Melinda, if you wind up in the hospital, I'll stick with you the whole time. I'll be your advocate. I promise. It's part of my deal with Jorgenson."

Earlier that week I'd finally tested that deal, once for a newborn with high respirations and once for a client who wanted meds mid-labor. I'd served as a doula, wiping brows and whispering encouragement. Bill had ignored me. I left the hospital both grateful for Bill's backup and fuming that we had to work that way.

Melinda bit her lip and examined Kevin's Lego construction, far more elaborate than what he'd built two months ago. Then she stood. "Can we get on with this?"

By the end of the appointment, my back muscles were lumpy with knots. I needed to figure out what was driving Melinda, what else I was responsible for midwifing besides her ill-placed baby. When I'd first met her, I assumed she was pulled forward by her passion for growing things and tripped up by pride. She reminded me of Carol Simic. Now that the baby had folded itself into the nest of her pelvis, I was less certain. Her stubbornness seemed to spring not from ego but from some lower source, as though rising from the earth through her feet. With Melinda I couldn't tell the push from the pull, the resistance from the exuberant life. I didn't know how to be her midwife. Instead I invested my energy in wishing: Given a nudge, the baby might yet turn.

.

35.

Ambulatory Mamas

EARLY JULY EXHALED humidity into my attic room. Hot and sticky, I dreamed of floating on Little Long's simmering surface, semiconscious, upheld . . . and shook myself awake. It was Sunday morning—no need to simply dream. I climbed into my suit and shorts, slung a beach towel around my neck, and walked out the back door barefoot—why not?—into the gleeful world of cardinal song and white-throated sparrows. The sidewalk concrete was cool, the streets shaded. In fifteen minutes I was at the town limits. The cornfields were hip deep, leaves bending and erasing the furrows. Out here the pavement was warm and coarse. Red-winged blackbirds scolded and swooped from telephone wires. The sun sunk hot fingers into my back. I left County Road N and descended the sloped street. I hung my towel and pager from a dock post at the public boat launch and strode into the water.

The surface was sluggish, pocked by bubbles, limey smelling. Here, willows and silver maples cast green shadows, and ducks rustled in the reeds, occasionally parading, bottom heavy, onto the warm dock. To my right, the houses' sliding glass doors blazed with reflected sun. Across the lake, a single silver fishing boat crept along the shore. A morning wind opened stretch marks on the surface. I pushed through the water's initial shock with a rush of strokes. Under the water, needles of light pierced through to the silty basin bottom. The lake lifted me. I turned over, skull cupped by water, limbs propelling me toward a wisp of cloud on the southern horizon. By the time I'd reached the center of the lake, the trailing white had burned away.

I thought of Dad in church at that moment, standing in his elevated, isolated spot behind the chancel rail, deftly paging through the hymnal and offering up round-toned praise. Worship buoyed Dad. Swimming did the same for me, cleansing, refreshing, not just skin but also that secret inner beacon that beckoned me to take on the world, or midwifery at least, despite my better judgment. I wanted to heed that beacon in my interactions with Dad, with Melinda, with Bill Jorgenson, but kept losing sight of it. And the costs—a failed relationship with sweet, solid Leif, potentially my midwifery practice—at times seemed too great.

Down the way, a passel of kids tumbled from a house, rending the quiet with their high, happy chatter. Deer flies descended from nowhere. I swam back toward the beach, each stroke bringing me closer to the muck of my life. Melinda had fourteen days until her thirty-sixth week, when external versions work best. She'd yet to show any interest. Dad's public pronouncement a month ago hung unexplained and unacknowledged between us. And was it really feasible for me to make a living in this town? I'd been avoiding breaking the bad tax news to Cathie. My client load was unpredictable. Flies landed in my hair; I whipped the towel like a lasso and stood on the dock to dry.

Back out on the road, the pavement seared, and I regretted my impulsive choice to go barefoot. I picked my way along the ditch, watching for glass. Behind me a horn blared. I turned to see a dented red pickup hauling a trailer and boat—Bill. I waved. He slowed just ahead, blocking the eastbound lane. I kept walking, now conscious of my mussed hair, wet shorts, and bare legs.

Bill bent across the front seat and pushed the passenger door into my path.

"Well, if it isn't the resident subversive. Hop in."

"I'm happy walking."

"Don't be stupid. You're not wearing shoes." The band of Bill's fishing hat was discolored, the brim frayed. His nose had burned and peeled and burned again, a splotched, cancer-prone red. "I've had a mind to call you. Can we chat now instead?"

I looked toward town. "I'm wet."

He patted the seat. The well of the passenger's side was littered with McDonald's wrappers and gas station receipts. Yellow foam mushroomed from a split in the vinyl. The hinges crunched when I pulled the door shut. Bill shifted and leaned into the gas, his white-whiskered chin extended over the wheel.

"Good swim?"

"Blissful." I lifted the towel from my neck and covered my pallid thighs. "Catch anything?"

"A few Z's. And some smallmouth bass."

"Where?"

"On the Rum. Out by Stanchfield Minor." The motor whined; he wrenched the truck from first gear to second. "That's as much information about my secret fishing spot as you'll wheedle out of me."

I held my hands up in surrender. On the south side of the road, the corn bowed in broad sweeps.

Bill yanked the stick shift into third and took an exceptionally long time clearing his phlegmy throat.

"Now, I'm not one to meddle in other people's business, but a man can't help but feel protective. And, if truth be told, it's not me, it's the hospital regs I'm trying to abide by, their goddamn quotas and standards and whatnot. If it'd only happened once, I'd think it was a fluke. But now it's twice."

I had learned to wait out Bill's irritating preambles.

At the edge of town he concentrated on downshifting, the truck wheezing against the forward thrust of boat and trailer. "What exactly are you teaching in those birth classes of yours? Because I've had two women refuse to stay put. Supposedly students of yours."

"What do you mean?"

"They fight getting IVs. They get out of bed. Walk the halls. One even left the premises. An orderly had to chase her down."

I bit back a smile. Cindy and Dominique had both called this week with their happy news.

"I'm peeved, Hannah."

"And walking is an issue because—"

"By the time we get her back and hooked up to the monitor, she's already pushing. Hell's bells. We wind up in crisis mode, she's spitting out the baby so fast. And the other lady kept hopping out of bed. It throws off the readings. I don't have time for crap like that. Next thing you know, the insurers will hunt me down." Bill glowered at the road.

I felt proud of my students, and emboldened. "You know those baby monitors are inaccurate," I said.

Bill swung the steering wheel left, around the schoolyard crawling with my church-skipping neighbors, and stepped on the emergency brake in front of my house. "That may be true, but let me tell you, I would have given a pretty penny for one at your birth."

I was supposed to feel small and grateful and awe-inspired. Instead I sensed a window opening: My birth was not some distant, inert event; it was dynamic, relevant, a force shaping Bill's generosity and my own conflicted path. *It matters,* I heard Maryann whisper. Out loud I asked, "Why? What happened?"

"Let's not digress," Bill said. "The administration sets the regs. I'm just saying my job's gotten harder since you came to town. The plan was for you to lighten my load, not teach my patients how to resist me every step of the way."

"That's *not* what I'm doing. Come to class and see for yourself. I teach women to ask for what they need during labor, that's all."

"Exactly!" Bill smacked his fist against the seat. "They don't know what's best. I do. Damn it, Hannah, you're getting on my nerves."

Sun beat through the cab roof. I was sweaty and sticky again, despite my swim.

"When a woman walks during labor, she progresses faster," I said. "Your administrators aren't taking that into account. Besides, it sounds like the insurance companies are making your job harder, not me. I'm just easier to pick on."

I pulled the handle and the door crunched open. When I looked back and saw Bill's stomach pushing out his dirty white undershirt and his clenched, sunburnt jowls, I had trouble remembering why I'd held this man in such high esteem. I let loose an audible sigh and met his eyes. "Listen, Bill, I'm sorry things are getting harder for you. I never intended for that to happen."

He wagged his finger at me. "If it wasn't for your folks . . .," he began.

"What about them?"

"Never mind." He shook his head, leaving me poised at the edge of my unspeakable past. "You feminists get under my skin. Okay. Have it your way. Teach my patients their options. Just know I'm not happy about it."

"We both want the same thing, Bill. Healthy births, healthy moms. We've got different methods, that's all." I turned and slid down to the fiery pavement.

"Listen, Hannah, you're a good kid." He peeled off his hat and used it to wipe the sweat from his head. "I'm trying to look out for both of us. It's harder than I bargained, that's all."

I studied Bill's sorry nose, his strangely frantic eyes, and felt in me that familiar tension between sinking fear and this burgeoning bravery, between some hidden, festering shame and the miracle of my birth. I slammed the cab door and leaned into the open window.

"I appreciate your efforts," I offered by way of reconciliation. "And the lift. Let's keep trying, shall we?"

Bill thrust the truck back into gear. "You take after your dad, you know that?"

I was glad to hear it.

Bill offered a two-fingered salute, and then his truck and trailer lurched forward. A thread of lake water stained the street behind him and began to steam.

36.

Coronations

TWO WEEKS LATER, I sped past Chester Prairie's outer ring of tract houses with their treeless lawns and explosions of wilting rhubarb, then between corn rows tall enough for children to get lost in. Hot wind bent the stalks eastward and blew the black smell of baking soil through the open windows of Mom's old Dodge. The land swelled and contracted. The pavement rolled the car over fields and sunken marshland, and I felt for this place an affection too large to have originated with me. Surely it passed through my grandparents' blood, both sides farmers and children of farmers who worked the rough hills of Sweden until they emigrated, building their new homes from sod cut off the plains. Or my love arrived more immediately through my mother, who planted a garden worthy of any farmer's wife. Sunday afternoons she would sit on the arm of the sofa beside my father and his newspaper. "Let's go for a drive," she'd say. Speeding across the countryside, Mom would take in the fields and sky as though they were basic nourishment—communion, perhaps, although she'd never call it that.

Melinda was at thirty-six weeks—time for a home visit.

Maria and Sunny had taught me the wisdom of scoping out the birth site in case there's no running water or the parents need help making the room sanitary. When a midwife appears at your house doing an ordinary checkup, pouring a glass of water and helping you up from bed, birth at home becomes imaginable. Confidence around birth is portable. You tote it with your kit and unfold it like a warming blanket. The mothers feel it.

The road's rise and dip made me jubilant, and the hot-soil smell worked like coffee. When I spotted the green farm wagon and organic vegetables sign, I slowed for the turnoff. The drive wound down through a thicket of trees, crossed the Rum River, and emerged on high ground at a tidy farmyard—the house a yellow clapboard foursquare with large windows and a porch, the pole barn a nondescript metal prefab big enough for equipment only. Overhead, a rusted windmill rocked in its socket. Chickens pecked the gravel and scattered. I cut the ignition.

As of Wednesday a week ago, the fetus hadn't moved. Melinda reported swimming daily at the high school, doing underwater handstands between each lap. She was also doing body tilts five times a day. When I had asked about Mike, she'd said, "It's safety this and safety that. What's really safe and what makes Mike feel safe are unrelated. In the end, it's not up to him."

I had reiterated my policy and set a deadline: "If the baby doesn't turn in two weeks, I won't deliver it." Melinda had nodded, her face expressionless.

When Maryann called to offer a few pointers, I told her I wasn't going to deliver a breech but I'd take her advice in case of an emergency. "Good," she'd said, "because I'm going to give it anyhow." During her half-hour lecture, I vacillated between annoyance at her persistence and pride that she assumed me capable. In the end she'd said, "You know why they crown royalty? To remind them of crowning at birth. They're born into a new role. Whatever you do, honey, wear your midwife crown."

Extending beyond the south side of the barn was the tail end of a hoop-framed greenhouse, where Melinda said she'd be working. White industrial plastic stretched over arched ribs. I squeezed past a gigantic fan roaring in the doorway. The light was opaque here, the air stuffy and moist. A raised plank aisle cut between tomato plants drooping over their cages, prolific with heavy, flawless fruit. Past the tomatoes were peppers and eggplant and the herb beds, fragrant waist-high basil, sage bushes, a carpet of parsley. At the far end there was a slop sink, a hose slung on a hook, and another fan drawing in fresh air above the doorway. Melinda bent over a notebook at a workbench. Her overalls hung loose at the bib, tightened around her middle then dangled widely at her legs. From the thick denim rolls at her ankles, I guessed they were Mike's. Her bare arms, elbows pressed into the table, were flexed and muscular. Sun blazed through the arch of taut plastic and shone on her skin, giving her the radiance of a woman in prayer. I'd never seen her so soft.

The plank walkway ended, and I stepped onto packed earth. "Morning," I said loudly.

She straightened and took the pencil she'd been chewing out of her mouth. "You found us!" Curls sprang from her fat braid and her smile was eager, generous. "Kevin, Hannah's here. Come say hello."

There was a small scuffle under the table. I crouched to my heels. "How's it going down there?"

"I'm cooking," Kevin said. His blond bangs stuck to his forehead in pointy triangles. He held up a wooden spoon caked with dirt.

"Whatcha making?"

He looked down at an aluminum pie tin, a trowel, and a headless action figure. A few half-buried matchbox cars pointed their bumpers upward like sprouting bulbs. "Muffles."

"Waffles," Melinda said.

"Mmm. Can I have some?"

He frowned, dug into the ground then raised the spoon. My enthusiastic chewing got him to grin.

"Impressive," I said to Melinda, gesturing around the greenhouse. "You do it yourself?"

Melinda shut the pencil between pages of her notebook. "Mike lends a hand on the weekends and evenings. In the spring especially. And I have a few interns. Want to see the fields?"

We left Kevin and climbed a path of dandelions to the top of the rise. There, the unkempt grass ended in a crisp line and garden began. I guessed she was working four acres; beyond kale, chard, broccoli, cabbage, and other vegetables lay a vast blanket of corn. A few mullein and dock weeds had cropped up between the rows—hardly the rude mess I'd expected.

"I didn't realize you worked on this scale. You must sell more than at your stand."

"Oh, that." She brushed off her roadside business. "No, I supply restaurants in the Cities and a couple food co-ops."

Her enterprise demonstrated business savvy and bullheaded determination—and a love of growing things. My respect for Melinda burgeoned.

"This is my seventh year. Next year we won't lease out the western acreage, and I'll triple the corn. It takes ten years without chemicals before you can claim organic status, so I'll just sell it in town."

"A big undertaking."

Her smile was lustrous.

We turned toward the house, Melinda calling repeatedly for Kevin and finally towing him by his grubby hand while I held open the screen door.

Inside, the kitchen smelled of laundry soap. Breakfast dishes were piled in the sink, a tabby cat leapt down from the counter, and a washing machine slushed in the corner, clothes piled in lights and darks on the linoleum. Kevin whined for juice then made a beeline for the kitchen table, draped with red-checkered oilcloth. He sat underneath, working a sippy cup.

"How're you doing?" I asked Melinda, pulling out a kitchen chair. She ran the tap, testing the temperature with her wrist before filling two glasses.

"Sluggish. The baby hasn't budged, if that's what you're after."

The glass was already perspiring when she handed it to me. The water smelled of sulfur. "Any other movement?"

Melinda sat a few feet away from the table, her hands on either side of her swelling abdomen. "Kicking. Starting at four in the morning, right in the groin. It wakes me up, and then I'm famished. This morning I devoured a whole ham sandwich, and I don't even like ham."

I laughed. "Guess the baby does. Are you able to nap?"

"Yesterday I went down with him." She nodded toward the table. "Not my usual practice. It's hard to lose daylight hours. But then, if I'm starting at four—"

I whistled. "That makes a long day. Besides, you're doing everything for two." I left it at that. "How about shortness of breath?"

Melinda took a long sip. "Nothing I can't handle. What do you want to see? The bedroom?"

"That depends on where you envision giving birth. If the baby turns."

A grin spread across her freckled face. "If you really want to know, I imagine squatting in the greenhouse. But I'm willing to compromise, despite what you think. So I guess the bedroom."

"Is there room to move around?"

Melinda heaved herself up. "I'll show you."

She led me across the living room's worn rag rug strewn with Kevin's toys and up steep, painted steps. The blinds were down in the bedroom, the bed unmade, the blue walls empty. The hoop house would be more welcoming. I could imagine the summer night, the translucent walls preserving the day's warmth, the hushed company of tomatoes and whispering dill fern, how the moon would whitewash our faces, Melinda's blood fertilizing the soil, and the baby landing in a place intended for growth. Sunny and Maria would have plugged in a hot plate to warm water, spread a tarp, and let it happen—so long as the baby wasn't breech. I wished I could make a birth like that possible. Then I considered the chaos of it, the dirt and the danger.

"This will work," I said with false cheeriness. "There's room to walk in the hallway. Maybe we could move out that chest; we'll need space for Mike to hold you. Where's the bathroom?"

Across the hall was a closetlike room with a miniature clawfoot tub, toilet, and an enamel sink plastered with toothpaste and hair.

"Sometimes a bath can provide relief during labor." I chose my words carefully. "It might be smart to scrub it ahead of time."

Melinda's nod was barely perceptible.

Back downstairs, we went through the box of supplies I'd asked Melinda to gather: plastic bedcover, disposable underpads, a hot water bottle for the receiving blankets, diapers. A few items on the list she'd have to add at the last minute, like a stock of food in the fridge and cookie trays for me to lay out my supplies. I saw myself on autopilot, normalizing every aspect of the birth as though the breech position was temporary. I feared that proceeding this way fed Melinda's hopes and made me complicit in a deed in which I wanted no part.

"Olive oil," I continued.

"What for?"

"To rub on the baby's bottom. Remember how the first poop is sticky, like tar? Meconium's sloughed-off cells that've accumulated throughout gestation. The oil makes it easier to clean. You'll also need honey for your menstrual pads. It's a natural antibiotic."

Melinda relaxed into the sofa. She looked at me with cautious admiration.

I raised the question of erythromycin and vitamin K for the baby, both standard medications administered in hospitals which I offered as options but strongly recommended. Some parents dislike injecting their newborns; others jump at the chance to prevent any serious illness. Melinda squinted. "They just did that on Kevin without asking?"

"They're both standard in the hospital."

She considered a moment, and then said, "It's nice to have a choice. Let me talk it over with Mike."

We listened to the heartbeat through the handheld Doppler.

The underwater shush-shush-shush drew Kevin from his kitchen-table tent. He leaned his body against the couch. "That's the baby," I explained.

"Sprout," Kevin said, resting his ear on his mother's tummy.

She scratched his head. "We're looking forward to meeting Sprout, aren't we?"

He gave her exposed skin a wet kiss.

When Kevin pushed off, I asked, "Will Kevin be at the birth?"

Melinda hoisted herself onto her elbows. "Do you think that's a good idea? We were going to take him to his grandparents'. I mean, I never considered him staying here."

"There's no reason why not, so long as someone's around to explain what's happening. It can be easier for kids because then they know exactly where babies come from."

Melinda evicted a pillow and lay back down. "I guess I assumed it'd be too traumatic. I don't know why. He's watched the neighbor's cow give birth."

"Talk it over. You'd have to find someone else to be with him. Mike'll be focused on you."

I measured her—thirty-six centimeters, on the mark—and pressed my fingers into the springy sphere of her belly. Sure enough, there was the spine, the knob of a head: Sprout's butt snug in her pelvis.

I pulled over a kitchen chair and sat down. "Have you thought about those referrals?" I asked. "Now's the time to do an external version."

Melinda shut her eyes.

"Melinda, it's not invasive. It's slow, nudging the baby bit by bit, through the skin."

"I don't think so."

"What makes you reluctant?"

She rolled her head to look at me. "A gut feeling."

"Okay. We need to be realistic then. It's fine preparing for a homebirth in case the baby turns, but we also need a contingency plan. Here's a list of midwives who deliver breeches"—I'd found four in the state of Minnesota—"although I should warn you none of them will travel. And they're not abiding by Guild standards, which I don't approve of. None have backup doctors." The thought made me ill. "I'd prefer you see an obstetrician."

Melinda's body contracted, pelvic muscles hitching her up; she gripped the sofa cushion, and the muscles in her arms grew taut.

"I don't get it, Hannah. One minute you're asking whether I want to give my kid erythromycin, and the next you're denying me a homebirth. What exactly do you stand for?"

I exhaled as quietly as I could. "I'm concerned—for you and for the baby."

"No." Melinda stood, roughly, to look down at me. I sensed her full strength, muscular limbs, skin tanned from outdoor labor, her ripe womb. "I know that. I also know how many breeches come out fine. And I'm assuming you do too." She pointed her finger at me and I thought, *So this is what it'd be like to deliver a baby at gunpoint.* "That's not what I'm asking. I want to know what's guiding you. Because there's concern for my safety, and then there's watching your own back. I've been down that road before, having people say they're caring for me when really they're violating me, shooting me up with drugs, taking my baby away out of concern for *his best interest*," she sneered, "and it's not going to happen again." She paced to the window, drew back the heavy curtain and let in muggy July light. Her back was a dark, rigid pole.

The defense I had ready—that I was guided by a bigger picture, a midwifery practice both practical and sustainable in a hostile climate so I might serve the largest number of women—suddenly seemed inappropriate. I remembered the platitudes I'd offered Carol Simic, felt a rush of uncertainty, and wondered if once again I was blinded by hang-ups I couldn't identify. What *was* guiding me? The way Melinda sought refuge in the view, a lush rise of corn, reminded me of Carol, who had taught me that a midwife's role in a pregnant woman's inner world was quite small. Perhaps this tight turning away was the closest Melinda came to crying. I deliberately pushed her question aside and approached the window. A hand on Melinda's shoulder would be too much. Proximity would do.

"Kevin's birth was a terrible violation. I'm sorry that happened."

Melinda sagged. "It wasn't just the hospital, although that was awful. It was everybody. The baby came out fine. He was healthy, and that was supposed to be enough. But what about me? Mike and my mom and everyone were focused on how plump he was, how his nose was just like his father's. And I felt this gush of love, like it was worth it for him, but underneath there's this secret that I had to be totally degraded for my baby to enter the world. And if I said so out loud I'd be selfish, because now I was a mom with a beautiful baby." She pressed her fingers into her womb. "I've decided to be selfish this time, Hannah. I've learned that part of being a good mother is staying true to yourself. It's not good for Kevin that I surrendered something so essential." She lowered her voice. "I resent him sometimes. I hate that."

Melinda's skin was lit by the window's diffuse, green light; her eyes were sad. Her confession set my head pounding. She'd named the unnameable—a mother could resent her child. Mom, despite her affection, despite her seemingly perfect mothering, had resented me. I was sure of it. Inside me, a mess of inarticulate hurt and anger and compassion arranged themselves around this awareness, and then I pushed them aside for Melinda. I could barely take in her beautiful, vehement conviction. I reached for her arm.

"It's not selfish," I whispered. "You're just being honest."

"You really think so?" Melinda seemed fragile. Her wrist was cool.

"Yes," I said, and then considered whether I meant it. Pretense and any resentment that ensued would only trip us up.

"Yes. It's your birth. You deserve respect." This was true in the hospital or out, breech or not. I took her hand. "It's possible to be treated respectfully *and* have a safe birth. That's what I stand for, Melinda, to answer your question. I'll do my best to guard your dignity, whatever happens. And your health. And the baby's. I hope you'll believe me."

She searched my face for evidence.

"If we're in the hospital, I won't leave you. I'll do everything I can to support you. I'll be the mama bear."

Melinda squeezed and released my fingers. "I ought to get back to work," she said, shifting her gaze to the fields.

I gathered my equipment and tussled Kevin's towhead. "You give your mom and Sprout lots of love, you hear?"

Kevin nodded gravely. We said our goodbyes, and I retreated to the car, where the vinyl seat burned my skin.

On the drive home I imagined Sprout, butt leisurely sunk into the Adirondack chair of Melinda's pelvis, her womb arced above like a plush red heaven, the atmosphere a thick ninety-eight point six degrees. Here was a strange amniotic planet. The sun neither rose nor set, and there was no reason for Sprout to imagine otherwise. Why move when your universe is shaped for you alone? Why leave? Perhaps Sprout had chosen to undermine Melinda's strident will or collude with Mike's nagging conventionality. Perhaps Sprout already knew fear, of cold air, of change. Or perhaps Sprout was busy counting invisible, internal stars, committing them to memory.

As I had that very first morning I'd met Melinda, I felt an aching affection for Sprout. We were compatriots in our reluctance to face forward. Sprout was self-contained, complete, settled, and—I felt certain—not going to turn.

37.

Insemination

THE SPERM ARRIVED in an aluminum tank the size of a space capsule; when Lori unscrewed the top, the steam of dry ice escaped. Soo Young and Lori's studio apartment included a kitchenette, table, and two chairs, a full-sized mattress on the floor and a few square feet of floor space. Lori sat cross-legged on the bed with the vial under her armpit, warming it up to body temperature. I knelt at the foot of the bed with the speculum. Soo Young wore nothing but an oversized Twins T-shirt, which twisted around her waist as she squirmed.

"And I thought this would be romantic," Lori said. She honked into a red paisley handkerchief. I wiped laughter tears from my eyes. We couldn't proceed until the bizarreness of the situation no longer triggered hysteria.

They had settled for a med student donor who drove a Harley and built houses with Habitat for Humanity. His picture in the "male order" catalogue showed a thirty-something, curly-haired dude straddling his bike. "All right, Daddy-dearest," Soo Young said, arranging herself on the bed and trying to frown.

I placed my hand on her hip to ease her twitching and

inserted the speculum. Soo Young grunted. "Not funny," she said.

Lori stroked Soo Young's smooth thigh. "Incoming master-baste-er."

"Don't," Soo Young sputtered.

Afterward, despite my advice, Soo Young did a handstand against the kitchen cupboards because she'd once seen a woman secure a pregnancy that way in a movie. Lori took a photo.

Before I left, I recommended some fervent—horizontal—lovemaking to get the hormones raging. "That's no hardship," Lori said.

I descended a grimy stairwell and emerged onto Main Street. Brick buildings and glass-plated storefronts, gas station on the corner, post office flag snapping in the wind—a town predictable on the surface, but sheltering within its rental apartments and tract housing and isolated farmsteads this radical intimacy. Maryann had told me to wear my midwife crown, and walking across town I understood I'd been granted a privilege, my birth bag a passport to the interior lives of my community. With Soo Young and Lori, I wore my crown easily, lightly. I set my own needs aside, serving them with authority and confidence. I worked from that sense of ministry I now shared with Dad.

Why, then, was it so hard with Melinda? I rounded the corner and saw her in my mind's eye against the bright glass of her living room window, drinking in the greening fields. All that burgeoning lushness, decisive pecking of hens, rain and warmth and black soil—they were her birthright. Of course she wanted this baby at home; it was only natural. I slapped a mosquito from my neck. Melinda had somehow knocked off my crown, and I was fumbling around, trying to retrieve it.

* * *

The week sprawled before me, hot, unscheduled, and sticky. At home I opened the kitchen and front doors, hoping for a cross breeze; I stirred a pitcher of instant iced tea and spread

Cathie's taxes across the kitchen table. The forms, once my refuge of competence, were now lifeless. I wanted to practice midwifery. The three appointments on my calendar for the rest of August—Melinda's on Monday, one of my Christian moms later in the week, and a new client interview—were meager, especially considering I would relinquish Melinda to Bill. Apprehension rose in me like the frantic saw of cicadas. How could I interrupt the beautiful continuity Melinda desired for her body and her baby? I was sweating and uncomfortable and couldn't concentrate. Maybe Dad had an extra fan in the attic. Maybe I should direct my energy productively, to cleaning the parsonage attic or—yes—Mom's sewing room. Awareness of Mom's resentment toward me weighed me down, doubled my own resentment. Maybe clearing out her possessions would bring me some closure.

On impulse I stood and dialed the Birth House. Maria answered. After catching up, I asked for her advice. "A breech birth at home?" she said. "In that political climate? *¡De ninguna manera!* Don't be ridiculous."

To hell with Maryann's crowns.

I'd no sooner hung up than the phone rang.

"¡Hermana!"

The wire crackled with distance. Stuart was hurried. Cal's grandmother had died, and they were taking the next flight to Chicago. They'd be in Madison for a couple of weeks around the funeral. Was I open to surprise visitors a week from Friday? They could borrow a car.

"Mi casa es tu casa," I replied. Company! Stu and Cal, coming to Chester Prairie! After saying goodbye, I shelved the taxes, ordered a coffee cake from the bakery, washed the windows, and cleaned the car. I walked to the library to research vegetarian recipes and write out a shopping list. Crouched between the stacks, I chose a potpie recipe that called for tofu—did Red Owl carry it?—and a bean salad. Chuck stood at the checkout desk while the librarian passed a red laser beam over a stack of books on Mexico. I was glad to see him. He bounced on the balls of his

feet. "Reading up for the youth trip," he explained. "How about you?"

I flashed the spiral-bound *Veggie Delites* and effused about Stuart and Cal coming from Allende and how Chuck could now meet them before his trip. Chuck's listening eyes were the color of lake water streaked hazel with sunlight. The front of his black T-shirt read, "WWJD: What would Jesus drive?"

"I'd love that," he said. "When?"

"A week from Saturday, say four o'clock. Stop by the house for a beer." The prospect of a gathering of friends was thrilling.

Chuck took a clumsy step backward into the librarian's desk. "That's just great. Really. Thanks. I'll be there."

He slid the books off the counter and stepped aside. When I was done checking out, we shared an awkward pause. Then he asked, "Say, is your dad okay?"

"I assume so." I hugged the cookbook. "Why?"

Chuck leaned on one foot, then the other, then bent to dump his books into a backpack. "I don't want to sound . . . I mean, he hasn't seemed himself since . . ." He threaded his fingers and cracked his knuckles. "Hannah, your dad didn't like me from the get-go."

I laughed. "No kidding."

"But now he's unpredictable. He gave me his blessing on the Mexico trip. Literally. 'Chuck, your heart's with Christ, and I give you my blessing.' " He held his hands behind his back and rocked stiffly in a perfect imitation of Dad, making me hoot. "Not that I'm complaining. And that sermon he preached about the midwives? He digressed from the lectionary. Hannah, he *never* digresses from the lectionary. The one time I tried, he tore me to shreds. You know, 'Our responsibility to honor tradition trumps mortal inclinations.' "

"That was because of me. He's not exactly subtle."

"I figured. He's just . . . less convicted now. Whatever you're doing"—he cupped his hand around my upper arm—"I'm grateful."

His touch was kind. "I'm not doing anything," I said.

"Just so you know." Chuck was so earnest, I laughed again and the nervous tension between us eased a notch. He ducked to retrieve his backpack. "I better go. See you next Saturday?" When he turned, I saw the white bicycle silkscreened across his back.

I ordered daisies from Cathie's teenage worker and printed up the monthly financials. At the bank my small deposit of midwifery fees and the few hundred in my account seemed enough, and the liquor store's glistening walls made me jubilant. We'd go for a swim! We'd drive out to Darwin to see the stupid ball of twine, or spend an evening down in the Cities, or just sit in the yard and talk and talk. With Stuart coming, I remembered the expansive part of me, shaped not by the limitations of protocol or fear but by connection, by passion, by the potential to create one's life. Telling Melinda no would be a loving boundary. She belonged in the hospital. I would make of my practice a safe container, a magnificent womb, its fertility unmatched and its walls pliable but firm.

38.

Fabric

MIDWEEK, I LET myself in the back door of the parsonage and put on coffee, not bothering to interrupt Dad. I had invited two of the Quilters to help me sort through Mom's sewing things. The annual church bazaar was approaching, and, according to Dad, the Elsie Circle was "going great guns" making pillows and oven mitts and aprons with quilt-square bibs. They could use Mom's scraps, and anything they didn't need they would sell at the Twice Nice booth—spare thread, extra scissors, rickrack.

The doorbell rang at ten sharp. Maggie and Trudy stood beaming on the front porch, Maggie in a homemade floral housedress, Trudy sporting a pastel sweat suit with nicely hemmed cuffs and rose prints sewn across the chest. Trudy was tall, her skin unnaturally brown from a decade of Florida winters. She brushed my cheek with a kiss.

"Greetings, greetings!"

Maggie thrust forward an exuberant mass of orange, fuchsia, and yellow zinnias cut from her garden, and wrapped me in her arms. I ushered the women in and fueled them with doughnuts and coffee in Mom's teacups. With zinnias rocketing from the vase, the women's bursts of chatter, and the chink of china, Mom might have been lurking in the kitchen, she seemed so near.

Dad must have sensed it. He emerged from his study, his countenance severe but eyes bright. "Ladies!" he said in the doorway. In two swift steps he had a hand on Maggie's shoulder. "Up to holy mischief, I see." In Trudy's ear, he stage-whispered, "Beware of this one. She's a nuisance."

The women fussily invited him to sit.

"I'd enjoy nothing better. Unfortunately, I have a meeting." I pointed out the flowers and he glanced at me, a quick look of confusion and regret, before thanking the women.

After he left, I endured a barrage of *Your father's a saint* and *The church runs him ragged*. They each downed four cups of coffee. Maggie clapped her hands, rubbed them vigorously, and declared, just as Mom used to, "Let's get to it!"

Upstairs, I positioned chairs within easy reach of the dressers and brought a pile of empty cardboard boxes down from the attic. The room smelled of decaying McCall's patterns. I opened the window. I had expected sorting fabric to go swiftly, but the women unfolded each swath to assess its size and potential—quilt for the children's hospital in St. Paul? felt Christmas ornaments?—and to deliberate plans. Despite the agonizing pace, Maggie's and Trudy's delight at finding brown and white gingham or a full drawer of rickrack was infectious, and their exclamations at my mother's good taste kindled my memory of how Mom had coached me for my first interactions with these women: *Say thank you to Mrs. Hendricks, Hannah. Remember to excuse yourself from the table.* When we closed empty drawers, I felt the hollow thump in my chest. Maggie and Trudy had a vision for each scrap and button, just as Mom would have had. Nothing could better honor her memory.

I found a shoebox and packed the thread, some on wooden spools, some with needles stuck in the paper tops. Our initial excitement eased, and we settled into a routine. Maggie opened a drawer of cotton prints. Trudy unfurled a swath of teddy bears on a yellow background and asked, "Now who's expecting?"

"Mike Hollinger's wife," Maggie said. Her perm was now loose enough to jiggle. "When's she due, Hannah?"

"Mid-August."

Trudy folded the material and pulled over an empty box. "Are you Bill Jorgenson's assistant? I saw you in his truck the other day."

"No. I do homebirths."

"Really!" Trudy unfolded a few yards of pink cotton printed with rocking horses. "Women still do that? When I gave birth to my Susie, the doctor knocked me out completely. I didn't do a blessed thing."

I wound blue thread around its spool. Likely Mom had been drugged at my birth as well. "What was that like for you?" I asked.

Trudy shook her head. "Just how it was done. Suze had trouble breathing so we stayed in the hospital a few weeks. You don't hear *that* happening anymore." Her mouth hung open while she remembered. "Actually, those were good weeks. All that pampering by the nurses."

I stood and pulled the cord on the ceiling fan. A puff of dust descended then we felt the marginal relief of moving air. I wondered what the consequences were of a whole generation of mothers physically removed from the births of their babies.

"Is Melinda having a boy or a girl?" Maggie aske. "We should get stitching."

"She doesn't know."

"What about that yellow flannel for backing? We could alternate the rocking horses with this." Maggie held a white floral print between quivering fingers.

I pulled straight pins from the faded turtle cushion and collected them in an earring box. The women moved on to a drawer of corduroy, its furry ridges out of the sixties, while I packed sewing machine parts. Maggie dreamt up plans to make gargantuan pillows for the youth room. Here was the legacy of my mother's era—women whose lives and bodies were given in service of others at a cost they refused to acknowledge or perhaps didn't recognize, bending graciously within the boundaries expected of their sex, creative within the confines of practicality, expressive only as much as was supported by the social order. Maggie settled on a design for the pillows—zigzags of brown, black, orange, and yellow. Thoroughly retro; the youth would love it. I adored these women. I wanted to continue their good work in my own fashion. I opened the red plastic case for the sewing machine. Inside was a cubby for the pedal, space for the box of parts, and yellowing instructions. The extension sleeve slid off the machine and fit sideways against the case's wall. I wound the cord and levered the machine inside, where it inhabited the crannies and protrusions precisely. My satisfaction at the fit was also my mother's.

"What about this?" I asked, snapping the buckles. "It works."

"Don't you want it, Hannah?"

"I couldn't sew a straight line if I were sober."

The ladies chuckled.

"There's a charity in the city that teaches immigrants to sew." Maggie scratched her scalp. "Catholics. If you put it in my car, dear, I'll drive down next week."

I set the case in the hall and began labeling boxes.

"Now look at these!" Trudy exclaimed, opening the last drawer. "Don't these bring back memories!" She unfolded two matching baby quilts done in faded floral gingham, one green, the other pink, both the four-square log cabin pattern.

Maggie rubbed a corner between thumb and forefinger. "My, my. Now these are relics." She held one within inches of her face to examine the stitches. "Looks untouched."

Trudy frowned. "What a waste, stuffing good quilts in a drawer."

Quilts are for beds or for hanging and ought never, ever be folded. That my mother had committed the quilter's cardinal sin felt ominous. I set down the marker to look. "What are those?"

Both women turned to me, surprised.

I knelt. The quilts were light, the fabric softened with age. Thin strips of rose faded into pink in opposite quadrants, and pine green into pale lemon. Each square retreated into a center of light. I passed my hand over their surfaces. "What are they from?"

"When your mother was pregnant."

"Two?"

The women exchanged glances. Trudy twitched. Maggie placed unsteady fingers on my arm. "Your mother was supposed to have twins, dear. Didn't she ever tell you?"

I leaned back against the dresser. My face grew hot with embarrassment, at being caught unawares, at exposing a family secret, at not knowing something so essential about myself. A dresser knob dug into my back. My heart spun. I shook my head, and Maggie withdrew her hand.

"Barb probably had her reasons." Maggie refolded the quilts, careful not to duplicate the old creases.

Twins. The whole world spun. I could barely think. "What happened?"

Maggie looked to Trudy, uncertain.

"Her father should tell her," Trudy said.

"Your sister was stillborn," Maggie answered. "There was some complication, I never heard what, but she didn't make it. Barb took it hard."

A sister! The awful ache I'd known my entire life, that desperate longing for connection, washed through me. I sat down, pressing my hand to my forehead.

"We should get going," Trudy said. She struggled to close a cardboard box.

"Hannah, dear." Maggie reached again for me. "Your mother was a very private person. Losing a child is unbearable. Don't judge her too harshly for not telling you."

My mother had lost a child. An image of Carol Simic curled in anguish burned in my mind's eye. But any compassion for Mom was swiftly plowed under by fury. Why hadn't they told me? A sister. She was mine too, to love and grieve. I stood, pulled Trudy's box toward me, and crammed the flaps one under the next. I wanted the women to leave.

"Here." Maggie stopped me and placed the quilts into my arms. "You should take these."

A sister! Shouldn't I have suspected? The women straightened the room while I numbly lugged boxes downstairs—the snaps, safety pins, hooks and eyes, pinking shears, antiquated patterns in their fading envelopes, the tape measure made of fabric, the lace and rickrack and miscellaneous buttons—all the material of my mother's creative life exiting the house, and good riddance. She'd spent so much energy denying truth when the truth was simple and sad. A death. Nothing to be ashamed of. Whether they'd intended it, my parents' silence was punishing. Mom's fabric would be transformed by her friends, her legacy of beauty perpetuated. I wanted to cry.

Carrying the sewing machine, I stepped out into riotous summer, where sun and heat pulsed off the pavement. Across the lot, a man dismounted from a bike in front of the church offices, turned, and waved. The air above the polished hood of Maggie's white Impala warped his image, and for a moment I thought he was Leif. I wanted to run across the pavement and spill out this awful truth. I wanted to be comforted, to be held in fierce and loving arms. But no, it was Chuck looking like a Mormon missionary in his black suit and bike helmet. I waved briefly, opened the rear door, and maneuvered the case onto the vacuumed carpet. Up front, a bag of lemon drops sat in the ashtray, and the tidy order of it all clamped down on me—I couldn't breathe. I wanted to run away, from the sidewalks, the mown lawns, the church's righteous steeple, and a whole town concealing what it didn't understand and couldn't face. My mother had formed me to fit inside this place snuggly, but to do so she'd cut off something essential, and now that I knew I wanted to smash the box, I wanted to break free and return to myself, to the truth, to the Hannah who once shared life with another spirited being. I slammed the door.

39.

Thirty-Eighth Week

DO YOU KNOW what percentage of American babies actually arrive on their due dates? Four. So much of modern maternal care is an illusion. Really, the body is an animal, bucking, reproducing of its own volition, fierce in its timing, and luxuriant in its beauty. The great challenge of tending the body is how to both assert and release control, because of course we can cure illness and mend bones and induce labor, and yet many of the workings of nature, especially birth and death, are damaged by our touch. "Hold 'em lightly," Maryann says of her patients. Imagine a wounded songbird shivering and restless in your hands. How long do you cup that feathery life? How much care is wise, really? When does care become captivity, and release, regardless of its consequences, the better gift?

* * *

I turned from Melinda, on her back staring at the spackled ceiling, to Mike, slouched in the overstuffed chair I'd determined to replace. He spun a Lincoln Log between his fingers. It was

Monday morning; ninety-degree heat had slowed the town to
an irritated crawl. The brick house baked us. After two years in
New Mexico, I'd lost my tolerance for turbid, unbreatheable air.
Overhead, the ceiling fan whipped its pull chain in a taut circle.

"What's the verdict?" Mike asked.

"No change."

Mike put his face in his palms. Melinda rolled her head to see
his reaction. I offered her my hand; she pulled herself upright
with difficulty. I'd envisioned this appointment a hundred
times, constructing the best tone, tweaking a word here or there,
reminding myself, *be firm, be clear*. Now that the moment had
arrived, nerves made me heady while the broken secret of my
sister throbbed in my chest. All that longing for connection I'd
for years directed toward my mother was perhaps meant for my
wombmate, my second self. *A sister*. I couldn't shake off the
pain.

"Sometimes babies have good reasons for the positions they
choose," I said. "We don't necessarily know better." In the terse
silence, I thought of the stubborn breech delivered vaginally
without mishap; a year later a tumor was discovered on the
baby's brain, there since before birth. Had she been delivered
headfirst with the tumor pressing against the vaginal opening,
she might not have lived. Or the footer, born through C-section,
with a ten-inch umbilical cord—too short to have survived a
vaginal birth.

I offered Melinda a chair and, when she indicated she was
fine, took it myself.

At Mike's feet, Kevin lined up Lincoln Logs to play like a
xylophone: a wooden tap, tap, tap, along with the anxious
drone of cicadas in the lilac and the fan's whir. Sprout had
dropped butt-first, squeezing torso and legs into the birth canal
while keeping steady watch on the womb-skies. Melinda was a
centimeter dilated. The tent of her T-shirt was drenched. She
breathed through her mouth and wore flip-flops on her swollen
feet. I reached for her chart. I needed the modicum of authority
those pale manila pages offered.

"I can't deliver your baby," I said. Kevin ceased his rhythm and stared at his mother with round eyes. "I'm disappointed it's not going to work out. I can be at the hospital with you, act as your doula, and do your postpartum care at home. I'll be your advocate. I'll help you get the closest thing possible to the birth you want."

Melinda looked around the room like a cornered cat.

Kevin unloaded a dump truck of logs onto his father's loafers. Mike and I looked from him back to Melinda on the exam table, her ill-fitting maternity stretch pants—obviously hand-me-downs—and her sweat-darkened curls pressed to her forehead. She struggled to keep her posture. Her gaze skimmed the top of Mike's head. Her eyes hardened. I imagined she was remembering the hospital, the renovated maternity wing with faux-wood floors, rose-patterned curtains, the stainless steel emergency cart loaded with masks and sterile episiotomy scissors tastefully hidden behind closet doors, seeing herself three years younger, her lithe, capable body bound to the bed by an IV and baby monitor because she's laboring beyond Hiawatha County Hospital's regulation twelve hours. Mike does his best to be encouraging. The nurses ignore them both. A masked Dr. Jorgenson pats her hand, saying, "Not to worry, kiddo. We'll induce you," at which Mike looks visibly relieved, and Melinda hasn't the strength to argue. Amid a frenzy of medical intervention, the contractions come too fast and too hard; Melinda wails and Mike can't bear it; he reneges on his oath to stave off the epidural, and Melinda's will is broken. She concedes, what else can she do? She rolls over for the fine plastic tube to be inserted in her back like a straw so her body can drink in numbness, and she floats upward, away from the pain in her pelvis and heaving uterus, until Dr. Jorgenson pulls over the vacuum extractor for that extra oomph, yanking the blue baby upward and out of that contrary, inept body. Like a magician, he flourishes little Kevin, cuts the cord, and hands the baby off, Melinda doesn't know to whom or why, the initial panic and silence eerie but no one explains, and her tongue is too bloated to ask.

I had seen this birth. Numerous women had told me the same story. My own birth was similar, no doubt, and shackled to loss. Melinda was fighting for dignity and for the power she suspected resided in her body but had yet to experience. Still staring into the sunlight, she placed her palms on either side of her uterus as though conferring with the child.

"Melinda?" Mike asked.

She shook her head.

I pulled out a page on which I'd written contacts for everyone I knew who delivered breeches naturally. "If you want alternatives, here are two docs down in the Cities who might take you. I recommend the one at St. Paul Pres; I could hook you up with a great nurse midwife there. Then here"—I pointed out the third contact—"is the one place you could go for a nonhospital birth. It's called The Farm, in Tennessee. Ina May sometimes takes women at the last minute."

Melinda faced the window where the afternoon was still and sultry.

"I know, that's far. I'm sorry there aren't better options."

Mike reached for the page of contacts.

"No," Melinda said. She turned her gaze toward me. "I'll do it myself."

"What?!" Mike leapt, scattering little brown logs, and grabbed Melinda by the elbows. The desperation in his voice confirmed the power of Melinda's decision. He shook her. "Are you crazy? Jesus Christ!" Kevin began to whimper. Mike spun, walked to the door and back. Wet patches seeped into the armpits of his white shirt. "How the hell are you going to do that? We'll wind up in the emergency room anyhow. Christ. What's your problem?" He raked his hands through his hair. "What about me? Am I supposed to stand around while you bleed to death? *I* can't deliver this baby."

Melinda's look sharpened; her voice was low and calculated. "If this birth becomes an emergency then it will *be* an emergency, and we'll treat it like that. Until that happens, this is what I want to do."

She swiped her face with her hand. I couldn't tell if she was brushing away tears or sweat. Kevin pushed himself to his feet and made urgent "eeh, eeh" sounds, reaching for his mother. In one rough motion, Mike swooped him into Melinda's lap and resumed pacing.

An ache crept up my temples. If Melinda chose an unassisted homebirth, our contract was broken and I was no longer responsible for the outcome. Why, then, did I feel culpable?

"What are you trying to prove?" Mike demanded.

Melinda curled around her son and unborn child.

Mike stormed back and forth. "At least consider these options, Mel." He waved the contact list in her face. "I'm sure we can find someone you like in the Cities. Hell, I'd even go to this Farm place. Melinda?"

She was still, her nose nestled in Kevin's auburn curls.

Mike flopped back into the chair and buried his face in his hands. The muscles on his back convulsed through his dress shirt.

"Mama." Kevin squirmed around in her lap. "Daddy's crying."

"Yes, he is."

"Why?"

Melinda thought. "Because he's scared. I'm scared too. Sometimes it's okay to feel scared."

Kevin's eyes were dark. "I'm scared," he whispered.

Mike looked up, red-eyed, his face wet.

"Oh, I know, honey." Melinda pulled him close and rocked back and forth.

Mike stood and lifted Kevin into a hug. "It's okay, sport. You don't need to worry."

My role was receding. In its wake was an emptiness where I thrashed, trying to stay afloat. "If you decide you'd like some instruction," I offered meekly, "I could teach you the basics, what's possible in the next week or so."

Melinda shook her head no. Mike put his hand on her knee

and adjusted Kevin in his arms. "Thanks. Anything you've got."

I pulled a few books from the shelf while Mike kicked the stool in place for Melinda to climb down. Others had given birth at home, in cars, under worse conditions and with less information, and survived. Bessie had called malpresentations a sign of specialness. Maybe Melinda knew something I didn't. I handed Melinda her purse, Mike the books.

"I'll call," Mike told me.

They pushed through the screen door. The image of their departure seared itself into my brain: two intrepid forms and a boy clutched to his father's side, backlit by a summer so bright, it hurt.

40.

Expansive Part

I HAD A sister whose death coincided with my birth, whose memory had accompanied my family for thirty-six years. I knew her only as a longing and as my mother's distraction. Twins supposedly share memory and language and identity; I had none of this. Yet the fact of her brief, erased life felt absolutely true. It answered my earliest question.

For a week I neglected to return Dad's phone calls, my anger at his complicity mounting with the August heat. What had my parents gained by their silence? Not the avoidance of grief, not happier lives, certainly, and not a daughter more beloved for surviving. I wanted to claim my sister. Her presence and absence were part of me. My parents had denied me this awareness, and what else? A witness to my past. Honesty. Transparent affection. My heart boiled with loss.

Thursday, I finally made perfunctory dinner plans with Dad and spent the morning in my nightshirt doing laundry, scrubbing the kitchen floor, and otherwise madly bringing under control the one thing I could—my house, just as my mother always modeled. I washed light fixtures. I dusted picture frames. I thought about Bill, who had colluded in my parents' cover-up, although I couldn't imagine either of them brazen enough to ask it of him. The mystique around my birth now made sense—I was a miracle baby, the one who survived—and yet it didn't, because there had been no need for deception. I wiped down the molding, the base shoe, the coving. I bleached the insides of garbage bins. I thought of Carol Simic with new respect. By grieving openly, she wouldn't inflict decades of ache on others. She wouldn't deny her child's death.

Much as I was looking forward to Stuart's visit—his sympathy would be a balm—the timing was bad. I'd be distracted, if not by my newly discovered loss then by my terror for the Hollingers. Mike was reading medical texts at an uncomprehending pace, phoning me every evening with strangely mathematical questions: "So it says to turn the baby's head. Would that be ninety degrees? Or more like forty-five?" What could I possibly say? Distinctions like these meant nothing without unimaginable presence of mind.

Stinking of sweat, I washed the insides of windows, wiped the sashes, and dusted each blade of the venetian blinds. Outside the hot spell raged. House finches took dust baths in the garden. The playground's swings hung limply. Most houses were sealed tight, air conditioners whining from side yards. I took refuge in a cold afternoon bath and finally dressed.

At five, Dad rang the doorbell. He passed me a paper sack rolled at the top. "Pasta salad. Tess Carson made it up for me."

"What would you do without those ladies?" I said flatly.

He grinned. "Have some peace?"

Dad wore the uniform of his after-work hours: tan slacks and a light-blue button-down shirt. His neck was free and flat. Pale hairs were exposed on his arms.

He relaxed at the kitchen table while I spooned salad from the yogurt container onto plates, my mind frantic, my heart torqued. Bowtie noodles with chopped chicken and celery, smeared with mayo and sprinkled with dried cranberries, did not whet my appetite. Tess had also thrown in rolls and a container of green Jell-O salad.

"I ran into Chuck the other day," I said with false calm. "At the library. You're letting him take the kids to Mexico?"

"That man," Dad huffed, "is a thorn in my side." His words were rote; they lacked the usual irritation.

"He's not *that* bad, is he?" I'd found myself looking forward to Chuck's company on Saturday.

"I've had two complaints from neighbors about the ruckus on Sunday mornings. I warned him to tone it down. Claims the volume makes for a full-bodied worship."

"Does anyone show up?"

"Well, that's it." Dad cleared his throat.

"Maybe he's onto something."

"What? The desecration of worship as we know it? The end of all reverence?" He set his wire-rimmed glasses on the table and rubbed his eyes.

"Who comes?"

"Kids. A lot of the younger families. People I don't know."

"Would you consider hiring him?"

"I may not have a choice."

"You don't sound too upset."

Dad turned his strong profile toward the window. The severe slope of his nose, his high cheekbones, his soft mouth, and the tired, curved line descending from his eyes gave him the appearance of a beneficent monarch. "The man's got a way with folks, I'll grant him that." He slapped the kitchen table. "Enough. Tell me about your day."

"Busy." I blathered about Stuart's impending visit, set down the plates, and handed him a fork. "They'll drive here late tomorrow and stay the weekend."

Dad grunted and bent his head in prayer. I studied his thick, healthy hair and wondered whether his extreme devotion was spurred by guilt. Knowledge of my twin was an unexploded bomb between us. When Dad picked up his fork, I continued, "I'd like you to meet them, Dad."

He took a bite.

"Stuart's an important friend."

"Well then, bring them by."

I chewed celery and chicken without tasting them.

"How was your day?" I asked.

"Summer doldrums. A trustees meeting. Not too many phone calls. Sunday's done."

"Even the children's sermon?"

Dad agonized over those five minutes with the kids clustered at his feet.

"Recycled. I'll use the falling backward one."

He would have the kids stand one at a time and test how far they could fall without looking before he caught them. This supposedly illustrated faith. Some kids stuck out a leg to stop themselves. Most glanced behind to make sure he was there. As a child I'd dropped within inches of the carpet, so utterly certain of my father's capable catch that the congregation gasped. Even then I knew my deep fall said less about faith than it did about my need for Dad to hold me.

Dad said, "Mike came to see me yesterday."

My head jerked up. "Mike Hollinger?"

"He asked for prayers for Melinda. And counsel. Said the baby's breech and you're not going to deliver it."

"I thought what people shared with you was confidential."

"Why not, Hannah? Why aren't you helping them?"

"I promised Bill I wouldn't do breeches. And if it's illegal for me to do homebirth, it's a really bad idea to do a breech. I could get arrested."

Dad massaged his swollen knuckles. "I didn't know what to tell him. She needs care."

A moment passed before I realized Dad was asking for help. He wanted me to assist with Melinda's birth. "What about 'falling backward into God's arms'?" I said.

Dad stared at me.

I held his gaze. "Of course she needs good medical care. I told them to go to Bill. She's refusing."

Dad's brow dropped. "Why would she do that?"

"She had a bad experience the first time, with Kevin. A series of minor complications. Bill's heavy on intervention. He induced then gave her drugs for pain after she'd asked him not to." I wiped sweat from my eyes.

"That's all?"

"She's a healthy woman. She should have been able to deliver the baby naturally. They also took Kevin away without telling her why. Never mess with a new mom like that."

"Your mother came through worse just fine."

He said it defensively, as though Mom's suffering was the standard against which all others should be measured. I did my pitiful best to breathe. "What happened, Dad? Maggie and Trudy found two baby quilts in Mom's drawers. Maggie told me about my twin."

Pallor stole across Dad's face. He pushed his plate away and bent over, propping his forehead in his hand. I watched my father crumple.

"Why didn't you ever tell me? It's cruel. And unnecessary." My heart was beating so hard, it might have hammered Dad into the ground.

"Before God and all the heavens, Hannah, we never meant to be cruel."

I waited. Dad's face muscles twitched. The darkness under his eyes deepened. He suppressed a sob then regained himself.

"We were young and poor. We'd just barely gotten here. We weren't ready. Your mother especially, and twins . . ." He spoke to a spot on the Formica table. "Your mother wanted to become a nurse. She was waiting for me to finish seminary so we'd have some money."

I crossed my arms.

"And then everything about your birth was an emergency. The weather was awful, delivering twins was dangerous, you were breech—"

"I was?"

He looked up. "That's what Jorgenson said. He did a C-section. You were footfirst and . . . the other . . ." He shielded his face from me. "She was stillborn."

I placed myself back in my mother's womb, yang to my sister's yin, our entwined dance of life and death doubly unwelcome. I yearned for her. I needed to claim her. "What was her name?"

Dad looked away. "Ruth."

My stomach lurched. *Whither thou goest, I will go; and where thou lodgest, I will lodge: thy people shall be my people, and thy God my God.* Later I looked up the rest of Ruth's speech to her mother-in-law: *Where thou diest, will I die, and there will I be buried.* My sister resided in my bones.

"Your mother asked that we not discuss it." Dad's voice rumbled and broke. "She said . . . she said she didn't want you to feel . . ." He rubbed his eyes with the palms of his hands.

"What?"

"Responsible."

I sat back. My skin burned with sudden heat—I *was* responsible for Ruth's death. I knew it. I'd survived, and she hadn't. My guilt had gravity, and endurance. Guilt was my bedrock.

Then I thought of that tender moment with Carol Simic, when she told me she was trying to be good enough for the baby, to earn her way into heaven. "You get it, don't you?" she had asked. She recognized my strain. I shook myself—why shouldn't we be good enough, *as is?*—and traced my guilt backward, through my apprenticeship and childhood and birth to my mother, and knew by this bloodline, as sure as I've known anything, that Mom blamed herself for Ruth's death. Perhaps she'd wished the pregnancy would end, perhaps she'd felt punished by God, but whatever her private anguish, she'd held herself so bitterly accountable, she'd marked us all.

"I agreed out of respect for your mother, Hannah, but it never seemed right. We buried . . . her . . . in the cemetery and didn't buy the surrounding plots. We couldn't afford them. Your mother's nowhere near. I don't know what she wanted. We never talked about it."

My legs stuck to the vinyl seat cover.

"There's a marker. It says Ruth." Dad's voice was low and pleading.

I knew it; the cemetery had been my backyard when I was growing up. The small marble block was set level with the earth, four letters carved on the surface, no dates. It was under a large elm, an acre away from Mom's grave.

"I'm glad you know now." Dad took a paper napkin from the wood dowel holder and wiped his eyes, his mouth. "Your mother took it very hard. Try to understand, Hannah."

Dad wanted my forgiveness. I shook my head.

"Thank God Almighty for Bill. He did some quick work. Your mother survived, you survived." Dad stood. "I pray in gratitude every day, Hannah."

The admission warmed me, but only so much—Bill's handiwork and God's miracle both cast large shadows. Dad slid his hands into his pockets and jiggled his keys. "I'll be paying a visit to Mike and Melinda tomorrow morning," he said.

I sighed. I wanted to cry but held back, lodging the pain inside. "What are you going to do?"

"Say a blessing. I don't know."

"Let's hope it helps," I said. "I wish I could do more."

"Have you prayed about it?"

"No. I haven't."

"Well, then," he said, as though that explained the Hollingers' predicament. He gazed out at the schoolyard, where the playground equipment glinted with angling sun. "The sanctuary's always open, you know." I looked up, but he was focused on the distance. "Milton says he sees you occasionally." Milton was the church organist.

"I like the quiet," I said.

"Prayer isn't about personal enjoyment, Hannah." He pressed his hand onto my shoulder. I turned in surprise. "It's a relationship. It's about listening." He held my eyes as though this advice somehow atoned for the past thirty-six years of deception. Then he released his grip and turned to the kitchen door. "You might give some thought to the parable of the good

Samaritan. Bring your friends by on Saturday."

Dad walked out, letting the screen slam behind him.

So I was a Levite ignoring an injured stranger, a heartless EMT speeding past an accident because I was off duty. I reached for the plastic tub and a fork and furiously mashed Jell-O into a lumpy, translucent liquid. I could heed nothing but the blood pounding in my ears. I may have felt unseen much of my life, but my sister, little Ruth, had been utterly erased. All that grief! Bill's miracle had not remedied it, Mom's secrecy had not blotted it out, Dad's moral authority could not rectify it, God's grace would not redeem it. The grief had festered for years and would continue.

41.

Hour of Patience

I PARKED AT the Hiawatha County Hospital on Friday morning and walked the length of the dreary lot. The automatic glass doors accordioned open. The lobby doubled as an ER waiting room; folks in varying degrees of discomfort squirmed in sanitized plastic seats while news blared from an overhead TV. I approached the front desk just as Zarida burst through a side door in white orthopedic shoes, pea-green scrubs, and a nursing coat printed in pink and baby blue seahorses. "Adolf Sorensen?" she called out, then spotted me. In two swift steps, she offered me a faux hug.

"Whatcha doin' here, Hannah? Nice to see you."

"Looking for Bill." My bitterness at her ratting on me now seemed petty—she'd been doing her job. "You look great."

Zarida grinned. Her features had gained substance since I'd seen her in the grocery store—her cheeks were lit from within rather than plastered with makeup. She leaned in confidentially. "Pregnant."

An unfamiliar sensation caught in my throat. For years I'd happily surrounded myself with fecundity, but in that moment, out of nowhere, I was jealous. Zarida's hand rested on her belly. Did I want a baby? Yes, in fact, I did. The feeling was fervent, and strangely sweet.

"April twelfth," Zarida said. "Don't be insulted if I don't call. I want that epidural. Although Nina Smith said you were awesome." Nina was one of my Christian moms and Zarida's neighbor.

An elderly man leaned into his walker and approached with a teenager at his elbow. "Hello, Mr. Sorensen." Zarida dipped her knees to look into his eyes. "Is this your grandson?" Zarida winked at me. I gave her a minute wave.

I opened a fire door to an underused, dimly lit stairway. The hospital had been renovated in the late seventies—internal walls torn down to make more individual rooms and wider halls—but the cement block exterior was the same as it had been thirty-six years ago at my birth. My open-toed sandals slapped against waxed linoleum tiles. At maternity reception, I leaned on the counter to chat with a young woman in pigtails, who peered through fashionably large, black-rimmed glasses. Her voice over the PA was brash. "Dr. Jorgenson to the front desk."

Bill was five paces away when he registered my presence. "Hannah." He grabbed my arm and pulled me back to his office as though I were his mistress, appearing where I shouldn't. "Decorum, woman."

Bill's lab coat hung with sloppy, indisputable authority. An undershirt peeked out where his gray shirt met his belt. His eyebrows were white against the red fury of his skin. I did not want Bill to touch Melinda.

"We need to talk," I said.

His beefy hands disappeared into lab coat pockets.

"Can I sit?"

"Fine." He lifted some folders from a discarded waiting-room chair and dropped them on the carpet. Stacks of papers lined the floor, buried the desk, and warped the pressboard bookshelves. His décor consisted of a framed medical degree and an antique rod and reel mounted above the window. Bill took his desk chair, pivoting to rest his feet on a document box.

"You know the Hollingers," I began. "Mike and Melinda?"

"Sure. I delivered her first. A girl, I think."

"Boy. Kevin. He's three now."

"Haven't seen her since."

"She's due with her second any day. A frank breech." Bill straightened. "I've wiped my hands of it. She wants to do it unassisted. Mike'll see that they get here if anything goes wrong."

Bill's overgrown eyebrows met in a prickly line. "You were dealing with a breech?"

"Prenatal, Bill. And now I'm turning it over."

He sputtered. "What's the deal with having it at home? Does the baby come out more *organic*?"

I didn't respond.

"It's child abuse."

I couldn't argue.

Bill sighed and rustled through the mess of papers for a blank pad. "Okay. Give me the specs."

I took Melinda's chart out of my bag and filled him in on the prenatal details.

"Natural is important to her. She wants the baby vaginally, and if everything goes smoothly there's no reason for her not to. She's got a roomy pelvis, her first was under eight pounds at birth, and as far as I can tell the head's well flexed. If she knew you'd give it a try, she might come in without a fight."

"What is it with you people?" Bill threw his pen on the desk. "We can *control* the outcome of a Caesarian."

I crossed one leg over the other and leaned forward. "I'm just telling you what Melinda wants. Once she walks through the door, she's yours."

"Damn right." Bill leaned his office chair back until he could see me through the bottom of his bifocals. He'd agreed to back me up because of Ruth's death—I was certain of it. I replaced Melinda's chart in my bag, my hand trembling.

"Tell me about my birth, Bill. I know I had a twin. What happened?"

His eyes narrowed. He swallowed, his Adam's apple leaping. "Let's stick with the case at hand," he said. "I suppose you'll be Melinda's labor coach."

The office was too small, too cluttered. I crossed my arms.

"Tell me why you're backing me up."

"Kindness?" He opened his hands between us but his tone was disingenuous. "Generosity?" I stared at him. We listened to the air conditioner blow through the building ducts, the drone of the PA in the hallway, the footsteps of nurses passing. His bifocals obscured his eyes.

"I'm going to request my records on my way out. I'd rather hear the story from you."

Bill's jowl sagged; he jabbed his beefy pointer finger at me. "Your birth was not my proudest moment, Hannah." Then he looked away, threading his hands through stark white hair. "Your parents were . . . discreet. I appreciated that. But it's not a secret." He removed his glasses and set them aside.

I expected him to go on, and when he didn't, I said, "Tell me."

He pounded a fat fist in his palm. "I never thought . . . Well, how old are you? Thirty-four?"

"Six."

"Thirty-six years ago, medicine was different. Hell, I remember prescribing morphine for this lady with migraines for a good three months before I figured out she was faking it." At my look of disgust, he said, "That wasn't an uncommon treatment, and I was a rookie. Don't tell me you've never made mistakes."

I uncrossed my arms.

He grunted. "My point is, I'd only been practicing a year or two. As a GP. Broken legs. Flu. Damn, geriatric aches and pains. I'd done the requisite hundred-some births in residency and only a handful on my own when your mother came along." Bill's voice rumbled in the tight room. "I didn't think much of your father, being religious and all. Your mom was nice enough. Twins made me nervous. I'd seen a few, that was it. I don't know how long Barbara was in labor before they called me. Too long. We were in a cold snap, wind chills minus twenty or something. God-awful. The kind of cold where you'd spit, and it'd bounce off the sidewalk."

"Bill—"

"My truck wouldn't start. I borrowed a neighbor's, but still, I lost precious time. When I got there, Barbara was six centimeters with feet descending. Yours. I panicked. I'd never seen anything like it, and here was this charming pastor's wife, totally unsuspecting, ready to push. You know your mother. She didn't let out a peep. The only way I could tell she was hurting was her eyes." Moisture beaded on Bill's temples.

"You panicked?"

He pressed his thick palms to his forehead. An electronic buzz jarred the room, and we both watched the red light blink on his phone. "I ordered general anesthesia, and we transferred her to surgery."

"You *what*?"

"I pushed the baby back in. It was either that or forceps and a huge episiotomy. She wasn't fully dilated. And the baby was big. You were."

I reeled with the horror of interrupting a descending baby with a twin still in the womb. "Was there evidence of fetal distress?"

"Your heart tones were crazy, the other baby's were bad, what could I do? It was awful, Hannah." He bit his knuckle. "My worst moment. I hope you never see anything like it."

I felt ill. My sister had not died of natural causes. My beginning had obliterated hers. Her small, sacred spark smothered . . . But no, even this wasn't my fault. Ruth had died because of a botched delivery, because of ignorance, because my mother wasn't ready.

"Does Dad know?"

"He does."

"Did Mom?"

Bill hesitated. "I told her. I'm not sure she understood."

And I saw my parents, young and unprepared for children, overwhelmed by the news of two, my father accepting the pregnancy as God's will, and my mother—who knows what her reaction was? But then only one child arrives alive. Is this an answered prayer or a punishment? Dad's version had morphed into a parable of God's grace, Bill swooping in to save Mom and me from the brokenness of our earthen vessels. My father preached salvation by grace alone. And Mom? I shook my head. Mom parroted Dad, but what had she really believed?

Bill's eyes were moist at the edges. He gazed over my shoulder at an empty wall. "I know it grieved your folks. I know it. I've tried to be a good friend to your family since."

Bill was tragic. He had no idea how beautifully a woman's body works when she's trusted, and I pitied him because his practice was hampered by this ignorance. I swore mine would never be. What I wished my own mother had known—care that fostered trust in her body, that depended on it—I determined I would provide for the women I served. Bill fumbled around in his back pants pocket and extracted a handkerchief, the same wrinkled linen variety as my father's. He dabbed his forehead and neck.

I averted my eyes. I'd been inhabiting my mother's story—a story of guilt and fear and hijacked dreams—and awareness cut me loose. Finally I could escape this heavy history of collusion. What would hold me instead? More than anything, I wanted a swim. The lake, I realized; the lake could hold me in its weedy depths. I remembered the dead man's float, how I could spread my arms and sense an umbilical cord binding my center to the undulating muck of the earth. The lake fused me. It returned me to my source.

I looked back at Bill. My measure for a lifetime of decisions—what's right, what's wrong—had been misguided. I was a midwife, not just at births but in every moment. The question guiding my every decision could be, "What is being born?" I considered this, and then I knew the answer.

I leaned forward. "Come with me," I said. Confusion creased

Bill's brow. "Come out to the farm. I could deliver Melinda's baby if you were there. That's the way it should be, Bill. It's the only solution that's in the mom's best interest. And the baby's."

Bill slumped in his seat; his tanned hands were blotched with liver spots. He stared at me for a long time. Redness rimmed his faded blue eyes. "In my heart of hearts I agree with you." His voice rumbled. My breathing stopped. For an instant, in a closed hospital office, Bill and I held a solution.

He unfolded his glasses and slid the wire frames back onto his nose. "I can't go there, Hannah. I have to deal with insurance companies breathing down my neck, hospital regulations, a lawsuit-trigger-happy populace . . . Your heart's in the right place. I just can't see my way clear to it."

Surrounded by mounds of documents, the blinking phone bank, the muffled noise from the ward—and resigned that Bill and possibly no one would ever sign up for this revolution—I sensed that same blanket of quiet descend on me that descends at births, when my hands have the impulse to reach out and catch a wet and fresh living being. This same sensation had drawn me in from the beginning, under Maryann's steady gaze. I had to continue moving forward.

"I understand." I rose. "I'm glad we had this conversation." I extended my hand.

Bill didn't take it. He huffed from the chair and wrapped me in a tentative hug. "If it helps, you can do your doula thing with the Hollingers. I'll take good care of them. I'll do my best."

I relaxed into him. In his own bumbling way, he had loved my mother too.

42.

The Other Side of Pain

I WAITED UNTIL after dark that night. Stu and Cal weren't due till midnight, and the sanctuary would be empty once the church staff went home for dinner. Inside, carpet muffled my steps. Dull light from the streetlamps filtered through the stained glass and glinted eerily off the brass candlesticks on the altar. Most of the space was cast in shadow. The stillness that had washed over me that afternoon in Bill's office now filled the church—a calm, a listening, not to the sounds of the physical world but between them, down and under: a great, fecund silence.

When I leaned awkwardly over the altar, balancing on my stomach and groping for the birth kit, I was also reaching for something formless and mighty. Maybe I sensed the God Bessie Jones had talked about—a being who sees beyond circumstances. My father's voice returned to me from some distant sermon: "Even the darkness is not dark to thee." I had serious doubts about God, but this undercurrent of silence preceded every birth, and I trusted it—I do to this day. Underneath your question about my newsworthy birth, aren't you really asking how you can trust yourself to do this work? Trust the work instead. The self then falls away, a feather molted in flight.

I lifted out the gym bag with the oxygen tank and stretched over a second time, grasping the kit's canvas handles, my feet rising off the floor.

I would deliver Melinda's baby. The clarity of my intent rang out in the silence and shook me. I carried the bags down to the first pew and sat, willing my rational mind to catch up with this gripping certainty. I had wanted to land feetfirst on the earth, but had been shunted back into a tangled dance with death. "How you're born always matters," Maryann had said, and now I saw the consequences of my beginning and Ruth's end everywhere. I wished Bill had responded to my own feetfirst descent by working *with* it rather than pushing back with an arguably more dangerous protocol under which he was absolved of blame. I wished Bill had trusted us. Sunny's comment now made sense: If we loved women, we'd trust their bodies. I wished Mom had been better loved.

I could choose a different story now. With memories of my sister in my marrow, I could begin again.

I would deliver Melinda's baby. If all went smoothly, Bill would learn of my betrayal after the fact. Perhaps he'd refuse to back me up for future births. I wouldn't be the first midwife without a backup doctor. Perhaps Minnesota's homebirth advocates rallying at the Capitol would sway the legislators or the new governor to change the law. Surely over the long haul, health care would make stumbling progress forward. And if something went wrong? Well, Mike and I would force Melinda to go to the hospital. I'd bear the responsibility. The Midwifery Guild might catch wind of it and drop me from their roster; whoever was on call at the hospital, even an orderly, could press charges; I could get slapped with a ruinous fine; I could do prison time. Would I have the gall to attend another birth? Dad would support me. In his constrained and unfathomable way, he had come to understand my work just as I'd come to appreciate his life of service.

What if Melinda or Sprout should be hurt? Or die?

I shivered. Stuart called death a vital organ. The reality of death pulsed throughout the sanctuary—my mother's, my sister's. My heart was ruptured and all of me ached, but I was wholly, brilliantly alive.

I would deliver Melinda's baby. My surprise at this decision was undergirded by that reservoir of silence. I tried to breathe it, to lean into the place beyond security and beyond my control, as I wished Bill had done.

The chancel door opened—I jerked to my feet—and light sliced through the sanctuary. Blood pounded in my head and chest. Too late, I remembered my prayer ruse and regretted standing.

"Hannah?" The shadowy form morphed into Chuck. He closed the distance between us and took my hand. The gesture was pastorly and kind. "I interrupted you. I'm sorry."

I extracted myself and sat back down. "You scared the crap out of me." Enough light from the hall now shown on Chuck's face that I could see it was blotchy, his eyes red. "You okay?"

He nodded toward the simple wooden cross hanging from invisible wire above the altar. "Just questioning the authenticity of my vocation. How about you?" He swiped his eyes with his sleeve and sat, his arm extending across the pew-back between us.

I laughed. "Preparing to commit professional suicide."

"What?"

"I'm going to a birth I'm not qualified to attend." I kicked the birth bag. "If something goes wrong, I'll get locked up or sued. Even if the birth goes fine I could lose my practice. Don't ask me why I'm going."

"You and the Hebrew midwives."

"Except it's just me, going it alone."

"God's always in the picture, Hannah. We just don't know where."

I examined my fingernails.

"That's the nature of faith," he said.

"I haven't *got* any." I glanced up at him then down at the floor. "Sorry. Life with my father pounded it out of me."

"Oh." He massaged the tattooed spot on his neck. "Pounded? That's a pretty accurate description of how I feel."

"Dad's making your life miserable."

He smiled. "He's . . . well, challenging."

"He's not God's proxy on earth, you know. Despite how it seems."

"Oh, it's not all his fault. Sometimes I feel like I'm hollering into the void. A response would be nice now and then." He stretched both arms out, gripping the pew very near my arm. "What's this?" He nudged my bag with his toe.

"A birth kit. Incriminating evidence."

Chuck's full-chested laughter swelled into the great space. "The contraband, huh?" He reached for my shoulder and squeezed it. "That's what you've been up to. You're the perfect antidote to Pastor Loren, Hannah."

"Thanks for your discretion." I stood up.

He nodded. "Here, let me help."

He lifted the oxygen tank, I shouldered the kit, and we walked up the aisle into the night. The moon, yellow and bloated, hung just above the roofline. Humidity cooled against my skin. When I realized Chuck was going to walk me home, I paid attention— his high-top sneakers, his easy gait, how I'd grown to trust him, how much I enjoyed his company on the empty night sidewalk. Crickets sang from the bushes and a lone goose beat the air above us on its way to the lake.

"Melinda Hollinger?" Chuck asked.

"Yes."

"I'm not surprised. Loren went out there this morning."

"Her baby's breech, and she wants it at home. I told her I don't do breeches. But I'm afraid she won't let Mike transport her if something goes wrong."

"So you're going out there to rescue her from her stubbornness?"

"I'm going out there to stay true to my calling."

"Ah," Chuck said. "So it *is* about faith. Not"—he raised a hand against my protest—"your Dad's kind. Faith in your work, or in your relationship with the Hollingers."

We rounded the corner by the school, the brick walls and dense canopy of tree limbs casting us in darkness. The kit's strap cut into my shoulder. We crossed the street and approached my house. Chuck stopped at porch steps and handed me the gym bag.

"You'll come tomorrow to meet Stu and Cal?" I said. "Mid-afternoon?"

"I'm looking forward to it." He smiled. "And thanks for taking care of Melinda."

"Good night, Chuck."

He raised his hand and turned. After I'd unlocked the door and placed my bags inside, I went back out to the porch and watched him walk away. I liked the way he pressed his hands into his front jean pockets, his relaxed shoulders, and his buoyant gait. After he turned past the school and I could no longer see him, I waited, enjoying the sense of him striding through the night.

43.

Fathers

A STEAMY ITALIAN falsetto bounced off the upstairs bathroom tiles and woke me the next morning. Sleeping on the sofa had cricked my neck; a tussle of sheets lay heaped on the living room floor. The guys had stumbled in at one a.m., too bleary to socialize. The night had been muggy, my sleep so leaden I wobbled when I sat up.

I shuffled to the kitchen in the T-shirt and shorts I'd slept in, scooped coffee into the filter, and punched the button. The sun was already above the school roof, streaking through the kitchen window and lighting a mason jar crammed with open-eyed daisies. Behind the wall, plumbing vibrated.

I picked up the phone and dialed—I'd gotten home too late to call. Mike answered.

"I'll come," I said. "It's crazy, but I'll be there."

Mike let out a prolonged sigh. "Wow. Thank you, Hannah. What changed your mind? God Almighty, this is a relief."

"It's a long story. Let me know as soon as she goes into labor or if her water breaks."

The light on my answering machine was blinking so I

pressed the button—Soo Young, pleased as punch. Would I do their birth? With a wooden spoon, I mashed frozen orange juice concentrate into tap water and rejoiced at sunshine gleaming in a jar.

The coffee maker sputtered and, upstairs, Stuart added a finishing flourish to his aria, making me eager—I wanted to tell him about Ruth, and about Melinda. I wanted a friend to know.

The stairs creaked. "You decent, girlfriend?"

"As good as I'll get."

Stuart squinted at the bright kitchen. His Bermuda shirt printed with pink flamingos was untucked and ridiculously long bare feet extended from the torn cuffs of his jeans. He had cut his hair short since our apprenticeship. Now it was towel-dried, standing on end. I loved seeing his familiar, goofy smile.

"Sleep well?" I asked.

"Like a log."

"More like a sawed log," Cal added. A delicate whiff of cologne entered the kitchen. "He's dreadful. Did he keep you up?"

Cal looked like a catalogue model, shirt pressed, slacks trim, every dark hair in place, and a diamond stud in his left earlobe. Stuart's gaunt height was cartoonish in contrast. Stuart slinked his arm over his partner's shoulders, and they both gazed happily around the kitchen. I loved their love.

I sat them at the table while I sliced the bakery coffee cake and poured coffee. "Not *that!*" Stuart pointed to the can of Folgers, to which Cal replied, "Mind your manners," and I said vindictively, "When in Rome." We discussed a midmorning swim. Stuart had forgotten his trunks; we'd stop by the parsonage to borrow Dad's.

"Does that mean I'll meet the old man?" Stuart frowned into his cup.

"I guess. I can't promise a warm reception. He knows I've got friends for the weekend, but he doesn't know . . ." I cocked my head to indicate the invisible bond between them.

"Chicken."

"Hey. I've got a lot on my plate now. Remember that mom with the breech? I've decided to deliver it." Stuart raised his hand for a high-five, and I smacked it. "I'll need some serious consults while you're here," I said.

"Are you going to tell Hannah our news?" Cal beamed. I looked from Cal's movie star eyes to Stuart's pale blue ones and sensed a familiar but incongruent electricity.

"Guess," Stuart said.

The coffee was thick, bitter, magnificent. "You're moving back to the States."

Stuart emitted a puff of disdain.

"Cal got a grant?"

"We wish."

I couldn't imagine what would make them glow like my clients. "You're pregnant?"

"Ding, ding, ding!" Stuart bounced in his seat.

"What?!"

Cal folded his hands on the table and leaned forward. "Stu's got a mom who wants to place her baby in an adoption. A sixteen-year-old."

Stuart grabbed my hand. "Can you believe it? After assuming it'd never happen. We're going to be dads." His fingers enfolded my knuckles.

"Holy moly. That's crazy. When?"

"Late November. Of course a lot can happen between now and then. We're trying not to get too excited. Stina was living on the streets until we got her hooked up with Claudia, who manages Cal's gallery, so we could make sure she got a bed and the right nutrition, and the girl thinks I'm the bee's knees—"

"No surprise."

"—and she's hoping to cross the border in January. She's got a cousin in San Diego with a job lined up for her."

"It can't be legal in Mexico. For you to adopt, I mean." I felt strangely numb.

Stuart brushed off the notion. Cal said, "It's not. We go round and round about it, because it'll be nixed if the government finds out, and we won't be able to leave the country. But Mexico's social services are practically nonexistent, and this baby would end up in the dumpster otherwise, then some orphanage. Plus we're living in this artists' colony on the edge of town where everyone's wacko and there's lots of gringos. Officials steer clear. We think we can get away with it. Claudia's single and Mexican; she'll be our cover mom, plus do some daycare while this one's running around birthing babies." He thumbed Stuart. "She's offered to legally adopt and cross.the border for us and then transfer parental rights here, if it comes to that."

"Wow." I tried to digest it. Even Stuart could have a baby. "Congratulations. A baby's going to change everything."

"No kidding." Stuart cavorted about the kitchen, tossing invisible dandelions. I'd seen a great many expectant parents in six years, but I'd never seen anyone yank their hair in illimitable joy.

"Hannah, you've no idea what this has done to me. Can you believe I bought the 'Gay men can't have families' line? Me! I never considered being a father, never even let myself want it. But then I'm counseling Stina and delineating her options—it was early enough that I suggested an abortion, but no-go, so I ask about the family, and she won't touch that one with a ten-foot pole, and she's skittish about the government, having lived on the streets and because she's skipping town, and then she says to me, '*Tomé está cria tu.*' You take this child." Stuart whacked his head with both hands. "It was a conversion experience."

"What if—" I began.

"She could change her mind. That's not the point, Hannah. The point is that Stina already gave us this amazing gift, *that it's possible.*"

"You too?" I asked Cal.

He blushed. "Our house has seemed empty ever since Stu came home that day. Diapers will take some getting used to, but, yeah, I'm sold."

"The man's already painted a cradle. Navy, with quetzal flitting around. His latest craze is mobiles. He'll be the next

Calder."

I laughed at Cal's sudden shyness and stood to wrap Stuart in a hug. "I'm so happy for you." He jumped up and down, taking me with him. "Can I be the auntie?"

"*Tía* Hannah. You got it."

The morning was all sunshine, coffee, and company—Stuart and Cal listened at the kitchen table, rapt, while I told them about the sister I'd never known, my parents' deceit, and Bill's blundering. Stuart said, "You're toting a heavy load, woman," and I finally fell apart, crying while my friend held me. Ruth's death was awful, but it was death, just death, and in Stuart's arms I could distinguish the messy cover-up from the sad but ordinary end of a life.

* * *

We dropped by Dad's on the way to the lake. Cal and Stuart reminded me of who I wanted to be, so I burst through the parsonage kitchen door at eleven in the morning, smack in the middle of his Saturday devotions, and called, "Dad?" The guys hung back in the dining room, admiring my parents' wedding china in the built-in while I knocked on his office door. "Dad?"

I heard a grunt and the rasp of floorboards. Then he towered over me, his brow wrinkled with some theological conundrum. He seemed vulnerable, eyes cloudy and shoulders slumped. He took a moment to focus on me standing in the hallway in a bathing suit, sarong and flip-flops.

"I brought my friends by."

Dad glanced at his desk where the Bible was open and his pen lay across a half-filled page. He wore black slacks and a black shirt, his unhooked clerical collar the only sign it was the weekend.

"Dad." I touched his arm. "I changed my mind. I'm going out to the Hollinger's."

He studied me. "Did you pray about it?"

Chuck's comment that I practiced my own form of faith

made me hesitate. "Sort of," I said.

In a swift motion, he buttoned his collar tight. "Al Jenkins died this week. His funeral's this afternoon. At the nursing home."

"I'm sorry."

"He had a stroke. He was eighty-four." Dad headed down the hall and turned when I didn't follow. I could lose him any time, my magnificent father who had buried one daughter and refused to see the other. "Prayer is deep listening, Hannah. It's how we prepare the soul to receive divine grace. Only seeds that fall on fertile soil bring forth grain."

"Honesty makes the soil fertile, Dad." He stiffened. I hugged my chest. "And we make our own grace. Come meet my friends."

I walked past him into the dining room, where I saw, from Dad's perspective, Cal's hand resting elegantly on a chair-back and Stuart's gangly, Bermuda-shirted enthusiasm.

"Stuart and Cal"—I gestured—"my dad, Loren."

Stuart extended his hand. "Good to meet you, Mr. Larson. I heard oodles about you while we were in Sangre de Cristo."

"Stuart's the one I apprenticed with," I prompted. I wished Stuart's generous soul was as obvious as his bony elbows and ankles. "He's a midwife in Mexico now."

"A midwife?" Dad said thickly.

"And Cal's an artist."

"An artist?"

My eyes briefly met Stuart's. I glanced away, biting my lip.

"Mostly photography. At least that's where I make my money. I've been branching out into other media lately."

"You've got a lovely home, Mr. Larson. They don't make houses like this anymore. High ceiling, the coving, built-ins . . ." Stuart swung his arms to encompass the room.

"It's fine craftsmanship," Dad offered.

"How long have you lived here?"

"Thirty-seven years."

I willed Dad to invite us to sit, to offer us coffee. He seemed to have lost the few gifts of hospitality within his pastoral repertoire. I even considered asking Stuart and Cal to church the next morning so they might see Dad in form—a magnificent preacher regarded highly by his parish, rather than this frowning, stoic presence.

"Can Stuart borrow your swimming trunks?" I asked.

Dad examined Stuart's scrawny middle. "I doubt they'll fit. There's a pull cord, though. You could tie them on." He turned up the stairs.

I offered an exacerbated grimace by way of apology. Stuart whispered, "Tell him we're expecting."

I smacked his arm.

"He's a doozy, Hannah."

Cal put his hands on his hips. "Like you're one to talk."

Dad returned with the trunks pressed in quarters.

"Thanks, Mr. Larson. I'd hate to miss out on a swim. We don't get to much in Mexico."

"Why Mexico?" Dad asked.

"It's where the babies are. At least those I can deliver. And there's a strong arts community in our town." Stuart locked eyes with my father. "Some of us need to find pockets of safety on the fringes, you know. The unacceptable lifestyle and all."

I looked from one to the other. Dad was unreadable.

"You know, Mr. Larson, your daughter's a remarkable woman. It's one thing to stand up for what you believe where it's safe, and another to do what Hannah's doing, negotiating a political climate where natural birth, well, where it's not socially sanctioned. Everyone at the Birth House thinks so highly of her."

"I'm proud of my daughter."

I stepped backward in surprise. Dad's eyes were fixed on Stuart, his shock of silver hair regal, his jaw set. I said, "That's nice to hear, Dad."

He refused to look at me.

"Best not let the day get away from us," Stuart said cheerily. "Thanks for the loaners."

Dad gripped the dining room chair with his left hand and extended his right. "Good to meet you."

Stuart and Cal took turns shaking it. I considered giving Dad a hug but decided to spare him the awkwardness.

* * *

Down at the beach, Cal steered me away from the shady spot where I wanted to spread the picnic blanket and pointed at a bleached stretch of sand directly in the sun. While Stuart did a deck change, Cal stripped down to a skimpy Speedo, meticulously folded his clothes, and arranged himself to take advantage of the rays. "Like a turkey on a spit," Stuart said. Indeed, while Stuart and I plunged into Little Long, hooting at the cold and then streaking out to the deep center, Cal rotated himself, careful to extend both arms and legs, bronzing every inch of skin. "No time at home," he had explained.

The lake buzzed with water-skiers tracing figure eights while a few father-son fishing boats hugged the marshy shore. Kids cannonballed off rickety docks. Stuart and I raced then treaded water, bobbing with the waves and piecing together our respective news from the Birth House. With the latest sixty percent leap in insurance rates, Anita estimated they'd last one more year. Sunny had launched a New Mexico consumers advocacy group, a couple hundred homebirth mothers who rallied monthly at the legislature to change Medicaid policy; apparently the babies-on-hips were making enough ruckus to persuade the lawmakers. Both Carol and Janice were pregnant again. We frog-kicked aimlessly while Stuart described the women he worked with, how they managed without husbands for whole growing seasons and sometimes years, fighting to tend their beautiful newborns and numerous little ones on money wired unpredictably from the States. "There's no electricity in these shanty towns, so they steal juice from the main lines and string extension cords from shack to shack. It's a total fire hazard."

I held my head above water, trying to imagine Mexican poverty and Stuart's immersion in it, reveling in the chill. "Who's minding your clients while you're gone?"

"No one. But that was the case before I arrived." When I frowned, he said, "I need a break, you know."

A whistle shrilled over the water. Stuart pointed toward Cal, who waved from the beach. "Your pager!" Inside my floating chest my heart grew loud. I swam to shore, breathing every third stroke.

"Thanks." I grabbed the pager and my purse and walked up the hill to the pay phone out by the street. I dialed and waited half a ring.

"Hannah, thank God," Mike answered. I listened as fabric muffled the mouthpiece. Then I realized he was crying, so I plugged my open ear to shut out the crows and kids' shouts and the roar of a car speeding past. I closed my eyes and tried to inhabit the farm and shaded house with Melinda outside, likely, and Mike in the kitchen, receiver unsteady in his hand.

"Take a deep breath, Mike. That's it. Has she gone into labor?"

"Just now. Come quick. I'm so scared."

"How often are the contractions coming?"

"She just had her first."

It could be days yet, weeks even.

"What about heart tones? Can you hear the baby's heartbeat?"

I heard pages turning. "I counted a hundred thirty-five heartbeats per minute."

"And blood pressure?"

"She won't let me check it anymore. When I did it at seven this morning, it was one twenty-six over seventy-four. She threw the cuff across the room and said I was worse than the hospital. But the baby—"

"Everything sounds fine, Mike. Perfect even. I could come now, but labor starts and stops a lot. You know that from Kevin. Melinda might be better off without me until her contractions are regular, and that could be a long time yet."

"I've got to take Kevin to the neighbor's. He's too much."

At the Birth House we used to joke that birth was a piece of cake for the moms; it was their partners and parents who

truly suffered. Mike needed a midwife as much as Melinda did—
someone familiar with the rise and release of pain, someone
to normalize Melinda's bearlike instincts and give surefooted
instructions. "If you're certain she's okay, I can wait." Mike blew
his nose. "But she won't let me touch her. She wasn't like this
last time. How am I supposed to watch her vitals if she won't let
me touch her?"

"Lots of pregnant moms are like that in labor. Hang in there.
When it really matters, she won't care." Melinda was creating
with her fury a safe den for herself and the babe. She was
exceptional, extraordinary, foolish. "Have you asked her if it's
okay for me to come?"

"I told her."

"Mike, I won't come if she doesn't want me there."

"She does. She might not say so, but she does."

I opened my eyes, locating myself back at the top of the
public access ramp, the phone box screwed to an electric pole,
and the midday sun beating through the Norway pines. The
endorsement wasn't resounding.

"Is everything ready?" I asked.

"I even scrubbed the bathtub. Melinda's in the greenhouse."

"Good. When contractions are every four minutes, that's
when you can expect action. Why don't you call me when they're
coming every seven or eight?"

We hung up. The locket of birth on the Hollinger farm clicked
closed and released me back into summer—the sloped, fiery
pavement, the sink and salty smell of sand, Stuart's browning
boyfriend with a photography magazine shading his face, and
Stuart himself, clambering onto the dock with one hand holding
up my Dad's trunks, his blond hair smeared against his brow. I
threw down my bag and joined him.

"That was my breech mom. Early labor."

I sat, dipping my burned feet below the surface. Stuart shook
his head like a dog, splattering my hot skin. The dock lurched.
After a moment, a school of sunnies ventured from the shadows
and brushed our legs.

"The dirty details, please."

"She's an organic farmer, rotten first hospital experience, total homebirth convert, and the baby's frank." Stuart turned toward me. I backtracked, giving him a complete history as though this were a case review at the Birth House, relieved to have him alone and to relate the whole story. "I've got to trust Melinda. Someone has to. It took me some time to realize that." Stuart frowned. "She's strong, she's healthy. Maybe she knows something I don't."

Stuart lifted his feet from the water and faced me squarely, hugging his pale knees. "I think of you as the authority on the greater good. You have a birth practice, Hannah. Don't give it up lightly."

The wind had picked up, skittering across the lake's surface and chopping it into a billion sparks. "I'm terrified of that breech. I'm scared to death of losing my practice." I swung my feet back and forth, watching ripples compress before my calves. I thought of the Russian babies frog-kicking through sun-streaked water, how they know their own volition, and I thought of circus babies turning circles in the air and then caught, expertly, in loving hands. I couldn't have such a beginning, but I did have the potential to give it to Melinda's baby. "I have to go. It's what I would have wanted for my mom."

We watched a metal dingy putt-putt from one marshy cove to another. Down the shore, a metallic clang rang out from behind a house and a troop of kids raced out of the water and up the grass, probably to a lunch of baloney sandwiches. Suddenly the absurdity of Mike's call struck me. "Melinda just had her first contraction," I told Stuart.

He snorted. We laughed until my side ached. Then Stuart said, "Want help?"

I wiped my eyes. "You're on vacation. Besides, it could be weeks."

"Do you want help, Hannah?"

To have Stuart, who during our apprenticeship had become my birth partner, yielding to me as the primary midwife and stepping forward at the needed moment, his company making me graceful, capable, and bold . . . I could imagine nothing better. Stuart's eyes were a clear, washed blue. They reminded me of a newborn's, wide to everything—to me, to loss, to possibility.

I took his head in my hands and kissed his brow. "I'd love for you to come." He beamed. I swabbed my eyes with the towel and grabbed the dock's anchor pole, hoisting myself up.

"Help an old man, will you?"

I gave his forearm a hardy pull. He sprang upward of his own accord, nimbly, throwing me off balance. "Hey!" I shouted, teetering over the water. The dock screeched against its pilings. Stuart laughed, but he didn't let go.

44.

Barred Owl Rising

IN WESTERN AFRICA there's a tribe that believes that a man impregnates a woman by whispering to her the ancestors' stories. His words slip into her ear, wind down her throat, and spiral within her womb. There the stories curl into human form and begin growing. Only then does the couple make love.

What happens at our beginning matters, as do the lives that precede us and the thousand moments when we choose to pull back or be born. Our task is to find the true stories, the stories that give life and love. Only then do the words we whisper spiral into a new creation with its own will, its own tears, delight, and transformative power.

I tell you my story by way of example. Really, I want you to know your own—otherwise you live someone else's, and that won't do. When you squat at the cusp of new life, the hands you extend should be yours, fully inhabited. That's what it takes to be a good midwife. Then your every fingerprint is a blessing.

* * *

That Saturday afternoon in my tiny backyard, Cal and Stuart sipped gin and tonics and I, Coke—who knew when Mike might call? I wore my story like a new body. It hummed, unfamiliar and keen. Surely I glowed. Sun ignited the trees. Potted geraniums decorated either side of the back steps. When Stuart told Cal about his plans to stay, Cal tossed up his hands in a distinctly Stuart-influenced gesture and resigned himself to his sorry lot as the midwife's husband. He would drive back to Madison alone and leave Stuart to take the train or change his plane ticket, if it came to that. We talked about diapers and malnutrition and insurance, about the art market and families of origin. Our idleness warmed and softened my jangly nerves.

At four, Chuck shyly rounded the house carrying a spiral notebook under his arm and a paper bag of fresh-picked corn. He accepted a beer, plopped down on the grass, and proceeded to grill Stuart and Cal about Allende. Chuck had been in touch with a relief organization that delivered boxes of food to much of Stuart's clientele. At the end of August, he'd drive straight through, twenty-five hours, with a van of confirmation kids and a couple of parents; they'd stay a week, sleeping on the pews of a local Pentecostal church. The guys schemed ways to rescue Chuck from what they were convinced would be a nightmare and Chuck insisted would be a blast. The Saturday market, Cal suggested, and a trek out to see the desert.

I relaxed into the lawn chair, aware that this phenomenon— friends chatting on the grass on a lazy summer afternoon—was nothing I'd known growing up. Ice clinked in my glass. The pop's sweet fizz gave me chills. I thought of Melinda out in the field harvesting red and green peppers through early labor, her womb readying itself, Sprout sinking into her pelvis. I watched Chuck tip his face to the sky, his laughter full-chested and easy. When Cal heard that the youth group was bringing sandwich meats and mac and cheese for meals, he insisted on hosting the crew for a Mexican feast. "That's too much!" Chuck protested. "There'll be thirteen of us." The guys insisted. Cal sketched a map in Chuck's notebook.

"You should come, Hannah," Stuart said.

I shook my head.

Chuck cleared his throat. "Actually, I could use another chaperone."

"I've got clients due," I said.

Stuart wagged his finger at me.

"What?" I demanded.

"That's too bad," Chuck said. "I'd enjoy your company."

Conversation tumbled forward until it was natural for Chuck to join us for dinner. We moved the kitchen table out from the window, lit candles, poured wine. The guys enthused over the vegan potpie, though in my opinion it seriously wanted hamburger. After much crowbarring from Stuart, Chuck revealed that he was on ordination track, which caused Stuart to pounce: "How *does* a Gen X Lutheran dude make sense of God?" My blood surged at Stuart's daredevil questions. I raised my glass to hide a smile.

Chuck flushed as he told us about God being like dark matter, the ninety-five percent of the universe's mass that no one can account for binding things together and giving the world weight and meaning.

"That can't be orthodox Lutheran doctrine," Cal said.

"You didn't ask for the party line."

"No wonder Dad thinks you're a threat," I teased, a little giddy.

Chuck's clear brow knotted in consternation. "I'm not, though. That's what gets me. I love the Bible stories, and I love how liturgy reenacts them, keeps them alive. I'm as traditional as they come."

"Treading in J.C.'s footsteps," Stuart said.

"Don't exaggerate." Chuck turned decisively toward me. "What do you believe, Hannah?"

"Me?" Compared with the golden clarity of Chuck's beliefs, mine were an angry mess. "I guess I'm agnostic."

"Hannah and I have our own religion," Stuart said. He thunked to his knees, raising cupped palms in abject adoration.

"All praise the thinned perineum!"

I laughed aloud—he was so right. If Chuck's holy text was Jesus walking around Galilee, mine was the resplendent progression of pregnancy and birth. Here was meaning; here, mystery. Perhaps this was the faith of the Hebrew midwives. Perhaps, in some roundabout way, this was what Dad had meant by his sermon. Two nights later, sleepless in the Hiawatha County Jail, I would have time enough to consider and claim my praxis: *Care offered fearlessly with smarts and great love telescopes beyond our imaginings.* To this day I follow it.

The cloak of dusk gathered around the house. Wine glasses magnified the candles. Crickets tuned up. None of us wanted the evening to end, so we turned on the lights, sped through the dishes, and began a rowdy game of Oh Hell clustered around the kitchen table with a pot of coffee and box of Oreos. The fans of playing cards expanded and shrunk. At nine thirty the phone rang—Mike, reporting contractions every seven minutes, heart tones one hundred forty, and a blood pressure of one thirty over eighty. Melinda was cooperating.

"Still normal," I said. "She's under a lot of exertion. Pulse? Temp?"

Melinda's vitals were spot-on. I walked until the coils of phone cord pulled straight, turned, and traced my steps. The men watched.

"Mike, I have a friend in town who's done a few breeches. He's offered to help." Mike effused gratitude. "What about Melinda?" A hand muffled the receiver then Mike passed on her permission. "Give us half an hour. It's essential that Melinda not push. Stay in her face. Be absolutely strict about it. Do you hear me?"

I hung up and slid into birth mode—calm, clear-minded, sliding my finger down the checklist, slipping feet into sandals, aware of Cal and Chuck conversing at the table while Stuart grabbed shoes and a jacket.

"Call me," Cal demanded of Stuart. "Otherwise I leave first thing."

I slung my bags over my shoulder, accepted Chuck's help with the oxygen tank, and led the way to the car. A warm wind had risen from the west, shaking the tired leaves of August and cooling the sweat on my skin. I opened the trunk, wedged in the tank, packed in the bags, and, once Stuart had climbed in the front, was glad for a private moment under the streetlamp with Chuck. I wanted to preserve it, and so before I reached up to slam the trunk, I met his eyes and kissed him briefly, sweetly, on the lips. I was coming more alive and here was confirmation, along with his quick flush and fingers pressed to my waist. I took this blessing with me directly west across sloped fields, the corn tasselled and heavy in the night. At a rural road I turned north, spitting gravel, then up a dirt drive over the creek bed with its shaded willows and silver maples. Dust billowed when I pulled the brake in the farmyard. Stuart watched me from the corner of his eye. I cut the motor. When worry extended a slithery tendril, I closed my eyes and remembered with moist pleasure the pressure of Chuck's lips.

I left the key in the ignition, squeezed Stuart's hand, and said, "Let's go."

"Amen, sister," Stuart said. "You call the shots."

On the front porch, I turned the Hollingers' unlocked doorknob. Stuart moved into the kitchen, rolling up his sleeves to tackle a sink full of dirty dishes.

I found Mike and Melinda in the upstairs bathroom. Melinda was naked in the shower, stunningly large, glistening, absorbed. No one had bothered to draw the shower curtain and so spray and steam filled the small, white-tiled space. Mike pleaded with her and turned to me as soon as I appeared in the doorway. "The water's too hot. Don't you think that's too much, Hannah?" His jeans and T-shirt were damp.

"She's fine," I said.

Melinda took the spray chin up, eyes closed. Her curls had sprung, her breasts lolled heavily to the sides, her belly streamed with water.

"In fact, it's working great. Melinda, is it okay that I'm here?"

Her arms hung idly at her sides. She took in breath after slow breath, and nodded minutely.

I closed the toilet seat. "Sit, Mike. Can I get you something to drink?" He collapsed, leaning sideways against the wall. "Hot? Cold?"

"Whatever."

Downstairs, I found half a pitcher of iced tea in the fridge and a stained coffee maker on the counter. I dug through the cupboards for decaf. "Here." Stuart took it from me. I poured two glasses of tea and cracked in some ice cubes. Back upstairs, I handed one to Mike and placed the other on the sink. Melinda had shifted to her knees with her hands pressing either side of the tub. The water beat over her curved back. Porcelain and tile magnified her groan, which emerged coarsely, a muffled, rusty hinge. Mike leapt to his feet. I pushed him back down. "Drink," I ordered. "Did you two get any sleep last night?"

"She did. I was up most of the night." He looked it too, eyes bruised, jaw unshaven.

"Is she still at seven minutes?"

"Six."

"How long at that frequency?"

He looked at a shiny new watch on his wrist. "Twenty minutes."

"Any sign of her water breaking?"

"How can I tell with her in the shower?"

I squatted down, back to the doorframe so I could look directly at Mike. "You're doing an excellent job keeping track of things. Listen to me, Mike. We may still have a long way to go. Why don't you get some rest? In Kevin's room. I'll take over and wake you when the time comes. Stuart's downstairs. He can help if I need anything."

Mike pressed the glass of tea, now dripping with condensation, against his forehead. "I don't know." He sighed and took a long drink. "I couldn't have done it, Hannah. You have no idea. I don't know what would have happened."

"You love her." I touched his knee. "Even trained midwives

have a hard time when the mom is someone they love. It's too much."

Melinda shifted in the tub, raising her neck like a turtle. "Damn. The water's getting cold."

I leapt to turn it off and collided with Mike. "Go," I ordered.

"Honey?" he asked Melinda.

Melinda's body contracted with annoyance. "It's fine. I'm fine. Go rest." I guessed this was the hundredth time she'd said as much.

Mike lumbered out, and I helped Melinda over the tub's rim. Beginning with her hair, I toweled her off, rubbing vigorously, patting her shoulders and arms, which sank under my pressure. I moved down to dry the enormous swell of her center, her widespread hips and firm legs, using the touch I'd learned from Maria and Sunny and Stuart—attentive, careful, a touch adults rarely offer each other but know from caring for children. I knelt to dry her feet and felt reverent and humble. Above me, Melinda braced for a contraction.

"How is it?" I asked.

She grabbed the towel rack in one hand and the sink ledge in the other. "Ugh." Her face tightened; she receded into her pain, and I waited. Finally, "I'm okay. God, I'm famished."

"When did you eat last?"

Her freckled nose wrinkled. "Mike would know."

I lifted a cotton nightgown from the hook and helped her dress. "I need to see how far along you are before I know what's best to do next. Here"—we shuffled into the bedroom—"let's lay you down." I reached for a pillow, but she didn't want it. "Any fluid? Gushing, leaking?" She shook her head no. I placed chux pads over the cookie sheets I found on the dresser, laid out my instruments, tucked the receiving blankets inside a pillowcase with a heating pad, and found some towels. "Okay, then. Can you butterfly your knees?"

The position—exposed, her nightgown scrunched up, ankles at her buttocks—jarred her out of that hormone-induced contemplative state we midwives call Laborland. Her chest stilled. She raised herself to her elbows. Her eyes, sharp with lamplight, followed my hands. For the first time since calling Mike, I felt unsure of my choice to be there.

"This won't take long," I said, partly to convince myself that we'd be back in that floating state soon enough. I put on gloves. Had the baby's position been normal, measurements wouldn't have been necessary, although most women appreciate knowing how far along they are. I couldn't afford to let the breech surprise me. With my left hand touching Melinda's skin along the baby's back, my right fingers entered her widened vaginal opening. The bones of her hips and pelvis had parted and spread; the cervix was now elastic, stretching its wondrous mouth. Inside, I took a quick measurement—barely two centimeters, just beginning, the baby's bottom not yet engaged—and retreated. Melinda pulled her nightgown back to her knees and propped herself on her elbows.

"How much?"

"Two. Let's grab you something to eat."

"I'll make myself a sandwich in a minute." Melinda scrutinized me. "What are you going to do, Hannah? How are you going to cover your ass?"

"My ass?" Heat rushed to my head, and I threw down the gloves. I'd expected at least a glimmer of gratitude. "I'm sticking my neck out for you."

"I don't want your charity. I want a midwife. And I certainly don't want you making decisions here based on your future career. You've jerked us around enough already." The contractions had stopped. "Why should I trust you?"

"Because I care about you." There was no place for me to sit other than the bed, so I loomed over her. "Because I care about this birth. I'm still figuring out how to practice, Melinda. I'm a work in progress."

"I don't want to be your guinea pig." Melinda's eyes were hard. Her body quivered with the strain on her arms, or—finally I saw it—from fear. I sat. Breath filled my lungs. My exhale was measured. I despised not being able to control the outcome of her birth. I despised being inadequate, even with Stuart's help, and yet absolutely no one was adequate to attend Melinda's breech—not Bill or the most skilled surgeons with their readied knives, not Bessie Jones down in Florida or Michel Odent in France—because there were no guarantees; there was no reason for Melinda to trust anyone. The knot tying up my throat made me feel like my father—silent, perhaps not out of reserve or judgment, but because he had no answers.

I gripped Melinda's knee.

"I'm sorry I've been inconsistent, Melinda. I'm human." The bitterness in her eyes faded. "We both are. But one thing I know is that you're the authority on your body. You know how to deliver this baby." I shook her slightly. "And another thing is that I'm a guardian of safe birth. I'm here to support you. I can help your body do what it knows how to do. But I need you to cooperate. If I'm in over my head and we have to transport, I'll tell you. Whatever happens for me afterward, I'll deal with it."

And later, I did: the criminal investigation, jail time, the publicity, the sidelong looks from townsfolk. Dad's hurt and forbearance as he paid my bail. Bill's blustery termination of our agreement. Zarida's lofty non-apology: "You know I had to report it when I heard, Hannah. I may not be a doctor, but I believe in the Hippocratic Oath."

Little Kevin had spent the night of the birth with the Hollingers' neighbors, who were also Zarida's in-laws, so of course the news spread. But Melinda and Mike refused to cooperate with the District Attorney, and Chester Prairie Lutheran harbored the tools of my trade nicely. Despite the dropped charges, I faced months of uncertainty—had I done the right thing?—until Chuck one day sat me down, knee to knee, my hands in his warm hands. "Knowing what you know now," he asked, "would you do it again?" I thought back to Melinda's labor, my heart clearer then than ever before or since. Yes. Unabashedly yes.

In the next moment, Melinda's attention slipped away. The angle of her chin eased; her eyes grew dull. Rather than respond, she released herself back into the container of confidence and trust, and struggled to sit up for a contraction. "Try your side," I suggested, nudging her over. The muscles in her back tensed and rippled. When I stood, years of uncertainty fell from my shoulders. Melinda released a guttural moan. Once it passed, I helped her out of bed and down the stairs where she beelined for the coffee.

Stuart dried his hands and winked at me.

"Melinda," I said, "this is my friend Stuart. He's a midwife in Mexico, and he's had experience with breeches." She gripped the countertop, eyes scrunched, oblivious. I flashed two fingers at Stuart, and he nodded. Stuart poured her a cup and wrapped her hands around it after the contraction passed.

"I feel honored to be here. You have a beautiful farm."

Melinda raised the mug to her lips and allowed Stuart to usher her to the table.

The refrigerator was packed with yogurt, individual containers of what I guessed to be veggie stir fry on rice, wheat bread and sandwich makings, and generally enough food for weeks—Mike's doing. Between contractions, Melinda downed two bowls of cereal topped generously with frozen homegrown strawberries opaque with milky ice. I made myself a sandwich but only took a few bites. "I've got to walk," Melinda said.

Melinda strode out the front door barefoot, and I didn't stop her. Soon enough we'd get her horizontal; we would need gravity and whatever it took to keep pressure off her cervix. For now, exercise was a good distraction. I followed Melinda across the yard. Overhead, the black curtain of evening pulled tight. Nighthawks called "eew, eew" and chased the season's dwindling mosquito population. Crickets sang in the grass. My sandals were open-toed; the lawn was cool.

We walked up to the rows of mounded potato plants, sprays of kale, cabbage, and broccoli along packed-earth gutters. The air was warm, damp at the edges. Rustling corn walled in the garden. Following Melinda's shadowed form, I knew again why I loved birth—how, if we let it, this cord of instinct pulls us. Melinda's feet sunk into the soil she'd cultivated; she doubled over. I placed my hand lightly against her spine. She straightened, moved forward as her muscles called her. I trailed one step behind. We reached the acre's boundary, turned, walked a few paces to a pumpkin field where globes of night-orange lurked under elephantine leaves, and turned back east. Parchment yellow fringed the stand of silver maples along the creek. The moon was rising.

By the time we reached the yard, the fuzzy light had coalesced into a blank, glowing orb. Only a few stars poked through the humidity. A cat emerged, burnished its head against Melinda's calf, and skittered off. Melinda grabbed my arm and pulled. I guessed the contractions were coming every three or four minutes. "Good," I told her. "You're doing good."

"Can I push?" Her voice was thin, pleading.

"Let's see how far you're dilated."

I took her elbow. Every window of the house was lit, as though amid the black cornfields and the black dome of sky, here was the blazing axis of change. I closed the screen quietly. We made slow progress up the stairs. The door to Kevin's room was shut with Mike behind it.

Melinda fell back onto the bed. I lifted her feet one at a time, her skin cold and smeared with mud, and toweled them off. "Give me a minute," I said. I washed my hands in the bathroom, took out gloves and fetoscope. I would bypass taking her vitals; her skin was warming normally, her breathing regular. Melinda writhed on the bed. With a baby bottom in her pelvis, lying down compressed her womb and pushed the baby's head against her spine. "Not so comfortable, huh? This will be quick."

Melinda's skin was firm but pliable. She had to progress at a steady clip until she was big enough for the baby's head to get through, while also preventing that baby bottom from descending. "Excellent." I snapped off the gloves. "You're at four centimeters."

She rolled to her side, her "Oh!" shocked and sharp. Down the hall, feet hit the floor and Mike appeared, dazed, hair disheveled. I guided his hand onto the small of Melinda's back.

"There," I said. "Good. Mike, stay in her face. She needs to breathe through the surges, float through them. No pushing. Keep her lying down. Do you hear me, Melinda? You need to stay horizontal until you're fully dilated, or the baby will come out too soon. We don't want any pressure on your cervix. No pushing."

She made a pinched animal sound.

"I'll get Stuart to fix a snack."

Down in the kitchen, the counters were clear, the washer and dryer hummed, and Stuart's head was in the oven. "Good grief," I said.

He emerged, dropped a scrubby in a bucket of ashy water, and stripped off rubber gloves. "How's she coming?"

I reported on Melinda's progress, and we sat to review the plan. Once the baby's butt was engaged, Melinda had to follow Friedman's Curve: She had to dilate two centimeters an hour or arrive at ten centimeters by six a.m. If not, we'd insist on driving her into town. If she was ready before then, we'd heed the Hour of Patience to ensure full dilation—absolutely no pushing. Then Mike would position her in a standing squat or, if she refused, she could hang her bottom off the edge of the bed. The head needed room to flex; the body needed gravity for quick descent. The legs would flop out easily, or, if not, I would reach up to bend the knees. I should not allow the baby to rotate into a face-up position; I should not read the baby's heartbeat through the cord.

"I'll monitor heartbeat," Stuart said. "You stay on task." When the tops of the shoulder blades were visible, I'd sweep down the arms unless they came out on their own. I'd support the baby until the nape of the neck was visible, and arc the baby up, sweeping its face over the perineum. All this I knew.

"And if the head's stuck?" I asked.

If the head was stuck, the hospital would no longer be an option. We'd have eight to ten minutes, maximum, before anoxia and permanent brain damage set in.

"You do the Mauriceau-Smellie-Veit maneuver. I'll coach. Hand inside, palm up under the face, middle and index fingers on each cheekbone." We rested our elbows on the kitchen table and practiced in tandem. "Pull down, maintaining the head in flexion. I'll do serious suprapubic pressure. It works."

The V of my fingers shook. I realized I was lightheaded; it was one in the morning, and I hadn't eaten since dinner. I devoured the remains of my sandwich while Stuart assembled bread, cheese, hummus, and sprouts for Mike and Melinda. He found a serving tray; he poured mugs of coffee. "This one's decaf." He pointed. "The others are loaded. Shout when you want me."

Mike was spooned around Melinda, murmuring into her neck, arms crisscrossing her chest. I set the tray on the bureau and walked around the bed. Melinda's cheeks were moist; pain veiled her eyes, and she breathed heavily. I brushed an errant blond strand from her mouth. "You're doing so well. After the next contraction I think you should pee. We don't want your bladder distended."

Immediately she gasped, and scrunched up her legs.

"Ride it out, ride it out, ride it out," Mike chanted, his low voice wrapping the room.

On the toilet Melinda arched, palming the porcelain tank behind her. Her chest heaved. I thought of Sunny's sphincter lesson and how the body opens, the rings of muscles in secret communication with one another. When Melinda emitted a ragged wail, I put my hand on Mike's arm. "Making noise is good."

When I tried to get her back on the bed she resisted and complained of being famished, so I brought the tray into the bathroom. She grabbed the sandwich.

Mike sat on the tub ledge, frowning.

"She needs nourishment," I said. I joined Mike on the tub, handing him a plate and clutching my coffee, which was how the three of us ended up crammed in the five-by-six bathroom, Melinda ignobly enthroned, stricken suddenly with hysterics because it was a bizarre dinner party and thank God Mike had cleaned.

The contractions were persistent now, violent waves rippling through her back and abdomen. We got her into bed, where she wept with the desire to push. When I peeked I could see the taut membranes. That they hadn't yet ruptured was a good sign—there wasn't too much pressure on her cervix.

"I want to push. Oh, God, why can't I push?"

Here was transition, the stage when birthing women lose hope and midwives must carry it for them. Sunny used to say that when the mother felt ready to die, we should roll up our sleeves. I call it the Great Impossible: Even hippie women, sworn to drug-free birth, beg for an epidural; even brash, brave women plead for mercy. The mother gives up, and only beyond that point, having relinquished hope and proceeded anyway, does she push out her baby.

I kept the knowledge that Melinda was almost fully dilated to myself—we still needed to wait another hour. Mike held her and resumed his mantra, "Ride it out now."

I showed Mike good pressure points and how to massage her thighs to relieve tension. Melinda emitted ragged throaty noises as she tried not to bear down. They labored while I made sure Stuart had water on the stove and a few large mixing bowls on hand. I ate, held ice water to Melinda's lips, fed Mike a piece of quiche, and let Stuart massage my neck. Stuart and I suggested new positions for the couple, orchestrating them like yoga instructors.

Time passed. Labor opens a window onto eternity, not because of the progression of pain or the hours, days even, of wakefulness, but because of a woman's complete attention to the rough, muscular workings of her uterus expanding moment by moment, and the witnesses' alertness to subtle changes, in stamina, in focus, each instant attended with either care or distance. The child that hovers on the other edge of labor and the dangers of bringing that child into the air ask that we inhabit each nook and cranny of a minute and every minute of an hour.

I ran a washcloth under the cold tap and held it to Melinda's forehead. Damp spread across the pillow. When she looked at me, her eyes were drained of defiance; they were dim, dependent, gazing up from the bottom of a lake. I leaned in, ear to her stomach and arm extended to read my watch. A soft thu-thump passed up through layers of skin.

"Let's see where you're at," I said gently.

At three thirty I reached up—ten centimeters, the thick ring of the perineum gone, the baby's behind still blessedly wrapped in membranes. "Yes!" The pokey little butt bones where I'd only ever touched skull brought a rush of adrenaline. "You're there. I'll get Stuart, and we'll be ready to push."

Melinda gasped. "I have to poop. Now. Get me up, get me up," and Mike and I hauled her by the arms. She straddled the toilet like a birth stool and pushed. The rush of fluid was her water breaking. The baby's butt had hit the pelvic floor.

Now Sprout could come quickly. "Stu!" I shouted down the stairs. I checked that Mike had made the bed atop a rubber sheet and laid out towels. I turned the shade of a reading lamp to dampen the glare. There was just enough space to maneuver at the foot of the bed.

Mike helped her off the toilet. Once in the hall, Melinda peeled away from him and down the stairs, grasping railings on either side. "Where the hell are you going?" Mike shouted. She paused for a contraction, pitching forward dangerously. "Don't push! Don't push!" Mike shouted.

Stuart's voice rose from the living room. "There you go. Would you like to lean on my arm?"

I stood for a moment, gape-mouthed, but then finally saw what Melinda saw and knew what she would do. All Melinda wanted was to live in her body. "Yield," a voice—my voice—said.

"Mike"—I stopped him at the landing—"let her go. Do you have a plastic tarp? Or maybe we can take this sheet. Here, give me a hand."

Mike fumbled with the fitted corners. I yanked the rubber pad out and folded it. Downstairs, the screen door slammed and footsteps echoed on the wood planks of the porch. "Carry this"—

I thrust the sheet into Mike's willing arms—"and that stack of towels. We need pillows and blankets. Unplug the heating pad there, and bring out that whole pillowcase. Keep it clean. You'll need to make several trips. My kit"—I kicked it on the floor—"and the oxygen tank. Also, a strong flashlight."

"Will a lantern do?"

I stacked the two cookie trays of sterile instruments and carried them downstairs. The kitchen was thick with steam and coffee. I paused by the dryer, piled with folded jeans and a three-year-old's T-shirts, warmth at my back and a chill seeping through the screen door. Night insects billowed around the porch light; beyond a few feet of grass I could see nothing. Corn-sweetened air entered my lungs. Who was I to judge Melinda stubborn or proud? Perhaps she was, or perhaps she'd known, the way women have known since the beginning of time, exactly what was necessary. So many of us have forgotten. I would try to remember too. I would attend what was at hand. I shouldered open the screen and entered the night.

A fine gauze of fog had settled over the grass. Once I left the ring of porch light, I saw the moon, full and fuzzy with humidity. The yard was hushed. Crickets scratched in the brush, and I could hear the river stirring beyond the tree line. Wet soaked my sandals. My bare arms prickled. Ahead, the greenhouse suddenly lit up, luminous and fluorescent, Stuart and Melinda's silhouettes inside.

"No!" Melinda shouted, and the vision vanished. When I pushed through the hoop house door, the curved plastic walls were milky. Melinda was a crouched shadow. Stuart held her.

I set the trays on the workbench and touched Melinda's back. "How're you doing?"

Melinda's words were garbled. She gripped the ledge of the planting table, squatted, and strained.

"Listen, Melinda. We have to be able to see. Mike's bringing a lantern. If it's not strong enough, I'm going to turn on the lights."

Her head was level with the table, facedown. At her bare feet, a trowel and the glint of an aluminum pie tin were half-buried in dirt. I surveyed the square of packed soil here at the end of the hoop house, an area perhaps ten by ten bordered by the table, the door, a coiled hose, slop sink, crates of pots, and the plant-beds. When Mike arrived, I had him spread the rubber sheet in the center. He fussed with the wick of an old kerosene camping lantern; he struck a match. A sizzling hiss and light blazed in our small circle: Stuart's gaunt features alert but calm, Mike's uncertain hands, Melinda's nightgown clinging to the curve of her back, the flexing muscles of her arms, the determined clench in her jaw and seeming absence in her eyes which was really complete presence.

Something landed in the dirt.

I snapped on a glove. With one hand on the small of her back, I knelt and reached below her nightgown. My fingers slid. "I need a heart rate," I ordered Stuart, who crouched to press the Doppler against Melinda. Sure enough, when I brought my hand to the light, it was smeared brown. "Meconium," I said. My heart shifted to high gear, clearing my mind of everything except mother and unborn child, who was now in distress.

"We're okay," Stuart said. "One fifty-two."

The baby's position was, momentarily, an advantage. Had Sprout defecated into the amniotic fluid, the little bugger would be in danger of inhaling it. But the waste was outside Melinda's womb. I wet a washcloth in the slop sink—the sputtering spray was icy—and wiped her off. Melinda panted raggedly.

"You're nice and open," I told her. "Like a big, satisfying yawn." Her cheeks twisted. Stuart stroked her hair. I focused through my hand and Melinda's back to her convulsing interior. "Good. You're wide open. As big as a lake." Melinda's sound was gravelly and desperate. "As big as the moon."

Mike hunched in the doorway.

"We need another tarp and bring out a pot of boiling water. Carefully. I'm serious, Mike, don't burn yourself. And then I'll need bowls. Stu, draw up the Pitocin." We had to prepare for hemorrhage and full resuscitation.

Melinda's countenance shone pale in the yellow light, her hair flattened and clingy with perspiration. For a moment there was only the acrid scent of tomatoes. I kneaded her shoulders.

"Can we take your nightie off, Melinda? Will you be chilly?"

Her contractions came in rapid, powerful waves. She plucked at the light cotton. "Get it off! Get it off!" I wrestled it over her head while Stuart plugged in an electric space heater he had found beside the workbench. The coils reddened. Mike set hot water and mixing bowls by the sink; he piled extra pillows and linens on a tarp between the herb beds. Stuart prepped the oxygen tank.

"Mike, I want you to grab her from behind. Can you do that? Can you hold her up?"

He stepped on the rubber sheet. "Shoes!" He looked at the mud now marring our sanitary birthplace and levered off his shoes. In stocking feet, he grasped Melinda's armpits, catching himself as she dropped, knees bent, thrusting downward. I wedged myself between Melinda and Kevin's play area. The space was crowded with the acidic stink of sweat. It was too dim. "I need the lantern down here." Yellow light descended, revealing the tiny blossoming bottom. I steadied myself with one hand in the dirt. Two legs flopped out. They dangled limply. The torso was thin and pale. There was no need to interfere; the baby showed no signs of rotating into a more difficult position. Stuart slid the Doppler along the bulb of Melinda's uterus, closed his eyes, and said, "A hundred." Low, but not too low.

"You're doing great. The legs are out." I bent underneath to see. "Yes, it's a girl."

"A girl?" Mike was disbelieving. Melinda's squeal of excitement morphed into a groan. Shoulders, arms, and head were still wedged in that womb-world with the cord, a throbbing white strand, caught between.

"Next time, give it all you've got. Stu, I need a sterile towel and gloves."

Melinda leaned into a contraction and came out gasping, choking on sobs. "I can't. I can't do it. Oh, God."

The tiny torso slid another inch. "You *are* doing it, Melinda." The baby's arms were raised as though praising her maker, or reaching for home, familiar and safe. "It's a beautiful world out here, baby."

"Abby," Mike whispered.

"Little Abby," I said.

"Oh, God," Melinda cried out. The domed plastic walls muted Melinda's cry, as diffuse as moonlight. "Oh, God. What have I done?" Her weeping dissolved into a contraction. Her face was vised between pain and the effort of pushing.

A bowl appeared. On my knees, I washed my hands in scorching water and took the gloves from Stuart. "I see the shoulder blades."

"Good," Stuart said. "Now reach up. Exactly."

I wrapped the towel around Abby's slippery hips and nudged her shoulders clockwise, hoping for more stretch against the pelvis. Her right arm swept out, and then the left. The little one hung grotesquely from her neck. I cupped her in my left palm with her narrow back toward me. Her skin, thick with the film of newborns, was ghostly white. She was gazing up at some internal universe. "Abby. You can see the moon out here. And your mom's tomatoes. And your mom and dad, who love you and are eager to meet you. You even have a big brother. All right now. We need you to come out."

Melinda's head lolled limply to her shoulder.

Mike turned toward the driveway. "Should we—"

"No." Stuart held up his hand. He turned to prep another bowl of hot water.

"Push through it, Melinda. Your baby girl's on the other side of that pain."

"I can't." Melinda's voice was unrecognizable. Mike locked his arms around her chest. She pulled against him, earthward, down toward the black Midwestern topsoil, her neck arched against his chest, her eyes shut. I angled my watch toward the lantern—we had two and a half minutes before we risked brain damage. Fortunately the cord lay along Abby's right arm—less pinching. But I couldn't know for sure.

"I'm getting decels," Stuart said. "Get her out of there."

Melinda said, "Oh, God."

"Melinda, listen to me. Give it all you've got."

"I can't." Melinda wept, beyond exhaustion. "I'm sorry, so sorry."

"Yes you can. One more shove, and she's out. I know you can do it."

"We're dropping," Stuart said.

"Push!" I shouted. "Now!"

Melinda staggered forward with a coarse groan, wedging me under the workbench. Just as Abby passed into shadow I saw the occiput bone; I lifted and turned her tiny bottom. Her face swept over the perineum.

Melinda reared back; Mike stumbled, caught her, and I lurched forward, my hands slick with fluid. Just like that, Abby was out, plopped into my open palms along with a steaming flush of blood, silent a horrible moment while Melinda collapsed onto the rubber sheet and I crawled out from under the table trying to gauge the baby's color in the poor light and whether I should apply oxygen and whether Melinda's bleeding had stopped, but then Abby let out an angry squeal that was the most wrenchingly beautiful sound I've ever heard, and Melinda actually laughed amid her sobs.

Stuart raised the lantern, passed me the bulb syringe, and examined Melinda. I suctioned mucus from Abby's nostrils and mouth and took her vitals. She was wispy-haired, round-headed, coated in slippery white film, a bruise beginning along her butt, genitalia swollen from the rough descent but otherwise intact and fierce in her dismay. The soft spot on her head pulsed. I placed her on Melinda's chest. The air around us was heavy, pungent, fertile. I double-checked Melinda's uterus to make sure it was still contracting. The bleeding had stopped. Stuart wrapped Abby in a warm receiving blanket, pulled a tiny cotton cap over new ears. Mike wept, his face knotted with grief and joy; he lay beside Melinda in the dirt and blood, resting his head on her shoulder, where he could see Abby. They held each other and cried. When Stuart helped me up and embraced me, I realized I too was weeping, great emptying sobs of relief, because whatever the fallout might be, the worst was over. Abby and Melinda were alive. I buried my head in Stuart's chest, clinging to his shirt.

A groan from Melinda set us back in action. Stuart got me fresh water and gloves and wiped Melinda's forehead with a damp cloth. She bled only briefly before the placenta emerged. I placed it in a spare mixing bowl. The red, round loaf of tissue was networked with veins and the cord was strong. The tree of life was healthy, meaty, in its own way just as stunning as the baby, because it was an entire organ grown to feed life into a child and then be cast off. *I have this potential,* I thought. What had been abstract was finally real. I felt again the press of Chuck's lips, his hands at my waist. I would go with him to Mexico. I would, as you know, marry him.

"Would you like to cut the cord, Mike?"

"Me?" He propped himself on an elbow.

"Sure." The rise and sink of Melinda's chest was slowing. I turned Abby on her back and unwrapped her. "Sweet girl. This won't take long." I clamped the thick skin spiral and showed Mike where to cut. Stuart propped Melinda on pillows so she could watch. With a snip Abby was fully in the world—the August night, the moon-washed hoop house, the surrounding open acreage soaked in darkness. Surely, in some way, she would remember.

We rubbed her down and showed Mike how to swaddle her with a fresh, warm blanket. In the lamplight, Abby's eyes looked black as the sky; they were surprised, with sweeping lashes the same dandelion-seed color as her wisps of hair. She yawned dramatically. Her tongue was miniscule and pink. "Oh," Mike said, pressing her cheek to his own.

Melinda shivered; she was naked, and her sweat was cooling. I unfurled a spare quilt, the fabric velvety with age. The backing was familiar yellow flannel, the front alternated squares of floral and rocking horses. *Of course,* I thought. My father must

have delivered it along with his pastoral assurances. I wrapped
it around Melinda, holding her a moment inside my mother's
hidden but persistent love before easing her onto the pillows.

"Look at how gorgeous your placenta is." I tipped the bowl
for the couple to see. "What would you like me to do with it?"

"Don't tell me we're going to eat it," Mike said.

Melinda laughed, reaching for Abby. "It's good fertilizer.
Bury it in the compost." I stood. "Out back. There's a shovel.
Get it down deep."

Once outside I began to shake; my knees were unsteady, my
jaw rattled with cold. The moon had sunk just shy of the tree line,
and, in the east, between the black lace of branches, the morning
sky was brightening. A breeze had picked up, rustling the weeds
and sunflowers behind the greenhouse, and some small creature
scurried in the underbrush. I found the shovel leaning against a
framed bin and dug a hole toward the back. The soil was loose
and leafy. I tipped the bowl. Blood and placenta poured into the
humus, and I knew I was also burying some thick, fleshy organ
that for years had nourished—what? a tiny bud of faith?—until
this night, when it had finally outgrown its purpose. I sloughed
it into the earth. Despite all that happened in the following
months, what was born that night would abide. I shoveled grass
clippings and vegetable peelings and the first fall leaves over the
hole while somewhere down near the river, from the clustered
trees, a barred owl called out in rising, breathy amazement.

Author's Note

Birth, I believe, is the final frontier of women's rights, health, and spiritual wisdom in the United States. I hope Hannah's story honors the many midwives who practice in adverse circumstances, especially in states where homebirth remains a felony. Although homebirth in Minnesota was legalized under the Ventura administration, it still receives no institutional support. Homebirth and birth-center birth continue to thrive in New Mexico.

I am immensely grateful for the many people who gave this story their time and love: Kelly Sonnack, whose insights, patience, and enduring advocacy are an enormous blessing; Marcia Peck, Carolyn Crooke, and Terri Whitman, the faithful trio; Christine Sikorski, who twice generously helped shake up this manuscript; Joan Norris, who is as good an editor as she is a midwife; Marcy Andrew for the inspiration and her connections; Elizabeth Gilmore, who modeled the fullness of midwifery and who supplied Sunny and Maria's birthing stories—the only true stories related here; Mark Powell, Emma Gemmell, Sheryl Stowman, Rebeca Barroso, Kerry Dixon, Jerry Whiting, Jessie Groneman, Reita Reid, Sue Torkelson, Kelley Rae Jewett, Maggie PaStarr, Kris Tromiczak, Susanna McDowell, Claire Wilson, Christy Santoro, Lindsey Kroll, the Northern New Mexico Midwifery Center, the women at the Portland, Oregon, MANA Conference, and the many midwives I've forgotten to name. I am indebted to Mary Lay, Ina May

Gaskin, and Michel Odent for their research and life's work. For her great generosity and design work, I thank Linda Koutsky. Thanks to Jenny Larson for her photography, Beth Wright for holding my hand through the publication process, my team of last-minute readers—Nancie Hughes, Helen and Len Andrew— and the hard-working crew at Köehler Books. I am profoundly grateful to have benefitted from the generosity of the Minnesota State Arts Board and Minnesota taxpayers. Lastly, a burst of gratitude goes to Emily Jarrett Hughes, whose story instincts, steadfastness, and affection undergird every page of this book. Much love to you.

CPSIA information can be obtained
at www.ICGtesting.com
Printed in the USA
FFOW05n1512210314

9 781940 192185